The Prophecy of the Sacred Cross

Book 1 in the Parables of the 24th Elder
Trilogy

The Prophecy of the Sacred Cross

Book 1 in the Parables of the 24th Elder Trilogy

Peter Silas

Incarnate Press

Incarnate Press
an Imprint of Incarnate Press, LLC

Published by Incarnate Press, LLC

Cover design by Aleks Davis. Cover © 2013 Peter Silas

Logos Incarnate and the colophon are trademarks of Incarnate
Press, LLC.

Printed in the United States

First Edition 2013

Paperback ISBN: 978-0-9889424-0-0
EBook ISBN: 978-0-9889424-1-7

To my father, who brought to me a world of mystery

Table of Contents

Preface

It would be typical to say something like, "based on events conjured in the deepest portion of my mind, this work is based on fictitious characters, events and places that have no relationship whatsoever with reality whether in the past, present or even the future...."

The future, however, is the one subject that I will refuse to wholly reject is associated with the expression known as *The Prophecy of the Sacred Cross* because, let's face it, there is always a part of each person's imagination that lends itself to some aspect of hope – hope that is not limited by what we perceive to be reality but rather is assisted with a mysterious twist into the fantastical unknown. And that is where the Church, with her mystical nature, comes into play.

In all of His ineffability, He gave us the Church and with this gift we can find ourselves grounded between the known and what lies beyond our understanding. Grounded on this premise, I began writing the *Parables of the 24th Elder* trilogy with two goals in mind. The first is to connect abstract ideas through a relationship between the secular world and a life in Christ. Being a Christian, however, is not required to gain wisdom from reading this novel because as you read you will soon see that certain parallels remain no matter your beliefs. I would hope, though, that you would have a better understanding of how the Orthodox Church offers more than a seemingly bland mix of excessive prayer and fasting.

Secondly, two groups I aim to reach through my writing: young adult and adult readers. To the young adults, I offer a connection between the Church and fantastical concepts; perhaps religion and faith can also bring a new and exciting adventure that is grounded on more than dark magic and undiscovered planets. And to the adult reader, I offer a more intellectual examination into spiritual warfare – all without losing the flavor of a new, fictitious storyline. I therefore challenge you to read this book with an open mind. No, the concepts I offer are not based on real events or people. No, I don't suggest the events in my storyline are *going* to happen or that even the dogma of the Orthodox Church is congruent with this adventure in any way, shape or form. However, ask yourself the following question. Could the future lend itself to something as exciting and fun as a Christian fantasy novel? I cannot give the answer to this, but I can say that, with God, anything is possible.

Peter Silas

Book 1:

The Prophecy of the Sacred Cross

Prologue

Twelve year old Timothy found himself in a very strange building, climbing winding stairs; each floor looked exactly like the last. Eventually realizing that something was chasing him, climbing turned into running, and running turned into stumbling. It was not until a strong presence was felt upon his shoulders that he looked back: there was nothing but descending staircases broken up by empty wooden floors.

"Where is my mother?" Timothy gasped, realizing he was now alone.

He distinctly remembered having entered the building with his mother, but could not recall precisely the moment when they had separated.

Starting again up the stairwell, Timothy heard the sound of an elevator arriving at the floor above him. Confident that he was no longer missing his mother, Timothy rushed up the stairs, veered off into a corridor and turned down the first corner he came to. The elevator was straight ahead, and so he hurried to look inside – but by the time he reached it the door had closed. Curiously, he looked up to find dozens of floor numbers and, noticing that number ninety-nine was lit, he looked down to the side of the elevator.

"'Ninety-eight,'" Timothy read off of a placard.

Timothy immediately ran back to the stairs, still suspecting that his mother was on the elevator. Running much faster than the last time, he found himself suddenly at the end of another hallway, peeking around its first corner.

"How fortunate!" Timothy declared, nearly out of breath.

He had arrived just in time to see the elevator door open up. But trying to make his way forward, he found that his legs would not move. Despairingly, he could only look ahead and expected that he would once again be too late. The door this time, however, did not close. Instead the path before him became a brilliant tunnel of light and inexplicably drew his eyes closer to the elevator. Finding there to be only darkness within, he became drawn to the sharp contrast it had with his surroundings. In fact, the more he focused on the darkness beyond the light the closer he felt to it – as if the elevator was traveling toward him through the tunnel. Like a reflex, he reached out in an effort to touch the door frame but in reality it was still several feet away.

The light in the hallway then diminished, and conversely the darkness filling the elevator converted into a glowing brightness. Once this disparity came to its peak, Timothy felt able to move forward and walked through the open door.

"There are stairs in an elevator... how very interesting!" Timothy said in awe.

A set of two dozen steps upward lay in front of him, and he peeked back through the door to make sure that he had in fact entered into an elevator.

Hoping that he was following his mother's footsteps, Timothy began to climb up the stairs as the absurdity of the situation diminished from his mind. The passageway was dark and narrow, but his thin body frame allowed him to pass with ease. As he approached the final few steps a source of light returned above him, penetrating through cracks in what appeared to be yet another door.

"That is strange; a cellar door at the top of a set of

stairs!" Timothy called out, half-laughing.

It was a hatch positioned at an angle, designed so that one would have to pull it open rather than push. Fortunately there was a rope hanging down from the handle bar, to which he took hold of it with both hands.

"It's stuck," Timothy muttered, unable to pull it open. "Shouldn't gravity be assisting me with this?"

Discouraged, he stepped down with one leg, bent his knees and again grabbing the rope became exhausted, until it finally opened. Without hesitation he jumped up and pulled himself through to the roof of the building, finding himself outdoors. Except for minimal light coming from the faded stars and moon in the sky, it seemed to be as dark as the passageway.

The light that had sifted through the hatch proved itself to be fruitless.

"I am so afraid," Timothy blurted out loud, as wisps of air began to pass through the night.

"No matter what happens…," a very familiar voice replied from above, briefly soothing his fears.

The wind carried the voice away to the edge of the roof, bringing his eyes to a roof ladder hooked over a cement lip. Still searching for his mother, Timothy felt no other choice but to approach the edge of the building top. He peeked over the ridge and looked downward, finding speckled white dots: like in the sky, they were countless and seemed to go on for an eternity.

"I've got to get a better view!" he proclaimed, stepping up on the cement.

At that very moment he felt again a strong presence behind him, similar to the one he had encountered on the stairwell. Timothy decided to look back toward the center of the roof and saw a shadow moving across his view. Startled, he stumbled backward and, unable to catch the railing on the ladder, plunged into the night.

"One-hundred, ninety-nine, ninety-eight, ninety-seven," a fell voice pronounced, counting down each floor he passed by.

Timothy looked up to the top of the building and like an explosion it revealed an unending brightness. It was so powerful that it forced him to briefly shut his eyes. Upon opening them back up, still able to see the radiating light, Timothy grasped in his mind something rather extraordinary. Yet different in concept, what he was now seeing was strangely reminiscent to his experience on the ninety-ninth floor, where a lightened tunnel had seemingly brought him closer to a darkened elevator. This time, however, there was a tunnel of darkness and it was moving him away from a source of light. Additionally, he recognized something peculiar: the barbarous voice was coming from the light, yet he had heard a pleasant sounding voice while on top of the roof in darkness.

"My father told me something purely good could not have in it any part of something dark," Timothy reflected.

Still counting backward, the voice was now suddenly at fifty.

"Forty-nine, forty-eight, forty-seven," the disturbing voice continued.

With every number came a window before his eyes, which through each he could see the stairwell that he had laboriously climbed. He closed his eyes, this time for good, and nausea began to resonate through his chest; sweat poured down his face. Forty-six then became forty-five and forty-four became forty-three.

This continued until the final number one, and within a heartbeat his head hit a pillow. Timothy woke up and a cold washcloth lay upon his forehead; seeing his father off in the distance, he felt his mother lift him up to her arms.

Chapter 1

"Timothy? Timothy!" Mrs. Jenks declared, disrupting his daydream. "Timothy, it is time to break into your assigned group!"

Seventh grade was the first time Timothy realized for certain that he was going to be recognized differently than the average person. He frequently told his parents that he felt it was unfair how he was categorized: not for his intentions, but rather based on how others judged him. If one could picture an archetype of a very intellectual boy, who dressed up regularly for a day in a public school as if he was still in private school and who always knew the answer to a question, then that would be Timothy. Unfortunately, Timothy was far too shy and not the least bit outspoken. Inconsistencies such as these led to the differences in how Timothy was treated. On the one hand, most of his teachers recognized both his aptitude and unusual ability to remember abstract details. Because of this they would give him the benefit of the doubt, usually praising his performance on examinations and writing a giant letter A on his papers. On the other hand, his class mates saw a quiet, socially-awkward and religious boy who was very passive and appeared to lack confidence. This, in addition to pure jealousy, always led to him being outcast from various social networks; it often led to him being teased and mocked.

Timothy walked across the hall to sit with the other four students, who all had superior reading abilities for their ages. It was very troubling for him that none of them were his friends. Most of the friends he had had all failed the third grade, except for one who was not in his reading class.

"Okay group, please open up your books to page sixty-two," Miss Shull instructed.

Mrs. Jenks had stayed with the larger portion of the class to teach a lesson on prefixes and root words. Timothy was thrilled this was the case, as Miss Shull had a very soothing voice and always smiled as she talked. Mrs. Jenks, on the other hand, had a very cross face and would often snap at the students. This made Timothy very uncomfortable and at times discouraged, but to other students it seemed quite normal.

"Do I have any volunteers to start reading? Timothy, would you care to read?" Miss Shull inquired.

"Well, that would be fine," Timothy responded.

He began to read the advanced topic with his usual precision. Timothy was very articulate and Miss Shull would nod every time he finished a paragraph. Often times she would forget to ask another student to take over, and neither would the other students ask for their turn. His reading continued for a few moments, but before long the bell rang.

"Don't forget, kids, please bring your copy of the book home with you and continue reading through chapter seven; Mrs. Jenks is likely to give a quiz in the morning!"

Timothy walked back to his desk and picked up his backpack. Feeling fortunate that he had survived reading without being made fun of, he let out a big sigh and rushed to his next class: World History. It was one of his favorite topics. He could not wait to turn in his paper on the current Greco-Turkish War II, and the historical events leading up to it. The challenge had been to find a way to present it without having religion being the primary focus.

"I am sure I will do well. I was careful with it after all," Timothy told himself, stopping by his locker.

Timothy put a few books away from his backpack. Turning around, he became off-balanced and fell backward to the ground; something had bumped into him.

"Move out of the way! Why don't you go pray or something?" another student yelled at him.

Timothy looked up and it was a boy from the football team. A bully by trade, he continued walking and broke out into laughter along with his friends. There were a few other students who witnessed the aggressive behavior, but they closed their lockers and walked away as if nothing had happened.

Alone, Timothy stood up and sullenly walked to class.

"Good morning students," Mr. Lowry said, just after the bell rang. "Today is a big day. I trust you all have your projects to hand in! But before that, we need to finish your lesson on the progression of American society.

"Recall that we discussed how big of a change our country went through a few decades back, in the tens and twenties. Up until then, there was this notion of a god being connected to our constitution, which limited how we could progress toward real change. Now, all religion has been separated from our government and our school systems and we are better off because of it. Are there any questions about the facts I just reviewed?"

Mr. Lowry looked around the room, and found one student raising his hand.

"Yes, Timothy?"

"Good morning Mr. Lowry. I do have a burning question. Why is it that people are supposed to hide their religious views, in particular when speaking of Christianity, but at the same time it is okay to talk about if one is condemning it? All of the textbooks seem to be somewhere along the spectrum between agnostic and atheist; are those not religions in and of themselves?"

"Excellent question indeed Timothy, although I think your views show you to be a bit young and prove that you lack a certain understanding. Would anyone here like to explain this to our friend Timothy?"

"I would!" a young voice called out. "It is because his family is religious and his dad is a priest, and they think they are better than us and that we all might as well go to hell! What a loser!"

Giggles and sneers throughout the classroom were directed at Timothy.

"I should have kept my mouth shut. Why do I never keep my mouth shut?" Timothy said under his breath.

"Alright students, settle down now!" Mr. Lowry said with a grin. "Let's move on from this particular topic. So with all of these variables known, can someone please tell me in what ways are we benefitted by limiting the conceited flaunting of personal views in the public sector? How far can we push –?"

Mr. Lowry stopped his sentence, as the principal appeared in the doorway with Timothy's father.

"Excuse me Mr. Lowry, but can we please see Timothy?" the principal whispered.

Mr. Lowry paused for a brief moment, uncomfortably gazing at Timothy's father. "Yes, of course. Timothy, could you turn in your assignment on your way out? On the side table there is fine."

Timothy placed his assignment as instructed and walked over to his father. They began walking down the hall as the principal increased his distance behind them with each step.

"Tim, we need to take a trip to the doctor today.

Your mother and I need you to be especially strong and answer any questions he may have for you."

"Dad, can I ask you a question?"

His father grinned. "Yes, of course Tim.

"Why can't I find myself to be normal like most other kids?"

"Because you are not most other kids: you are Timothy. And you are my son. Have some patience! We have just a short drive ahead of us."

They proceeded through the exit and there idling was his father's car. Father John opened the passenger door for Timothy, reminding him to fasten his seatbelt. Timothy then looked over to observe his father's usual routine of sitting down, buckling his own seatbelt and placing his flat cap on the top of his head. They were the same motions made in the same manner that Timothy could remember watching ever since he was a little boy. Something about it was especially comforting.

They drove down the winding driveway, only a few short miles from that point to the highway. Father John looked at Timothy a few times, before he finally was able to speak.

"Now Tim, when we return home... you must remember that I will not be home tomorrow night through the weekend. Your mother will be home of course, and you know how to reach me by phone. The meeting that I am attending is very important."

Timothy's father sensed that his only son was very troubled by this news. It was rather unfortunate that Timothy felt a desire to spend more time with him, as he felt that he did not see his father as much as most of his schoolmates saw theirs. Part of this desire was evidenced by memories Timothy had when his father would come home right after work and be available to sit down with the family for dinner, or when he would go fishing with Timothy on the weekends. Recently, however, his father did not come home until late in the evening and most weekends not at all.

Father John was a very important man, but only relative to his new endeavors. Very few understood the essence of what it was that he did. To many it only seemed to be a family tradition – from one generation to the next – for the father of each respective generation to dedicate his life to a church. But to Father John and those who understood his faith, it was more than a church: it was the Church.

Timothy responded after a long silence. "Well dad, you know... I try my best to pray about missing you and being able to understand what you are doing for our parish. Sometimes I can't get past the feeling of missing you."

"And I miss you, Tim; I miss you all the time. It is the nature of our faith to feel very lonely, and the times we are in do not help. Someone has to keep our mission going and in order to do that it requires diligence and perseverance. Perhaps one day you will have the chance to play your part as well."

They drove for about fifteen minutes until arriving at the heart of Laketown's business district. Father John then turned off of the main road, which led them miles into the country. The scenery immediately changed into a peaceful assortment of nature. Green pastures, ponds and groves of trees were randomly placed along the way. Reaching a large lake, the road turned from pavement to dirt and he pulled into a long driveway that ended with an empty parking lot.

"'St. Paul's Center for Spiritual Counseling,'" Timothy read aloud, looking at an ornate sign attached to a very old building.

Despite only having been there once before, Timothy remembered well his last experience. The doctor's office was the only occupied space in a very old and partially renovated facility, which was only reachable by walking through empty, drafty hallways. The parking lot was quite a few steps from the main entrance, and Timothy also remembered having to walk a ways through the chilly late fall air. It was just as well that he had forgot to bring his jacket to school that morning, as the weather was warmer than average.

Walking to the building with his father, Timothy let out a sigh before halting half way to the entrance.

"Timothy, what is it?" Father John rhetorically asked, for he knew very well that his son was perplexed by something disturbingly familiar.

Father John was attuned to recent experiences that Timothy had had, sometimes at a rate of several times per week where he would sense something to be strikingly unusual. Each time Timothy would react in the same manner, although he would always reveal the disturbance to be unique.

"Well I have been here before. Yes, I know I've been to this place," Timothy said, correcting himself, "but I mean that I have been here at this exact point in time. Everything seems so familiar, and it feels as though there is something around me that I cannot see."

Father John put his arm around Timothy's shoulder and pulled him close, sharing a silent act of compassion. To many who observed them, there would be seen a very mystical composition to their relationship as father and son. It was as if they were able to understand deep meanings within their conversations and mannerisms, without actually needing to have a sufficient content of dialogue. Part of this was the articulate manner that they would speak in, but that paled in comparison to the indescribable mysticism that both their verbiage and demeanor revealed.

They continued through the parking lot, which turned into a courtyard just before the old, brass doors that served as the only entrance. Opening them, Father John let Timothy walk in first and they began walking down a large space. Aside from support columns, the entire first floor was an open concept.

At the other end of the building, they reached the stairs to find that the elevator was out of service. It was just as it had been the last time they visited, and it took four flights of twelve stairs each to reach the counseling office. Once reaching the fourth floor, they walked down a long corridor, which led back to the front of the building. The end of the hallway then led them to the only door on that particular level.

"'St. Paul's Center for Spiritual Counseling,'" Timothy repeated, this time to himself.

The label consisted of fancy gold leaf lettering that rested on top of ceramic covered glass. Directly inside of the solitary door was a very large waiting area, surrounded by four wood plank walls. On two of the walls there hung beautiful, hand painted icons of saints from all ages. Across from them the third wall had three more doors, very similar to the door they had entered through, except that there was no writing on the glass. Otherwise, there was little else to be seen. There was neither a receptionist nor reading material and very few chairs to sit in. Timothy and his father immediately took a seat in the waiting area, but only for only a brief time as the middle of the three doors opened.

"Glory to Jesus Christ!" Timothy's doctor avowed, in his usual excited tone.

"Glory forever! Thank you Father Andrei for your ability to see Timothy on such short notice," Father John replied, embracing his colleague with a triple kiss of peace.

Father Andrei was now foremost a priest; he had attended medical school and became a psychiatrist in his first career path. Father John was intent on referring to Father Andrei as a doctor to make it easier on his son, as he was afraid for him having to make excuses otherwise to leave school. It was unfortunate that many times Timothy had been taunted for his faith, but the sentiments of others were not conducive to a boy of his likeness and it was most necessary to allow Timothy the ability to find himself with a certain level of normalcy around his peers. In Father John's wisdom he found ways to limit the persecution Timothy had to deal with as Timothy's situation could not afford to be tested any further.

Wearing his usual garb, Father Andrei was dressed in his inner cassock along with a very weathered, yet profound vestment-sized pectoral cross. Revealing his thinning dark hair, he chose not to wear any head covering while counseling.

"Timothy, what a pleasure it is to see you again," Father Andrei smiled. "It has been a year to the day; I could say it is very inconsequential to see you under such circumstances otherwise."

Father Andrei then nodded at Father John, signaling that he was ready to begin the session with Timothy. To that, Father John promptly turned around and exited the office space, as he was looking forward to a walk through the vast greens that surrounded the building. There was much for him to think about, and it was rare that he had any time to process his concerns.

Father Andrei led Timothy through the center door

and into the counseling room, closing the door behind him. Timothy then had a seat on the couch, which was the only piece of furniture other than Father Andrei's chair.

"So Timothy, here we find ourselves once again," Father Andrei began, turning his cheerful face into a rather gloomy expression. "Your father has explained to me that you had a troubling dream last night. Would it be possible for you to share with me the details of the dream?"

Timothy became increasingly anxious. Father Andrei's words reminded him of the dream that he had there vividly described one year ago to the day. He recollected how he had explained to him that he found himself walking about in complete darkness, searching for some light that could help him find his way. "The further I traveled," he had continued to tell Father Andrei, "the further from any light I felt to be until this feeling of nausea came over me. It vibrated in my body. Soon I felt hopeless and it was the only feeling I knew until I found myself absolutely still and no longer searching. Light then began to fill the entire room and the world turned on its side. But the world wasn't sideways – I was somehow horizontal and felt a soft pillow under my head until I realized that I was in my bed. Then I saw something great: a man, who looked so much like the icons of God's only son, sat next to me. I felt all of this grace, or something like that. Before I could breathe he told me that I need not worry no matter what happens."

Timothy next remembered how he had suddenly awakened from the dream, but had not actually woken up. It had been synonymous with reality.

"No matter what happens, just like in my dream last night," Timothy said, finally responding after his brief daydream.

"I'm sorry, Timothy? What are you saying?" Father

Andrei asked, appearing a little confused.

"Oh, no… I am sorry. I was thinking of my dream from last year and realized that it contained a similar statement to the one I had last night."

"Timothy, your mind bears a heavy burden," Father Andrei insisted.

"Yes," Timothy responded, as a tear fell from his eye. "I feel like there is something I am supposed to do. Or rather I must find – or even something I should be! I don't really understand all of this."

"It will be alright. I'm here with you, just as God is always. Take your time. But it is very important that you are able to explain to me your dream from last night."

Father Andrei then proceeded to have a daydream of his own, reflecting back to his conversation with Father John earlier that morning. He recalled seeing the pain in his good friend's eyes, concerned for his son being able to process his dreams. And like Father John, he had a suspicion that both of Timothy's dreams were directly related. He only needed for Timothy to give a detailed recount to confirm their suspicions. Unfortunately, Timothy had much difficulty with talking to people about his dreams, and his own father was no exception.

"Trust in me Father John," Father Andrei had told him that morning, "if these two experiences are to bear no difference, then I am confident that Timothy will once again find himself to explain to me his dream. Perhaps he is embarrassed to tell you, as he was last time."

"Okay, so this is how the dream started," Timothy said, bringing Father Andrei's mind back to the room. "I found myself walking up several flights of stairs. I am not sure how many I actually walked up, but I can say for sure how many there should have been. Every floor I came to looked like the last. And there was a final set of stairs before a door that looked like it would lead to a cellar, only it was above me and not below me."

"Tell me more about this 'final set' of stairs, in as much detail as you can provide me," Father Andrei instructed, before Timothy could let out another word.

"Well they were very narrow, or at least the passage way was, and... oh, there was an open door that led me to this passage way... an elevator door! And, before the doorway, it was like I was seeing a tunnel before my eyes, and it was as if my eyes had grown closer to the space inside the elevator without my body actually moving. All I could focus on was the lightened room and the sharp contrast it had with the darkened elevator space!" Timothy explained, suddenly becoming engaged.

Father Andrei was puzzled. Although Timothy was well-spoken for his age, at times his mind worked much too fast to coordinate with his speech.

"My dear boy, please do start over again... from the lightened room and the darkened elevator."

"Sorry Father Andrei, this is very difficult! When I reached the top floor, number ninety-nine I think it was, I ran down a hallway and saw an elevator in front of me. I had hoped that my mother was in it. Unfortunately, I suddenly could not move; the elevator had to be at least twenty feet away from my reach at that point. Then the room became very bright, although the space inside the elevator was becoming extremely dark."

"Anything purely from good and of light never had in it any part from evil and of darkness," Father Andrei remarked.

Timothy nodded in agreement, and then continued describing his dream.

"Once all of the light and dark business settled down, I was able to move and I made my way into the elevator. I found a final set of stairs in between a narrow passage way and at the top of those stairs was a cellar door. It was inverted, if you know what I mean. It looked like I should be above it to climb downward, rather than being below it to climb up. Also there were cracks within the door itself that light seemed to also shine through. My eyes became very focused on this. Wouldn't yours?"

Father Andrei smiled.

"So I pulled on a piece of rope, trying to open the door," Timothy went on, "but it was very hard to open. It felt light but was somehow stuck. I tired myself out and nearly gave my hands rope burn."

Father Andrei raised an eyebrow to this, but continued listening as he did not want to steer Timothy from his thought process.

"You know, Father Andrei, I also remember a detail about the stairs that led to the cellar door. There were exactly twenty-four."

"Twenty-four," Father Andrei repeated. "Numbers are very strange, aren't they?"

Timothy's voice became much softer. "Finally I opened the cellar door, but after all that there was no light on the other side of it aside from some dimmed stars."

Timothy explained the rest of the dream just as it had happened, and once he reached the part where his head had hit his pillow, finding himself in his mother's arms, Father Andrei remained silent with a only a blank stare.

"That must have been very difficult for you to talk about," Father Andrei eventually said, sympathetically.

"Yes, it was very scary. I am thankful I woke up just in time."

Chapter 1

"I have only one last question for you, Timothy," Father Andrei asked after another pause, "how have things been for you at school? More specifically, how have people been treating you and interacting with you? I do remember how saddened you have been in the past, especially regarding how you feel you are looked at as very different from others."

"Not good at all," Timothy confessed. "I know that the last lunch period I sat down at a table with a few students from my reading group. I get the feeling that they do not like me, as they are not very friendly. The only time someone seems to admit that I am there is when I say something, as moments later someone may look at me very briefly and with a very confused face. I know that at times recently I have been called church-boy, and I even remember that last year we voted on the most popular student among other titles. I won the 'most likely to join a church' label, which is strange because I already go to a church. Anyway, the history teacher, Mr. Lowry, wouldn't have that. He went to the principal who then decided that no one was allowed to bring up going to church because not everyone has the same beliefs as me. I am not even the one who brought it up, although it seemed it was taken out on me."

In his usual fashion when contemplating something profound, Father Andrei closed his eyes. Reopening them, he did not waste another moment before he responded to Timothy.

"These are very difficult times indeed. I have something I want to share with you, Timothy. I don't think you will fully understand this now, but I am fully confident that you will find this useful at some point.

"In regards to how others view you, you could put yourself in their shoes and feel sorrow for their situation. For instance, could one truly have a mutual relationship with someone who is able to read their mind? He or she puts a wall up, which serves as their only guard, but only to discover that someone can still undoubtedly peer into their most innermost desires with glaring eyes. Then that someone interprets what they see, abstracting it into words, which one could not have surmised of their own self.

"Much is the same in a relationship between two people, such as yourself and your peers. Whether it is two friends, two colleagues or even a man and a woman who are in love: if a person faces humility or feels weak and vulnerable based on another peer's insight or words, then one of two things could happen. The first thing that could happen is that the person who had felt humility, weakness or vulnerability would no longer be able to face their peer in the same manner as before; they would have realized that their relationship could not be mutual in any way possible. If this were not to happen, then the person would instead revert to subconsciously refuting the insight that the peer possesses."

Timothy looked especially confused, but at the same time very intrigued.

"What I am trying to say," Father Andrei continued, "is that this might be your very case. You are an example of a boy who possesses a great deal of intelligence among other characteristics, and especially compared to most others of your age. Surely, a great deal more than any other boy of your age that I have met. No one else that you associate with perhaps understands this phenomenon and to them you are quite different. This is rather intimidating to many, even to people who have been around a lot longer than you have, and it brings unnecessary attention to you. For your part, your mind only sees concealment from others and in turn you experience pain. You are an extraordinary boy, Timothy.

Be aware of your surroundings and remember always that there are those who love you dearly. You are never alone, even when you cannot see another person nearby."

Timothy did not respond to this directly. He stood up, bowed his head and cupped his right hand over his left.

"Bless, Father," he stated.

Father Andrei gave him his blessing, and then steered him out of the room where Father John had since returned.

"Timothy, I am going to have a chat with your father for a moment. Will you be alright to wait for a few minutes?"

"Yes Father Andrei. I have a lot of thinking to do, anyhow!"

Father Andrei put his hand on Timothy's head and walked out of the office with Father John. They proceeded a ways down the hallway so that they would not be heard.

"Father Andrei, is it as we expected? Are these dreams connected to my father and the state of the world? Are these possibly signs that Timothy's mind and thoughts are being penetrated by darkness?" Father John crossed himself with his right hand, top to bottom and right to left.

"Something very odd is happening indeed. Timothy has always been unusually mystical and is a sign of wisdom to come. During these times that exist in the current state of the world I would be dishonest if I told you that he is not a target of the ungodly. Let us not get ahead of ourselves and judge the origin or even begin to pretend that we can apply our own meaning to God's plan! Keep a watchful eye on this boy, and meanwhile I believe it might be time to bring this up at the emergency council meeting this weekend. We can also make sure Timothy is added to the prayer lists across the diocese."

"My own father, bless his soul, always told me how this time might come during my lifetime. I never believed it to be a possibility so soon. I thought that there was more time. And Timothy, he is so young," Father John said, becoming teary eyed as they had turned around to return to the office.

"Be strong, and be sure to call me if there are any more occurrences before I see you tomorrow," Father Andrei explained.

Father Andrei's face and tone had become more solemn than Father John had ever remembered. Father Andrei then opened the door and walked to Timothy, briefly putting his hand on his shoulder. Without uttering a farewell, he continued on into his counseling room and closed the door behind him; Timothy looked over just in time to see Father Andrei disappear. Timothy then stood up, gave his father a hug, and they made their way back to the car.

Chapter 2

It was a cool, crisp night. There was a half-moon in the sky and not a cloud to obstruct the bright reflection of light that emanated through the air. These were the nights during which Timothy preferred to fall asleep. Although he was not particularly fond of the colder temperatures late in the autumn season, he certainly looked forward to bundling up underneath his bed covers. Timothy would often pretend he was camping in the middle of the wilderness, surrounded only by a sleeping bag and tent. Instead of looking through his southeast facing bedroom window, he would imagine the moon's glow, shining on him through a pine forest as the owls hooted and crickets chirped.

Having been a very long and thought provoking day for Timothy, he had practically fallen asleep during the car ride from Father Andrei's office. He certainly had no objections climbing into bed at eight-thirty that evening. Five hours into his sleep, however, Timothy heard a loud banging on the door nearest him. His room was such that there were two doors: one to the outdoors and one separating the rest of the house. The door closest to him was the one leading to the outdoors.

He jumped out of bed and then, realizing he was much too loud, began tiptoeing toward a window to the right of the door. It had a pleated shade that he often would peak through in the early morning to see how much snow accumulated, gauging his chances for a snow day from school. But this was a different scenario; it was very much still dark and the moon was nearly covered by clouds.

As he moved closer to the window the knocking continued, now much louder. For a moment Timothy stalled but in accordance with his usual curiosity he continued forward. Opening part of the shade with one hand and holding onto the window sill with the other, Timothy looked through the window. He did not see anything unusual and moved a little more to the right, being careful to neither make a noise nor set the shade in any noticeable motion. As he briefly looked downward, since his cat would often find herself right below his step, yet another knock came. Timothy immediately looked back through the window and there before his eyes was a man with his face all but pressed against the glass. Horrified, Timothy stepped backward and, finding his cat, fell onto the floor.

He immediately picked himself up and started to run out of his bedroom toward the hallway. But before he made it three steps, the man had somehow opened the outside door. Timothy stopped and turned back his head, and there the man appeared before his eyes as stiff as stone as the door rocked back and forth to gusting winds. Unlike through the window, his face was not discernible as it was hidden in shadow, caused by a large hooded cloak hanging over his head.

At first Timothy dared not to run, like prey before a predator; the anonymous man also stood still and this went on for what seemed to be a very long time – until without notice the intruder finally made his move: he opened his mouth wide and let out a scream in an ensemble with fear. Deeply resounding with an evil twinge, the sounds of havoc left Timothy with no other choice but to run into the hallway and escape through the front entrance.

"I know my way around here so very well, with my eyes closed," he muttered to himself, still running. "The darkness should not deter me."

Timothy found a path that led through the woods. He had often taken walks down this path when he felt most alone, and now was a time that being alone felt extremely welcomed. With any luck, he would have the advantage of having navigated there through the wilderness for several years. Hopefully, Timothy thought, the stranger was not familiar with the area.

Continuing onward, Timothy realized that he was no longer being chased. He decided to slow down in order to catch his breath and listen to his surroundings. Fortunately, the only sound he could hear was that of his feet treading through the leaves on the ground, which was calming for only so long as he realized the possibility of the horrid creature detecting his whereabouts.

"I cannot hear anything, not even the crickets. Not even the owls! Why are things so quiet out here?"

Still walking, Timothy found himself near the edge of the woods where an open field of tall, wet grass lay just ahead of him. Looking out into the darkness, a butterfly then revealed itself under the moonlight, suddenly shining down through a break in the clouds.

"You might perhaps be the most beautiful creature that I have ever seen," Timothy said, speaking to the hovering insect.

Its colors were in fact magnificent; its flight was majestic. The butterfly circled about in front of him, and then charged forward as if to lure him. Timothy did not hesitate and pursued it all the way to a river. Interestingly, it had led him precisely to his favorite spot between two large rocks that he often would rest on. The butterfly then continued out to the end of a dock that peered deep along the water's surface. As if it was calling to him, the butterfly seemed to encourage him to follow suit, until it finally dove over the edge and out of sight.

Timothy crept along the soft wooden structure and at its end he fell to his knees, slowly bringing his head out over the edge. His eyes then widened to a glow in the water; he had initially seen his reflection, but soon after it transformed into a face much older. Remaining motionless, Timothy noticed the man in the reflection moving his lips.

"What are you telling me?" Timothy shouted.

Looking closer, he realized it was in fact an older version of his own self. He wore a white, trim beard and was holding a scepter.

"Listen to me," his reflection said. "If you can handle a place such as this – one so far away but yet so close. Not a soul can here reach us, through one's own accord. Younger yet you shall one day be. Pain and joy will then both be found."

"What is so far away? And aren't I quite young enough as it is?" Timothy asked, after a brief silence.

"Look out behind you," the reflection whispered.

Timothy gasped as the reflection disappeared. He refused to turn around, despite a shadow moving over him. Large raindrops then began to hit the river surface and, synchronized with his heart, they increased in frequency until they fell at a steady speed.

"This is just a dream. This is just a dream," he began to repeat, as the world about him began to spin and his eyes became out of focus. "This is just a dream. It's only a dream."

"Timothy, it's only a dream," he heard his father say, shaking him delicately.

Timothy opened his eyes and briefly glanced at his father. Then, looking outside, he observed a steady rain.

Chapter 2

"Just a dream; yes, it was only a dream," Timothy stated.

"Timothy, if you don't wake up now I'm afraid you might be late for school. Come now, I will let you get focused and breakfast will be waiting."

Timothy rubbed his eyes and nodded. His father walked off out of the room and he turned his eyes to his alarm clock: it was 6:45 AM. Like his father, he was accustomed to waking up very early, sometimes as early as five in the morning. This was the first time that he could remember sleeping past six, and he immediately jumped out of bed.

Having his own bathroom, he first washed his face and then got dressed. He was somewhat wobbly putting his shoes on, but it did not present concern in his mind; physical symptoms, such as that, were becoming the norm in his daily life. In fact, not a night seemed to pass by where he did not have a dream that resulted in acute disorientation. No symptoms would prevent his normal routine, however, as he inevitably stood before his make-shift altar, where three icons were hanging above it on the wall. They were of his favorite. In the center of the three was an icon of the Holy Trinity; to the right hung an icon of Christ and then to the left was The Most Holy Lady Theotokos.

"Dear Lord, Jesus Christ, have mercy on me, a sinner," he piously chanted.

He repeated this for a good five minutes, following it up with the Lord's Prayer. Upon finishing, he recalled the caution Father Andrei gave him about using the Jesus Prayer in excess without the guidance of an elder.

"You must have a clear mind and keep Jesus in your heart," Father Andrei had told him. "It is extremely powerful, this prayer, and you mustn't wander astray or invoke any other abilities except that which comes natural to you. Not even I have become very advanced in using this prayer, my boy."

Timothy crossed himself and bowed his head, venerating each of the three icons. Father John was always amazed at how his son would find time to pray on a daily basis, even if only for a few minutes. Where the average person might see their life to contain limited time for extraneous measures, being forced to rush about their life due to material constraints, Timothy would conserve his energy for quite the opposite. If he possessed strength at all it would be in his impeccable ability to organize his routines and an awareness of how they relatively affected one another.

Finishing his prayers, Timothy walked out of his room and still in the hallway he stopped just short of the kitchen. To his left was a guest room where his father would allow traveling monks to stay free of charge. The door had been closed for the past few days and Timothy had been constantly contemplating why he never saw any light coming from the room. This specific guest seemed to remain in the darkness and keep to a very reclusive life style. Timothy was quite curious to learn more of the traveler, despite a recent eerie sensation that would cause him to occasionally shiver every time he walked past that room.

"Timothy, breakfast is done," his father shouted.

He continued on into the kitchen. It was seven o'clock and he realized he had only a few minutes to make it to the bus stop.

"Father, I think I might not be able to sit for breakfast!"

"You'll catch a break this morning. I just heard the morning news and there is a one hour delay due to icy road conditions in the higher elevations. You sure did pick the best time to sleep in! Sit and enjoy, I have made you oatmeal and toast."

"Yes, it is Friday," Timothy replied, taking a seat. "I will have to wait until tomorrow for bacon and eggs!" he said half-jokingly.

Father John placed Timothy's breakfast on the table and went back to the counter to grab his cup of coffee. He turned up the volume on their antique LCD television and sat down to give Timothy some company for breakfast.

"Dad, I haven't seen mother much the past few days; in fact, I have not seen her at all since waking up from my dream the other night. Where has she been?"

"She has been up late and sleeping into the early afternoon," Father John replied, after hesitating for a moment. "Whatever do you mean by 'since waking up from your dream'?"

"Well dad, you know... I woke up in her arms. I dreamt of her during that dream where I was falling, and then she was there waiting for me just as I woke up."

Father John did not say a word. Taking a sip of his coffee, he looked over at the television and detected a breaking news story. Turning up the volume even more, Timothy joined him in watching.

"In global news, reports just in of a never before recorded 10.2 magnitude earthquake off of the Tonga-Kermadec ridge, which is located along the south-west portion of the Pacific Ring of Fire. Widespread devastation has been reported in New Zealand and further reports have been confirmed of a mega-tsunami that made landfall to Eastern Australia just moments ago. Death-tolls are estimated in the thousands between each of the two countries. For more, let's go to our correspondent Jeremy

Trevens in Adelaide, South Australia."

"Thank you Jennifer. Chaos ensues on the eastern shore of Australia as reports have now been confirmed of widespread…"

Father John turned the television off.

"It seems there is so much trouble in the world today," Timothy insinuated. "I remember yesterday on the news they were talking about the war between Turkey and Greece. Do you think Mt. Athos will be invaded?"

Father John then reoriented his mind to that of Timothy's question, as he was chiefly focused on the catastrophe to hit New Zealand and Australia.

"What would make you think Mt. Athos would be invaded?"

"Well… I guess there is more to my reasoning than simply listening to the news yesterday. So, I was reading a book in the school library the other day for my research project. It talked about an earthquake just over forty years ago that had caused problems between Greece and Turkey, sometime in the late 1990's. Although the book made no mention of religion, I connected it to Mt. Athos because you had once told me how it has stood through so much in the past, being in Greece and a region that has so much religious tension. I have been concerned for their welfare ever since. With this natural disaster today it got me thinking again, that's all. What strange timing. You know, I have always thought there was some trend between the decline of religion and all of these problems in the world. It is as if there are now too few people to pray for the world."

Father John knew exactly what Timothy was getting at. In the past few years, natural disasters were becoming much more prevalent. At the same time, anti-Christian sentiment was spreading its influence in both the United

States and Europe and war was breaking out in many areas of the world. Timothy was making a very abstract link, as if to imply that the natural disasters were not so natural but instead preordained.

"Only God knows," Father John said softly.

"How about I brush my teeth," Timothy replied, finishing his breakfast. "I will be ready for you to drive me to the bus stop."

"That sounds like a good plan. I will grab my suitcase and meet you at the car."

Timothy went to brush his teeth and gathered his backpack and books, eventually walking out to the car. The engine was running as his father was patiently waiting for him.

"Tim, as you know I will not be home at all this weekend. I leave for New York State immediately after dropping you off at the bus stop. It works out nicely that you planned on staying over the Stephanopouloses, as I know you have been feeling quite lonely. I have shared my contact information with them in the event of an emergency."

Father John began driving toward the bus stop as Timothy did not have any response to his father's instructions. Two miles later, Father John stopped the car and Timothy gave him a big hug.

"See you Monday, father?"

"Yes. I love you very much, Timothy. Oh, and have a wonderful time tomorrow at the fair! Be brave on the roller coasters, will you? I know you and Jacob have been looking forward to this for quite some time!"

"Bye dad!" Timothy waved, watching his father drive off down the highway.

He joined the two others waiting for the bus and stood there with his arms wrapped around his upper body. It was another dark, chilly morning and the foggy conditions gave him a very eerie feeling. Sensing that he was being stared at, he looked up only to see them shift their eyes toward the main road. Both of these boys were once friends of Timothy who had years ago stayed back in the third grade. They gradually steered away from their relationship, but not solely because of being a full grade apart; rumor had it that Timothy's father was a priest and their parents had erred on the side of caution.

"Hi there, it's cold this morning, huh?"

Timothy purposely said this outside of his usual articulate form. He always made an effort to relate to others by assimilating to them in this way, but usually his exertion came across very unnatural. It wasn't that Timothy wanted to fit in with others, but rather it was that he was aware of how others perceived him and was afraid of causing them to feel uncomfortable. Recalling Father Andrei's speech about how others react to what they do not understand, he looked the other way. He realized it was best to not say another word.

"Sure, Tim," one boy responded after letting a few moments pass by.

The other then blatantly stared at him, silently looking into his eyes. Timothy exchanged a glance, but being the one to typically initiate eye contact with others, he was taken aback until he soon noticed something very peculiar: the boy's eyes were very dark and his face was unusually pale. His eyebrows then became cross, which caused Timothy to look away and eventually the boy returned his gaze to the highway. The bus could not have arrived at a better time.

The ride to school was very quiet, for a change. Sitting alone in his usual routine, Timothy looked out of the window the entire time. He thought about his upcoming classes for the day and what he had been learning the past week. This lasted for half of the trip to school, until the bumpy ride began to make him feel nauseous. He was unsure of how he would even survive the next day at the fairgrounds, given that he could barely make it through a bus ride. Nevertheless, he was absolutely thrilled to be able to spend some time with Jacob. It was by far worth the risk of feeling queasy.

The ill feeling did not subside, to which he recalled his dream from two nights ago. Comparing how he felt while falling from the building with on the bus, he recognized that his experience during the one hundred story descent had not revealed a typical provocation of motion sickness.

"It is as if the nausea in my dream is related to a different essence, rather than that of my own," he enquiringly thought.

The bus stopped and opened its doors in front of the school. Grayson Junior High was named after his town Grayson Village; however it actually resided in the city of Laketown. Its name was in fact the one and only comforting aspect Timothy found about it.

"Timothy, wait up!" Jacob shouted as Timothy entered through the large double glass doors.

Jacob ran up to Timothy, bumping into a few other students along the way. Timothy paid close attention to the sneers that were made at Jacob and then watched as he clumsily dropped a few papers from an armful of books. Unlike Timothy, Jacob was very unaware of his surroundings. It always caused Timothy to laugh, and this time was no exception.

"Hi there, Timothy," Jacob said, pushing up on his glasses with his free hand. "Are you ready to get on with the day? I could barely sleep last night, you know. I was thinking about the sleepover tonight and our trip to Sunny Lake Fairgrounds tomorrow!"

"Yes, I know what you mean; I am looking forward to leaving town and doing something different for a change too. I'm also glad that I missed first period reading this morning! I am getting tired of having to read aloud. Miss Shull is rather odd at times."

Friday was the only day of the week that his reading class was first period. Timothy looked forward to Friday's class schedule especially because after first period he had math, study hall and band with Jacob.

"Did you finish your homework on fractions and percentages last night? I barely got it done! I couldn't figure out the last problem," Jacob said, admittedly.

"Oh no," Timothy said out loud, realizing that he had completely forgot about his math assignment. "I fell asleep and it had not even entered my mind. I can't believe..."

"That's very unusual for you to be unprepared," Jacob interrupted. "Well, we do have one free assignment each quarter. Relax! You can't be perfect, and I think it's good for a change you are normal like the rest of us!"

Jacob shoved Timothy playfully as they approached their lockers.

"Whatever!" Timothy replied, with a huge grin on his face.

They both exchanged books between their backpacks and lockers to prepare for the rest of the day. The school bell then abruptly rang and they both closed their lockers at exactly the same time, walking across the hall to math class. As they entered the room, Timothy looked down at his shirt and noticed his cross hanging out of it. He tucked it in very cautiously; displaying any religious paraphernalia would warrant an automatic detention.

Sitting down at their usual places next to one another, they waited for their math instructor to begin class. Mr. Jones was writing out the usual math problems he would start each class with. He was very systematic and predictable, which made it very easy for students like Timothy to excel in his class.

"Good morning students," Mr. Jones said, in his distinctive monotone speech. "Today we are going to review yesterday's lessons on percentages and fractions. I have each of the ten problems projected onto the wall and we can solve them together. Before we begin I am going to walk around the room and collect your assignments."

Timothy took a deep breath. Mr. Jones walked up and down each row, at last reaching him.

"Timothy, can I have your assignment please?"

"I – I don't have it. I mean to say, I did not do this."

"O-ooh," the entire class sounded off, harmonizing together.

Timothy's face turned red and Mr. Jones raised his right eyebrow in disbelief. "Ok, very well. Jacob?" Mr. Jones continued.

Jacob handed over his assignment, and then Mr. Jones walked around to collect from the remainder of the students. Timothy looked around, embarrassed as some classmates were whispering and briefly glancing over at him.

"Jerks," Jacob whispered, in support of Timothy.

––––––––

Later that morning Timothy went outside. He sat alone on a bench and watched some of the boys playing soccer out in the field. The sunshine was abundant and he began to stare off into the woods as the rays of light were shining through the tree tops. Timothy could sit for hours pondering about the world and any other given topic that was on his mind. He rarely found himself with more than a few minutes, though, as something would usually interrupt his train of thought.

Beyond the field, Timothy noticed in the distance something moving about the woods. He watched as it trotted along, causing some leaves to fall off the branches as it passed by. Timothy stood up and began walking toward the tree line, out of the way of the other kids who were playing soccer until he was able to make out the creature's shape.

"What kind of animal is that? Almost like a deer?" he asked himself, under his breath.

He couldn't imagine what else on earth would be rustling through the woods, especially since it was very marshy and there were thorn bushes scattered all around. Besides, there were obnoxious kids running around the soccer field and that would be enough to scare any animal away. Timothy decided to walk a little bit closer, and at that point he found himself at the edge of the field. Suddenly the movement stopped and he could see part of the animal through the trees. It looked at him, and making eye contact he was astonished.

"It's a person?" he asked, making out the vague face through the tree branches.

He was very confused over what he was seeing, as its body still looked like a deer or a similar type of four legged animal. He was convinced that he was looking at the face of a human.

"Hey you, what are you doing over there? Spying on us? Make yourself useful and join us; we are one player short."

Timothy looked over at the boys who were on the soccer field, disoriented as if he had just arrived home from another world. He then snapped his head back at the woods, finding the creature to have disappeared. Disappointed, he moved in a little closer but there was nothing at all to be found but trees and bushes.

"Where did it…"

"Hey there, Timmy! We are talking to you! Yes, you! Wake up," a voice screamed.

The group of seven boys began to laugh at him.

"Have you ever even touched a soccer ball before? We wouldn't want you to get your nice fancy school clothes all dirty!"

Timothy sighed and mustered up enough courage to walk over to them.

"I know how to play. I have watched you all many times," Timothy sharply replied.

He began to look at each of the boys to see who exactly he was dealing with. One of them was Jason Miller, the same boy who earlier that morning had exchanged glances with him at the bus stop.

"I'm not playing with him," Jason shouted. "He's a freak, just like the rest of his family!"

Timothy noticed that Jason looked just as ill as he did that morning.

"Well, I don't have to play. It is okay," Timothy conceded, turning around and walking away.

The same boy who had originally called over to him spoke up.

"No, it's fine Tim. Ignore Jason. There are only ten or fifteen minutes left here before the next class starts and we'd like to play with even sides if we can."

Jeremy always took charge of the groups he was in. Considered the most popular boy in the school, it was rare that anyone would ever challenge him.

"Why don't you be on my team and you can stand at defense," Jeremy continued to say. "If the ball gets past me or Jason here then don't worry about any fancy foot work. Kick it as far away from you as you can, even if you have to put it out of bounds. You're good to go?"

"Sure Jeremy. I can do that," Timothy confirmed.

The boys began to play and Timothy watched as they kicked the ball back and forth. Jeremy and Jason were very athletic, and rarely did the ball ever get past them. They scored twice while Timothy stood in the same spot.

Timothy soon became distracted and looked out into the woods again. He was still very curious as to what it was that he had seen.

"Yes, just a deer was all," he muttered.

Timothy figured that it was no different than his dreams. Most likely, he had been only confused and disoriented, observing nothing other than a figment of his imagination just before waking up to reality. He turned back to the game only to find that the ball was headed his way with the other team running behind it.

"Kick it out of bounds!" Jeremy yelled out.

Timothy braced himself to kick the ball and before he knew it, he was shoved to the ground, lying in a patch of muddy grass. He heard cheers and knew that the other team had scored. Embarrassed, Timothy sat up and looked around. He saw Jason staring at him with a disgusted look on his face.

The school bell rang and the other boys left him on the ground, running back to school. Jeremy then stopped and looked back at Timothy.

Chapter 2

"Thanks Tim for your help, and sorry about my friends," Jeremy shouted before catching up to his friends.

Timothy stood up and began to squint as a burst of sunshine hit his face. He then gave into a half smile, happy to know that there was still one who could show compassion.

Hurrying inside, he stopped by the bathroom to clean up. Brushing the dirt and mud off of his sweater, he noticed a scrape on his neck and washed it clean. He partially unfolded the turtleneck he was wearing to cover it up and rushed off to band class. As Timothy approached his seat, he caught Jacob staring at him.

"Timothy, what have you got yourself into?" Jacob whispered. "It looks like you were rolling around outside. Are you alright?"

"I'm fine. I was playing soccer."

Jacob burst out into laughter. "I don't think I've ever seen you play sports before, Tim?"

"I know; it is very rare. The funny part is I was actually playing with some of the kids from the soccer team. I didn't do so well," Timothy admitted.

"Well that's obvious! How'd you end up with that gang?"

"I'm not really sure. It's a long story. Something in the woods caught my attention," Timothy replied.

Just then, the auditorium doors slammed shut as Mr. Finkly hurried down the aisle, presenting himself before the group of young musicians.

"Sorry I'm late! We have much to do here this afternoon; form into your sections! That's it, brass to the right and percussion to the left. Hurry now!"

Mr. Finkly tried to catch his breath as he opened the compositions on his conductor stand. The students always thought his mannerisms were very comical and had difficulty taking him seriously.

"I won't repeat myself. Let's get on with this show!"

Along with the other students, Timothy picked up his clarinet and began to run through the octaves. He did this effortlessly, having played his clarinet for four years. Jacob, on the other hand, was struggling with his French horn. This was only his second year playing an instrument and only had joined so that they would have another class together.

"Alright boys and girls, from the top now…"

Mr. Finkly raised his hands, pointed his conductor's wand at the students and the sound of amateur music began to play. Timothy, daydreaming about his vision from the woods, stared out into the auditorium and did not make a sound.

Chapter 3

The bus dropped the two boys off at Jacob's house at four o'clock that afternoon. Unlike Timothy, Jacob's house was on the main route that connected Grayson Village and Laketown. Not only did Jacob not have to rely on transportation to the bus stop, but he also had the luxury of the bus not arriving until twenty minutes before school started.

The Stephanopouloses were very wealthy and owned a very large townhouse. Behind the house was over twenty acres of woods and a very large brook, which the water running off of the nearby hills would feed into. Like Timothy, Jacob was an only child and usually had the entire property to himself for a few hours after school. He spent that time playing video games, except when Timothy came over they would work on his tree house. He was not allowed to work on it alone as his mother, Andrea, was constantly worried for his safety.

"What if a bear or a wolf was walking by, or what if you fell out of the tree," she would always repeat.

Walking into Jacob's house, they tossed their jackets aside and had a seat on the couch. Both were at first quiet, and Timothy began to anticipate what Jacob would say next.

"Timothy, do you want to try my new game? It's pretty sweet! It's called Galactic Wardens and just came out. You can create your own world, and eventually each galaxy competes against each other with their top fighter."

"Oh Jacob, that's okay! I know that you don't often have someone to play video games with, but I still am not fond of them. I can't seem to get the hang of them and you would certainly be better off playing without me, that I am sure of! Besides, we have your tree fort to work on."

"Yeah, you are right. I think one day I will get you to play again, but then again maybe I could follow your example!"

"Thank you, Jacob. Let me change into something else so we can go outside and get some work done. We've got to finish this before winter. I will be right back."

Timothy went to the second floor and down a long corridor to reach the bathroom. He had two changes of clothes in a small suitcase that his father had dropped off for him that morning, and was looking forward to exchanging his muddy sweater and turtleneck with something much more comfortable. Then, recalling the scrape he had gotten on his neck, he looked in the mirror and pulled down the collar.

"That's quite odd," Timothy commented, unable to find the scrape.

He looked on either side of his neck, but it was nowhere to be found.

"I could have sworn I had a scrape, right here..." Timothy said, bringing himself closer in a last effort to find an abrasion.

Timothy gave up looking and changed into a buttoned-down flannel shirt. He also had a new pair of durable work jeans that he received on his last birthday. This was the first time he had the chance to put them on, and Timothy was more than delighted to switch them with his dress slacks. He then carefully folded up his clothing and kneeled down to place it into his suitcase. Standing back up, Timothy took a few steps back so that he could get a full view of himself in his new clothes.

Chapter 3

"This is not right," Timothy proposed, suddenly feeling sad and removed from the world. "What do my clothes really mean? How important are these materials to anything at all?"

As Timothy pondered over these considerations, his mind wandered away from the room. The mirror became a portal to which he could see his thoughts. He began to feel a very heavy burden as he was envisioning a time from long ago, and there sat a hermit who was living in a hut made of sticks and stone. This hermit was wearing ragged clothing and was surrounded by candles inside of his small living quarters. Beginning to kneel, he lifted his arms up toward the ceiling. Joy took over this recluse's facial expressions and a single tear came out of his eye. This man was obviously content with the bare minimum that he had.

Timothy then felt within his heart the concept of something much greater than Earth itself; it was something that gave the entire universe its meaning. As he continued peering through the mirror, the area surrounding the hermit began to light up. It revealed a great space filled with glory, happiness and virtue for which words were not capable to describe. This ineffable vision then faded as soon as it started, and Timothy's eyes were brought back to the very spot he was standing in. Timothy was absolutely mystified as it was the first experience like this that he could recall where he was not dreaming to start with.

Someone then knocked on the bathroom door.

"Tim, what are you doing? It has been over ten minutes. If we don't get moving it will be dark before we know it and my mother will be home... Timothy?"

"Yes Jacob, I'm all set. I am fine," Timothy finally replied, opening the door suddenly and causing Jacob to jump backward.

"Oh, well okay… yes, you are fine!" Jacob said, as he raised the pitch of his voice at the end of the statement. "I made some hot chocolate for you, so let's go have some and be on our way!"

"Sounds good, Jacob. Let's go!"

Timothy walked past Jacob. Sensing something very peculiar about Timothy's state of mind, Jacob proceeded to follow him down the stairs and into the kitchen. They both sat down on stools at the kitchen's table bar and began to sip on their cups of hot chocolate. Jacob abruptly set his cup down after just a few sips.

"Wait!" Jacob blurted out.

"What?" Timothy inquired.

"Well, this wouldn't be the same without whipped cream! I almost forgot!"

Jacob rushed to the refrigerator and took out the can of whipped cream. He went back to Timothy's cup and began spraying it on top of the hot chocolate.

"Say when!" Jacob commanded.

"That's quite enough!"

Timothy chuckled as Jacob had sprayed an inordinate amount of whipped cream into his cup. It had overfilled and began to fold over itself, down the side of the cup. Timothy began drinking, but Jacob finished first as he had less whipped cream to deal with. He stood over by the sliding glass doors that led to the patio in the backyard.

"Take your time!" Jacob confirmed.

Slurping up the rest, Timothy left his cup next to Jacob's and they hurried outside. It was becoming overcast again and in conjunction with the fog it seemed closer to dusk than it actually was. The temperature was also much warmer than that morning, and so they decided not to bring their jackets with them. Reaching a small bridge that spanned across the widest point of the brook, Timothy stopped and looked over its side. The water was bubbling over the rocks as the minnows swam downstream.

"It is so peaceful. These creatures in their natural state, I mean," Timothy said.

"Speaking of these creatures, could you talk to me about the woods back at school? What on earth was interesting enough to cause you to go near those jerks in the first place?"

Timothy thought about what Jacob said. He did not know what on earth it was; the real question should have been about what it was doing on Earth to begin with. At this point, he was not too sure about anything he saw and he questioned whether or not he should just admit that he was daydreaming. Timothy then realized it was quite dangerous to be curious about visions for which he knew not the source. Were they good natured? Were they really dark visions, made to look appealing by their initial impression, like in his dreams?

"I am not so sure," Timothy finally admitted.

They walked over the bridge and into the woods. There were still a few more minutes of walking before they were to reach the tree fort.

"I think," Timothy said, deciding to continue, "that what I saw was some kind of four legged animal. But it was odd because the second look I gave caused me to think it was a person. Something sure was very peculiar about it, even despite its appearance. These times are leading to strange occurrences."

"What do you mean, 'times'?" Jacob questioned Timothy, genuinely perplexed.

"Don't you notice all that is going on in the world? How about all of the civil wars around the world? Do you wonder about the catastrophes, or even the predominantly selfish and self-absorbed attitude that people seem to have? Tradition is a thing of the past; progression from what was seems to be quite inevitable."

"To tell you the truth, Tim, I have trouble thinking of anything more than getting my homework assignments done in time to play video games."

Timothy looked at Jacob and let out a sigh of frustration.

"Hey Tim… look, it must be hard thinking about all of these problems. But maybe you should talk to someone about it all? I don't know. It doesn't seem so healthy for you and you are only twelve! And, I notice how it's like you're in a different world. I'm the one that is supposed to be unaware of what's going on, remember? But besides all that, what does all you are saying have to do with weird creatures running in the woods?"

Timothy did not immediately respond to the question, and turned to a wheelbarrow as they neared the tree fort. It was lying in the middle of a pathway next to some other supplies for the project. He began to push it the remainder of the way to a grove of oak trees, which was sandwiched between forests of enormous pine.

"Well Jacob, when was the last time we had ice in early November?"

Jacob still looked confused.

"Forget about that, Jacob. I just have this feeling that things are so strange and I notice how I am having all of these dreams and seeing things that I do not find to be completely normal in an absolute sense. I don't know, maybe I am just overtired from these dreams. It's nothing really. Let's get on with building this tree house!"

"Tree fort," Jacob corrected Timothy.

Chapter 3

They smiled at one another and then climbed the ladder into the tree fort. The structure itself was nearly complete. The base and walls were fully constructed except for a few boards that had to be secured on the floor. Most of the work that remained was carpentry and cosmetic fixes, in addition to applying shingles on the roof. That is where Jacob came in handy. Very skilled in that respect, his father Paul had owned a very large home improvement business. Jacob had apprenticed with him for the past four years. Due to the state of the economy, however, Paul recently was forced to sell the business and subsequently found a job with the federal government.

"Alright Timothy, I will start handing you some supplies. Let's see, we have the hammer, nails, door hinges and window frames. What else... oh, over there are the shingles... we can get those up here at the end. Ready?"

"Ready!" Timothy confirmed.

They worked for the next hour without interruption. Jacob took the lead as they efficiently made progress. Talking about their week at school and the plans they had tomorrow, they began to wind down. The fog had lifted and the clouds parted as the sun began to set. The wet trees glimmered through the rays of light coming from the west, until the sun nearly found its way beyond the hills and shadows began to creep up on them. Timothy then climbed down to the ground and began to look around at the nature. Taking a deep breath through his nose, he sensed the attractive smell of the forest around him.

"Tim, are you fetching the shingles under the tarp over there? If we can get them up in the fort we can call it a day. Thankfully we have the platform hooked up to these pulleys so it shouldn't take too long."

"Yes, I am heading there now. Let me grab the

wheelbarrow and I will get them over to you in a moment's time!"

"Well if it is any moment longer we can call it a night!" Jacob sarcastically blurted out.

Timothy only had to move a few feet before approaching the pile of shingles. He lifted the tarp off and began loading the wheelbarrow. His arms were tired but he forced himself to finish loading all that he could fit. As he placed the last set of shingles in the wheelbarrow, he started to think about all that he had imagined the past week. There was more to this adventure, he thought.

"Keep a positive attitude and open your heart to the indescribable," Timothy told himself.

Timothy lifted his head up and saw what rays of light were left from the sun, shining down in one spot but a few dozen yards in front of him. A beautiful deer, this time unmistakable, then crossed in front of his sight and fixed its stance under the sunlight. It raised its head toward the skies with a majestic effort as Timothy stood still, mesmerized by what presented itself to him.

Jacob, still in the tree fort, called out for Timothy but Timothy did not hear a word he said. Looking out through the window frame, Jacob saw part of Timothy staring off into the distance, but had no clue as to what Timothy was looking at. Jacob stepped closer to the empty square in the wall to gain a better vantage point. He was so determined that he did not pay attention to where he was stepping and his feet neared a small gap in the floor where the boards not been fully placed together.

Timothy began feeling an inner strength that he had not experienced ever before as the deer turned away and ran back into the woods. At that very moment the sound of wood cracking vibrated through the air as Jacob, twenty-five feet above ground, fell through the fort's base. Timothy turned around as the sound made it to his ears, and just before Jacob hit the ground an invisible mass of energy rapidly moved from Timothy's gaze. Barely noticeable to Jacob, he was suspended in the air for just a brief period of time. It was just enough to break his fall as he proceeded to hit the ground.

"Jacob!" Timothy screamed.

Without hesitating, Timothy ran over to Jacob who had not yet moved his body. He shook Jacob's shoulder, but did not garner a response. Timothy began to cry, yelling out to the woods.

"What happened here!" he screamed, closing his eyes.

Trying to determine the next step to take, he stood up to run for help. But before moving a step forward, he heard a brief moan followed by a rustling on the ground.

"Wow Tim that hurt!" Jacob muttered, beginning to sit up. "I can still feel my legs; I think I am okay! I can't believe I fell that far and –"

Timothy interrupted Jacob. "Don't you say another word, and don't you move. I am going to run back to the house. I think your parents may be home by now. Will you be fine here for a moment?"

Jacob nodded and Timothy ran back to the house. Andrea had just come home and was putting away her coat. Timothy let her know what had happened and they ran back to Jacob, who had by that time ignored Timothy and stood up. He was brushing himself off and looking up at the tree fort, not having sustained one injury other than appearing to be slightly confused and dizzy.

"Watch that last step," Jacob laughed.

———

Later that evening, Timothy and Jacob began to set up their tent in the backyard. They had hoped to have had it set up much earlier, but the commotion caused by Jacob's falling from the tree fort had prevented their efforts. After walking inside the house, Andrea and Paul had pampered Jacob and his mother in particular had not ceased constant hugs associated with words of advice.

"How many times did I tell you being out there is such a dangerous affair! A twelve year old boy who thinks he can conquer the world! You take after your father, that is for sure," she had repeated herself. "It is a miracle that you didn't kill yourself. I don't see how you fell down that far and didn't break a bone!"

Jacob was more than used to this and it had not bothered him one bit. His father usually smirked at him when his mother smothered him with love, but that time had been an exception. Timothy, for his part, had sat in one spot the entire time, paying attention to the family dynamics; he had been particularly focused on the interactions that Jacob was having with his mother.

"Alright, we are set for the evening," Jacob said, hammering the last tent pole into the ground. "I have extra blankets here and we should stay fairly warm. Dad is coming out in a moment to start the campfire."

The night revealed a clear sky. The moon brightened up the backyard and created for Timothy that nostalgic feeling that he longed for; being among the beauty of nature and being thankful for the marvelous creations instilled a sense of peace. Timothy sat on a log in front of the campfire and once again began pondering over all of the strange happenings he had recently experienced. He began to accept that it was his calling in life to experience and contemplate the depths of meaning to life. Perhaps this was somehow tied to his family's tradition of the firstborn in each generation becoming a priest. The only part about this that bothered him is that he desired solitude and longed to devote himself to a personal relationship with God; he was not sure how he would handle being around so many people as a priest, despite his affinity for loving others. His father would constantly remind him that everyone who serves their Creator has a certain calling, whether it is in solitude or in communion with others.

Mr. and Mrs. Stephanopoulos wandered outside, bidding Jacob and Timothy a good night.

"Don't stay up too late now," Andrea said as Paul started the campfire. "We have quite the day ahead of us tomorrow!"

"Yes mother!" Jacob responded. "Tim never stays up past nine anyhow."

Jacob's parents walked back inside and Jacob sat down on a log across from Timothy. They both stared into the fire for a few minutes without saying a word. Jacob then broke the silence.

"Do you have any good stories to tell? I remember last time we did this you had a really scary story that nearly knocked me off of my seat," Jacob began laughing hysterically. "Remember when the coyotes howled right at the end and I gasped so loud I thought I woke my parents up?"

"That was a riot! Well, I do in fact have another story to tell of. This one is not just a legend. This really happened," Timothy went on to say, as Jacob leaned forward to hear more of what he was saying.

With stories, Timothy proved to have quite the imagination that could command the concentration of a person who had several other thoughts already preoccupying their mind.

"It happened in the early 19th century. There was a married couple, in their early thirties at that time. They went to visit their priest for counsel as they were convinced that demons were taking over their bodies. What they didn't realize before visiting the priest is that they had been bitten the night before by strange, human-like animals in the middle of the night before. These animals had special powers where they were able to penetrate their victims' skin with venom, without them even knowing it until it was too late and they slowly turned."

"Turned into what the human-like animals were? Sounds very much like vampires," Jacob said, examining carefully the details that Timothy offered.

"Turned into… supernatural monsters, capable of turning invisible," Timothy added. "Well, what happened as they continued to talk to the priest was that they began turning into the animals that had bitten them, as I was saying. Their teeth turned into fangs and their fingernails became super-sharp claws. Afraid for the welfare of their priest, they jumped up and dove through a stained cathedral-sized window and ran off into a field behind the church.

"What can be confirmed for sure is that the monsters that had originally bit the married couple were waiting for them outside. You see, the married couple broke the law of their new nature. This law stated that they must attack the first person that they engage with after being turned. Well, the animals could not let the married couple get away with this alive or else their own line would be corrupted and they themselves would turn into dust. So, as the monsters watched the married couple run off they engaged them in a hot pursuit, jumping several feet at a time so as to catch up to them." Timothy then halted his story for a brief moment.

"Well… did they get away?" Jacob said, rooting for the newly-turned monsters.

Timothy lowered his voice. "The couple kept moving until they reached a cliff and they had nowhere else to go. With nothing left to do, they did only what their new form permitted them to do at this stage: they changed into incorporeal form. And at that moment, something very powerful happened; the monsters chasing them could no longer see them, despite being the same kind of creature with the same exact capabilities. You see, when they were able to avoid harming the priest they gained power of the virtue of grace through God. At the same time the couple turned themselves into an invisible form, they became one with that very virtue that is naked to the eye and incapable of being understood through material essence. The monsters that had chased them, only capable of understanding the material, were destroyed by this. They met their fate and the married couple then turned back to their original selves, defeating the curse that had originally captured them."

"Wow that is deep!" Jacob said, looking around him to make sure there were no monsters creeping up to him. "How do you think of these stories? I think it is really interesting how they had a choice and through God were able do the right thing. I'm not really into God like you, Tim, but you sure do make me think about things."

"Sometimes I just think of ways to express how I feel and relate to people, I guess. You know, the choice was interesting but you hit it right on the head when you said 'through God.' Often we feel trapped and overcome by the negative in our lives, and then forget about how greater powers are at work. We are not perfect and cannot rely on only our knowledge of what we see or what we experience.

To think we are, in our own mind, the only thing that matters! It goes far beyond this, my friend. Sometimes to think out of the box means to open your mind to your heart and have unconditional faith."

Jacob looked into the camp fire and thought this over. He also pondered over how lucky he was to have a friend like Timothy. He thought about all the times Timothy was there to support him through the trials and tribulations of life. Timothy was also there when he fell out of the tree fort, Jacob thought, and he began to wonder if somehow Timothy had the ability to keep him safe.

"I felt Timothy looking at me briefly before I landed," he thought to himself.

Timothy was also thinking about the accident, and could not comprehend how Jacob had survived the fall without any significant injury. He thought that it was rather odd that he had turned around at the moment before Jacob hit the ground, and furthermore he could not put his finger on how time seemed to pause as he had laid his eyes on his best friend. It was a force that he could not describe to himself and he only knew of the indescribable to have one origin.

Jacob yawned and they went in the tent to their sleeping bags.

"I bet tomorrow is going to be real exciting," Jacob said. "I look forward to this fair every year. The rides, the candy, the animals and even the freak shows! Each year seems to be more exciting than the last..."

Jacob fell asleep as he was mumbling the last few sentences that he spoke. Timothy lay awake for some time after this as he processed the thoughts running through his mind. He was not looking forward to the fair at this point, as he felt a strong urge to be alone. He desired to contemplate all of the confusing events that had been happening. There was no one in the world, he thought, that could begin to believe or understand what he was experiencing. Jacob was no exception, as Timothy was at times made to feel he looked into everything with too much depth.

As Timothy fell asleep, he began to have strange dreams about the fair. Everything material he could see seemed unreal, like it was distorted and from a different world than him. In one dream, he approached the gates to the fairgrounds and there was a tall man wearing a white robe who was collecting tickets for admittance. Timothy handed him his ticket, and the man gently placed his hand on his shoulder as to stop Timothy from moving forward.

"Today is the day when things will become much clearer. Keep your eyes opened and your heart ready. You will know what to do when the time comes."

Timothy nodded and proceeded through the gate.

Chapter 4

Wandering in the back yard, Timothy observed the sky while waiting for Jacob to wake up. It was now six-thirty in the morning and the sunrise had just begun. Amazed by how vividly bright the sky was becoming, Timothy stared to the east in awe as the shadows over the brook slowly diminished.

"If only moments like this were to be captured," he thought to himself.

Soon after dawn emerged, Paul and Andrea came out to Jacob's tent to wake him. They noticed Timothy on the other side of the brook.

"Bacon and eggs come and get it!" Paul shouted from afar.

Timothy perked up as he remembered mentioning bacon and eggs yesterday to his father, who would often pick up on subtle ways to cause happiness within his son.

"That sneak," Timothy whispered, "he must have told them what I was craving!"

Timothy, feeling immediately starved, ran across the small bridge and into the house. He sat down and eagerly waited for his plate of food, joining Jacob who was still rubbing his eyes and yawning. Andrea told Paul to have a seat with the two boys as she finished serving each plate.

"This is absolutely delicious, Mrs. Stephanopoulos!" Timothy proclaimed. "I've never been so hungry in my..."

Timothy stopped his sentence short and thought about what he was saying. He realized that he was not hungry at all, as the food no longer tempted him.

Chapter 4

"It's alright, Timothy! You owe it to yourself to enjoy and indulge yourself every now and then!" Andrea said. "I have to admit your father told me you were looking forward to this breakfast."

Timothy nodded and forced himself to eat the rest, so that he did not offend Mrs. Stephanopoulos. Once he finished, he stood up and asked if he could be excused.

"Certainly, Timothy," Mr. Stephanopoulos responded. "We have some towels upstairs next to the shower. We are leaving in about an hour!"

After showering Timothy went back downstairs to the living room, patiently waiting for Jacob and his parents. He was bothered by the fact that he was no longer looking forward to the fair, but he only thought about this briefly as his mind soon wandered back to the events that had taken place the day before. Timothy replayed over and over in his mind the moment before Jacob had hit the ground, and he could not reason in his mind the supernatural event that seemed to have saved Jacob from severe injury.

The four of them packed up the large sport utility vehicle with bagged lunches they had placed in a cooler, and then secured four lawn chairs in the trunk. This particular fair was to have an enormous display of fireworks and so they made sure to be prepared. At just before eight in the morning, and with a three hour drive ahead of them, they hurried along so that they would arrive at the fairgrounds just in time for the gates to open.

Timothy sat in the back with Jacob as Paul began driving down the main road and toward the interstate.

"So guys, what's the first thing you want to do when you get there?" Paul asked.

"Arcade!" Jacob yelled.

"That sounds good, Jacob." Timothy added.

Timothy felt very anxious about the day before him. Trying not to ruin it for Jacob, he continued to talk about the arcade.

"So did you hear about any new games that came out? I know the fair always has the newest and best."

"They have Galactic Wardens! I saw it on the advertisement online. They have this awesome new technology where it is a virtual environment. You can put this head gear on and it brings the picture close up like you are actually in each world fighting off invaders!"

While Jacob continued to talk about it for several minutes, Timothy looked up at the rear view mirror and saw Paul smiling. For a moment, it almost looked to Timothy like Paul was smiling at him as if they were on the same exact level of understanding. It was as if he was saying, "thanks for being a good friend to my son."

Continuing down the throughway, they neared the half-way point; the rest of the way would take them along a state highway. There, the scenery was absolutely beautiful and none of them could wait to see it. It was also the first gorgeous day in quite some time, as the temperatures were going to climb into the low sixties. This was actually the last weekend of the season that the fair took place – each year seemed to have a warming trend around that time.

Finding a rest stop right before the exit, Paul slowed down to turn onto the short off-ramp and into a small parking lot.

"Anyone need to use the bathroom?" Paul asked.

All four of them got out to stretch their legs. Andrea sat down on a bench outside of the rest area building, looking at the view of the mountain ranges in the distance, while Paul walked with Timothy and Jacob inside the building.

While Timothy decided to walk around the gift shops, waiting for Paul and Jacob, he noticed a vendor stand that had various religious books for sale. It seemed to have a section for every type of religion and so he casually pondered through them, including everything from Mormonism to Buddhism. After browsing for a few minutes, he came across a particular book that seemed very old and worn.

"'The Believer's Guide to the Celestial Realm,'" Timothy read aloud. "That's interesting; it has an Orthodox cross on the front cover."

Timothy looked at it closer and realized that the cross on the book cover was the nearly the same size as the one he was wearing. In fact, it looked exactly like the same. Approximately one inch in height and three quarters of an inch in width, it was wooden and rather weathered. It also contained a slanted beam on the bottom of it.

"What a strange coincidence," he continued.

He opened the book and began filtering through the pages when a very old woman came around the corner of the bookstand at which he was standing. She was dressed in a very simple, off-white tunic and an unbuttoned woolen sweater.

"My boy, how nice of you to find this book!" she exclaimed, speaking in a very mysterious tone. "Do you know what it is that you have in your hands?" she smiled, eagerly awaiting his response.

She then looked around to make sure that no one was listening.

"Well, no ma'am, not exactly… is it a book about the heavens and creatures, perhaps? I did notice the Orthodox Cross on the front of it."

"Why yes! And it isn't just any book. You must take

this! Keep it close to you and make sure to carry it with you for the rest of the day. Do you hear me! You mustn't let go of this!"

She grabbed a hold of his shoulders, startling him. He tried to move back and away from her, but she did not let go and started to shake him as her smile grew larger by the second. Just as Timothy came loose from her grasp, Mr. Stephanopoulos approached from behind and intervened.

"Hey now lady, that's just enough! What is the matter with you? He's just a kid!" Paul turned to Timothy and looked at him closely. "Are you alright Timothy? What happened here?"

Timothy looked over Paul's shoulder and realized that the woman had disappeared.

"I don't know she must have..." Timothy said, pausing to think about what he was saying. "She was just confused, I guess. I'm alright. I just need a moment. I think I want to buy this book."

"No problem, Timothy. Jacob is at the store across the way down there buying some candy. I'll go find him and meet you at the truck, okay?"

Timothy nodded and went to the kiosk's purchasing counter. He placed the book on the counter, waiting to be checked out, but the clerk instead smiled and handed the book back to him.

"This was paid for by the elderly woman you were with so no amount is due. Enjoy!"

The vintage cash register rang as the man finished his sentence. Astonished, Timothy took the book back with him and walked back out to the vehicle, where Jacob and his parents were sitting and sharing a few snacks from the convenient store. They were laughing and enjoying each other's conversation, and Timothy smiled as he watched them the entire way. It made him happy to see a family such as that: one that shared happiness, joy and love. To Timothy, the lack of family values was the one aspect of society responsible for many issues that his peers at school were going through. He felt so sad when thinking of this, because he knew how fortunate he was to have a family that was there for him and that supported him in every way possible. Jacob was also very fortunate, although he was not as aware of this as Timothy was.

"Hi. I'm sorry for the delay!" Timothy apologized, climbing into the back seat.

"Don't worry about it Timothy," Paul said. "I am surprised you are not more shaken up than you are letting on. Jacob has an orange juice for you – and some trail mix too if you want."

"No thanks," Timothy said, refusing the snack that Jacob tried to hand him. "I am still full from breakfast, but thanks."

"So what was up with that crazy woman, Tim?" Jacob asked. "Dad told me all about it! What a strange world it is. I am almost afraid to go off on our own at the fair!"

"Oh, I am not really sure. She just mistook me for someone else," Timothy replied, feeling very uncomfortable to not tell the truth.

Timothy slipped the book into his backpack as Jacob was looking out the window. He was hoping that Paul had not told Jacob anything about the book so he could relax and process yet another strange occurrence. Timothy knew that Jacob would have become even more curious about his experiences the past few days and was in no mood to retell the events.

Paul drove back on the interstate for a short time before taking the next exit to the highway. It was just a little over an hour and a half to Sunny Lake and Timothy closed his eyes in hopes of resting the remainder of the ride. The Stephanopouloses began marveling at the beautiful scenery and were quiet the rest of the way, and so several minutes into the ride Timothy fell into a light sleep.

Timothy was used to being in an out of sleep during long car rides. Besides the fact that it helped him to avoid car sickness, he also enjoyed the dreams that he would experience. They were the usual very short, nonsensical type of dreams that one would have being half asleep while listening to background noise. This time, however, was not the usual case. Timothy dreamt he was at church, standing with the rest of the parishioners during the liturgy and before Communion. While Father Andrei was standing at the altar with the two middle doors open, Timothy found himself robed in deaconate attire. Carrying a censer, he walked up into the sanctuary and hung it on a wooden stand.

"Six winged and many eyed," Father Andrei said, looking at Timothy.

Timothy then began to rise up through the air, with two massive wings emerging from the back of his vestment. Turning toward the communicants in the parish, they all bowed in a concerted effort before he vanished through the ceiling.

"See you later Oregon!" Jacob screamed.

Timothy jumped in his seat and woke up. He realized that they had just crossed the border into California. They were at that point a little over an hour from the fair grounds.

Timothy looked out the window as they drove through northern California. Every time he passed through the Oregon and California state line he recalled the story his father had told him about some history between the two states.

"At one point in history, part of northern California and southern Oregon tried to secede from their two respective states and form a new state called Jefferson. As history tells it," his father had told Timothy, "Pearl Harbor was bombed that same day and the entire plan of them seceding folded."

Timothy always found it interesting how two significant events could affect one another. In his mind, this had to be more than a coincidence.

"And if it was the universe that required two equal forces to balance out each other," he thought to himself, "then where did the forces come from and who was behind them?"

To Timothy, God's plan was to work through nature, balancing out an equation. Nature did, according to Timothy and all that he knew, come from the Creator of the universe.

Just after eleven o'clock they reached Sunny Lake. Its Fairgrounds now hosted the largest annual fair in the State of California. It surpassed that of the state capital just three years ago and Timothy had been attending it with the Stephanopouloses ever since. The proud lofty mountains surrounding this area, in addition to the beautiful redwood trees, drew attention from many places throughout the region.

Paul drove through the traffic, which he mistakenly had not included in his travel estimation. It was eleven-thirty in the morning by the time they rolled into the parking lot. Fortunately, they were one of the last vehicles to enter before it was extended to lots across the street. As he found a space, Timothy and Jacob stared out of the same window and their jaws dropped at the size of the park. It was as if after each time they went, they forgot just how magnificent their last experience was. Several roller coasters, Ferris wheels and the beautiful Pacific Ocean were just to name a few of the great qualities they saw.

Walking up to the entrance, the line was exceptionally long and they could not even see the ticket collector for over a quarter of an hour. Jacob was rather impatient, as he could not keep still and intermittently he let out a giant sigh. Timothy on the other hand had no problem with this, as patience was one virtue that he often exemplified. In addition, he had much to contemplate. He had realized by this time that the day was going to be very important, but he did not know the reason why.

They were finally in a position where they could watch the line dwindle down, one person at a time. Timothy looked ahead at the gentleman collecting the entrance tickets who was very similar to the one he had dreamed of the night before. He was a tall, lanky man with a beard and grim face. Timothy could hear the man repeat himself with every ticket stub he collected.

"Thank you, enjoy your stay," he said each time, using the same stern tone.

Moments later they reached the entrance and the man collected their tickets. Part of Timothy was hoping that the experience handing his ticket to this man would turn out exactly as his dream had; he would be relieved to know that his imagination finally led to a tangible relationship with reality. The other part of him realized that this experience was completely different than what he had seen in the dream, and he laughed at himself for thinking it could have been anything but.

"Thank you, enjoy your stay," the ticket collector said to Timothy.

Timothy looked up at the man and noticed him

smiling. Not only was it the first time Timothy saw him make a facial expression, but he also bore a distinct resemblance to that of the woman from the rest stop. It was as if the man understood who Timothy was and what Timothy was about to experience. Timothy kept looking at the man as Jacob pushed him forward through the gate; Jacob was in no mood to delay his time at the fair.

"Alright, we are in!" said Jacob. "I have been waiting for this for so long... let's get to the arcade! And don't forget about the fried dough! And cotton candy!"

"Now, now, settle down some Jacob! We have got to figure out what our plans for the day are here," Jacob's father instructed him. "Now, I have this cell phone I bought the other day for you both. Keep this in your backpack in case of an emergency or if we aren't able to meet up at the time we chose."

"Honey, we didn't decide on a time," Andrea said, partly teasing her husband.

"Yes, you're right; I was just making sure someone was paying attention! So what time would be good for everyone? Do you want to go have lunch now and then we can let you boys go to the arcade and have some fun? Or do you want to have a late lunch after some play? What do you think, Timothy?"

"I am finally beginning to feel a little hungry, I must admit. However, I realize that Jacob needs to play in the arcade before too long so I am flexible."

"Let's get something to eat first," Andrea interjected, looking at her son. "Your friend is hungry and I still consider him our guest. Your game can wait."

"Aw mom... alright, you're right. Let's get some lunch. Then we can go off and have some fun for a while," Jacob responded, earnestly hoping someone would agree with him.

"Yes Jacob, that's fine," his father replied. "After we eat we can then separate until three o'clock. Then we can establish what the rest of the day will look like. Don't forget that the fireworks are at seven sharp."

Paul led them on to the food court. They all had a large lunch, except for Timothy who ate lightly. It was nearly one in the afternoon by the time they finished lunch and once separated, Timothy and Jacob went to the arcade as Jacob's parents wandered around enjoying the different games and shows.

"Finally Tim: we can get on with our day! They have Galactic Wardens here; I saw it in the advertisement online," Jacob explained, realizing that he was repeating himself. "I said that earlier during our trip here! Anyway, I couldn't get you to play at home so now you can see it here. The graphics will be awesome."

Inside the arcade station were dozens of video arcade machines, pinball machines and virtual emulators. Other than the virtual emulators, most of the games offered were considered retro as they were games from before Timothy and Jacob's time; in fact they were restored arcade machines from the 1980's, over half of a century prior. Because of that the Sunny Lake Fair was now renowned across the country, as those games were nearly impossible to find elsewhere. Nearly packed full, Timothy and Jacob had a hard time finding a game to play together.

"Let's go wait for the Galactic machine, since we won't find anything soon anyway. I don't mind waiting in line and it will be worth it!" Jacob exclaimed.

Timothy followed him and they waited in line for quite a few minutes. He looked around at all of the people absorbed in the games. Everyone he could see seemed so happy and thrilled, as though gaming was the only thing in the world that could please their senses.

"Thank God I'm not like that," Timothy thought to himself.

"Timothy, pay attention; we're next! Okay, here's how it works. First, put on this headgear. That's it. There are two joy sticks. The left controls the movement of your avatar. The right controls weapons. Click the button on the top of the right joystick to select weapons and use the middle button to fire. For the left joystick controls, the right button moves right and the left, well, moves you to the left. That's easy enough! I am going to pick a warrior from the planet Navonod. I have special powers to be able to deflect ballistics and turn invisible – or incorporeal, as you like to say – when a sword tries to swipe through me. So I would suggest that you pick a warrior from Kirtap because you will be able to freeze your opponents before they attack. Also, you have the capability to turn ballistics into magnets, forcing them away from your own magnetic field and causing them to hit your opponent. Does that make sense?"

Timothy was always amazed at how intelligent Jacob was when it came to coordination skills and understanding tactics. It sometimes reminded him of how everyone has some kind of talent and when you put all of your energy and confidence into it, one can be very successful at it. Timothy felt very different about himself, however, because his energy was always directed toward something so immaterial. He felt inferior at times as it was not very measurable.

"Okay. I think I know what you mean, Jacob. Let's give it a try."

They played for a few minutes. Timothy did not stand a chance against Jacob, but Jacob did make sure to go easy on him. He would allow Timothy to bring his character's morale down just enough to make it exciting, and then he would systematically bring Timothy's down until they were even again. As Timothy started to get quite involved in the game, which was very unusual for him, he saw out of the corner of his eye something very peculiar. In a split second a shadow had wisped by. It caused him to have chills as he looked around, fearing that something was watching him or even worse was directly behind him. Timothy recalled his dream where he was looking into the river as his reflection told him to look out, and how a shadow had crept up behind him right before he woke up. Only this time, he did not refuse to look.

"Got ya," Jacob proclaimed, before realizing that Timothy wasn't even paying attention. "Timothy, what gives? You're not supposed to make it easy on me. It is supposed to be the other way around!"

Jacob then realized Timothy looked afraid and rather pale.

"Sorry Jacob, I thought I saw something. I don't really feel so good at the moment; can we take a break?"

"Of course Tim, let's go have a seat."

"No, I just need some open air. Let's go for a walk, if you don't mind."

"No problem, it is kind of hot and crowded in here anyway. Besides, there are some people behind us who have been waiting for some time."

They walked outside and around the park. Silent at first, Jacob decided to prod Timothy for some more details about why he was acting so strange lately.

"Come on Timothy, I am your best friend. I know there is something bothering you that you aren't telling me. You aren't yourself and it is starting to make me feel like it's me or something."

"No, Jacob! Of course it isn't you," Timothy pleaded, "not at all. I am just not sure how to explain it. And I don't want anyone worrying about me. My father is worried enough, and already twice in a year's time I have had to talk to Father Andrei about troubling dreams. They both happened on the same day of the year, too. Wait," Timothy stopped and held onto Jacob's shoulders. "You can't say a word about his to anyone. And please don't think of me differently."

"Okay, I promise already! It is okay, really. Go ahead and tell me. What's with these dreams? I am sure they are just dreams," Jacob assured him, as they began to walk again.

"Alright, you have never let me down before. I need to get this off of my shoulders to my only friend at some point, besides… so you know how I have been praying a lot more lately? And how I have felt closer to God and wanted to experience more of the joy I feel when praying to Him?"

"Yes, you told me a little about that. That's how everyone in your family has been; I figure it just runs in your family."

Timothy looked at Jacob and they began to laugh, as Jacob realized he spoke in a way that seemed negative.

"That's not what I meant, Tim," Jacob continued. "I just meant that your father became a priest, and so did your Grandfather and his father before him, and so on and so on. You told me all about that remember?"

"Yes, of course. Well that is true, and so that's all I thought it was. But now I have been having all of these dreams. I know what they say, that you shouldn't put too much stock into dreams and that they are only suppressed thoughts and what not. But you know, deep in early

Orthodox tradition, especially in some parts of Eastern Europe, there were theories based on dreams. It was recommended to never look into dreams, of course, without prayer and consulting your spiritual father. With proper insight some of these visions and dreams were interpreted. In addition, there are also many symbols from the Bible linked to dreams; think about the fish, or the lamb, or the dove."

"I know what you mean. I heard something about the butterfly once, not sure where, but that is also a symbol. It had something to do with being reborn or reemerging from a cocoon. That stuff is pretty interesting!"

"Wait, what did you say... a butterfly?"

"Yes, a butterfly. That's about the only one I really heard much about but I do remember reading about lambs and doves in the Bible."

Timothy stopped again. He appeared deep in thought for a moment and then smiled.

"Yes, I had a butterfly in my dream! Well, I am not going to begin to interpret what all of this means. You know as I said before, Father Andrei seems very interested in my dreams lately and I notice my father is really concerned for me. The point of what I am saying is that everything is starting to seem so peculiar. It is worse than ever. I have visions about ascending toward light, falling into darkness and I even see strange creatures. I didn't want to tell you, but that crazy woman from the rest stop gave me this weird smile, and it was the same smile that the guy at the entrance gave me. This does all seem so strange, but I think something is going to happen and I don't know what."

"Alright Tim, I hear you. Calm down for a moment; this isn't like you. Nothing is going to happen to you. You are just a kid, like me. Yes you are different, but all of this hocus-pocus type stuff... it's all in your mind and I think you are really stressed out by school and all that. Maybe you need to take a break from focusing so much on God and maybe relax about your assignments. Maybe find something fun to do for a change when you are alone. Maybe even get a new hobby?"

"You are right," Timothy nodded, appearing to agree with him. "I am sure I am just stressing myself out too much. I should be like all the other kids: just relaxed and down to earth."

Once agreeing, they continued for a while until Timothy stopped once again in his usual abrupt fashion.

"Yes Jacob, down to earth. Instead of up above! I am not focused on what is momentary here on earth and that's what my issue is. Perhaps this is a sign. I think I need to stop talking about this, and let life happen."

"That's it, Tim! Go with the flow!"

Jacob clearly had no inclination of what Timothy was really referring to. They were both satisfied with the result of the conversation, and continued walking in silence for a few minutes. Before long Jacob's cell phone rang.

"Hello dad," Jacob assumed. "Yes, things are fine... we are all set... no, maybe we can meet at five for dinner? Three is just around the corner and we wanted to get some rides in... okay thanks. Talk to you soon; I love you!"

Jacob hung up the phone and put it back in his backpack.

"So we have a little more than a few hours to go on the rides! We will all meet up for dinner. Are you up for a ride?"

"Sure thing, Jacob! I am definitely in the mood now. Let's go; do you have anything in mind?"

"Well, there is the battleship. That's fun. You know, where you go inside a ship and it vibrates and moves around as you are attacked and sinking."

"That sounds good. Then maybe we can go for the rollercoaster. It might start getting very cool tonight so it would be better to go on that as soon as possible."

"You're right, Tim. Let's go."

The boys ran to the battleship and then afterwards headed for the rollercoaster. Jacob was really happy to see Timothy enjoying himself and was nearly baffled at how relaxed he suddenly seemed. They both laughed and talked about random things until the ride came to an end and they went to retrieve their backpacks. Finding themselves walking again, they looked for another ride to go to.

"What next, Tim? This has been awesome!"

"How about bumper cars? You really like those," Timothy responded.

"That's cool! Let's go. I think it is on the right side of the ride area."

They took their time walking until they passed a lemonade stand. Thirsty, they stopped for a drink.

"Wow, do you see those clouds off in the distance, Tim? I hope they aren't coming this way. I am having too much fun for a rainstorm! It's odd. The weather earlier said it was going to be sunny the entire day!"

Timothy looked over to the southwest and saw the dark clouds. They were very ominous looking, although they did not cover a wide area of space like a usual storm would. It was very isolated in nature.

"Yes, Jacob, they don't look too promising. Let's get to the bumper cars before it's too late."

They jogged off with their lemonade and had drunk nearly all of it by the time they reached the line. Jacob began looking around and fidgeting about, as if that would make the line go faster. It was obvious to them both that it would be at least a five to ten minute wait.

Standing in line, Timothy noticed something fluttering about his right side, swooping around the back of his head and over his shoulder. He looked up and he could not believe what he saw: a beautiful butterfly was flying about back and forth in front of his view. Timothy dropped his jaw.

"Just like in the dream," he said out loud.

"Say what, Tim? Are you going on about your dreams again? Hey, what are you looking at?"

Jacob realized that Timothy was not paying any attention to what he was saying. Clearly in his own world, Timothy was looking up in the air, following with his eyes something that only he could see. The butterfly was flitting back and forth until it charged forward in a very familiar manner. Its colors were that of a rainbow as its wings glimmered underneath the sun. Next it flew into the carousel line, across from where Timothy and Jacob were standing until it suddenly disappeared.

Timothy then became focused on a person standing there and smiling jovially, in a very similar manner to others from that day. There before his eyes was the most beautiful girl that he had ever laid his eyes upon. She seemed to be a year or two older than him and had thick, dark hair put up in a ponytail. Timothy became enthralled with her deep, yet bright colored eyes; it was his first time having an experience like that. He then realized that she bore a striking resemblance to the top half of the person-like creature he had seen in the woods.

She opened her mouth as if to say hello and waved her left hand at him. He wanted to look around to make sure it was him she was looking at, but could not move his head as everything about her seemed so bright and pleasant.

"Pinch me!"

"What? What are you talking about? The line is moving up Timothy; what are you doing?"

Timothy looked over at Jacob for a moment, and then turned back to the carousel. She was still looking at him as the sun began to shine extremely bright for just a moment. Within seconds, though, the dark clouds dimmed the sun to the west. At that point the girl's lips began to move, whispering.

"Look out behind you," she clearly indicated.

Timothy turned around and saw that two men in black trench coats were moving through the line, as if they were coming for him. They were well groomed, their hair was perfectly combed and covering their eyes were dark sunglasses. Timothy then had a sudden sense of nausea take over him, like in his dreams.

"Jacob… we have to run; we have to get out of here. I think I am in trouble."

Jacob stood confused until he saw the very same men that Timothy had become afraid of. But before he could process what was happening, Timothy had slid under the metal bars that formed the line that and was running off into the distance. Jacob then saw the two men also step out of line as they began to chase after him. The very next moment they vanished from his sight.

"What the…" Jacob responded, in fear.

Timothy found himself running faster than he ever had before. He secured his backpack's straps with his two hands and began to pick up the pace. It seemed to him that the two men were gaining ground on him, but he decided not to look back. Suddenly he noticed that there were no other people around and the clouds completely took over the sky.

"May I have your attention please," a loud voice said

over the fairground's intercom speaker, "the rides will be closing temporarily until the storm passes by. If not already inside a building, we encourage all to take cover underneath the tents in the southern part of the grounds in order to stay dry. Refer to your park map for directions."

Timothy experienced another feeling of déjà-vu as he heard the voice speak. He soon recognized it to be strikingly similar to the one from his dream where he was falling. Panic began to take him over as he continued to run and he nearly forgot to breathe.

"Hey! Over here," a voice whispered.

Timothy stopped running and looked to his left and there was the same girl from the carousel line. She moved her hand, waving him over.

Timothy did not take even a second to think and ran to her. They proceeded down an alley in between two old brick structures, which housed tigers, ponies and other show animals that were to be displayed during the carnival show later that evening. As she continued to run in front of him, he looked at her attire and was marveled at how well she could run in her skirt and Mary Jane style dress shoes. She then looked back at him and smiled, as they continued running. Timothy then turned his head back and, just as they turned the corner, he saw the two men enter the alley about one hundred feet away.

"Take out your book and get rid of your backpack!" she ordered Timothy.

Timothy did exactly as she said and ditched his backpack. He then noticed that his cross had come out from under his shirt and attempted to place it back, as it was annoying him.

"Leave that as it is, Timothy."

Timothy was absolutely mystified and gained a

sudden sense of security. Until now, he had not ever met another person who caused him to be confused. He could not read her at all, and felt a power emanate from her that was intellectual in nature. It was beyond what he could comprehend. This gave him comfort, until it began to rain and thunder was heard in the distance. At that point the girl grabbed him by his shirt and pulled him through a doorway in the back of the brick structure.

"Brace yourself; this will be quick," she said, instructing him to remain calm.

They went through the building and then up very old, creaky stairs that led to the second floor. As she directed him through a barred gate that was left open, he caught a glimpse of a few tigers lying on the ground, outside of their cage. They had no chain around their necks but they remained tame. Just as soon as he finished looking at the tigers in disbelief, she brought him around a wooden beam that was supporting the tall ceiling above them. Following her lead, he squatted down.

"Lift up your heart!" she shouted out, using a beautiful tone.

At that moment, Timothy heard the two men walk up the stairs and approach the gate. But before Timothy knew what was happening, the building began to shake and a bolt of lightning struck the roof. Feeling a warm sensation around his cross he closed his eyes and suddenly vanished with the girl, as the building collapsed on their pursuers.

Timothy immediately opened his eyes, finding himself sitting on a beautiful sandy beach. Gigantic bird-like creatures were flying through the air and the sky was brightened without the source of light to be seen. He looked up and saw the same girl that he had followed, only she was wearing a white tunic and her hair was no longer in a ponytail. She also was quite older than what he remembered.

"Where are we?" Timothy politely asked, standing up and brushing the sand off of his pants.

"Oh, I bet you are really confused at that point. Let me see, you probably are looking at an ocean of water, a beautiful sky and creatures that you cannot fathom," she giggled. "Yes, you will not yet understand what you see. For what is all around you cannot be yet grasped. You still need the material things you are used to in order to justify what your senses tell you. Nevertheless, it will make sense soon I am sure. We are in safety. Let us proceed."

She took Timothy by the hand and guided him along as they walked away from the body of water. Timothy then noticed he too was different: looking down at their hands, his was much more mature than before; he also appeared older.

Chapter 5

Jacob stepped out of line and took his cell phone out of his backpack. He began to dial his father's cell phone number and then abruptly stopped, having only entered the first three digits; an extremely loud voice came over the intercom and broke his concentration. Noticing the crowds leaving the area and heading for shelter, he turned the other way and made his way around the carousel, hoping for some sign of Timothy.

He found himself on the only pathway that led in the direction Timothy had disappeared into. At that point it had become extremely dark outside. Taking into consideration Timothy's strange experiences, not the least of which included two odd men, he questioned why he was not calling his father to find help. Part of him did not know how to even begin to explain what he just saw. Regardless, Jacob convinced himself that he would find Timothy.

"Hopefully I won't find those dreadful men," he told himself.

Sneaking down the pathway, he suddenly saw a horrific bolt of lightning that crashed downwards and shook the very ground where he stood. Several hundred feet away, the sound of a building collapsing took over the air surrounding him. Jacob immediately linked this to an imminent fear for Timothy. As he looked up in the air and saw smoke billowing upward, his instincts led him toward the disaster and he proceeded to run further down the pathway.

As he neared the site of the destruction, part of the

building protruded through the road before him. Jacob looked to his left and saw an alleyway, parallel to half of the structure that still remained standing. His heart began to beat extremely fast and it became increasingly difficult for him to swallow as tears welled up in his eyes. Thoughts then entered his mind regarding the whereabouts of those two men and he experienced additional uncertainty for his own welfare. Ultimately, the image of his friend being hurt rose to the forefront of his thought process to which he hurried down the alley. He reached the corner of the building to his right and poked his head around it. All that he could see ahead was a narrow dirt road, sandwiched between a stone wall and the rear of the building.

Charging forward, Jacob was not watching his footing as his sight was concentrated only on the distance. Several steps later he tripped onto the ground, face first.

"Oh, that hurt," he grimaced.

Jacob sat up and turned around to see what had obstructed his path. It was Timothy's backpack, lying out in the middle of the road. Initially Jacob felt a sense of relief as the backpack confirmed that he was following the same route that Timothy had taken. Then, pausing as he held Timothy's backpack in his hands, he realized that his best friend was inside of the building to his right; looking forward down the dirt road, it showed to be a dead end.

———

Father John woke up at four-thirty in the morning that same day. Now at a monastery in New York State, the sleep he just had was not enough to overcome his feeling of jetlag. There was a full day of services and council meetings to look forward to and, being the resolute man that he was, he swiftly rejected any thought of despair that attempted to penetrate into his mind. He entered into the small living area, which along with the bedroom made up the quarters that were provided for him by the monks. Taking out his Orthodox prayer book, he read through the morning prayers for the next few minutes.

It was not an hour before a knock suddenly shook the door to his chamber. Father John quietly strolled to the door, opening it slowly. A familiar face stood before him.

"Well if it isn't Father Andrei, as if I had not just seen you days ago!" Father John exclaimed. "God bless. What a beautiful morning it is!"

"Yes, indeed, indeed," Father Andrei replied.

His face barely lifted a smile and the mere attempt was immediately noted by Father John. They both stood at the doorway for nearly a minute until Father John broke the awkward silence.

"Why don't you come in for a moment, if you will? There is a little more than an hour left until Hierarchical Divine Liturgy; it is at six-thirty, correct?"

Father Andrei walked past Father John without an immediate response. He had a seat on a short stool in front of the only window that, other than candles, was the chamber's only source of light. He then looked up at Father John, who stood there suddenly quite solemn.

"Yes, six-thirty it is. You know, it would usually be seven. But, there is much to discuss, I suppose. I'm not really sure how to say this, but there is much controversy at this time: it does not seem that everyone quite agrees with the upcoming discussions. I hear that the Ecumenical Patriarch of Constantinople has called for similar meetings in response to ours, and Alexandria will be next. It is one thing that we are not recognized as autocephalous by

Constantinople, but the Russian Patriarch now doubts our direction. All of this discussion of dreams and world disaster... and the Book of Revelations! Well no pun intended, but it is a bit unorthodox, wouldn't you agree? America as a country is known for its progressive direction, especially as of late and no matter how much we state that we are still synonymously representative of the Orthodox Way, you must know that our ideas are going to be rejected just by association alone."

"My father would not agree. If he was only alive today to bring us his blessing –"

"If it was not for your father, we would not have had this much insight, that's for sure. He was always very mystical; Timothy does takes after him. But he is not now around, and there is little time or leverage we have to advocate for what he envisioned. Plus, the secret council meetings he held put all of us in hot water. It has taken us all of the past two years to recover our reputations. In addition, it is well known throughout the Orthodox communities of the world how much stronger in numbers we became at that time because of his rhetoric and leadership. The patriarchates are not keen on us becoming stronger again if we are to carry a similar message! I don't know. I don't know if it is wise, but I do trust you Father John."

"What's got into you, Father Andrei?" Father John asked, putting his hand on his shoulder. "It was you who consoled me the other day, as I was in fear for Timothy. Now I am here to return the favor. Look, Timothy is following in his grandfather's footsteps. Timothy, bless him, has this gift of seeing this web that Satan is weaving, although he not yet knows it. He is being attacked with these troubling dreams, just as his grandfather suffered. It is now quite obvious to both of us that he will be involved with all of this, although I never expected so early in his life. This along with all of the other signs shows us how time is running out. It is just like my father said it would be: the end of Orthodoxy as we know it is near. Our membership is declining – and not just here in America! Is that by itself not a sign that we are to reintroduce my father's ideas? Also, his ideas and success commanded attention from abroad, like you said. How could such a small group, such as us here in America, be able to garner that attention if it did not have a greater meaning or purpose?

"Beyond this, I admit that I can't explain the intricacies of the situation and I don't know every step that we need to take. But there was one thing my dear father did confirm on his death bed: the day was near that Christians across the world would need to come together as one body, remaining strong in prayer and communion with each other.

"You know, Father Andrei, I can't believe we were so blind to think that Christ's return was delayed because of my father failing! I can see now so much clearer. It is quite the opposite indeed. It seems that He will return whether things are in order or not. If we do not find a way to solve our differences with one another, then the consequences I cannot even begin to fathom. Somehow my dear son bears some part in this responsibility, but we can at least do our part by laying the groundwork. So yes, my father's very message we shall bring back. Our council must support us. One way or another, I am certain the trouble Mt. Athos is in, along with the destruction elsewhere, will sooner or later wake up everyone up!"

"You do speak wisdom, my good friend. I am just anticipating some heated discussion and I don't care for the past decade of controversy to come up again. Our council may see it as backward movement if they think there is any chance this would alienate us from the Orthodox patriarchs abroad... "

"I don't care for controversy either, Father Andrei. Every one of us in the Orthodox Church is on their toes lately. It can't be denied that things have gone awry. But let's remain calm and collected as through the Holy Spirit we will be guided. It's apparent to me that we need to reintroduce the prospects of how a changing world affects our mission as Orthodox Christians."

Father Andrei smiled genuinely and stood up. They embraced one another with a hug, both assuming the conversation was over. Father John went into the other room and approached the shallow closet across from the bed. Taking out his cuffs and stole, he then returned to Father Andrei's side. They both left the room and headed toward the chapel where Liturgy was to be held.

Entering the chapel, they set their cuffs and stole aside until they were to partake in Communion. In a counterclockwise fashion they each venerated the three icon stands: one at the center of the nave and one on each side of the steps leading to the Holy Doors. The Holy Doors were in the center of a wall covered in painted icons and on each side of the wall were two smaller doors. They took turns making the sign of the cross before each one. The priests who would be serving were chanting outside of the sanctuary, reciting the entrance prayers. Fathers Andrei and John, not selected by Metropolitan Ezekiel, joined the remaining priests and monks.

The choir then began chanting as the Metropolitan and his deacons made their way into the monastery's parish.

"More honorable than the Cherubim, and beyond more glorious than the Seraphim," they continued to chant.

The Byzantine style chanting was beautiful beyond

words and the scent of incense was refreshing. The baritone voices sent vibrations through the entire room in which they stood. As if all their cares had gone away, the service reminded them of heaven on earth, if there could be any material descriptors that could possibly do justice to such a vision.

About forty-five minutes passed by in what seemed to be only a few moments. The gospel reading was read and Metropolitan Ezekiel began his sermon. Still standing, as there traditionally were not many seats in an Eastern Orthodox nave, they lifted their eyes up to the iconostasis, which he was standing in front of.

"We gather here today, representing all that the Orthodox Church stands for. In communion together, as one body, we stand here while the fullness and richness of our experience is being carried on. That is, carried on by the bishop who was intended to be the center of His Church but yet still a humble servant of the Lord. This act preserves our traditions, which began over two millennia ago and was given to us by Christ and His Apostles. Fasting, Holy Communion, Confession and the like: they show how the strength of God works in us and the how the intercession of the Holy Spirit continues to penetrate in our hearts, allowing us to use what energy we have in a positive manner. I am certainly honored to be amongst you, brethren, to share this time in the Love of Christ, who is consubstantial with both the Father and us."

Metropolitan Ezekiel continued on and finished his sermon, which commanded the attention of all. An hour later, after Holy Communion and the dismissal, Father Andrei waited for Father John outside of the chapel doors. It was an overcast day and in the northeastern states the chill of winter was foreboding. It was hardly avoidable, as an inner cassock was not an effective barrier against the cold; Father Andrei, quite preoccupied, was however not affected. Father John then exited the chapel and with Father Andrei they began to walk to the council meeting. Although on the other side of the monastery's grounds, the giant archway that served as the meeting hall's entrance could be seen from afar.

"I would have to say it is such a blessing to be here today. Metropolitan Ezekiel has such a profoundly beautiful voice and so beautifully did it resonate throughout the chapel. Combined with the ornate features that surrounded us, it was so very much glorious and quite breathtaking!" Father John concluded.

They continued down a stone pathway that cut through astounding gardens and shrubs. These plants were still vibrant with life, not having yet passed into the fall months as early as they should being in a climate such as they were in.

Blessed was everything about the monastery that they were staying at. St. Peter's was only one of three active Eastern Orthodox monasteries of the Orthodox Church in America. The buildings sat in the middle of a forest, which itself spanned an area of over one hundred acres. Surrounded by a ten foot high stone wall, the monastery was truly a fortress of faith; truly blessed were the monks who served their Lord on those grounds. Their miraculous works had protected their sovereignty in every way that a physical barrier could not.

St. Peter's was also the official meeting place for not only emergent meetings, but also for the all-American council, which now met yearly. Being in a remote area of upstate New York was ideal as it allowed the Orthodox Church's fathers to avoid the widespread anti-Christian persecution that had spread across North America. Also, any patriarchal visitors from abroad would usually arrive at St. Peter's. The Patriarch of Russia, Tikhon II, however, had not set foot in North America since the controversy of secret council meetings had begun. The recent isolation that the Orthodox Church across the world was experiencing furthermore diminished correspondences that each previously had with one another.

Entering through the archway to the meeting hall, Father John and Father Andrei both casually approached the large conference table. It could seat upwards of fifty persons and for anyone who was present beyond that number there were seats that surrounded the perimeter of the room. They were the first to arrive and both sat at the table on the opposite end where the Metropolitan and bishops were to sit. Father Andrei took out his daily prayer book to recite some prayers in his mind.

"Father Andrei, would you like to explain our most dire situation or do you prefer that I do most of the talking?" Father John said, not noticing he had interrupted Father Andrei.

"I think they would much rather hear it come from you," Father Andrei responded, setting down his prayer book. "You have the benefit of you being your father's son, and if there will be any agreement from anyone, it would surely have much to do with that premise," Father Andrei said, without hesitation. "Although, if there is no agreement, that could also be the reason."

"I do agree. It could go both ways, I assume. You know, I have a good feeling about this. We have the benefit of all of the bishops being present today, save one. Bishop Peter I think it is?"

"Yes," Father Andrei replied. "I do find it to be odd

that he will not be here. He has attended every other meeting of significant importance that I know of. Actually, that is what prompted me to act so strangely this morning. I had heard that he had visited with Metropolitan Ezekiel and after that was on his way to Russia to meet with Patriarch Tikhon II. They met to discuss…"

Father Andrei paused as the first two of the six bishops entered the room. Father John tilted his head toward Father Andrei as if anticipating he needed to continue his thought.

"I talked to our own Bishop Andrew," Father Andrei continued in a whisper, "and he told me that as we speak they are contemplating the dangers of discussing Timothy's dreams and connecting it to your father's ideas! That's why there is talk about our sovereignty here in America being compromised. Russia won't have it! His Grace Peter says it could be the final straw if you were to succeed. You must know that he is a so called expert in eschatological matters, cosmos and the psyche and could make a good argument for your dismissal. That is, in order to keep us in good standing with the patriarchs and save the Orthodox Church in America from being no longer recognized. Don't get me wrong. I'm not defending him… whatever the truth happens to be, something is amiss here with him not showing up to this meeting!"

"Good morning and God Bless," one of the bishops stated, using a prominent tone.

Fathers John and Andrei immediately broke up their conversation as if there was little importance to it whatsoever. With a great smile, Father John stood up and Father Andrei followed his lead.

"Bless, Your Grace Bishop James; also to you, Bishop Nikolai," Father John replied.

Bishop Nikolai nodded with a very straight face.

"I am Father John, and this is Father Andrei. We are from the west coast."

"Ah yes, the main reason for our meeting," Bishop James replied. "Your bishop told me all about each of you. Very interesting times we have found ourselves in indeed. I truly look forward to finding a possible resolution."

Bishop James was Bishop of southern California, Nevada and all the way across through Texas. He was very close friends with Father John and Father Andrei's bishop, who was Bishop of northern California, the northwest and all of the states in the Pacific. Also, he presided over parts of the Mountain Time zone that were not under jurisdiction of Bishop James.

"Yes, we look forward to that as well. We have experienced much joy through serving under His Grace Andrew," Father John added.

The two bishops had a seat near the head of the table. As they sat, the remaining three bishops who were expected to attend, including Bishops Andrew, David and Luke, entered and also took their seats. Over the next half hour entered ten other priests who represented the five other dioceses, aside from the one that Fathers Andrei and John were from, joined the meeting.

Metropolitan Ezekiel at last entered with two of his deacons. All fifteen bishops and priests stood simultaneously to honor His Beatitude. Metropolitan Ezekiel was a very tall, heavy-set man with a prominent white beard that formed its way down to his sternum. Always revealing glowing eyes and most often a smile, he was regarded highly not only by his fellow bishops but also by the patriarchs across the world. Thus he was elected as metropolitan two years before, taking over for Timothy's grandfather, Metropolitan Victor.

Chapter 5

Metropolitan Ezekiel conducted the opening prayers and, once all but himself were seated, called the meeting to order.

"My dear fellow church leaders and representatives, we are meeting here today in dire times. There are three main topics on the agenda today, all of which are in many ways related. I have prayed for this very moment so that our minds can be lifted and our hearts warmed as we look for possible conclusions. I do realize that in many ways we have our differences on various particulars when it comes to the management of the Church's governance and directives. I ask that we all allow for full consideration in regards to what each of us has to offer. Additionally, I regret to inform that Bishop Peter will not be with us here today. He is caught up, so to speak, in Russia and seeking guidance as well as offering support to a nation that, like ours, is also in dire need of prayer and comradery.

"First, our ranks are diminishing. As you know, in recent years many parishes and diocese have ceased to exist. Along with many of the monasteries, this has been a trend reported by the other Eastern Orthodox patriarchates across the world – and by a greater percentage than we have here in America. Likewise the Roman Catholic Church, particularly in Western Europe, has also been suffering persecution and losses in membership. Here we are in the year of our Lord 2041 and clinging to survival, both in financial terms and membership.

"Secondly, the Church alone is encountering times of seclusion. As we are all fully aware it was long ago that we were issued autocephaly from Alexius I. However, the Tomos of Autocephaly was not accepted by all patriarchs, particularly that of Constantinople. As long as the Orthodox Church of Russia struggles to survive in their new government and the issues I previously addressed continue, we will lose the communion that is so strengthened by prayer and faith. In other words, we will be even further secluded.

"Thirdly, we hear from Fathers John and Andrei who wish to bring to this council some ideas as well as perceptions that may very well pertain to the conundrums that we face today. Personally, I am open to explore ideas that fall within the reason of our faith. It has always been first and foremost not only the tradition, but also the responsibility of the entire council as a whole to bring wisdom into light. I am the first among equals as the saying goes, so here I am to promote the discussion. Is there one of you who wishes to begin evaluating the issues now presented?"

"I would like to speak," Bishop Nikolai said, standing up and encouraging attention from all.

Bishop Nikolai had taken part in the secret council meetings held by Timothy's grandfather and knew exactly what it was that Fathers John and Andrei were bringing to the table.

"I think that we need to steer away from these discussions of meandering," he continued, "in the realm of what is most unknown. It is surely not for us to look into, conforming to the plan of God in whatever way we see fit. It has always been our tradition to leave the end of all times to be a mystery. To suggest that we can now see this unraveling is a most preposterous suggestion! The Church is fine the way it is!"

Silence could only be heard except for a few uncomfortable movements of the old wooden chairs over the stone floor. Metropolitan Ezekiel took it upon himself to continue the discussion.

"I think that we have not even given a chance to hear our dear brothers Father John and Father Andrei, who have traveled far to share what they feel to be very pertinent. Should we not give them the benefit today?"

"We listened to His Beatitude Victor for quite some time and it was to no avail," Bishop Nikolai immediately retaliated. "All that speculation of his... that it was somehow revealed to him through an angel that we must come together with the Roman Catholics as the Ancient Catholic Church? It caused irreparable damage as well as controversy within the Orthodox Church here in America. Now we sit here with our right to self-governance endangered just by bringing this up again! I rest my case. It would be best if this discussion is to occur that we get right to the point. I think your first two points speak for themselves, Your Beatitude. My only advice to engage times such as these would be for all of us to emulate the reclusive habits of our dear monks on Mt. Athos instead of pretending that we have some prophecy to fulfill!"

"Let's listen now to the two fathers here," Bishop David added, smiling in the direction of Father John and Father Andrei, "and besides, let's note that the monks' sovereignties are in question as of late."

Bishop Nikolai withdrew himself back into his seat, without airing any hint of rescinding otherwise.

"Well, let us hear what you have to say to this council, fathers. The floor is yours," Metropolitan Ezekiel said, before another word could be uttered by anyone else.

Father John immediately rose to the occasion.

"My dear brothers in Christ, I realize that the actions taken by my father were not looked at in a positive way by most. I say with confidence that his goals were good natured and from what he thought was to be the direction of the Holy Spirit Himself. Admittedly, there was damage done to the

Orthodox Church here in America. I can't imagine the embarrassment caused to all of the bishops present at those meetings, particularly for the two bishops who were not forced to retire," Father John said, turning to Bishop Nikolai and also referring to Bishop Peter. "Strain was surely placed between us and our brothers and sisters in communion abroad. Now, however, we find ourselves in dire times. War has broken out near Mt. Athos. Russia is in danger of collapsing. The ancient foundation of the Early Church and its survival is at risk and if that is to be defeated I am confident, as my father was confident, that the rest of Christianity will follow the same path.

"My father, Metropolitan Victor, experienced some difficult times that were similar to that which saints of old wrestled with. I mean this in a literal sense. Attacked by Satan's demons, he had horrible visions to tolerate and yet it was prefaced by a blessing: a visit from an angel sent by God. We know from what he told both the council and me that he found a cross and was instructed by the angel to do two things. First, he was advised to work toward bringing the Orthodox Church closer together. The world's final struggles were apparently near, which would require a great amount of prayer. Secondly, if he reposed without success, he was told to have his cross passed down his family line to the youngest generation still living.

"And now I come to my dear son Timothy who now bears that cross. Father Andrei listened to a dream of his, just a few days ago. It was one year to the date of another troubling dream. They were very similar to what my father had experienced! How can one so young experience something so abstract? How has he possibly gained insight into the depths of the welfare of the Eastern Orthodox Church? Just yesterday he was telling me of the recent massive earthquake and linking it to Mt. Athos. I beg that we take this as a sign to revisit how my father advocated to "come together," as he put it. I suggest that we increase the future prospects for survival by forming a foundational community within these very walls, in order to build our churches stronger yet. Additionally, we should begin to reach out by strengthening our ties, first with the Orthodox Church of Russia and then next the Roman Catholics. We ultimately need to stick together. I am confident that we will see the benefits with an increase in numbers! Let's use prayer as our weapon and fight whatever evil is preventing us from coming together. The East must have woken up by now to these dire times of war and persecution. Time is running out and we must readdress what my father started through guidance of the Holy Spirit!"

"Father Andrei, do you have anything to add?" Metropolitan Ezekiel inquired.

"No Your Beatitude; I think he summed it up rather nicely. I did speak with Timothy as Father John stated," Father Andrei said, standing up confidently. "I think that this boy is extremely intelligent, but something else must be at work here. For him to suffer as he has, we cannot ignore how similar it seems to what his grandfather went through and to what his grandfather promoted. I am not afraid to admit it! I feel that this is a calling from God to strengthen our faith and unite under one church."

"But how can you say this; it would almost seem to be heresy! Are we not already His Church? Which churches do you mean, if not so?" Bishop David inquired.

"Perhaps," Father Andrei said in deep tone, "it is time to look at what the Ancient Catholic Church once was: united."

Chatter immediately broke out in the room.

Metropolitan Ezekiel's face turned pale and the glow diminished from his eyes.

"Order," Metropolitan Ezekiel shouted, "order! We shall take a break and resume these discussions this evening after vesperal services that begin at four. Order!"

The final prayer for the meeting was forfeited and groups of bishops and priests rushed out of the room. Hours passed and Vespers was conducted. It was just a little after six o'clock when the council reunited. Chatter again erupted as if they had never left the meeting hall earlier that day.

"Let us begin," Metropolitan Ezekiel sternly instructed.

The room eventually quieted down and Metropolitan Ezekiel stood up.

"I prayed long and hard about this," Metropolitan Ezekiel continued. "Fathers John and Andrei, I appreciate what you have to offer here. But it has been long since anything such as reuniting the Ancient Catholic Church has been suggested. What do you propose, an Eighth Council after all these years? I do not know exactly what warrants these ideas or concepts, but surely a boy's dreams and thoughts could not bring upon such discussions? Perhaps we are in need of solutions and miracles, but I think that your boy Timothy will survive like the rest of us, Father John. It has been thought that your father experienced a great miracle to see an angel, but this has not been yet officially recognized and I don't see how we can look into this further without causing undue strain. Let us leave coincidence aside and not dabble with what relationship we have left with the other patriarchates! We still have our standing conference with the North American bishops. Perhaps we can strengthen our prayer locally. There are ways to strengthen our objectives without interjecting unproven agendas."

Chapter 5

At that moment a monk entered through the great doors of the meeting hall. He stood there for just a moment, searching the room.

"Father John! Could I please speak with Father John! There is a most urgent message!"

"I am Father John," he identified himself, standing up. "What is this urgent message?"

The messenger, with a worried look on his face, ran over to Father John and grabbed onto his hands.

"Father John... it is your son, Timothy. He has been in a horrible accident. You must return home immediately!"

Father John looked at Metropolitan Ezekiel whose eyes were widened. Slowly turning his head, including every other person in that room within his gaze, he rested his sight on Father Andrei. Father Andrei, now trembling, stood up and placed his hand on Father John's arm. Father John then immediately turned toward the exit and started to hurry through the great archway.

"Wait, Father John," the monk continued. "He was air lifted to St. Catherine's Medical Center in southern Oregon. He is in critical condition... and Father John! Your wife is also there. She was admitted shortly after Timothy."

"I hadn't yet been able to tell Timothy of his mother's illness," Father John wept.

He continued out of the meeting hall and hurried to his room to gather his belongings. Driving off speedily, he took the very next flight home.

Chapter 6

Timothy and his guide were walking quietly, not yet having uttered a single word. It was not long before the sandy white beach that he had found himself on turned into an expanse with towering trees. The trees were positioned so perfectly that they were arranged in straight rows, regardless of which way he looked. Approximately fifty feet apart each tree lay, although their sizes were so largely proportioned that a precise measurement would have proved impossible. Looking up, Timothy could not make out the tree tops as they seemed to have grown beyond the skies.

Confused, Timothy could not even guess at the time of day. Although he had walked quite a while by his standards, the sky revealed no change to its lighting. Shadows were scarce, leaving everything fully exposed as if to suggest shame did not exist. Everything, from the distant creatures in the sky to the branches on the trees, seemed to move about with long graceful strides causing Timothy to perceive his own movements to be out of sync. In this way, there was a different pattern to this new world that conformed to an impression of greatness, which Timothy could not yet begin to understand. Frustrated with his inability to grasp the new world's complexity, he soon became irritated and lost his manners.

"Now I would really benefit from some additional information," Timothy snapped without warning.

His newfound companion, who was less than half a tree-distance in front of him, stopped herself instantaneously and turned to him. Timothy then stopped too, and took a few steps backward as he realized he knew not to whom he was speaking. In relation to his choice, the concept of cause and effect took hold of his mind as he anticipated a negative response.

"What would you have me say that you could find to be useful?" she rhetorically inquired with a straight face and strong eyes.

"Well first off, do you have a name? Secondly, how old are you?" Timothy said, now more politely.

"All intelligent creatures would indeed have a name. It is inconsequential at this point for you to know mine other than to satisfy your curiosity, however this was how you were intended to find out after all. My name is Eryana: the Angel of Elders and guardian of their path.

"As for my age, I am always asked that question; it often leads to a long discussion. When I explain that I am 6,045 Earth-years old, the next question is usually, 'how does one argue the evidence that points to the planet Earth being millions of years old,' to which I reply that the first few thousand years were one thousand times as long as an Earth-year that you now know. You are better off to take me for my word or else you will drive yourself mad in an attempt to understand."

Eryana was angelic with her approach, but she had some physical characteristics that he would have not have guessed an angel to have. Slightly taller than Timothy, she seemed to be approximately six feet tall, although he could not say for sure. She had long and thick black hair that contrasted with bluish green eyes. Her face was moderately tanned and her hands and feet had a golden hue, which matched the thread of her exceptionally tailored white robe. Peeking out from her robe was a sterling silver breast plate, and resting on her waist was a bronze sword that looked ridiculously heavy. Strangely he had not noticed the plate or the sword until she had replied to his question. Without a doubt she was the most statuesque being he had ever looked upon, and that was perhaps the attribute most congruent with her angelic nature.

"You look very familiar in some ways," Timothy continued, "and some things are starting to make sense! Tell me you weren't in the woods the other day. At least part of what I saw reminded me of you. I found myself in a very awkward situation because of that, and I was all muddy playing a game I was barely any good at!"

"Yes," Eryana replied. "I was there, although in a form that made sense with your plane of existence. Have a seat, will you?"

They both sat down, each conveniently finding a separate smooth rock. They were facing each other with just the right amount of distance between them for Timothy to feel comfortable.

"I don't want to waste any of your time, but I am extremely curious to find out more about my predicament," he said, after situating himself.

"We are on no particular schedule. Time is of no consequence here, and your experience will continue until you are ready for it to end. Everything you need to know will be revealed as necessary. Just be true to yourself and to your instincts. Human nature has its relevance here!"

Timothy took a few moments to process what she was telling him. He was every bit confused as he was intrigued at what she had to say. His understanding of theology allowed him to enjoy very much this intellectual challenge that was far more existential than any of his experiences on earth, which now seemed to have been rather mundane and onerous. The differences were like day and night.

"So then… where exactly are we and where are we going? Am I still alive or am I in heaven?" Timothy asked politely, cutting to the chase.

"We are in the in-between world, as you would find it easier to understand. This is the heaven below Heaven and the safe-haven above earth. Once reposed from your world, most remain here until the time of judgment, which all will encounter. Additionally, this space was once where Adam roamed with Eve before the fall of humanity and Satan's subsequent hold over earth. A great disassociation occurred at that time, and this realm now resides on a dimension separate from earth. As far as your welfare, your heart still beats. But your spirit is now with us and the manner in which you shall continue has yet to be determined."

"Well, I was always taught by my church that the spirit and body are the two parts of a soul and they can't be separated…"

"That is correct, Timothy."

"But, you are saying the opposite: my spirit right now is not with my body? That would indicate that I could not again continue on earth," Timothy replied, amazed at how his verbiage seemed more intellectual than usual.

"It is still," she replied. "But in truth it is also with us here, on a journey to protect you from harm and expedite God's will for you. I cannot say how the Will of God shall impact you or how your journey here will end, but what I can make clear is that I was sent to protect you from Satan's minions. Here we are to show you what you need to see. For His plan depends on this."

"Satan's minions; is that who those two creepy men were? They looked like vampires to me! They had sharp teeth and were pale and deathly looking. I thought they wanted to bite me and I can't get over how –"

"Let me show you something," Eryana softly said, purposely interrupting the overabundance of questions.

Eryana stood up and approached Timothy to which he reacted by also standing. She embraced him, wrapping her arms around his back. Suddenly great wings emerged from behind her as she flew into the air, rising up with the tree trunks and eventually reaching above the tops.

"So the trees do have tops! I was beginning to wonder…"

Timothy looked down and could no longer see the ground. Then looking up, he saw thousands of angels, not birds. They were traveling to and fro and each appeared to be on a mission, although they were not hastily moving. Stern yet pleasant faces they carried and glorious were their auras.

The angels seemed to be in a dedicated airspace, traveling in quite a uniform manner. In fact, it was so organized that there were two separate lanes which seemed to have invisible boundaries. One angel, heading toward the portal between earth and Eden, turned its head in Timothy's direction. Timothy could not help but first notice his long golden hair and sharply chiseled face. As their eyes met, Timothy noticed a single tear sliding down his cheek that caused him to feel quite troubled on a personal level. Then turning his head back to Eryana, he immediately became distracted from the traveling angels.

"You do have wings," Timothy mentioned, as if just recognizing the detail that had been hidden up until their ascent.

They were everything he had expected them to be and much more. The four wings each spanned greater than Eryana's entire width. The upper most two were nearly the length of her body, and the bottom two were a little less than half of that. It appeared to Timothy that the latter served a purpose in addition to flight, but he was dumbfounded as to what it would have been.

"Well – what did you expect? We are not omnipresent; we must get from point to point," Eryana replied, smiling warmly. "See around you? This in totality is what you know to be Eden. You can't see it from here, but ahead lays the Kingdom of Heavenly Creatures. Within the Kingdom of Heavenly Creatures are three more lands, and one of them contains the Vestibule of Faith. Also notice that there is no horizon to be seen in any direction. I know it is strange, but this land does not permit for any ability to fathom its entirety. Not even by us, the Heavenly Creatures!

"We have far to travel," she continued. "Trust in me, Timothy. Your questions will be answered in its own due course. If this view is any indication of the perplexity of these lands, then take that as a sign. Your questions could go on and on just as the distance ahead lay."

The distance did in fact go on and on, and he soon understood why he could not see the horizon. Like a concave view, the land ahead curved outward rather than inward, eventually becoming so large that his eyes were unable to decipher anything at all. In addition, Timothy saw colors that were beyond what he had ever processed. The sky had varieties of blue and gold and the land rolled between several types of green. Great grey mountains lifted up into the air. In its totality, Eden was sophisticated yet natural at the same time.

"Follow me, will you?" she asked, having slowly brought him back to the ground.

To that Timothy nodded, and he remained behind her but this time much closer.

Through the woods they walked over hilly terrain.

Unlike most forests, the ground was soft and the grass thick. There was little change to the scenery and Timothy still was not able to sense how long they had been traveling or to determine what time of day it was. Also, he grew not hungry and consistently found himself to be full of energy. In some aspects of this journey he was filled with joy, especially when comparing what he saw to that of earth and factoring in the mutable state of his existence. In that way, any thoughts that he would have normally found to be associated with negativity became directed into his heart. From there, they seemed to lift up toward the sky.

"So tell me some more about the demons. Why are they after me? I've had all of these dreams and visions lately and I'm certain they are connected in some way."

"Your life was in danger. If you were to return now, it still would be. You are a person of interest whom Satan himself does not want to see succeed. As far as that goes, that is all I can say right now. The two demons themselves appeared to be lieutenants of his army. I did not recognize those two fallen angels in particular, but they must have been entrusted to do something that was mission critical. I have been following you for some time now, and it came to the point that I could no longer ward them off. You had to be immediately removed from your situation, although this was somehow an appropriate time for you to enter the next stage of your life."

"So fallen angels make up the entirety of his demonic forces? And they just roam around in plain sight?"

"For the most part they are all fallen angels, but there are also men who are part of his army. Remember earlier I mentioned that most people of your world, who die, remain here in Eden until the time of judgment? Well, the other some made choices on earth that led them to be demonically possessed. We call them the 'Willingly Condemned.' Once this type of person meets their inevitable death without having repented, their spirits falls to Satan's side, also until the time of judgment. Keep in mind that each of these persons is given the chance to repent before they die. That is where this topic becomes extremely complex, and therefore I will not continue to delve into it any further.

"In terms of the demons roaming in plain sight... that is also not a simple notion to describe. They are able to mix in with others, but they are limited in the actions they can take while visible. You see, they are best with trickery if visible but best with destruction while invisible. While corporal, they preferably travel in darkness because light decreases their power. This forces them to either travel in greater numbers or else to become invisible again. Additionally, there are rules and a balance that must be maintained that they have to follow when they appear in a tangible form; you will learn more about that as you grow in wisdom. The bottom line is that it is contradictory to their mission if they are discovered for who they are. Their aim is to fool you into thinking that they are sent from God Himself! Timothy? Are you with me?" she asked, realizing she gave too much information at one time.

"I am here. I cannot stop thinking about vampires, I guess. The demons seem so much like that. I know vampires are fictitious, but it sure is interesting how man, using material concepts, is able to grasp what is otherwise hard to explain. For example, the demons you described definitely compare to our horrific tales of vampires. It is as if someone sometime long ago had seen a demon, and in order for it to be understood in earthly terms, they created the image of a vampire. Does that make sense?"

"Absolutely Timothy, you are a very intelligent boy. Well, now you appear a man! Everything on earth has a much deeper truth to it. No person is able to completely understand the complex nature of the mystical realms encompassing their earthly existence, but to some degree one can use reason through the intellect. So, when someone happens to see something they are unable to conceptualize, one turns it into something she or he can understand. Ultimately, the mind works in ways so as to justify what one knows or sees. This relates to concepts that you should be extremely familiar with, as you demonstrated just now. I know that some on earth say that Judas, a Disciple of Christ, was the first vampire! In one way that parallel is not so far off after all!"

Timothy smiled as they began to laugh. What Eryana had told him made complete sense and he was so thrilled to be challenged by what she had to say. At the same time, he also recalled some of what Father Andrei had told him during his last counseling session: the human mind, contorting much of what it knows, finds a way to reason so that one can be comfortable. In a relative sense, Timothy knew this all too well from his relationships with others as a child. Fascinatingly enough, he did not experience this discomfort at all in his relationship thus far with Eryana. He felt accepted and that, to him, was authentic.

Walking a little further, Eryana stopped short and extended her right arm so that Timothy was unable to continue walking any further. Her arms were very long and they gave Timothy a powerful impression. Even Timothy, much bigger and stronger than he was on earth, seemed to have not even a degree of her strength.

"What is wrong?" Timothy inquired, startled by her sudden halt in movement.

"Shush," she quietly spoke, "there is something unusual that I heard."

Timothy looked around and only noticed the tree trunks, which they had been walking through for an indeterminate amount of time. The trunks were, however, much more condensed and populated than before. To Timothy, that detail was awfully foreboding and so it caused conflict to flow through his mind. Up until that point they had been roaming through what seemed to be a safe haven, having escaped any potential for demise.

Contradictory to the ever-shining light emanating from the sky, fog began to creep around Eryana and Timothy. She looked back and forth to hopefully catch what she sensed nearby. Her great wings once again emerged from the back of her robe and Timothy walked closer to her, drawn by a feeling of protection that she gave.

"We are near the edge of the forest; hold onto me!" she suddenly commanded.

Eryana drew out her sword with her left hand. Her bottom wings wrapped backward around Timothy's waist as she charged forward, hovering near the ground while in flight. Timothy looked back and saw shadows creep toward them.

"I thought this was a safe haven," Timothy called out, as they rushed forward.

"It became that of a safe haven, although it once was the battleground. Small details! You know, I haven't felt this sensation since the great battle that took place here in the year of our Lord 1945!"

"Couldn't we have traveled the skies with the others?" Timothy suggested, as they continued forward. "Surely there is protection for us with your kin?"

"Those skies cannot be used for you. They are

dedicated for the Guardian angels who are traveling to and from earth on routine missions. It cannot be experienced by a human. And besides, we are not to distort the purpose of creation. Now continue to hold on to me!"

Eryana was now moving at an incredible pace and Timothy only saw the blur of tree trunks as they went by. He then began to feel ill, not because of nausea from motion but rather from the nausea of fear. He bowed his head into her feathered wings and closed his eyes.

"We are nearly there!" she informed Timothy, as if to give him confidence.

As soon as Eryana uttered those words, she halted and returned her feet to the ground. Timothy opened up his eyes, and coming out from behind the trees in front of them were twelve dark angels. Great wings they had, charred from the fire from whence they came. Piercing fangs emerged from their purple lips. At once they surrounded Timothy and Eryana.

"This shall not be yours!" she shouted at them, pacing around Timothy and ready for battle. "How dare you set foot again on this sacred land? It was sealed by our victorious efforts!"

The tallest led them as they sidestepped forward, crossing one leg over another. The evil creatures then pointed their deadly blades at Timothy's heart.

"We are your only hope! Do you find your angel's weakness to be appealing, boy? How can you know who to really trust, especially in something so complicated as this? I am much more familiar to you. I am the light for which you sought, and we allowed you the experience of falling away from us. Wouldn't you love to return to the top of that building again and taste more of the sweet bliss it offered?"

Timothy began to step toward the gigantic creature.

Chapter 6

Eryana then swiftly moved in front of him, preventing him from approaching the dark lord.

"Seize this pathetic excuse for an angel," the darkest of them commanded.

Eryana lifted her sword over her head with two hands to begin her defense, but it was not before she was overtaken by eleven of the demons. She began to struggle and they were barely able to hold her still. Timothy then fell down and began to crawl backward away from the evil.

"I can heal your pain, Timothy. Look up above me. That's it!"

Timothy looked up as the cunning leader waved his hand in a half circle, conjuring a vision that appeared especially for Timothy. The demons, still holding onto Eryana, moved off to the side.

"Now Timothy, do you see that woman? She is very ill. As I speak these words to you she lies ever so quietly in a bed. Don't you think someone you could trust, like your own father, would have told you about this? I am telling you now, as your friend. I can offer you help! If you leave with us, we can bring her back to health and you shall have all the joy in the world!"

"I – I don't understand. What is this?" Timothy asked, standing himself up. "This is not real. She has been fine. I just woke up in her arms the other day! Eryana, tell me this is a lie!"

Timothy looked at Eryana, who stopped struggling. She responded with a sympathetic glimmer from her eye.

Pain wrenched throughout Timothy's body and he fell onto his knees. Compelled, he looked up at the skies and dropped the book that he had still been carrying. Then, holding onto his cross, he cupped both of his hands around it until a bright aura abruptly surrounded his body. Letting go of the cross, his arms spread out into the air as a beam of light from his cross struck the dark lord. Eleven more beams of light from all directions then perforated through the other eleven demons and they became suspended in the air.

Eryana's eyes grew wide as the source of the eleven beams could not be found. But she knew exactly what they were. Without taking a moment to ponder, she leaped at the leader and struck her sword across his chest. Then, opening his mouth, he belted out a chilling scream. He disintegrated into the air and only his wings dropped to the ground. The beams of light then ceased and the remaining eleven demons, now freed, flew back to the Lake of Entrance. Eryana did not delay in taking hold of Timothy, who had just picked up his book and placed it into a pocket, and flew him off to the edge of the forest.

The fog dissipated as they traveled forward, allowing the sky's source of light to become prominent once more. In what seemed to Timothy to be equal to the time that they already had spent in the forest, they at once reached the border. At that point, he looked over Eryana's shoulder. She began to slow down and there stood a host of heavenly angels, firmly keeping guard. Timothy began to feel immediate relief as they approached a particular being that was standing front and center.

"What trouble do you bring to our lands, Arch-guardian Eryana, Angel of Elders? You seem to be with concern."

"Arch-guardian? Jacob would have loved this!" Timothy whispered, breaking out with a smile as his long face evened out.

The angel they had approached was certainly the head of the host, as his stature was taller than all of the others. His voice carried with it wisdom greater than that of

Eryana. Unlike those around him, the armor that he carried was instead on top of his clothing and his wings were exposed. Surrounding him in a half circle to his rear were nine angels, sitting upon four-legged creatures. To Timothy these animals resembled horses with wings, which gave cover to a large portion of their muscular bodies. Also they had three beautiful horns, one behind each ear and one between their eyes.

"Agread!" she at last replied. "Our land has been compromised!"

Eryana bowed and kneeled on one knee. Agread, the rank of Virtue, was the Stronghold of the Borderlands.

Eryana briefly turned back and gracefully smiled at Timothy. She then returned her gaze back to Agread who had lifted one arm into the air; he looked ready to issue a command to his warriors.

"Compromised?" Agread asked. "What do you mean? The angels in the sky fly back and forth carrying out their missions and we stand here protecting the border. Not a creature has made its way to infiltrate our guard."

Virtue Agread then stared into Timothy's eyes as if trying to read his mind. Timothy, unable to meet his eyes, looked to his right and then to his left. He unintentionally noticed the legions of angelic Powers in both directions keeping watch. At that point it had been only customary for Agread and his companions to preside over the border between the forest and the kingdom. During the last battle between the heavenly angels and Satan's demons, it was Agread and his host who had sealed the border from the forces of evil. That was the specific turning point toward victory. And so it became known that Agread's angels were the keepers of the kingdom's sovereignty, and they had remained in that capacity ever since.

"It was mid-way into the forest. I had not seen anything like it and swear by the authenticity that we witnessed. Eleven dark angels there were, led by a twelfth who contained within him an even deeper form of evil. A captain of Satan, which I have no doubt he was, was paralyzed by light and consequently was consumed by my blade. His wings are out there in the forest and will be proof thereof. We were saved by the Eleven Elders..."

Eryana stopped herself short. Unsure how to finish her sentence, her lips quivered subtly as she thought more carefully over what words to choose.

"And who should this be?" Agread inquired, unwilling to wait for Eryana to finish. "I see only a young man with you who has experienced but a few years of life. Certainly not an elder... and we were most certainly not expecting you to arrive with a human otherwise."

Eryana returned Agread's question with a sneer, hoping for him to notice her hint to desist. She shook her head and turned to Timothy. Reaching out her long arm, she encouraged Timothy forward by tapping on the back of his shoulder.

"Come forward, Timothy! This is Timothy Petrov: an Orthodox Christian who was in dire straits on earth, fleeing from Satan's grasp. We are here to protect him. No questions needed. I have orders that came directly from the High Dominion."

Agread looked into her eyes and saw that this was true.

"Very well, with that we will not continue conversation. You are safe now and that is what matters most."

Agread then again lifted up his arm and the nine riders allowed for Timothy and Eryana to pass.

Chapter 6

"Now," he told his soldiers, "go forth and find evidence of trespass. Find those treacherous wings and if possible chase down those filthy beasts."

Without pause the nine mounted angels went off into the forest, as their transport flew forward over the ground. Eryana then motioned to Timothy to stay in place as she approached Agread.

"Thank you, Agread. We will walk the rest of the way."

"We have a steed available for you both, if you wish," Agread offered.

"No, Timothy should be fine. I do believe he will start to tire soon, though. It has been just over a full day's worth of activity for him at this point, and this blessed land that he has encountered can only prevent for so long the laws of human nature wearing him down. Plus, there is more for him to learn before we arrive at his resting quarters."

"Indeed. So I gather he is it: the twelfth human to complete the Eldership? It was he who paralyzed the captain in the forest, wasn't it."

"Timothy was in danger on earth, and I received command to watch over him until his rescue was necessary. He is much different than the other eleven, in more ways than a lack of years. For whatever plan God has, we must honor that and realize that the Prince of Evil is desperate to stop Timothy from becoming an elder, using whatever means possible."

"Michael has called for a meeting and the leaders of our kingdom will be summoned," Agread replied. "Perhaps this is a sign that the final battles of our time are imminent and that our forces on earth are in danger. I will not keep you any longer. God bless, Eryana."

Eryana bowed once again. Turning around, she

walked back to Timothy. Agread nodded as they moved onward.

Chapter 7

Eryana led Timothy across the vast distance of the Borderlands. A simple dirt road broke up the delicate fields of dark green grass. Although the path was rather monotonous for Timothy, he was enjoying the chance to remain deep in thought. Since the fair, he had not been provided an opportunity to process even the minutest of details.

From the top of a rocky hill they could see the Grey Mountains, up close and standing tall. From the edge of the cliff all the way to the mountains stretched a veil of clouds from which angels were traveling in and out of. Finding a winding path downward, they descended below the misty barrier. Far ahead, magnificent gates were revealed to them. Therein lay the kingdom where all of Eden's intelligent creatures resided.

Finally approaching its walls, their journey from the Lake of Entrance to the Kingdom of Heavenly Creatures at last came to an end. The golden-tinted structure provided a sense of profound security: there would seem to have been no such existence of despondent life beyond that point. Great stone statues of Archangels Michael and Gabriel stood just outside of the gate to which Timothy then took a brief moment to contemplate on. Joining Eryana just in front of the entrance, Timothy presented himself in tattered garments, holding an old book in his hand. His face then displayed a look of discouragement.

"My dear boy, or rather, young man Timothy! I sense what you think. Remember how much truth can be found in our Lord's instruction 'blessed are the poor in spirit.' If anything at all, you are more than ready to enter here with me. Now keep your chin up and take my hand."

Eryana kneeled on one knee just to the right of the gate. She blew upon a horn that was affixed to a free standing silver rod. Gracefully standing back up, she led Timothy backward a few steps in order to make way for the doors to open. Slow they were, and patient was Eryana in waiting. Just before the doors began to close, they proceeded through the gate and into the great city. To Timothy's left and right he fathomed one hundred pearl archways as Eryana led him through a courtyard before reaching yet another entranceway. There, two heavily armored angels manually opened ornate wooden doors and without question allowed them to pass through.

Inside was a vestibule. Timothy looked up and saw a conglomerate of steps that began at one point but eventually split off into three very different directions: east, north and south. They had no visible mechanism of support but their weathered impression revealed they had been thoroughly tested.

"I think I am feeling tired now. I do not know how much energy I now have to walk up those steps!"

"You are at last feeling the exhaustion of your journey; no doubt can be made otherwise. What is specifically overwhelming you at this very point is the lack of earthly cares. Your mind does not know how to perceive the good state that bars the infiltration of evil. You now will embrace a strong pull toward God and your heart will be light. Focus on your breathing and do not resist the Love of the Holy Spirit."

Timothy took a deep breath and trusted his guide's instructions. Ascending up the initial flight, Eryana then chose to continue straight up the eastern stairway. They took an additional one hundred steps upward and reached a final doorway. Through the cracks of the doorframe, bright light shone through causing Timothy to uncomfortably squint.

"This is the eastern doorway. The Residence of Angels there lay; after you!"

Timothy pushed on the door and walked through. His mouth gaped open at first glance. Their surroundings now carried a completely different tone. Tens of thousands of angels there were, all walking along hundreds of pathways as far as he could see. Some were engaging in each other's company with great happiness on their faces, while others roamed alone contemplating whatever it was that off-duty angels contemplated. Although incomparably more glorious and a polar opposite of any vision of earth, Timothy was shocked by the similarities of these creatures to humans. They appeared to have a life of their own to live as each seemed to have their own unique and distinctive personality, carrying out their duties both to themselves and others.

The space that housed those visions of beauty was an illusion of sorts: he had entered a dimension within a dimension. Looking behind the door and all around, there was an open expanse that, like the view from above the treetops in the forest, also went on indefinitely. Here the sky was much lower and ongoing was the sound of angelic voices in hymn for the Lord. The source of this, like the light that filled the sky, he could not determine. As if having no other choice, Timothy began to weep.

"What is it, Timothy? What troubles you?"

"It's just... this is something I have been longing for. I have always felt that there was something I was longing for. That there was something I was supposed to do, or be, or find myself part of. I have said this before, although it was blindly. This is what my heart has been waiting to find."

Eryana put her arm around Timothy and consoled him.

"Very close to it," she added, now moving him along. "We must go to where you will be staying. The purpose of your being here is greater than just my saving you from demise. You will soon find out more of what is in store for you. First you must rest and gather your faculties and the House of Elders will restore this for you; you will certainly there be made more comfortable. Just a little more walking is required!"

By earthly calculations that was an understatement. To put it in perspective, there were several more miles of paths to undertake, equal to about a tenth of the total travel that Timothy had just completed. To make matters worse, he looked down and realized he had not any shoes on his feet. It was a miracle that his feet were not sore. It reminded him how Eryana had originally told him he would still need certain materials in order to justify his senses; perhaps now he was required to have much less.

"There certainly is not a straight answer about anything," Timothy quietly muttered.

Passing through the peaceful mobs of angels, they traveled on along marble roads. Timothy laid his eyes on the beautiful structures that the city center was comprised of. The roofs suggested the buildings were many floors high, but, peeking into the open entrances, Timothy saw that they were in fact only one floor, built with extremely high ceilings. Immaculate artwork was inscribed into the robust columns that supported an overhang for each building entrance. It was very similar to the woodwork design he knew from various Orthodox parishes as it imprinted a nostalgic image in his heart.

From time to time an angel or two would stare in his direction, which made him feel rather uncomfortable. He was a newcomer: a minority in a distant world. It was not that he had not experienced being singled out before – and perhaps part of his discomfort could have been attributed to the pain caused by religious persecution in past years – but instead he felt challenged by the unconditional love, joy and profound knowledge that stemmed from their deep eyes. How odd it was that Timothy was now the one feeling uncomfortable by the stare of other beings!

Moving out from the residence's busy center, there was a transition to a more desolate surrounding: the land became empty with nature and scattered trees could be found along the plains. It at that point occurred to Timothy that the road they were taking was not one trodden by the general angelic population. It was a road clearly specific to his journey. Although it was peaceful and maintained the same sense of security he found once entering the kingdom, he could not help to think back to The Forest of the Wise and the unexpected encounter with demonic creatures. How awful it would be, he thought, to have a similar surprise, especially before the chance to rest for the very first time.

A large compound on top of a steep hill became visible off in the distance, after an indeterminate number of steps were again taken. Still on a marble road, it had a much softer touch to the feet once Eryana led Timothy up to the building. There an archway stood in front and flanking the abode were an innumerable count of poppy trees that stood over blue violets and tall, yet well-kept blades of grass.

Finally, as if the events had been carefully planned out, a giant man-like being stepped out from the entrance and stood underneath the archway. They proceeded up a low grade stairway that had no railing and approached the creature.

"Gammond is my name; welcome to the House of Elders!"

Timothy looked at the gigantic being who cordially greeted him with open arms. Gammond was wearing a dark brown robe and had not a hair on his head. Timothy stepped back in an effort to better grasp who he would be embracing, but Eryana immediately encouraged him forward with a gentle tap on his back.

"Here I leave you for now, Timothy," Eryana revealed with a gentle tone, "and I trust Gammond with everything; you have no reason for concern. He has been the caretaker for the habitants of these living quarters for the past two millennia. As a true servant of the Lord he will see to your recovery. For my part, I must take to my business which is both old and new. I will see you after you have some rest, which your human soul still requires at this point. It has been an honor and shall continue to be!"

Eryana was fully aware that she was the only creature for him to depend on since his arrival to Eden, but there were important matters that had to be tended to. She turned around without another thought and wandered down the hill. Spreading her wings out from her robe, she then hovered off into the distance. Gammond waved goodbye and walked Timothy into the old stone building.

Timothy looked around as Gammond grinned largely. It was an enormous hall that was like any other in those lands: more spacious than what the building exterior had led on to be possible. Several staircases, three floors and a pleasant fragrance of incense filled the inside. Otherwise, only a single red carpet rested on the floor and beyond that nothing else could be found, except inside of a few rooms off to the side.

"Well, I should take you to your room. You must be quite exhausted. Upstairs we have a robe and sandals for walking. Follow me, master," Gammond instructed.

Timothy hesitated for a moment and then followed Gammond up the three sets of stairs that started in the vestibule. He kept a few steps distance from him the entire time.

"I notice that you are somewhat wary around me, Timothy," Gammond admitted, taking the last steps to reach the third level. "That is to be expected, especially since you are so young and may not quite understand what I am."

"Well, I am sorry! I just... I have never quite seen someone with your appearance. Maybe you are a bit uncanny... what are you?"

"Long ago and not too far into the beginnings of humanity, there were certain angels who roamed the earth. They weren't Archangels, but a level higher in the ranks. They were Rulers, or otherwise known as Principalities. They were entrusted to watch over various groups of humans... wait a moment, do you already know of this?"

"No, sorry, I tend to stare with wide eyes, as if I am peering into the minds of others. Or so I've been told. Go on."

"Alright," Gammond continued, as they continued down a bright hallway, "I can give the long version of the story. So, these principalities decided to be unconventional, so to speak. On earth they seduced the daughters of men – daughters of kings at that. As a result children were born and this was most troubling to the main sees of the First Hierarchy. Action had to be taken. Therefore the Dominions, at the top of the Second Hierarchy, had received a direct order from the Thrones of the First Hierarchy that God himself wanted this population immediately removed from earth. The problem here was the innocent: the children of these angels and humans. They could not be destroyed. Well, that is where the Arch-guardians came in. Eryana is one of them. No room on Noah's Ark for the children, the Arch-guardians rescued the offspring just at the right moment and brought them up into the heavens. In fact they ended up just outside of The Forest of the Wise, where you entered Eden. Long they traveled to make it here to the residence, each trusting their angelic shepherd like sheep in a pasture. Of course they could not live here freely in the Residence of Angels as half of their blood was human. There was going to be a much better use for them, indeed. They were to be servants of angels, saints and elders until the time of judgment. And here I am, a giant Nephilim at your service. Half angel, half man and rescued by the same who protected you! I have been the personal servant to each individual entering this household here on this hill since Jesus left earth."

Timothy thought about this for a moment as they entered his room, internalizing the details.

"Well, are you to say I am an angel, saint or elder?"

"My goodness, well, I... do not think about that. You are a special guest here for now. And you now know what I am!"

"What happened to the angels? The Rulers, I mean?"

"Well, they have fallen. They were the only angels to fall into Satan's command since the Great Fall during the times of Adam. New Principalities were then determined as a hierarchical position can be granted once the occupant either dies or falls."

"That couldn't have been a smart move on their part, for sure."

"Not at all," Gammond laughed, "not at all! Of course, here I am as a result."

Gammond's laugh turned into a straight face.

"So," Gammond continued, "here is where you will rest until Eryana returns. I have covered the windows to simulate darkness for you as I am sure that will help you in your sleep! Go ahead and change into that robe over there; a warm bath is waiting for you in the room next to this. I will see you later. Perhaps in the morning as you would call it!"

"Gammond?"

"Yes, Timothy?"

"How is it that I am not with my body, but I still have human requirements like those on earth? And besides, I was taught that the body and spirit, as two parts of a soul, cannot simultaneously be functioning and not united?"

"Some things must always remain a mystery, until one day it is revealed! That day I truly look forward to; it has been a long time here. Goodnight, Timothy."

Timothy was discouraged as he wanted to know so much more. Gammond took note of this, but nevertheless exited the room and closed the door. Timothy had his bath, changed and fell asleep. Dreaming, it seemed only a continuation of what he had thus far experienced in the new world: there was not a single recognizable difference between the concepts or scenery.

———

By the time Timothy fell asleep, Eryana had traveled across the Residence of Angels to the Offices of the Heavenly Hierarchy. It was the Chief Dominion himself, Corinth, who had required that Eryana, without delay, return to the High Office once she interceded for Timothy's welfare. The Lord had required this intercession, and subsequently had made possible for the thrones of the First Hierarchy to command Corinth's compliance on that matter.

Due to the urgency and sensitivity of the mission, Corinth had contacted Eryana directly. This was outside of normal protocol, however, as an unwritten rule existed that limited communication between angels who were more than one rank apart. (Ever since Satan had defected from Him and single-handedly solicited one third of the Second and Third Hierarchies, it was agreed by all of the intelligent creatures that the rule was meet and right).

Eryana approached the castle doors and knocked firmly. The doors immediately opened as a transparent veil stretched across the entranceway from top to bottom, which only intelligent creatures that had not fallen from the heavens were permitted to enter through. If any other creature not meeting that criterion attempted to enter, they would be sent to the Dark Chamber of Holding, trapped and bound with chains until the Second Coming of Christ.

Looking at the veil, Eryana recalled that there was once a time where an angel had not been loyal to the Hierarchy and was meant to fall with Satan. This angel had not the strength of will to face God's wrath, however, and so at the last moment he chose the side of God. Attempting at one point thereafter to enter the castle, he had been stopped by the veil and met the consequences of his temporary allegiance to Satan. The cries of sorrow that angel had let out were heard far and wide across the residence.

Eryana entered and, although trusting of the laws of the Offices, let out a sigh of relief once making it through for her very first time. Down a hall she went past heavily armored Powers who were positioned along each wall, until she reached another doorway. She passively knocked and it opened without hesitation. There stood Canter, Keeper of the Office Grounds.

Canter was a Virtue like Agread, but was only in charge of the grounds; he did not oversee any Powers in the Kingdom of Heavenly Creatures. He was nevertheless considered one of the most trusted angels in all the heavens, and was the only other aware of Eryana's impending arrival aside from Corinth and those in the First Hierarchy. Being the only mid-level angel in the castle, it was fitting for him to be in a room between the Powers and Dominions and to get past that room, Canter had to approve.

"Welcome Eryana. Follow me," he nodded.

Canter was known to make brief statements as he did not engage in unnecessary conversation. Silently he led her on through the room that was the archive for all heavenly writings. Large was how it was described by the heavenly creatures, but to an outsider the word large could not do justice: the writings had been conducted since God's creation of the heavens as the Cherubim themselves sang words into the transcriptions. Other than those records, all heavenly operations and events were otherwise only fully known by God himself. As such, to seek the Room of Transcription was the main reason an intelligent creature would travel to the Offices of the Heavenly Hierarchy.

Through vertical hallways, stairs, twists and turns they traveled until reaching the top of the castle. Finally reaching the level of the Dominions, it was truly breathtaking as the brightness of the entire floor was nearly abrasive to even an angel. It caused bearable pain to any creature that stepped foot there, unless you were a Dominion or an angel from the First Hierarchy. Also exempt from the sting of light was Canter: as they approached Corinth's abode, Eryana stood directly behind him with her face nearly in his wings, which was deflecting some of the light.

"We are approaching his doors; you may now come out from behind me," Canter instructed.

"Thank you," Eryana replied.

Canter vanished and Eryana was left there alone before the High Office.

"Enter," a mystically profound voice uttered.

The doors opened themselves and in that room she could barely make out Corinth's profile due to the shining outline of his body.

"I cannot imagine what it would be to stand before a Throne," she said under her breath.

"Welcome. Truly good was the work you completed," Corinth confirmed, as she suddenly found herself standing before him.

As nothing else could be seen except for his emanating brightness, she bowed her head so that the discomfort would ease.

"Thank you kindly, your Eminence. I seem to have brought Timothy out of harm's way just in time. Yet I am rather concerned about the conditions in which not only did I bring us out of from earth, but also those that we found ourselves in once in The Forest of the Wise. Both were a vision of hell and the latter was especially disconcerting. Agread himself did not comment much on the evil spirits that followed us into what was supposed to be a safe-haven," she exclaimed, now lifting her head up. "Please forgive my tone. If it was not for the intercession of the Eleven Elders, I know not what would have transpired."

"Eryana... please understand the times we are facing. I heard much of what happened. Word did arrive here from the Thrones," Corinth replied, stopping short of further explanation.

"Of course! But what of the thunder storm that nearly killed Timothy's earthly life while his spirit was escaping to the heavens? Where were the Principalities, particularly of North America, during my mission who could have offered protection from the natural disaster that nearly killed him? And where is the concern regarding Beelzebub's captain and his eleven lieutenants, which made their way through the forest? Surely something is amiss for them to gain access to our lands! Yes, Agread sent out his nine elite angels to search, but delay there was in his commanding of them. I can think of eleven trips I made over the past two thousand years, which had a level of difficulty that paled in comparison to what I just recently encountered!" Eryana finished as her eyes revealed a fierce concern.

"Duly noted; your concern is warranted, indeed. Now, I advise you to remove yourself from the emotion that is pouring out of your mouth. Trust in your Lord!" his voice stormed through the air.

Eryana bowed her head again and kneeled on her right knee.

"What are the orders from above," she conceded.

"Timothy must prove his worthiness of a select group such as the Twelve Elders. His spirit had not enough development on earth and so the Trials of the Trinity await him. If he refuses the quests or fails at them, his spirit shall be brought back to where he rests on earth. Then, upon his bodily death, he will remain in Tartarus where he will long for the joy that he has so far experienced until the Judgment Day of Christ.

"If he survives, on earth a second set of trials awaits him: performing three miracles. The welfare of both the Ancient Church and those he cares most for depend on this."

"But he is just a boy! How can Timothy be expected

to make it through the Trials of the Trinity at the age of twelve?" Eryana both pleaded and argued.

"You must take him past the Vestibule of Faith so that he can see through the Blessed Waters. There you can reduce his confusion and allow him to gain wisdom and insight. His path will then become much clearer and if his heart opens to the Truth then successful he might be in his journey."

"And if he can't let go of his earthly cares and decides he cannot attempt the heavenly challenge?"

"Then I am afraid his fate will be the same as the aforementioned," Corinth declared. "He must. Only he alone can ensure the revival of His Church, in preparation for earth's final battle against Satan who cannot afford to have that link remade. But for Timothy to succeed depends on his choices.

"The time is near for the age of the Twelve Elders, which has been so far thwarted by Satan and his army. Reveal to Timothy the prophecy regarding the sacred cross, which he bears. Explain it in earthly terms so that he can better understand."

A tear fell from Eryana's eye. As much as she found the requirements for Timothy to succeed unjust, she forced herself into compliance and bowed to Corinth. She pondered about the first eleven elders and how they lacked this deep challenge to overcome in a foreign dimension – in addition to having had trials and tribulations on earth. They at least had each remained in joy once passing through to Eden. Timothy, on the other hand, was challenged in a whole new way and had been given only a temporary taste of the true benevolence of God. And the consequences he would endure because of choice were crystal clear: if choosing to accept the Trials and within them attaining success, he would return to earth and encounter further tests in the quest to unify the Ancient Catholic Church. On the other hand, if for any reason Timothy chooses to not accept the Trials or he fails at them, he would find himself eventually waiting in Tartarus, longing for the Grace of God that he had so far briefly experienced. If only his life could have been more simple and innocent.

"Blessed are the ignorant, for one knows not true evil until they experience true bliss," Eryana said to herself, as she turned around and exited the High Office.

Canter then appeared to her and led her toward the castle exit. Eventually reaching the Room of Transcription, she turned around and bowed before him to which he began to hum sweet, graceful melodies. Looking over his shoulder she could see an open book suspended in air: through his angelic vocal cords, Canter was in fact repeating sounds of the Cherubim as another chapter of the heavens had been written.

Eryana hastily traveled back across the Eastern lands to the House of Elders. By the time she arrived at its entrance, Timothy had awoken from a full rest. She entered into the main hall and off in a side room was Timothy and Gammond, enjoying each other's company. Gammond was quite the storyteller.

"...so there ended the last battle for the Borderlands, and with earth's last world war coming to an end so did all hopes of Satan bringing upon the antichrist under his own terms."

"I hope you haven't filled his mind with too much now, Gammond!"

Gammond jumped up out of his seat, not knowing how long Eryana had been standing there. She was smiling, although in a rather accusatory fashion.

"I've been very selective indeed, Eryana! Why, he was so curious about the battle for the Borderlands … which he said he heard from you and Agread talking… and I thought just as well he should know the relationship between events here on heaven and on earth. It's all so harmless and I am certain that –"

"No, it is quite alright," Eryana interjected to calm his worry, "I am glad to see Timothy in such great spirits. Thank you for being such a great companion! So, Timothy," she said, taking a seat next to him on a padded bench, "how was your sleep?"

"Oh, just fine. It was very odd to not have a troubling dream! It was as if I wasn't really sleeping at all and everything around me was continuing to happen, even though I am sure in my sleep I wasn't really aware of my surroundings. Does that make sense?"

"Sure, perfect sense," Eryana confirmed.

She threw her head toward the direction of the hall so that Gammond would take a hint to let them be alone. Acutely aware of detail, he immediately bowed his head and turned out of the room. Eryana looked back to Timothy who was looking at the ground.

"I am still bothered by that vision I saw of my mother in the forest. She was there when I woke up from that dream I had a few days back; I know she was! Those are awful tricks that demons can play!"

"Timothy, this is certainly not to dismiss your feelings, but there is much we have to accomplish – and soon. Your concerns will be addressed and you must be strong and open your mind to your heart. Have faith."

"I knew there was more to it. That's fine, Eryana. Let's get on with everything. Confusion is not an ideal state of mind to be in either."

Chapter 7

"Good then, Timothy," Eryana said, smiling warmly, "let us go to the Vestibule of Faith. You remember me mentioning that earlier when we were above the treetops?"

"Yes absolutely! It sounded fascinating, although I am having trouble picturing it. Some sort of place that sounds secure, is it?"

"That is one way of putting it. You will learn much this day. That is especially why it was so important for you to rest in a way natural to you."

Eryana stood up and exited the room as Timothy followed her lead.

"And by the way, Timothy," Eryana continued, "that robe looks quite authentic on you! Very grand indeed it is."

"Thank you; yours is pretty nice as well!"

They both smiled with an open mouth, walking out of the building and down the low grade steps. They then traveled back to the center of the city, this time side by side. Rested, Timothy was much less concerned with the timing of things and took slow strides with his companion. Once in the marketplace, Eryana stopped at an unmarked building.

"We must shop here before leaving the Residence of Angels. There are some essentials that we need," she said, pausing after to give Timothy a chance to ask yet another question.

"What is this place anyhow? And I thought we didn't need materials in this place? I gave up my backpack before you brought me here," he said in a coy tone.

"You have had some rest, haven't you? The only true immaterial realm is where God exists, far above the First Hierarchy. But the materials we need here are not for greed! There is no human nature in this realm, but as intelligent creatures we too have certain essentials for our needs that are also pertinent to carry out our missions. But our markets do not quite work like yours."

"How so?"

"Well first of all, there is no charge or requirement for gaining something of need. If there is something of true necessity that one does needs, particularly for the angels of the Third Hierarchy, this market area is where we go. The Powers of the Second Hierarchy are not just warriors in the Angelic Army, but also help out by serving their kin. In this way, they use their God-given skills so that we can better accomplish our missions. For example, turn around. You see that building across the way?"

"Yes," Timothy said, still trying to understand her point.

"Well, that is a bath house. Our wings are cleaned there. The angels who travel back and forth to earth on their missions get a little dirty from the dust in the air. Keep in mind that there is no dirt or dust here, as cleanliness is next to Godliness. So therefore there are Powers who cleanse.

"Now take you, for example: still technically a human being even though in the heavens your spirit now resides. Your body has certain needs, such as energy for your mind to function; the rest you received at the House of Elders will be rare indeed. Do you see where I am going with this? This building here is where the Powers cook. They have potions that you consume so you can continue living – until you either return to earth or are officially made one with God of course! All of the essentials are in one concoction! The same is for all of the saints and elders who reside in the Northern Lands."

"I thought the elders lived at that building I was at?"

"No Timothy that is where they went when they first came here."

"How about all of the people who have died, aside from the saints and elders? Where do they stay?"

"You are very astute indeed! The same is also for all who have died on earth while they are waiting for their judgment here in the Kingdom of Heavenly Creatures. And they stay in Tartarus which is in the Southern Lands."

"Tartarus... isn't that like hell?" Timothy shouted.

"Now, now let's not get too off topic. Knowledge shall come as is necessary. If you are patient you just might find what you are looking for. Let us finish what we came here for in the first place."

"Okay, I'm sorry. I am just not used to all of this intricacy. I mean, I am realizing that the complexity that I thought I had in my life on earth is really simple after all."

Eryana smiled and they went inside the doorway to the Cook's Hall. Basically a warehouse, the inside was filled with thousands of stations where material potions were available for consumption. Far behind the stations were large carts that were apparently used to transport large quantities of the human necessity.

"Any Guardian angel of a reposed human comes here to acquire potions for them. They carry the potions to the Southern or Northern Lands, where those they had protected on earth now lay in waiting. That is one of their final missions as a Guardian angel. Follow me so we can get one for you. It is going to be quite a long day indeed!"

Timothy followed Eryana, but remained curious still.

"So you are my Guardian angel?" Timothy questioned, as they continued to walk.

"No, I am not. I just brought you here in the nick of time. You no longer have a Guardian angel, as I, an Arch-guardian, have interceded on your behalf."

"Oh, and also because I have not really fallen asleep, I assume?"

"No... enough with the questions for now!" Eryana said, half-smiling.

"Sorry," Timothy genuinely replied.

They continued walking inside until Eryana halted at one of the stations, deep within the building. There was a single cup resting on the station countertop, which resembled a tankard.

"Welcome Eryana," an armored angel spoke, approaching the other side of the counter.

"Many thanks Justinian," Eryana spoke, picking up the potion and turning toward Timothy. "Here you go Timothy. This should last you quite a while. You should not find yourself to need more in the near future."

Timothy took the cup. Bringing it close to his mouth he sniffed the steam coming from it.

"It smells so sweet! What is it?"

"Something you should know all too well. Drink up now!"

Timothy sipped the cup. He looked up at Eryana.

"It's the Body and Blood of Jesus Christ! Somehow this is apparent!" Timothy said, rather excitedly.

Timothy set down the cup and appeared extremely refreshed. He looked back and forth between Justinian and Eryana and nodded in excitement. Suddenly, however, Timothy became faint. His eyes rolled to the back of his head and he fell to the floor.

Eryana sighed and put her hand over her forehead. She then giggled, moving her hand up to her mouth. Looking up at Justinian, she saw a surprised look.

"First time for Timothy, is it? You didn't even warn him!"

"I did not give it a thought. I suppose this potion was too rich as he is so young. The other elders had no problem," she defended herself.

Justinian jogged around the station and bent down to Timothy, picking his head up off the floor. Despite his collapse, Timothy still had a joyful look stamped on his face. Eryana then bent down too, placing her hand on his cheek.

"Timothy, Timothy? It's alright now, come to," said Eryana.

Timothy began to open his eyes. He saw a foggy vision of the two beautiful angel's faces, one with golden hair and the other with dark.

"You're both so breathtakingly good-looking!" Timothy paused and then sat up, looking around. "What happened?"

Eryana and Justinian stepped back.

"You had something of a reaction!" she said. "You are here with me at the Cook's Hall, do you not remember? You have had an overdose of purification. Perhaps it will last you now in lieu of several sleep cycles," Eryana replied, turning to Justinian as they broke out into laughter.

Timothy's smile turned into a frown as he gathered he was the expense of a good-natured joke. He then stood up and looked deep in thought for a moment.

"So that was the Sacrament of Communion, so to speak? Now a thought just came to my mind. It is about all of these people in the Kingdom of Heavenly Creatures. Intelligent creatures I mean! What sustenance did they have to keep their mind going before Jesus' time? Obviously there was no Body or Blood!"

Justinian turned to Eryana, pretending to be equally curious along with Timothy.

"The Angel of the Lord breathed life into all through

the steam," Eryana explained. "Now the steam from the cup that still remains only symbolizes tradition. It is the actual substance of Christ rather than the Spirit through the steam that fulfills the mystery."

"That's fascinating!" Timothy replied. "Well, I believe I am ready to go now."

"We have two more stops here at this market. My blade needs sharpening, as that captain I defeated was rather thick skinned. And then I need my own sustenance," Eryana replied.

Timothy waved goodbye to Justinian and they left the building. Down the road a little ways was the Armory Facility. There they went inside, stopping at the end of a small line of angels who were already waiting for service. As Timothy gazed at the indoor structure he soon started to again feel a sense of awkwardness as a minority: a human intelligent creature. Although extremely anxious to leave the Residence of Angels into another foreign land, he thought it might reduce the discomfort caused by feelings of inadequacy if there he found fewer beings.

"I would think that there would be more angels than this in the marketplace here. I mean, with one Guardian angel for every human, and billions of humans having lived on earth, you would think it would be jam packed in here with weapon repairs from big battles with demons!"

Before Eryana could respond, they moved forward as they were unexpectedly next in line.

"Just a blade sharpening please, thank you," Eryana requested.

She then looked into Timothy's eyes.

"Well, Timothy," she started to explain, "most of the angels are actually looking after your kind, whether on earth or in the Southern Lands. In this manner there is a pretty equal flow of angels coming to and from these lands. The surplus is either comprised of the angels from the Second Hierarchy, any who are on break from a mission or those who watch over the saints. Saints need much less supervision in the kingdom. Actually, aside from the sustenance, the saints are completely independent."

"The Kingdom of Heavenly Creatures, you mean?"

"No, Timothy, I am afraid I have jumped ahead too far. The Kingdom of Intelligent Creatures is what I meant; that is another name for Eden and there saints can travel almost anywhere if they wish. The Kingdom of Heavenly Creatures, however, is comprised of these lands here to the east, and also to the north or south. Recall the three choices we had on the stairs once entering through the Kingdom of Heavenly Creatures' gate? Where you now are is, of course, the Residence of Angels, also known as the Eastern Lands, where the angels reside within the greater Kingdom of Heavenly Creatures, which then itself is within the Kingdom of Intelligent Creatures otherwise known as Eden," she clarified. "The Kingdom of Intelligent Creatures housed many more angels in the past before the battles of the heavens, but danger caused for many to be deployed to earth while the rest were consolidated inside of the golden walls. To avoid confusion, the aggregate lands are simply called Eden. The Eastern, Southern and Northern lands in particular are referred to as The Kingdom of Heavenly Creatures."

Timothy stopped asking questions, afraid for being overwhelmed with any more information. They stood there waiting for the Power to return with Eryana's blade. Timothy continued to look around inside the room and was still trying to get used to how the inside of every building was much more massive than the outside led on.

"No wonder they can cram so many angels in this

world," he thought to himself.

Eryana received back her blade and they left the Armory Facility. Down the way was another food shop, and there Eryana was given a small packet of oval-shaped pellets. She opened it up, swallowed the contents and returned the wrapping to the Power who was attending the station. Her eyes brightened immediately, although Timothy thought they were bright enough to begin with. She smiled once again and they traveled to the entrance, where they originally had entered the Residence of Angels.

Walking down the steps Timothy first noticed that it was considerably darker than where they came from. His eyes took a rather long time to adjust and so he put his arms out to ensure that he would not run into Eryana. Eventually reaching the bottom of the stairway, he could now see clearly: Eryana had already turned to the right, up another staircase.

"Follow me Timothy; we are on our way to the Northern Lands!"

"So what is south, the Southern Lands? When do I learn more about that?"

"Yes, that is the area I had spoken of. And you will learn if it needs to be revealed. We will not be going there at this moment for you to see. It is a one-way door that is only accessible to the Guardian angels who watched over those humans before they passed. Eventually, every soul will enter God's Kingdom through that door and to the Northern Lands. Speaking of which, shall we now continue?"

"I see," Timothy said. "Fine… let's continue."

He found the entire concept extremely eerie, but made sure to ask not another question. He then hurried to her on the stairway and they continued upward until approaching the Northern Land's entranceway. The door they found did not have light peering in through its cracks and it could not be opened with a gentle push. It was made of solid gold and reinforced with two steel beams. One beam was positioned vertically in the center of the door and the other horizontally lay just above the vertical beam's midline.

Eryana knocked three times and a voice spoke from beyond.

"When is the Trinity?" it loudly chanted.

"Both now and ever and unto the ages of ages!" Eryana chanted back, returning the password.

The door opened wide and a cool breeze swept past them. Beyond was a dark sky, brightened with more stars than could be seen during the clearest night on earth. There was no moon, but for purposes of illumination there not need to have been. Moving forward, Timothy gazed at the empty fields that surrounded both sides of stone steps. They led up a steep hill, which he mistook for a mountain.

Walking up the path, Timothy found lit torches adjacent to both sides of every seventh step. About halfway he paused to catch his breath and looked up at the top of the hill where the flames seemed to eventually merge into a single light. Among the bright orbs he could make out the outline of a cathedral and a sense of awe immediately filled up his entire being. All of his cares, for just a moment, left his mind. Eryana appreciated his temporary revelation and waited patiently a step ahead while he processed what lay before him.

Step by step they took, as if each was synchronized with the beat of Timothy's heart. Simultaneously the gradual onset of glorious sounds was heard: perfectly harmonized chants instilled hope into the illuminated air and a single bell chimed three times. To Timothy this indicated a service was about to begin. Then suddenly, as Timothy and Eryana approached the top step, a beautiful voice began to speak.

"What tongue is that, Eryana? It is not familiar to me."

"It is Hebrew," she firmly stated.

Timothy had heard services in Russian and Greek, but never before Hebrew. The ancient language seemed quite appealing and resonated throughout his heart. What a blessing it was for him to see and hear an environment such as that. Even more of a blessing it was to become as Eryana was about to lead him to the cathedral doors. Timothy anticipated that he was going to experience the richness happening inside.

"This is the Vestibule of Faith, dearest Timothy. Here, saints continuously worship God and pray for the salvation of all. They intercede according to prayers from below and work together with the angels there on mission, assisting with the work of the Holy Spirit. For God needs no aid but permits all to show their love for one another by keeping God's greatest work, the Image of God, in their hearts."

They entered the great structure and to the left of the narthex was another entrance to the nave. In the corner was a tall being holding a thickly woven rope in his hands. Timothy immediately recognized it to be a Nephilim, as his dress was similar to Gammond's. It was obviously this Nephilim's duty to ring the bells and how fortunate he was, Timothy thought, to be always so close to the holy services that went on inside that cathedral. The Nephilim bowed to Timothy and Eryana as they passed through into the nave.

Thousands upon thousands of men and women there stood facing the Beautiful Gates. A choir of Virtues stood in the rear right corner, proclaiming the Grace of God that the multitude of beings in the room was praying for. At that moment, a procession of fourteen men exited out of the north door of the iconostasis.

"Who are all of these people?" Timothy whispered into Eryana's ear.

"They are all of the saints who have passed from earth. The angels are Virtues, which are as we speak working miracles through their song; the saints are praying for this. Besides leading armies of Powers, another role of the Virtues is to help men and women on earth with their strife. They have beautiful voices. I know of one who sings the songs of the Cherubim into the scrolls of heavenly record.

"The first of the fourteen men are the Twelve Disciples of Christ, and following them is St. Paul the Apostle: High Bishop of the Vestibule of Faith; last in the procession is St. Timothy the Apostle. Now, behind the Beautiful Gates is the altar, as I am sure you have figured. What you do not know is that behind the altar exists the Stairway to the First Hierarchy, which eventually leads to God Himself. No creature except the Thrones, Seraphim and Cherubim may climb the stairway. But they would not need to since above they remain."

Timothy could not even begin to rationalize what was before his eyes. He felt weak while listening to Eryana as the energy flowing through the room was overwhelming. Any strength he had left had surely been given through the potion he had earlier consumed.

"How about the elders; where are they?"

"They live as hermits here in the Northern Lands. But if it is absolutely necessary, they will leave the Northern Lands and help out as asked of them.

"I wanted to show you more of this," Eryana continued, "but we must exit now and wander down the other side of the hill."

They both turned around and exited the Vestibule of Faith. Timothy was now in a trance. He followed Eryana over the other side of the hill like a lost soul until only the very top of the cathedral could be seen: an illuminated massive gold cross there stood high.

A path downward turned into a grove of spruce trees and bright lanterns hung from their branches. Further along into the lightly wooded area sat a bronze cauldron with gallons of clear water resting calmly inside. A bench made of a single slate of marble and four stone legs invited Timothy and Eryana to have a seat.

"Here we sit to reveal your purpose and make things here clearer for you. In this large pot is everlasting water that was blessed by Jesus Christ himself. This was done before he finally ascended into the heavens of the First Hierarchy," Eryana proclaimed, inching her face toward his. "The Blessed Water is the medium for which I will show you certain earthly events, Timothy. But first, I believe you have something on your mind that you want to discuss."

"Yes Eryana, in fact I do. I don't see how I can understand whatever it is that you need to show me without first understanding these dreams I have been having! I am convinced they are all related to what I am experiencing at this very moment. Can't I have some insight? Why do I dream about climbing stairs, elevators and my mother? Why do I dream about darkness, light and falling from buildings? About hearing strange voices that make me so very nauseous…?"

"Ah, yes, you had most troubling dreams. I was with you that night Timothy, although you did not know it until now. That night you fell one hundred stories until you woke up in my arms."

Chapter 7

Timothy stood up and backed away.

"What... what do you mean? I woke up in my mother's arms! I saw her and she had a washcloth for me. I was so warm with fever and so troubled. She was there for me and... and she must have heard me screaming in my sleep. She woke up for me!" Timothy pleaded, justifying what he had seen.

Eryana was quiet for a few moments. After allowing Timothy a moment to gain his composure, she replied.

"Timothy, please have a seat."

Timothy joined her side and was still breathing heavily.

"Timothy," Eryana continued, "your mother is very ill. We have been doing all we can to ward Satan and his curses off of her, but the time has come where our energy can no longer be of any help. Think Timothy, when was the last time you saw her?"

"Well, I guess it has been some time other than that night with my dream. I think that I saw her..." Timothy paused and thought.

His mind began to wander to the recent events he had experienced. He recalled asking his father where his mother had been lately and just before that he had passed by a dark room, which he had associated with a traveling monk. But there was not a traveling monk as that room had not been occupied by anyone in quite some time. Timothy realized his mother had been staying in that room all along. She had become ill, and his parents had not the courage to yet explain it to him. He began to cry.

"What of her?" Timothy cried. "What is going to happen? Your kind apparently can't help her, so what do you expect that I can do? Am I to return to earth as a weak boy, a foot shorter than I am here in heaven? It seems that it has been suggested more than once that there is some relationship between my situation and hers but I surely cannot be of any help!"

Eryana put her arm around his shoulders and sat closer to him.

"You will do what you have to do. You will know that God's plan has the best interests for you. You will be strong and not allow for false prophets to steer you away from the Truth.

"Your dream, Timothy... Satan himself was there, waiting for you to fall and hit the bottom of the world before you awakened. Power over you was what he needed most. But you are not so easily overtaken. I was there also.

"The dream in concept represents one moving between light and darkness. For you in particular, it signified a typical path of getting closer to God: receiving a glimpse of grace only to lose it shortly after. Secondly, it can be interpreted to mean that what you thought was good is really evil, and conversely what you think is evil was really good. That is how Satan and his demons use their trickery.

"Let me put it into more of a perspective, as it was really a combination of the two interpretations. The hallway where you found yourself signified earth. Earth, just as the hallway, was initially lightened with hope. The elevator, a material thing, then made you think that the path down the hallway led to darkness; material things can bring upon us nothing but deceit and demise and take away all brightness. But beyond the elevator you caught a glimpse of joy through the odd passageway at the top of a narrow stairway. Grace was beyond, as God is the only hope away from despondency. You went toward that grace and climbed to the doorway as if it was a portal to something greater above. But once you found it and entered, the light became foreign to you as God and the heavens are not easily deciphered by the naked eye. Unable to understand it, you then fell back into darkness, having only briefly experienced what God had to offer you. Then you realized that what was above you was really the light of heavens, compared to the darkness of hell to which you were falling back. Satan confused you by speaking to you from the light above.

"Earth turns into nothing but a dark vision of hell once one experiences the true Light. I woke you up, Timothy, because when you hit the bottom, Satan wanted to reveal to you a temptation and show you how profound it was to be back on earth once you awakened. He was counting down to you and waiting for you to come back to him."

Timothy began to understand what she was interpreting to him and then realized that the dream she described was a prelude to what he was now experiencing: he did indeed find a glimpse of Heaven, here with Eryana. Enduring temptation and returning back to earth would now be his next step. The manner in which he was to fall was his biggest fear.

"Timothy, the various concepts throughout your dreams are very similar. And Jesus Himself was revealed to you in the dream a year before. Take these gifts as a sign of what is to come. Allow them to give you strength. A set of three objectives soon lay before you. Before that, though, there is something you should know about who you are, who your Grandfather was and how that all relates to your being here with me at this very moment. Look into the Blessed Waters, Timothy. Look for a man. Wise he is, and in the same way, so will you be too."

Chapter 8

Elder Stamos prostrated alone in front of a cross that hung on the wall of his modest dwelling. Kneeling down, he lifted his arms toward the ceiling and then bowed once more, keeping his head close to the ground. A gentle breeze passed through the one room shelter as a large cloth sheet wavered in the doorway.

A joyful and God-fearing hermit, Elder Stamos lived in a wooded area in the outskirts of Athens, Greece. As he was not too far from a convent and several monasteries, his gift of wisdom was sought out by the nuns and monks. Quite often visitors would travel vast distances just to hear his uplifting words. He was known to inspire even the most destitute, leading them toward God to overcome life's greatest challenges. At age eighty-one, he had still not grown tired of balancing his time between worship and sharing his love with others.

Elder Stamos looked up at the cross and icons that covered the wall in front of him, and a single tear fell from each of his eyes. A force of grace that had originated from the very center of his heart then swept throughout his body. As he crossed himself he concluded his personal prayer, ready to have a small afternoon meal.

Stamos Halkias stood up and made his way to his kitchen area, although the entirety of his dwelling was a single open-concept room. Elder Stamos was content with the bare minimum in which he had, and provided himself with enough nourishment to only sustain his existence. Taking a seat on a hard wooden stool he slowly consumed a cold bowl of soup. He then finished and placed the bowl on a nearby table, just in time for a random visitor to reveal a silhouette behind the thin cloth.

"Enter my brother," Elder Stamos warmly welcomed the guest.

A man in his early thirties showed himself, dressed in attire that revealed he was something of a pilgrim. He appeared to be an Orthodox Christian, humble in what garments he wore. Carrying with him was nothing other than a small burlap sack that appeared to have very little inside of it. The man grinned briefly and returned his expression to a straight face as he approached the elder.

"Father bless," the man inquired.

"May the Lord bless you," Elder Stamos replied, making the sign of the cross over the traveler and then giving his own hand to be kissed.

"My name is Father Victor. I came from Russia to seek out your wisdom," he said, speaking in Elder Stamos' native language of Greek.

"I have been expecting you. It was revealed to me that a traveler was to arrive, seeking knowledge and that it would greatly change the course of my own earthly life," the elder replied.

Father Victor hesitated, caught off guard that his visit had so much relevance in addition to his own agenda.

"I am most excited to see you," Elder Stamos continued. "You must have had a long journey, given you walked through the forest and up the hill from the monastery. Would you like some water?"

"Thank you just the same Elder Stamos, but I am adhering to a strict fast today. I suppose I should just get right to the point as I do not want to take up too much of your time. You see, I am most troubled as of late. I had a vision. You are regarded as an authority on the authenticity of such phenomena and this is why I share it with you."

Elder Stamos nodded in acquiescence, as they both took a seat.

"I believe it was an angel," Father Victor continued, setting his sack down on the floor, "although I cannot say for sure. It was after several weeks of troubling dreams where my sleep was taken over by images of world catastrophes and dastardly thoughts, some from the deepest confines of hell. I was told by this messenger that it was of utmost importance to lead the various church organizations back to one another, and by this

I am referring to reinstating the Ancient Catholic Church. I was also informed that the time had come to seek out a certain elder, and that if I were to head out into the forests behind the Daphni Monastery I would find my way to him – well, you – and once I did it would all become clearer what to do. I did not at first take this seriously, but gradually my heart became heavy with concern."

"Mhmm...," Elder Stamos responded, contemplating.

"It is as if Satan is very irate about the fact that this vision appeared to me, and so I became confused on what to do. Following the vision I had a few more weeks of troubling thoughts and dreams that were similar to the first ones. That is when I decided to follow my heart in Christ and seek you out. I now feel so much lighter and know that it was the correct choice."

"I see," Elder Stamos delicately stated. "I can assure you that your vision was real. An angel sent by God did instruct you to perform God's will. You have a very important task ahead of you."

Elder Stamos stopped short of further explanation

and stood up, proceeding to carry his empty bowl to a large pot filled with water. At that moment, Father Victor noticed a very old piece of rope with a wooden cross attached to it, which was resting on a table next to Elder Stamos' chair. Just above the center of the cross was a shard that appeared to be somewhat calcified. His eyes lit up at the sight of it and what entered his mind was covetous at the least. Elder Stamos then returned to his seat, pretending not to notice Father Victor starting at it.

"Father Victor, there is about one and a half millennia worth of tension between the Roman Catholics and Orthodox Christians. I certainly will not pretend you do not know a thing about it, but you must have realized that if something so profound were to happen that it would predicate something so much greater to follow. Aside from this being the case, which none of us can presuppose, it would take great compromise – compromise that seven councils had also sought after."

"The Orthodox Way knows no compromise when it means sacrificing our principles, given to us by Christ," Father Victor responded, offering debate.

"Very true, and you are very wise beyond your years indeed. For the sake of argument, let us look at where the two churches do not agree. For example, consider these three: the form of bread during Communion, the Nicene Creed and the papacy. Neither are examples of principles given to us specifically by Christ but rather they were constructed by the men who continued His mission, inspired by the Holy Spirit. Although those issues are at the center of our arguments, Christ Himself surely does not endorse brothers and sisters to be stubborn, putting their worldly differences before the similarities they have of love in Him and others. And with that, I think you will find great challenges in what you look to attempt. Ultimately, the return of Christ will come in His own time. If the Ancient Church must come together according to the angel who visited you, then that time may be sooner than you think. One could surmise that Christ would require His Church to be in order and therefore there would be, in that case, no other choice but to compromise if you are to be successful in what He is asking of you. And consider this: the weaker His Church is here, the stronger the power Satan may have over those he tricks into following him and not Christ; the larger his army will be when the Lord returns."

To that, Father Victor had little response. The tone with which the hermit carried revealed a deep understanding and confidence that few could deny. Elder Stamos was surely a prophet in his own right and it appeared there was little he was not able to see in the most complex of matters. A few moments after processing everything he had heard, Father Victor's eyes began to wander back toward the cross he had spotted. He was drawn to it as if it was a rare treasure, like it was not anyone else's property or was something not known to the world.

As his eyes returned to meet Elder Stamos, he saw an astonishing sight. The space above and around the elderly hermit was illuminated and a calming presence seemed to take over the room.

"I am ready; my heart and mind are now one," Elder Stamos stated calmly, looking over at the opposite side of the room.

"I'm sorry... I did not catch what you have said," Father Victor said confusedly.

"Should I stand up? What about my friend here?" Elder Stamos asked, looking up from his seat.

Father Victor raised an eyebrow as he watched Elder

Stamos carry on a conversation with an invisible presence. But he was unafraid of the strange scene before him, as it was clearly related to his journey to the elder.

"Alright then, I see there is not much time," Elder Stamos said, now whispering.

Elder Stamos stood up and then knelt on both knees. Offering his right hand, he grabbed onto something in the air as if he was a child waiting to be led somewhere.

At the moment in which Elder Stamos lowered his head toward the ground, a deep rumbling sound resonated under the ground. Frightened, Father Victor immediately stood up and started backward, holding his arm back to search for the doorway. A vibration then carried through the ground, knocking him off balance. He tried a second time to make his way to the exit, but again was knocked off his feet by yet another shockwave. Looking up, he saw dust falling from the ceiling. Soon the dust was replaced by dirt, and then the dirt was replaced by pebbles until particles from the small structure itself began to come loose. The ground began to shake uninterruptedly to which Father Victor crawled under the kitchen table.

"My dear elder, come over to me before it is too late!" Father Victor commanded.

Garnering no response, Father Victor attempted to move toward the old man. But the shaking was now occurring at a greater intensity, and Elder Stamos collapsed onto the ground before he made it halfway to him. A loud crack then was heard and a supporting beam fell to the ground and on top of the hermit. Barely missing Father Victor, he jumped out of the way and went back under the table.

The earth was now trembling vigorously. Father Victor looked down at the ground and began to recite the

Jesus Prayer over and over again until the earthquake at once came to a halt. Father Victor, able to emerge from under the table, stood up and looked around at the damage. Every item on the shelves and table had fallen to the ground, and the only remaining object hanging on the wall was a large cross that Elder Stamos had routinely prayed in front of.

Pale and quivering, Father Victor approached Elder Stamos. Kneeling down and looking at him, there was no sign of life yet a peaceful sense of rest was in his final expression. Father Victor made a sign of the cross and bowed his head. Then, eyes watery and wandering, he observed the necklace that had fallen to the ground from the table. He bent down and picked it up. Not giving it another thought, Father Victor turned around, stepped through the wreckage and hastily went into the forest.

"But wait a moment," Timothy interrupted the vision, "my grandfather told me an angel wanted me to have his cross! I never knew he took it from someone. And he made no mention to the elder of this; he only told him the angel said to bring the churches together! What was the big secret about? He wasn't looking to steal it, was he?"

Eryana gave no response and briefly engaged Timothy's eyes. As she stared back down toward the pool of water, he remembered to trust that the necessary answers would be revealed.

The image of his grandfather running off into the woods was soon replaced by a monastery. It was a large stone building, three stories high and there was not a hint of civilization anywhere else in sight. Rubble surrounded the grounds and dusty smoke raised itself high into the sky. Inside the building the monks tended to the injured and were taking a census to ensure that all were safe from the destruction. Father Tikhon, a Russian priest who had traveled there with Father Victor, stood up and brushed himself off.

"Hieromonk David," Father Tikhon shouted, running across the dining hall. "Hieromonk David, are you alright?"

Hieromonk David stood up, brushing off dust. He appeared to be off balanced and had a gash across his forehead. He looked around as he heard Father Tikhon's voice, but was unable to place where it was coming from. Monks continued around him rushing about, as the scene was extremely unorganized.

"Please forgive me for not helping more here, but I must go look for Father Victor!" Father Tikhon said firmly, approaching Hieromonk David and holding onto both of his shoulders. "He should have been back long ago and with this terrible earthquake I am most concerned for him! I will be back soon!"

"He is a very careful man and perhaps he is on his way back as we speak. Still, do not delay; go now! I will be fine, and I certainly understand. Please be safe. May God be with all of us," Hieromonk David replied without hesitation.

Father Tikhon smiled, relieved that his request was not challenged. He hurried out, weaving in and out between large stones and other structural pieces until he reached the forest.

"I'm sure he would have been on his way back to check on us by now," Father Tikhon said out loud. "He will find his own way back wherever he is – I am sure of it."

The terrain inclined until he reached the steepest point of a hill. The dirt path was no longer noticeable on the ground, and he only could move forward as the open space between the trees allowed. It was becoming darker and that, combined with several downed trees, caused him to steer off track. Father Tikhon nonetheless gave his best effort to follow the upward slope until then, far to his right and a ways ahead, something was moving quite fast down the hill. It was none other than Father Victor and to that Father Tikhon hid, allowing him to pass by.

"Where was he coming from? It can't be!" Father Victor told himself.

Continuing, he was able to find again the path that he had veered from and after battling the remaining obstacles, Father Tikhon approached a clearing. There the hill leveled out and he could see ahead the battered hut. All was quiet as he approached the entrance to Elder Stamos' living quarters. Inside, he found the hermit lying still and breathless. Father Tikhon ignored him and searched the dwelling.

"Where is it!" he shouted. "Where is the cross?"

He began throwing anything and everything in his way over his shoulder and across the room. Father Tikhon anxiously rummaged through every corner and dark space he could find. His anxiety turned quickly into a panic until he was nearly out of breath.

"It is gone," a dark voice whispered, sneaking around the side of the building and into the dwelling. "It has been taken by a man dressed similar to you. He is well on his way back to the monastery as I am sure you have already noticed."

The dark voice was carried by a hunched over creature, with a large cloak covering nearly every inch of its body. Bright white eyes could be seen in the dark space underneath the cloak's hood. It appeared to be very frail, but Father Tikhon did not pay heed to the strangeness at all. It was not the first time they had been acquainted.

"Father Victor! He took it! How did he…"

Chapter 8

Stopping himself short, Father Tikhon sat down on a chair. Pondering, he scratched his head and rubbed his hands over his face.

"I was supposed to come here. The plan was for me to find this relic after the earthquake took care of the elder. What happened? How could this be? I must go get it! I must..."

Father Tikhon started for the door, but the creature reached out with its arm and stopped him from going any further.

"It's too late!" the dark being declared. "You will never recover it now; our mission must change its course. But there was one error made in this heavenly debacle. I was watching through that window from outside, as I was sneaking about. I saw the path taken by an angel with Elder Stamos' spirit, before his bodily death thereafter. But never mind you about that! Go back to the monastery. Accuse Father Victor of robbing this poor old hermit! Make him flee your land of Russia. Do this and you still have the chance of obtaining glory and wealth."

The images in the water darkened. Eryana was frozen, uneasy about the exchange she had seen between Father Tikhon and the dark creature. She had not expected to see the two of them converse, for she knew not the dealings of the creature with humans on earth. Even more alarming to her was that the entrance to Eden, leading to all of the heavenly creatures, had been exposed well before her recent encounter with demons in The Forest of the Wise.

"I don't think I can handle this, Eryana!" Timothy frantically spoke, turning his head away from the waters. "This is so disturbing. I don't have the stamina to continue with this; my stomach aches and my head hurts. I want to go back home!"

"Get a hold of yourself now and sit down!" Eryana commanded.

Timothy obeyed and had a seat.

"There is more to see," she continued, "and it might be very disturbing, but so much does the welfare of others rely on you tolerating this. Put your love for others above your own needs. Now come back, and look into the cauldron once again."

Timothy stood up slowly and quite cautiously. He stood by Eryana and held her hand for comfort. They both returned their eyes to the pool.

Father Victor returned to Russia. He traveled alone, as an exchange between him and Father Tikhon at the Daphni monastery in Greece had been heated with anger. In front of nearly all of the monks, Father Victor had been accused of allowing for Elder Stamos' demise. There was no mention made of the cross, however; Father Tikhon only stated that Father Victor had carelessly left the poor hermit for death. The monks there believed him as he had vowed to report the calamity back to the Office of the Russian Patriarch.

Days passed by and Father Victor entered into a cathedral in Moscow to meet with Patriarch Ivan, as he had been summoned. Walking toward Patriarch Ivan's office, he was nervous and not sure if he could trust anyone to explain the situation that he was in. Furthermore, the angel who had appeared to him had provided him with limited instruction. With his now estranged friend Father Tikhon having turned on him and looking to have him defrocked from the priesthood, he had decided that he would make no mention of any detail whatsoever until he received another sign from above.

"Good afternoon; may I help you?" a receptionist

asked Father Victor.

"Hello there, yes, I am here to see Patriarch Ivan. I am Father Victor."

"I see." the woman gravely replied. "Give me a moment, will you?"

The secretary walked into the patriarch's office and closed the door. After a moment passed by, Father Victor decided to have a seat while he waited. He began to think about the woman's ornery response, and how there had been others recently who had responded to him in that same manner. Since the events that had transpired at the monastery, he found himself becoming more paranoid each time he encountered an unfriendly individual.

"Alright Father Victor, he is ready to see you," the receptionist called out from her desk, startling him out of his deep thoughts.

"Ah, okay then. Thank you."

Father Victor entered into the office, and the receptionist closed the door behind him.

"Your Holiness, may I –?" Father Victor began to ask.

"Have a seat," Patriarch Ivan interrupted, with his back facing Father Victor.

Father Victor immediately took a seat as Patriarch Ivan turned around to face him.

"My dear Father Victor: we cannot say for sure what your intent was for leaving the elder alone after the earthquake. It is indeed odd that you did not return immediately to the monastery if you truly were looking to help him. Please, could you tell me some details so that I might help you?"

"How did one know for sure I had been with the elder?" Father Victor inquired.

Patriarch Ivan picked up from behind his desk a burlap sack, which had been carelessly left behind at Elder Stamos' hut. Father Victor lowered his head, ashamed for doubting the patriarch's knowledge.

"There are no further details to speak of," Father Victor replied, finally answering the question. "I wandered off after seeing that the elder had passed. I lost my way back to the monastery. Even still, there was surely no more help to give him and even if I had made it back sooner, the monastery had several severe injuries to deal with. I was simply looking for spiritual guidance from Elder Stamos, just as anyone else who visited him would seek. That is all."

"This certainly is an embarrassment for us here, and it does not strengthen our ties at all with the Ecumenical Patriarchate of Constantinople. However, I do not see that you should be removed from the priesthood as has been suggested. I have a much different idea. The Orthodox Church in America is looking for priests to expand their dioceses. We would ask that you go there. It is our only choice if you are to remain a priest. Your bishop has been notified of this." Patriarch Ivan stated this sternly, although his eyes proved teary.

"Wait, if I may speak more to this, Your Holiness. I was also scraped up during the earthquake. I did not leave unscathed as I tried to help him under a table with me for protection. Let me show you a few scrapes and bruises. One is particularly deep."

Father Victor stood up and lifted the left sleeve of his outer cassock up over his forearm.

"See here this one is… wait a moment; where did it go? I had several…"

Shocked, Father Victor let his sleeve back down. He took his seat again, and looked down at the ground.

Chapter 8

Mumbling to himself, he made an effort to understand how he had healed so quickly.

"Dear Father Victor, the scrapes are inconsequential to all of this and won't offset what you have been accused of. I am glad they have healed up nicely, but I am sorry. I have made my decision. And what is yours?"

Everything seemed troubling as of late to Father Victor. It made no sense to him how his years of servitude to the Orthodox Church of Russia could have resulted with an ultimatum. All of this seemed to come about over a matter that was purely revolved around hearsay. It was not his fault the earthquake had occurred, and he had in fact made an effort to help Elder Stamos. Additionally, a man who he once thought to be honest and forthcoming had destroyed his position as a priest in Russia. He now only had God by his side and could only wait for the next sign from above. Surely this was part of a greater plan. These details were made very clear to Timothy and Eryana, who through the Blessed Waters had received great insight into Father Victor's thoughts.

"I will take your offer and go to the Orthodox Church in America," Father Victor decided at last, standing up from his chair.

"Very well then, our secretary shall give you the details of your assignment. Stop by early next week for further instruction," the patriarch explained.

The cauldron then contained darkness within the water, as a new scene now showed for Eryana and Timothy to view. Timothy was now extremely curious as to the manner in which his grandfather had come to America; as far as he knew, it had been through his own accord.

The next image to brighten the waters was again that of his grandfather.

"My dear council, through the Grace of God I have now become your metropolitan. What a blessing it truly is and only possible due to the loss of my wife. I prayed she would recover from her stroke, and instead I now sit here before you in a new capacity. One question now lies before us: how can we be directed toward greatness in Christ, beyond that which we have ever known to be possible?"

Metropolitan Victor continued to speak before his council of bishops. Two of the bishops sitting before him were Bishops Nikolai and Peter, of New York and Chicago respectively.

"I have much to say, and I strongly believe that we are being guided by the Holy Spirit's will. Let me start with this: long ago, I was visited by an Angel of God. And it instructed me to work toward two goals. The first was to begin bringing the churches of the world together. Perhaps it was only right that I left Russia and ended up in a country that is so very secular, where there may be an opportunity in disguise. You see, culture itself may not promote the work that needs to be done, but that might be just what we need: little outside influence or pressure from a government that is not bias toward one religion or another. Here in America they seem to dislike all church organizations equally! All is certainly beginning to make sense, as it would seem that the time could very well be near when we will have no other choice. Therefore we need to start by beginning discussions with other church leaders, and upon our success of showing them the Orthodox Way, compromising where possible, we can in turn propose to the various patriarchates to follow suit. Yes, I know that we are at this moment statistically insignificant in the eyes of the Orthodox World, and all this might seem quite impossible. But they will have no other choice as their numbers are sharply declining and world disasters are striking the earth at unimaginable rates. This will only become worse for them. Through the Lord and prayer anything is possible and as such we in America will have an increase in numbers and the subsequent power of prayer will lead to fewer disasters striking us locally. This, my brethren, has to be true if at all the visit from an angel was indeed authentic.

"Secondly, I have a very special relic that I was led to. I have been instructed to pass this down to the generations beneath me. I was at first convinced that I was to be the sole guardian of this holy relic however a second visit from the same angel has guided me to pass it down as soon as possible. And so I no longer possess it, but my dear grandson Timothy now wears it. It offers protection from evil, increases one's ability to preach and proselytize and finally it has the power to heal. The healing power I know from personal experience. Likewise, it would seem that my own protection is now fading.

"It has been nearly eight years since I began talking of the churches coming together. Many found me a bit unconventional with these talks, but yet I still became Metropolitan of All America and Canada. Now two years as Metropolitan, well..." Metropolitan Victor paused and then resumed talking. "What say you all?"

"Your Beatitude, what is this talk?" Bishop Nikolai said, immediately rising up from his seat. "Of a cross? An object? A relic such as you claim should not be on a boy, let alone a boy in grade school! Let us bring it back to Greece."

"Bishop Peter," Metropolitan Victor responded, "how did you know of its origin?"

"What Bishop Nikolai means," Bishop Peter interjected, "is that we are sure this relic is special. We heard that it had been worn by a hermit in Greece. Patriarch

Tikhon II already has spoken of this legend. Let's bring it back to where it belongs if this is so!"

"I have not heard of this, Bishop Peter. Why don't we take a vote here at this council on how to proceed? All who agree with following the instructions of an angel to work at bringing the churches together through revealing the dire times of the world, and to preserve this relic accordingly, say yea or nay."

Ten of the twelve bishops gave a vote of yea to which Bishop Nikolai stood up and stormed out. Hesitating at first, Bishop Peter followed suit.

The pool then revealed a new scene. It was now a few weeks later and Bishops Peter and Nikolai had traveled to Russia to meet with Patriarch Tikon II, who, once becoming a patriarch, had changed his name from Tikhon to Tikhon II, as Tikhon was a previous patriarch in the history of the Orthodox Church of Russia.

"Your Holiness Tikhon II," Bishop Nikolai spoke, "we bring word to you that the relic has been given to a boy named Timothy Petrov who is Metropolitan Victor's grandson. We believe through this he is well protected by the Guardian angels; Metropolitan Victor spoke of this protection the cross gives. We were wrong to think Metropolitan Victor could have been the twelfth elder to be taken to Eden by an angel. It may very well be the boy!"

"Additionally," Bishop Peter added, "Metropolitan Victor plans to have discussions with the other Orthodox Sees. We fear he may tell of the history he knows of you and the ambitions to serve the will of Satan, if he has since made that conclusion. The power this relic has been given through the Grace of God may very well allow for his success, as small a footprint as they may have in America!"

Patriarch Tikhon II looked rather irate with himself,

as if he had completely overlooked this possibility. Yet again, he would have to explain to the dark cloaked creature the unwelcome news.

"I must have further discussions on the next steps to take. Stand by; do not return yet to the United States."

Two days had passed and Patriarch Tikhon II met with the creature once again. Timothy and Eryana saw yet another vision in the Blessed Waters.

"Judas, I have news. The cross has been transferred to a boy who is well protected. Metropolitan Victor may be ready to begin the other final step toward the reunification of the Ancient Church: one that could lead to an Eighth Ecumenical Council. It must be prevented at all costs!"

"I see, I see. This is most troubling. The other lieutenants and captains of Beelzebub were not able to see what was transpiring, and that also deeply concerns me. I am happy to have you on my side. We must immediately threaten to remove the Orthodox Church of Russia's recognition of America having an autocephalous Orthodox Church. That will provide for damage to Metropolitan Victor's authenticity, exposing him to be nothing more than a conspirator. No church will want to have discussions with him at that point! I will take care of the rest as now that we know his protection wanes, he will be sent back to his maker! As far as the other ten bishops, they will be tricked into retiring from their office."

"You are most wise, Master Judas. There is one more detail to not forget. Metropolitan Victor's son, Father John: we must not overlook him in this. The three remaining male Petrov's must be eliminated; who knows what either could do with the relic."

A final image appeared in the cauldron. Metropolitan Victor had become ill with disease, and no diagnosis or cure could be made. Having been in a coma for days, he was lying on a bed with his son Father John by his side. He suddenly woke up, and began to whisper.

"I have failed and have been sent back here to repose, my dear son," he told Father John.

Metropolitan Victor then passed on to the heavens, in wait until the Last Judgment of Christ.

"My dear father, I will be sure to continue with what you believed was right to do. May I avoid this curse that you seem to have succumbed to," Father John cried, bowing his head to the ground.

Eryana waved her hand over the pool and the water now only showed their reflection. Eryana looked at Timothy, and he returned her glance. It was evident that he now had a much deeper understanding of the situation.

"What of my father? He is in danger, isn't he? I am the one to continue with my grandfather's work; it is all connected with those I love, and I must be successful."

"There is much to ponder over, as I too have questions after seeing those visions. But the choice you now have lies before you. You are to be the last elder of twelve. It is up to you now to complete the necessary work in unifying men under God. For if success is to be had then there is no room for error before times prove it to be too late. You are in fact known well now to the enemy. But you were not supposed to enter into Eden with me so young, Timothy, but the Devil's trickery of men has extended into the high ranks of the Orthodox Church and it forced us to make haste in bringing you here. Ultimately, you do not have the power or skill to act in the capacity that is required of you at this time. If you had been brought here at a later point in your life, it would have been different. Therefore, you must pass three trialing events in order to grow in virtue. They will be painful, and they will test you to the extreme. But the Church of Jesus and those you love depend on this. If you find success, you can continue with your grandfather's mission, and at the same time those you love most may find hope at last through Him. If you are to fail, the forces of evil may instead replace their hope on earth with despair. Thus the state of the Church will break apart and all prospects of reviving the Ancient Catholic Church will rapidly dwindle.

"Your mother is very ill at this time and your father is in danger. Satan is looking to test you so that his plan remains uninterrupted. He will offer for their protection in order to coerce you into resigning from the challenges. You must be strong and trust that God will provide for your mother and you to unite when the time is right. But for now, you must leave her completely in His hands.

"We have one last stop to make before you are to decide. Come follow me into the Residence of the Gracious. There we have someone for you to meet. You may not be able to see with your eyes, but use your senses. It will then be clear to you exactly who you are."

Timothy broke his complete stillness by nodding his head in an effort to remain strong. His eyes, red and teary, wandered over to the forest. Then, Eryana waving him forward, he entered into the Residence of the Gracious.

To Timothy this forest was clearly enchanted. Mystical powers seemed to fill up every object by which they passed. Two gravitational forces, one toward the ground and the other toward the skies then began tugging at him. Walking side by side with Eryana, he began to rise up while his feet remained on the ground. Timothy was stretched to seven feet tall and he awkwardly moved forward with his guide. Eryana kept a straight face as if she did not notice.

"What is happening?" Timothy questioned, stopping

abruptly.

"Well I guess you have no reason to be intimidated by my stature!" Eryana responded, with a smirk.

"Hey! How did you know I once was intimidated by... oh never you mind!" Timothy embarrassedly expressed.

"You are not prepared to handle the mysticism that Heaven has to offer. Part of you wants to be closer to God above, and the other is too afraid to let go of your grasp from the security the ground seems to offer. I have seen stranger things, though. One elder's body, along this path, ended up going in so many directions that he turned into a big bubble! Now that was odd, even judging by our standards. Let's continue; we are almost there."

They continued down the path through the woods, and as they went further in every object became more and more distorted to Timothy's eyes. The trees now appeared nearly positioned sideways. Additionally, the bottom of their trunks had a smaller circumference than their tops. Off balance, but finally readjusting to his normal size, Timothy and Eryana approached a clearing of twelve huts. Out from one appeared a strange being in the shape of a man, but half of him was transparent and his face could not be decrypted by Timothy.

"Who is that?" Timothy asked, as they moved toward the eleventh hut to the right.

"Oh, he is one of the Eleven Elders. You don't quite understand what you see; that is normal. But what you see will be better understood as you become acquainted with your environment."

"My environment? Actually, I am going to stay clear of questions. I feel weak without energy and I think my mind cannot interpret your words for now!"

Chapter 8

They approached the door of the eleventh hut.

"Hello? Hello! Eryana is here and I am with a special guest!"

A figure similar to the strange being he had just seen came out through the door, without it actually opening. They backed up a few steps as he hovered above the ground; his powers seemed similar to that of the angels.

"Well hello there! Long time, no see! Although you certainly saw us back in The Forest of the Wise when you came to our rescue," Eryana continued, cheerfully. "I am here with Timothy. Timothy, this is Elder Stamos, descendent of St. Bartholomew the Apostle."

Chapter 9

Father John woke up in a geriatric chair provided for him by the nursing staff. After a cross country flight and the emotional turns in the health of the two people dearest to him, he had asked to stay overnight in Timothy's room.

On the third floor of St. Catherine's Medical Center Timothy lay in an intensive care unit, not two days since the building at the fairgrounds had collapsed with him inside of it.

"He's lucky to be breathing, even with life support," a neurosurgeon told Father John when he had first arrived. "He will most likely sustain permanent brain damage even if he does survive this."

Dr. Morris was the lead surgeon for the two surgeries that Timothy had had. If it wasn't for Timothy being airlifted to the hospital in a short amount of time, Dr. Morris indicated that it would have been too late. It was now only a matter of time to see how he would respond to the surgeries, and it was anyone's guess as to when he would wake from the coma.

On the second floor rested Timothy's mother, Candice. Father John had left for New York thinking he would be returning home to her smiling presence, but instead she had suffered a devastating stroke and like her son had entered into a coma. It had baffled the entire interdisciplinary team providing for her care: she was only 42 years old, in great physical shape and had a life rich with happiness and blessings. As of late she had been feeling extremely tired with severe headaches and so she had been resting quietly in the guest room during the day. Her primary doctor had only surmised that, between her day job and being a good mother to Timothy, she had overworked herself. Nevertheless, all indications pointed toward at the least a partial recovery.

Standing up, Father John walked over to his son. He took hold of his hand and began to pray.

"Dear Lord, please keep watch over my son Timothy. If this misfortune is in any way connected to me or my own father's doing, please spare Timothy's life and instead take mine. He has barely lived, and has hardly had the chance to experience the mysteries that you have given for us. He has so much to one day see. Why are you taking my family from me?"

Father John stopped himself, as he began to cry and realized his emotions were taking over his understanding of faith. He bowed his head and the crying turned into bawling.

"Mr. Petrov? Mr. Petrov, I apologize for interrupting, but there are a few visitors here who would like to see you and Timothy," a nurse kindly stated. "If you would prefer them to wait, that is fine."

"No, no, let me get a hold of myself," Father John responded, wiping his tears with a tissue before standing up straight. "Have them come in."

"Very well, just a moment," Timothy's nurse delicately spoke.

Not a minute later two familiar faces entered the room.

"Paul, Jacob, it is so nice to see you both! Please, come in and have a seat."

Father John cleared his throat and slowly regained his composure. They entered the room, but remained standing.

"We are so sorry Father John, for all of this. I should

have never let the boys off by themselves; this all could have been avoided if only –"

Father John immediately interrupted Paul. "Nonsense, it is no one's fault. Please do not blame yourself for this. Tragedy has struck my family for sure, but we must have faith and confidence that our God will provide for all," he persuasively stated.

It was convincing to Paul, but for his own part Father John knew that it was not so simple. There was more to these events, and perhaps they were signs he was to refrain from continuing with his father's work. That is, if he was going to ever have his family by his side again.

"How is your wife doing? Andrea is visiting with her right now, holding her hand. I know she hasn't been responsive the past day, but I am sure she knows when there are loved ones nearby."

"Well… she is in a similar situation as Timothy, strangely enough. She is also in a coma and it is anyone's guess as to when she will come out of it. I am told the entire right side of her body is of no practical use, and I don't really know what to…" Father John began to cry again and Paul came closer to him, offering a hug.

"Hey, we are here for you. You aren't alone here. And Jacob has something to give you, don't you, Jacob?"

Jacob was inching toward the door, obviously uncomfortable with the situation. He felt guilty for letting his best friend out of his sight. He was also afraid to come closer to Timothy, unsure of what exactly was going on and how he should react to it.

"Come now Jacob, don't be afraid. We are like family here. Father John is happy we are here with him."

"It is quite alright, Paul. It must be so hard for him, also. I will meet him halfway."

Chapter 9

Father John went to the middle of the room and went down on one knee. Jacob held his shoulders back and head down, finding it difficult to face Timothy's father.

"Jacob, it's okay. You are a hero. I hear if it was not for you, he might not even be with us right now. Thank you for running after him and doing your best to keep him safe."

Father John looked into Jacob's eyes, with an authentic look on his face. Jacob nodded and then returned the glance.

"You're welcome, Father John," Jacob replied. "I have this for you; it's his backpack," Jacob spoke softly, after a brief pause. "He must have dropped it before he went into that building. It still has everything in it that he brought to the fair."

Jacob handed Father John the backpack, still halfway unzipped from when Timothy took the book out of it. As Father John started to take it from Jacob, it slipped from their hands and fell onto the floor. A few items fell out of the backpack.

"It's okay Jacob, I've got it," Father John insisted.

He picked up a few arcade coins and a map to the park. A third item caught his attention.

"What's this?" Father John curiously asked.

He picked up a thin piece of paper, about the thickness of a carbon copy.

"Oh, just some receipt," he continued.

He opened the folded receipt and read it out loud.

"'The Believer's Guide to the Celestial Realm,'" Father John read. "Interesting... where would he have bought this? I didn't remember him ever having this book."

"Oh, he did buy some book! I almost forgot. He was at a book kiosk while we were at a rest area, halfway to the fair. There was some strange, old woman talking to him and shaking him briefly; it was very odd. Then he mentioned a book that he wanted to purchase. That must have been it," Paul confirmed.

"That's interesting – I have never heard of that book before. Let's have a look."

Father John unzipped the backpack all the way, rummaging through a sweatshirt and a few other items stuffed inside.

"It's not in there. Perhaps he left it in your car?" Father John questioned Paul, casually.

"No, there's nothing left of his in the car. He had everything in his backpack," Paul replied.

"Hmm alright, well that is the least of our worries at this point I suppose. But that certainly is an interesting topic. Timothy loves to read challenging works…"

Father John stood up and smiled at Jacob. He put his hand on Jacob's cheek, as if to tell him that it would be alright. At that very moment a loud beeping alarm sounded off at Timothy's bed. Father John turned around and saw the monitors flashing and suddenly a team of nurses followed by a doctor rushed into the room.

"What's going on with my boy?" Father John yelled out to the medical team, as they were opening up drawers to a cart that they had brought in with them.

"Sir, we are going to have to ask you to stand back!" one nurse yelled out.

Another nurse, more tactful in her approach, came up to Father John and put her arm around his back.

"Everything will be under control. It is alright if you want to stay in here; we have a code situation underway and are making efforts to resuscitate Timothy. His heart has stopped and there could possibly be an excessive amount of pressure within his cranium. Your friends, if they could step out for a moment?"

Paul nodded and he walked Jacob out, who had wide eyes and appeared panicked. Father John watched them leave and then turned his head back to the scene.

"Do something!" he yelled back at the doctor.

"Put the head of his bed up; there is too much pressure in his head!" one nurse shouted.

"No," the doctor leading the team responded. "Continue CPR; we need to get the blood circulating! Call Dr. Morris. We might need to get some scans done and potentially bring him to the OR table!"

Frightened, Father John lost his footing and the nurse who was consoling him helped him down onto a cushioned bench. Overtaken with fear, he became pale and felt an unusual presence around him. He lay down as darkness consumed the room. Not a voice in the room was audible to him except one from beyond that seemed to invade his head.

"Prayer will be of no use. He is next, and so will be you! Steer away from the prophecy if you are wise indeed."

The voice then laughed horrifically and, like the flip of a light switch, the darkness went away and Father John sat up. He looked over to Timothy's bed and he was no longer there. Only the nurse who had helped him lay down was in the room.

"Mr. Petrov? Mr. Petrov? Are you alright?" the nurse repeated, holding the back of his head.

"I am sorry, I must have fainted. I am not sure… where is Timothy? My boy!" he shouted, jumping up.

The nurse helped him back to the bench. "They brought him to have a few tests done and they will have a closer look in the operating room. They got his heart beating again. I heard they might need to relieve some pressure building up in his skull, resulting from an accumulation of blood. Dr. Morris will speak with you once he knows more. Your company is still waiting outside… would you like me to give you some space?"

"What does that mean? Is he declining? I must know more!

"Mr. Petrov, he seems to have recovered from the emergency. We need to take a closer look at him and Dr. Morris will let you know first thing if his status has changed."

"Alright, I understand. I'm fine. I mean, I will be fine. Let me go out there and talk to my guests."

Father John walked out of the room and still standing outside were Paul and Jacob. Neither was speaking and both of them looked ahead toward the wall.

"Hey Paul, look, I guess he's going to the operating room so they can take a closer look. I am rather tired now and my mouth is dry. I am going to get a drink from the cafeteria and then go to see Candice. Being close to her will help to relieve my anxiety."

"It's fine. We more than understand! We overheard the nurses say they think it is going to be okay. That's a good sign, right? Give us a call if you need anything," Paul assured Father John. "Andrea called my cell and I told her to go get the car started. We will talk to you later."

"Thank you. And thank you too, Jacob. Yes, I will talk to you both later."

Paul nodded and began walking down the hall with Jacob. Father John went back into the room and took his cell phone out of his jacket. Leaving everything else, he walked out of the room and headed for the elevator.

"I'll be back soon," Father John told the nurses at the unit station. "I am going to see my wife. I have my cell phone. Could you please call me when Timothy is through with his testing?"

A man lowered a phone receiver from his ear, nodded and then returned to his conversation.

Father John pressed a button to summon the elevator. He stepped back and held himself up against the wall while he waited, looking up at the ceiling. The elevator was still at the basement level and the illuminated numbers above the door did not immediately indicate that it was moving up. His gaze turned downward as he began to think about how Father Andrei had told him at St. Peter's Monastery more details about Timothy's dreams.

"He has very interesting dreams indeed, set aside from any meaning they may have to a religious effect," Father Andrei's voice stated in Father John's head. "He was able to comprehend a descent down one hundred levels of that building. He clearly described the lights behind the floor numbers and how he was so convinced that his mother was using the elevator to look for him. He then explained how he ran up the stairs to the next floor only to just miss her, and then finally she wasn't in the elevator at all. It was as if his conscience was telling him that not every path upward is what it seems or has within it an expectable result."

The elevator door opened and there was no one inside. Father John stepped in and, pressing the general floor button, it began moving downward until it stopped after only one level. The door opened, but no one was there waiting to join him. When he realized that the door was not going to close, he pressed the button and it continued its descent. Then at the first floor the elevator stopped and opened its door yet again.

"Candice?" Father John stated, confused. "What are you doing here? I was going to see you… this is a bit odd…"

The woman walked in the elevator, not saying a word. Looking over, he realized it was not Candice. The woman gave him a sneer as if to tell him that he was creepy.

"I need some more sleep," he said under his breath.

The elevator finally made it to the main floor and as soon as the door opened, he stepped out. Looking to the sign on a wall to his right, it pointed ahead for the cafeteria and restrooms. Father John marched down the hallway and toward the cafeteria. He felt hungry and yet at the same time the thought of food gave him an inkling of a stomach ache. He decided to buy only a bottle of water so that he could head straight for Candice's room. Arriving at a cooler he opened its door, grabbed a bottle of water and brought it to the cashier.

About to reach for his wallet, his cell phone rang. Father John fumbled while taking it out of his pocket as he could not wait to hear how his son was doing. Stepping out of line for a moment, he finally gained control over his phone and answered it.

"Hi, this is Father John," he plainly stated.

"Hi Father John, this is Bishop David. Do you have a moment to talk?"

"Master, Bless!" Father John said, before answering his question.

"The Blessing of the Lord be with you," Father David quietly replied.

"Well, I am at the hospital right now about to visit my wife. How can I help you, Your Grace?" Father John asked.

"Thank you, it is most urgent. I have been thinking about what you said at the council meeting the other day and I do see where you are coming from. The other bishops seem to agree after some sincere thought; even Bishops Nikolai and Peter would like to keep an open mind about all of this. Would you be willing to meet with us at some point, perhaps in the near future?"

Father John remained silent, unsure of what to say. There were enough ups and downs going on with his son and wife to be able to stop and process what Bishop David was telling him.

"I am sorry, Father John. Forgive me," Bishop David continued. "I had not even asked about your son Timothy and your wife. How is Timothy? Is he recovering from the tragic accident? How is he at this very moment, if you could give any details?"

"Uh, he is, well, in the operating room again. I do not know exactly and I actually thought this was the surgeon calling me. My wife I am about to see. Thank you for asking."

"Of course," Bishop David replied, in a sensitive tone. "We are all praying for the speedy recovery of both your son and wife. Look, Bishop Peter returns this afternoon from Russia. And Bishop Nikolai is also available. We were going to take the next flight out to discuss this all with you, if you have some time? We have already talked to your own Bishop Andrew and you have his blessing."

"I see. It is short notice, but all of this is quite important. How about tomorrow morning, if everything goes well here at the hospital? Can you make it out to St. Catherine's or nearby in the city? I am staying here overnight."

"Of course; yes, of course. We will call this number when we arrive tomorrow morning. We look forward to talking more about the state of the Orthodox Church and its relationship with the current world events, just as you had said. Perhaps we can then work with the Orthodox Church of

Russia on this."

"That sounds great, thank you Your Grace Bishop David. Talk to you then."

Father John closed his cell phone and thought over the conversation he just had. Amazed, he smiled at the prospects of perhaps a concerted, collaborative effort by all of the bishops in the Orthodox Church of America.

"I wonder how Metropolitan Ezekiel is feeling about all of this," he stated out loud.

"Excuse me," a voice from behind said, as a woman brushed by him.

Father John realized he had wandered to the middle of the walkway in the cafeteria and then apologized as he went back in line to pay for the water that he was still holding.

"That will be six dollars and fifty-nine cents," the cashier told him.

He shook his head, amazed at how much inflation had impacted something as simple as a bottle of water.

Leaving the cafeteria, Father John walked back to the elevator. About to press the button, he decided he would take the stairs instead, as his trip down to the main floor was so unusual. He assumed that it was just as well that he could use some exercise after lounging around at the hospital for hours on end.

At the second floor was the cardiovascular and stroke step-down unit, where victims of myocardial infarctions and cerebrovascular accidents would present once they were stabilized. He went to the unit's station to check in.

"Hi, this is Mr. Petrov here to see my wife, Candice Petrov."

"Oh, hi Mr. Petrov. Yes, you may go in to see her

now. The team was just making rounds and discussing her status a few minutes ago. I will let Dr. Morgan know you are here as she is eager to speak with you."

"Okay, thanks," Father John said with a tired face.

He turned down the hallway and entered her room, number ninety-nine.

"That's odd," Father John stated, reading the room number out loud. "Timothy's room number is also room number ninety-nine. Oh wait, no he is in ninety-seven. Why does that number sound so familiar otherwise?"

Father John blew off the feeling of déjà-vu and walked in. His wife was still resting as he had last seen her: wrapped up comfortably with blankets, up to her mid-section. A pillow was under her right arm, propping it up for support. He pulled up a chair and began holding her other hand. Bowing his head, he started to mumble a few prayers. He tried to open up his whole heart in an attempt to offer just the right words on his wife's behalf.

"Mr. Petrov hello, I am Dr. Morgan. We met briefly the other day when you arrived from your long trip."

"Oh hi," Father John replied, being quick to cease prayer and stand up. "The secretary was just mentioning that you were in this room with a few other members of her medical team?"

Dr. Morgan was very tall, with dark hair and dark blue eyes. She appeared extremely confident, as if she was truly a warden of his wife's dire situation. Her eyes offered not a hint of concern or worry.

"You know, Candice is a very confident woman," Father John added, opening up with personal conversation to Dr. Morgan. "She was very successful in her studies at medical school. It was during that time that I decided to go to seminary and we had Timothy, and so she gave it up.

Well, you standing there just reminded me of that. I could picture her so successful, caring for others. Other people are all she ever had concern for. Now it is her turn to receive care."

"It must be very hard these days to be a priest and have a family while living in the secular world. You are a good man and your family is very fortunate to have you to pray for them and be strong in faith."

Father John stood there, speechless. Usually religion was the last topic to be discussed in any setting outside of a church. Additionally, he was a little curious how the conversation had changed from his thoughts about Candice to the doctor's insight on his virtuous dealings.

"Thank you. That is kind of you. So, what is the prognosis?"

"Here, let's sit down. Shall we?"

"Of course, that's a good idea," Father John confirmed, sitting down in a chair next to Dr. Morgan.

"I would say there is a small chance that she will ever recover; I have to be blunt with you. Our original thinking suggested otherwise, but unfortunately we determined that she had lost too much oxygen to her brain, you see, and when that happens the cells cannot survive. It really depends on what we objectively see from her when she wakes up. Let's be hopeful that that is the case. Time will therefore tell. But to be honest with you, I feel it is as if she is holding on for something. We were baffled that it happened to someone of her health, but what is even more astounding is that she has made it this far. There must be something she is waiting for. I don't usually speak in terms other than medical science and what research shows us, but I can't help but give you that insight."

Father John looked down at the ground, not exactly

sure what to make of the new insight she had provided for him.

"Look, how about this. Timothy's room is well equipped to handle a patient like your wife. What if I arrange for both of them to be together in the same room? That would make it easier for you to visit both of them."

"I am still waiting to find out more about Timothy. He went in for some testing earlier and I haven't heard anything yet regarding how he is doing. What if he doesn't make it back to his room?" Father John cried out.

"Hey, Mr. Petrov, it's okay," Dr. Morgan consoled him.

"You can call me Father John, that's fine."

"Alright, Father John, and you can call me Catherine."

"Thanks," Father John said, revealing a small grin.

"Let me make a phone call for you. I'll be right back; maybe I can find out some helpful information regarding Timothy."

"That would be wonderful. Thank you, Catherine."

Dr. Morgan walked out of the room and conveniently across the hall was a phone hanging on the wall. She dialed a four number extension and asked for the status of Timothy Petrov's surgery. Father John could vaguely hear her from across the room.

"Yes, that's right. Timothy Petrov. A patient of Dr. Morris I believe. Yes, room ninety-seven. Floor three. Just came off the elevator? Alright, thank you."

Father John looked up earnestly awaiting Dr. Morgan's return. She was unmistakably smiling.

"Well, how is he?"

"He is fine. They have fully stabilized him, and the tests reveal that no further damage was incurred! He just was brought back to his room. For some reason he turned around and came right out of it. Don't mistake me: he is still in a coma. He will do just fine, though, with the life support that he has been on. Why don't you go back up to him? Dr. Morris is there waiting for you. I will arrange for Candice to be brought there by this evening."

"Thank you, Candice! I mean, Catherine! What am I saying?" John stood up and reached out to hug Dr. Morgan.

She nodded and graciously returned the hug. Father John then walked up to his wife and kissed her on the forehead. After that he left the room, heading for the third floor of the hospital.

Catherine watched as Father John walked off. She looked upward as the room filled with light. An angel lifted her spirit and she found herself in the presence of Corinth, at the Offices of the High Dominion.

"St. Catherine, thank you dearly for your work. It was just in time for certain."

"This was my pleasure, Corinth. I have it arranged for both of them to be in the same room, in preparation for Timothy's final decision. This should also ease the process for Father John and his coping."

"Well, the hospital was in fact named after you; I would be surprised if you did not have the required clout to provide accommodations as you see fit!"

St. Catherine smiled and then continued reporting to Corinth. "That was close with Timothy, I can say for certain. The dark powers are nearly overwhelming now and it is anyone's guess how long the Guardian angels can protect the room of Timothy and Candice – all while keeping Father John within the realm of safety. Perhaps this is a matter for a Principality to oversee?"

"Yes, indeed. I have spoken with Michael. He also

agrees. It seems as if Father John is attracting the attention of the top officers of Satan. Michael will personally oversee the meeting between him and the bishops. However, we must be careful to allow for the natural ebb of faith from earth without providing too much intercession; we cannot completely guide the events there."

"And of the Principalities, which do you see fitting?" St. Catherine asked.

"I will have Agread and one Power meet with Jeneral, Principality of the Americas. I have a feeling that there is going to be significant disaster there if we do not act soon. Jeneral is already very busy with the anti-Christian governments coming to power and having to fend off the impending disaster to hit southern California. But perhaps indeed he will have to also become involved in this new development. Thank you again, St. Catherine. I will let you return to prayer at the Vestibule of Faith."

"It was meet and right to do so. Farewell, Corinth."

St. Catherine left his office and exited through the Room of Transcription. Canter opened the doors and waved goodbye, and just outside of the castle was a winged steed, waiting to bring her back to the Northern Lands.

———

Night had passed by the Pacific Time Zone and Father John woke once again, this time to both his son and wife lying in twin beds next to one another. How blessed he felt to now sit with both of them, simultaneously. Conversely, he was still feeling anxious with the idea of leaving them to meet with the bishops, as a feeling of despair was present no matter how wonderful it sounded that there may now be some consensus on the dire times of the world.

In his small suitcase were a prayer book and rope. With these he recited passages for healing as he stood over each of their beds, first Timothy and then Candice. This was truly the best weapon he had against the spiritual warfare that he was beginning to sense. The worst that could happen, in his mind, was that his immediate family could perish from the earth and he would one day join them in heaven. As he was often recognized for doing, he remained calm by knowing this to be that of God's will; this particular time of despair was to be no exception.

Following the passages, he began to recite a prayer that he had once introduced to Timothy: a prayer of strength, known as the Jesus Prayer. It was surely the ultimate weapon against any and all evil.

"Lord, Jesus Christ, Son of God, have mercy on me, a sinner," Father John repeated.

Before initiating his morning prayers he jumped out of his seat. His cell phone was ringing and his heart began to beat rapidly.

"Hello?" Father John rhetorically asked, remembering who was going to call.

"Hi Father John, this is Bishop David – again. I am driving Bishops Peter and Nikolai and we are near the city. Would you like us to pick you up at the medical center?"

"I think I could manage driving myself, Your Grace, but thank you just the same. Where will we be meeting?"

"There is an Orthodox Church a few miles down the road from you – St. Michael's. I have permission from your Bishop Andrew of course, for us to meet there. The parish rector ensures that we can be alone. They have Vespers at five in the evening, so it is best we meet sooner than later."

"Of course; give me a moment to freshen up. I can be there in an hour."

Chapter 9

"Why don't we make it nine o'clock? That should give you plenty of time."

"Thank you, Your Grace. I will speak with you then."

Father John hung up the phone and proceeded to a washroom that the staff had made available for him to use during his stay. He dressed in his inner cassock and, wearing his regular fall coat on top of that, left the unit in a rush without telling any of the staff. His car was on the fourth level of the parking garage and so it took him ten minutes just to walk there.

He exited into the outdoor parking garage. It was unusually dark outside, as rainclouds were approaching from the west. The temperature was still predominantly mild for early November days, but the wind regardless brought an occasional chill to the air.

At first he struggled to find his car, as nearly every parking space was taken; not another person was to be found as he was searching.

"I know that I parked on this level; what section did I park in?" he asked himself. After a few minutes of walking about and thinking in regards to where his car possibly could be, he finally crossed its path.

"Ah, on the corner here, that's it," he reminded himself.

Approaching his vehicle, he heard something behind him. It sounded like the pitter-patter of feet. It was very quick to travel, and by the time he turned around there was nothing to see but a row of cars on the side opposite of his. The wind suddenly picked and, feeling somewhat cautious, he did not hesitate to take out his keys and open the car door; his car key battery was dead and the door had not automatically unlocked for him.

Father John was about to start the engine, but he started to feel quite unusual. It was as if he was not alone, even though the majority of his senses told him that he was. Then, a rustling sound in the back seat briefly sounded off. Father John turned around, but the rear seat was empty.

"What do you want with me?" Father John spoke out loud, halfway serious about feeling that there was someone following him.

He started the engine, backed the car out of the parking spot and drove out of the garage, eventually merging onto the highway. Father John then synced his cell phone to his car with the touch of an onscreen button. It was old technology, where most vehicles now had a separate built in portal that could be linked to any personal cell phone number, without having to actually have your cell phone nearby. He felt it was better to be modest and drive an older car; being humble was an important teaching within the Orthodox Church.

"I better call Dr. Morgan and thank her for what she did for me yesterday; I can't remember if I did or not," Father John thought to himself.

"St. Catherine's Medical Center," he spoke to the car phone.

"St. Catherine's Medical Center will be on in three, two and one," the digital voice replied.

"You have reached St. Catherine's. This is the operator; how may I direct your call?"

"I am looking for Dr. Morgan please," Father John instructed.

"Which department are you looking for, sir? There are two Dr. Morgan's here.

"The stroke center, um, Catherine Morgan. Dr. Catherine Morgan."

Chapter 9

"I am sorry sir there is not a Catherine Morgan here. We have a Gertrude Morgan in Geriatrics and a Jeff Morgan in Internal Medicine. Would you like me to direct you to one of them?"

Father John did not respond.

"Hello, sir? Hello? Can I please direct your call?"

Confused, Father John terminated the phone connection.

"What is going on around here?" he whispered.

He continued driving down the highway, reaching the exit for the Orthodox Church. He had been there once before, as it was not uncommon for priests to visit other Orthodox Churches; there were also few churches remaining in his diocese.

Driving up to St. Michael's Church, he parked his car on the street and hastily walked up to the front entrance. The left side of the double doors was already opened, although only a crack. He made his way through the narthex and into the nave. It appeared at first glance that he was alone until he heard footsteps slowly making their way downstairs. Before he could exit into the rear part of the church, where there was a common area for gatherings, a man dressed all in black came around the corner.

"Father John!" Bishop David called out. "Thank you again for making it here to visit us. Bishops Peter and Nikolai are upstairs waiting. Would the office there work? There is a comfortable chair waiting for you."

"Oh, thank you kindly," Father John replied, taking off his coat. "Your Grace, may I have your blessing?"

"The blessing of the Lord be with you," Bishop David replied, without hesitation.

"Is there a place for my jacket?" Father John continued. "It has been some time since I have been here."

"Certainly, up the stairs and on the right there is a coat rack," Bishop David explained as he led Father John upstairs.

Inside the office were Bishop Peter, who was sitting behind the office desk, and Bishop Nikolai who was sitting to Bishop Peter's right. There was an empty chair to Bishop Peter's left. Bishop David put his hand out toward a chair in front of the desk, signaling for John to sit there and Bishop David then took his seat next to Bishop Peter. Father John immediately noticed long faces on all but Bishop David and it did not surprise him at all.

"So, I am grateful we could all meet here today," Bishop David started off, "especially during difficult times in your personal life for which we all here have been praying for speedy recoveries, of course. Let's start off with the facts, shall we?"

Bishop David's eyes grew large and Father John was immediately uncomfortable. Also, Father John noticed a large gash on his forehead that seemed to suddenly become slightly swollen and red. Overall, there was something unnatural about the way he looked, as if he had become suddenly rigid like his colleagues sitting next to him. Just as soon as Father John noticed this, the bishop's eyes returned to their normal size and a smile returned to his face. The gash, however, remained obvious.

"Ah, I see you are noticing my forehead," Bishop David called out, appearing comfortable with his deformity. "Yes, I was injured during the earthquake to hit Greece in 1999. It seems of late to be acting up. Perhaps some scar tissue has been irritated and inflamed, hmm?"

About to smile, Father John lifted up one side of his lips, but it turned into nothing more than an uncomfortable acknowledgement of Bishop David's response.

Chapter 9

"So," Bishop David continued, "Bishop Peter just returned from Russia and had serious conversations with His Holiness Tikhon II. It seems that there surely is a defining moment that we have come upon. Russia, like America, is also struggling to keep its Orthodox parishes afloat: numbers are decreasing while the secular population is increasing, and the government is once again meddling in their affairs. And the persecution of parishioners, let alone the clergy, is becoming out of control. Prayer is not allowed in schools and neither is any type of symbol such as the cross tolerable. You must know this to be true here in America. And, along with all of the aforementioned, natural disaster is becoming more frequent, especially near regions that are heavily Christian. All-in-all, it would seem that the Eastern Orthodox Church is being forced into seclusion."

"Yes, Your Grace, and perhaps this is a sign that it is time to come together and look at our ancient roots: where we came from, what we have in common and prepare for this spiritual battle that has strengthened upon us," Father John concluded.

He looked over at Bishops Peter and Nikolai, and their faces had not changed from their original expressions.

"That is true. But, I think we should look at it another way," Bishop Peter added. "Bishop David did mention that we were open to talks about some of the ideas you have, which your father had taught you when you were young. But we had another conversation on our way across the country. And I think Bishop David now sees things differently, as will you."

"Excuse me, Your Grace?" Father John said, confused.

"You see," Bishop Nikolai began, as if they were taking coordinated turns, "the world is changing and we

199

must do what we can do to survive. Our own Orthodox Church, that is. I am afraid it is apparent throughout the Orthodox community that America's Orthodox Church is now weak, having ideas that will only lead to unnecessary change and ultimately destruction. Some slack was given after your father's mismanagement, but now their patience has run out. We are going to proceed with joining Patriarch Tikhon II and make the Orthodox Church here in America merely an extension of the Orthodox Church of Russia, under his control. You must understand, the differences between us and the Roman Catholics, let alone Protestants, are too great to ever come to resolution. Join us, if you also wish for a speedy recovery of your family. You will need the prayer of the Church; our path is the only capable of saving them. Look at it this way: ever since you have begun putting your nose into the revival of Metropolitan Victor's ideas, your family has greatly suffered. Is that not a sign?"

"I am sorry, it is just… I am a bit uncomfortable at this moment. Perhaps we should be having this conversation with additional spiritual guidance. Maybe we should talk with all of the bishops; Metropolitan Ezekiel included? I do not know even how they feel about this."

"That is enough!" Bishop Peter insisted, becoming quite agitated. "Metropolitan Ezekiel will come to see things our way. The other bishops already have. They have agreed that they have not done their part in helping Patriarch Tikhon II, and therefore they will step down from their positions if they can't accept following us. They see that it is God's will and that they are only in the way of our plans. You can join us now, and we will have a place for you and your family to reside at St. Peter's Monastery in New York. That will be our new base, you see. Away from the secular world where we can be in hiding, we can allow the rest of the world to take its natural course. And we can ensure that Timothy will return to full health once you agree to this. Our prayers we will lift up as long as you promise to relinquish the relic he possesses. If you do not voluntarily agree you might find your mind to not be as clear as it once was."

"I must be going, brethren. Thank you just the same," Father John sternly replied.

He stood up and started for the door, but it slammed shut as soon as he approached it.

"Sometimes," said Bishop Nikolai, "you have to lead a horse to water. And if you want it to help you on your path, you have to force it to drink," he continued, beginning to laugh.

Still facing the door, Father John hesitated as a strange feeling came over him, as if his mind suddenly became foggy. He felt compelled to turn around and face them, but instead he pretended to not have heard Bishop Nikolai's comment and moved closer to the door to reopen it. Then the same odd feeling came over him, but this time more intensely: he felt under control by a being that was seemingly inside of his body and mind. Attempting to fight it he started to reach for the door handle, but then immediately turned around and returned to his seat.

"Perhaps we should have more discussion," Father John conceded.

"That's it, very good," Bishop Peter happily said. "So as I stated, we feel that it is necessary to consolidate the Orthodox Church; we have that in common. However, it is most unwise to bring about conversations nearly fifteen hundred years old to resolve differences that do not matter. I will be the new Metropolitan of the Russian Orthodox Greek Catholic Church of America, signaling a return to the Church's name prior to the 1970's. Therefore, I will be working directly under Patriarch Tikhon II's watch. We will build a community on the grounds of St. Peter's Monastery, and isolate ourselves from the rest of the country so we can focus on our objectives. Religious freedom to a small degree still exists here in America, but of course we will have to look carefully at the next presidential election. Nevertheless, we are on the road we need to be. Additionally, we are confident that all disasters will spare us if we remain at that location; perhaps that is the only logic your father used that I agree with! The disasters to hit the populations that do not agree with us, on the other hand, will drive them to join us. The right way will finally be understood by the majority; we alone can lead them toward happiness. I just ask of you one thing only: please give us the cross that your boy possesses."

Father John, about to respond in agreement, heard again the pitter-patter of feet from behind. He turned his head, but saw or heard nothing more.

"I see where you are coming from. Perhaps Timothy won't miss it and it is the right thing to do," Father John replied.

"Very well, that is good!" Bishop David interjected.

Suddenly, Father John developed a warm sensation in his chest. He began to feel the Grace of God and all of the hope that the Holy Spirit had to offer him. To this he sat up straight.

"On second thought, I do not feel that this is appropriate. I will not agree to anything without a formal council meeting with all of the bishops, including Metropolitan Ezekiel," Father John firmly stated, contradicting his previous statement.

Perturbed, Bishop Nikolai and Peter's faces became reddened. Bishop David, on the other hand, stood up with his own change of heart. Father John saw as his face became more peaceful and the scar on his forehead less obvious.

"Perhaps Father John is right: are we to make such rash decisions?" Bishop David said with a calm voice. "The power of God is strong and our faith should permit for complete trust and submission to His true will. I think we should talk about this more. The path we are taking is not of the true Light, but rather it is of trickery, which leads into darkness."

Bishop David stepped back and had a seat, appearing once again angry. A very peculiar happening then took place: the half of the room that Father John was on became brighter, and as if a line was drawn before him the other side was taken over by darkness. To Father John's left and Bishop Nikolai's right was a light and dark angel, each respective to the contrast taking place. It was none other than the Archangel Michael, who had followed Father John to the church, engaged in spiritual warfare with a captain of Satan's army. To the human eye only material oddities could be sensed; neither angel could be discerned for what they truly were. Time then slowed, nearing a pause.

"I bid you leave at once, Archangel Michael, for you are outnumbered. I have three dozen of my finest angels arriving here at once. Release the hold of the gift of His grace from this corrupted man at once!"

"I beg to differ, dark one. For The Prophecy of the Sacred Cross shall prevail! You may have stopped Metropolitan Victor, but Timothy shall prevail and Father John will in fact be set free today with a sane mind, bereft of the hold in which the Devil has polluted the minds of several Orthodox bishops!"

Michael pointed his glorious spear out at the demon. The smell of fragrance filled the room and the glimmering of light sprinkled the air; each was discernible to the human senses, as they were revealed to Father John and the bishops as protruding from a large icon of Saint Michael the Archangel on the wall: from it sweet smelling tears trickled down to the floor. The dark captain then immediately cowered down on the ground, but then in the blink of a human eye he stood back up to spread darkness toward Archangel Michael. To the captain's dismay, lifting a shield Michael held the darkness at bay, and to only a celestial being such as the two battling could the awesomely phenomenal vision of light clashing with darkness be seen.

Father John then stood up as time resumed at a normal pace. He was now invigorated with courage.

"How could men of God, like all of you, not see the evil works that are threatening our survival as Orthodox Christians? Any other time but now it would seem absurd: it is as if there is a secret preparation for the Antichrist himself to come upon us, and when he does, the weak will be convinced to follow him."

The three bishops stood up as their eyes filled with arcane energy. The darkness in the room slowly crept beyond the invisible line between them and Father John stepped backward with a sudden sense of doubt and fear. Thoughts of his son and wife flowed through his mind, about how a simple task such as returning a cross and stepping down from the priesthood could solve all of the issues now facing him. He pondered over how easy it would be to not struggle any longer.

"You shall see our way, just as your stupid colleagues gave in," Bishop Peter said, now towering over Father John.

Time again neared a suspension. Behind the captain then appeared three dozen fallen angels, just as Michael had been warned. They filed in rank, paying no attention to material boundaries, and stood as a group through the wall and out into the air three stories high.

"It appears your position is quite lonely, Michael; you alone can surely not defeat our collective power!"

"Alone I would appear at first, but now you are outnumbered in spirit!"

With that statement the entire room brightened, so much that Father John and the bishops squinted. Protecting their faces and looking around at the illumination, they each stepped backward, unsure of the mystery they were now witnessing. Appearing between Archangel Michael and the group of demons, a great angel in both size and skill lifted its massive wings upward, as the very top feathers pushed through the ceiling with ease like they were sifting through water, until they met one another. With a swift movement the angel placed his right palm facing toward the evil in his path; his extended arm was as solid as steel.

"May the appearance of the Principality of the West be a sign of strength from the Lord our God," Archangel Michael declared. "May the humble servant Father John be protected from all Satan has to offer, and may he be on guard against anything that comes from the world beneath the world."

The Principality looked at Michael and grinned. Then, turning his gaze back, he belted out a cry of joy that caused the demons to flee into the sky with their captain trailing behind. The two glorious angels flew off together upward to the heavens above, and the room then turned back to a normal state of existence.

The bishops were now deprived of any power over Father John. They each had a seat and felt the drain of energy. Invigorated, Father John stood up and for his part he felt the release of power over his body. He looked at the bishops and, finding they were not going to challenge him any further, walked out of the doors and went to his car. After climbing in, he sped off and commanded his car phone to dial Father Andrei's number.

Chapter 10

Timothy woke up to the sounds of chatter between Elder Stamos and Eryana. A long day had led to a restful sleep and he felt like it was morning, despite the confusing presence of darkness over the Northern Lands. While the Eastern Lands were always bright without a sun, the north was permanently dark without a moon, save millions of bright dots speckled across the sky. Nowhere in the Kindgom of Heavenly Creatures did it suffer change according to an orbital pattern; one static existence was observed as it always had and always would.

Sitting up on a long, narrow bed that was padded with fluffy feathers, Timothy stretched his arms out. He looked across the room and rubbed his eyes, thinking that Elder Stamos was simply out of focus: the elder seemed to be no longer half transparent but instead generally a blur. Looking at Eryana, he realized again that this was not an effect of his eyes, but rather the inability to understand something that lacked the material components, which justifies to a man or woman the existence of essence.

"I feel somewhat sore, I would have to admit," Timothy told his company. "I hope not ever to stretch that thin again!"

"Hopeful thinking for sure," Elder Stamos replied, delicately.

"Come over here and join us, Timothy," Eryana offered, standing next to Elder Stamos.

They were presenting themselves in front of an opening in the wall, which heat was radiating from. This was not a typical heating element, such as a fireplace or woodstove. Rather only bright waves of steam could be seen originating from that point into the room.

"I am sure I have stated I've felt strange before to you, but could we sit down? Standing is a little too much for casual conversation."

Timothy certainly was not shy as he was becoming trusting of Eryana and the beings she would subject him to. He assumed it would be better to bring his feelings out into the open, rather than to discover his thoughts had been already figured out, often resulting in embarrassment.

"We can accommodate that."

Eryana stepped back and there appeared a table and three chairs, morphing their shape out of thin air. Taking a second look, it seemed to Timothy as if they had always been there, like an elusive mind-twister that revealed an already existing image: depending on how one focused their perspective, he or she may or may not see it.

"Here, take a seat," Eryana continued to say.

Timothy sat down with both of the intelligent creatures and for a few moments they just looked at one another. Eryana was smiling as Elder Stamos kept a fairly straight face, although Timothy could not understand his exact expression. After a few more moments of still wordless exchanges, Eryana finally broke the silence.

"Timothy, you were awfully tired when we arrived here. We feel it is best to explain what it is that is going on. As you are aware, this is Elder Stamos, whom you saw with me through the pool of water. The ten abodes next to us are the living quarters of Elders One through Ten."

"And I am the Twelfth Elder, and the hut to the right of us where I shall live!" Timothy smartly jutted in.

"That is correct, Timothy. You are the Twelfth Elder

– that is to say, the Twelfth Elder to be. But you shall not yet live there, and perhaps the order of events will never call for it to be necessary. There is… something more to explain here. You must recall me mentioning that Elder Stamos is the descendent of St. Bartholomew the Apostle?"

"A Disciple of Christ, right? I don't quite recall hearing much of him – no offense to you, Elder Stamos. So, there are twelve Disciples of Christ and Twelve Elders. I think that is where you are leading to. But I assume if I tried listing them all I couldn't come close to twelve."

"Very good," Eryana replied, knowing that Timothy had not yet grasped what she was trying to tell him. "Elder Stamos is the descendant of St. Bartholomew the Apostle, and each of the Twelve Elders is the descendent of a Disciple of Christ…"

Timothy paused, yet again taking some time to process what he was being told. "You mean I am the direct line – of the same blood – of a Disciple of Christ?"

"Yes, that is what we are telling you," Elder Stamos confirmed.

Elder Stamos now began smiling. As Timothy looked over at him, he could now make out the shape of his face. He looked quite younger than the Elder Stamos he saw in the cauldron. In fact, his face seemed to contain youth, nearly equal to what Timothy now had. Perhaps, Timothy gathered, the age you appear in heaven is some sort of equation based on your earthly experience.

"Like dog years!" Timothy blurted out.

"I'm sorry, Timothy?" Eryana inquired, a little confused.

"Sorry, I am thinking out loud. My mind is processing all sorts of concepts at the moment and I suddenly feel smarter. That is strange, do you not think?"

"No, it is actually normal, Timothy. Things are starting to make a little more sense to you. These things are not easily grasped in a material existence, and for the first time you are here seeing them for what they truly are," Elder Stamos added. "I know exactly what you are going through."

"So," Timothy continued, "which Disciple of Christ am I linked to?"

Eryana looked at Elder Stamos, smirking. It seemed that Eryana often noticed Timothy's young age and found humor with his attempt to acclimate to the new environment through articulation.

"St. Peter," Elder Stamos indicated. "St. Peter was an apostle who went with St. Paul to Rome, where they were made bishops. The significance of that and how it relates to you will be revealed another time.

"The relic that you possess is also significant. As we speak, demons from Satan's army are desperately trying to get a hold of it. It simultaneously is existing both on your body back on earth and on you at this very moment. We are afraid that if Satan gains control of it, the reunification of the Ancient Catholic Church will be delayed yet again. They postponed it with defeating your grandfather, as you may have gathered. But they miscalculated. You were the stronger of the two and besides, Metropolitan Victor and I were too close in time for him to be reasonably assumed as the Twelfth Elder. The relic has been passed down through the ages secretly, you see, from one elder to the next with the guidance of our beloved Arch-guardian Eryana: she is who your grandfather found himself to be visited by. And it is certainly a precious relic. It is a shard of St. Paul's hand bone, with which he wrote in the Holy Scriptures to St. Timothy. The secret of this shard's existence must be kept and maintained by the Eldership only, as it will permit for balancing that which the Antichrist will try to disturb. With it you, being the last of the Twelve Elders, are charged with fulfilling the Prophecy.

"I know this all must seem overwhelming, but trust me you: in time the order of events will show you to be entirely capable; the pieces to the puzzle will fit soon enough. Therefore we must prepare you sooner rather than later so that you will be ready, through both your willingness and the Grace of God, to continue on your earthly journey: a journey in which you did not finish but instead ascended here with Eryana. During that journey to come there are three miracles that you must perform.

"But first you must be committed to become a true elder, before you are to fulfill what is necessary on earth. However, you are so young in years and in spirit, and so this is where it becomes tricky: the only way to resolve becoming an elder without the proper credentials is to be rigorously tested by the Holy Trinity. Through trials and tribulations we become stronger, and thus through the Holy Spirit you can find yourself closer to God. And, the closer you are to God, the further you are from evil and the more prepared you are to keep Him in your heart while living on earth where one constantly struggles between two opposing forces.

"Timothy, the other elders along with Eryana and I will be schooling you so that you may be prepared for the Trials of the Trinity. If you fail these three tests, whether by choice or by inability, you will return to earth as you were. But if you succeed you will also return to earth with an invigorated spirit, so that you can work to complete the last earthly events before Christ's return and thus fulfilling the prophecy. You must understand, the prophecy ends with you whether in triumph or in defeat. There are so many who depend on you, elder-to-be! You must not fail, and you must ignore all temptation until you make it through the Trials of the Trinity! Are you ready to learn?"

Timothy sat still, looking neither at Eryana or Elder Stamos. This was clearly the turning point in his journey within The Kingdom of Heavenly Creatures. His faith in God was not by itself in question, but rather the relationship of his faith to the imperfect nature that he knew was innately part of his being human. It allowed for temptation to affect choice, ultimately measuring the strength of faith; how potent the temptation would be was the unknown variable.

Timothy had suffered little loss in his life aside from his grandfather, and so the image he had been faced with in The Forest of the Wise was too hard for him to bear. If he had any weakness it would be the love for his mother, and so it was in and of itself a temptation to quit his journey. This love, which he had come to know for all people during the few years of his existence, was perhaps what qualified him to be in this position in the first place. Consequently, in his love for others he was accustomed to setting aside his own needs. Ironically enough, if he was to be successful in this instance he would have to not put others first – which for him would be a miracle in and of itself.

Regardless of the dilemmas Timothy had to sort out, to continue or not was the imminent choice he was now facing and perhaps it would be the one and only decision he would have the opportunity to make without the forces of evil directly upon his shoulders.

"I accept; let us begin," Timothy said firmly, as if assuming the role of a wise man. "May the Will of God be in the events before us; may the strength given by the Holy Spirit instill virtue into my heart; may I have the ability to come closer to Him according to His plan."

Chapter 10

"So be it!" Eryana concluded, jumping up out of her seat.

"Yes. There is no time on earth to waste!" Elder Stamos confirmed. "Let me call for the other elders as this is the moment we have been waiting for! Do we have some energy to spare for Timothy?"

"Energy?" Timothy asked.

"Yes, Timothy. Recall the town center that we visited in the Residence of Angels? You had too much drink; I think you should tolerate it with greater ease this time along. Unfortunately I am unprepared as I did not think we would progress to this point so soon. I must fly in haste back to the Eastern Lands while Elder Stamos gathers the other elders. I think I should also find Agread. Timothy is going to need to learn a lesson or two about spiritual warfare, both in defense and offense!" she concluded, turning to Elder Stamos.

Timothy raised an eyebrow to that comment, but brought it to rest immediately as he realized that he was surely in for many surprises beyond that of tactics. Elder Stamos then instructed Timothy to lie back down, as it would officially be his last physical rest.

"Bodily rest is a concept for you to understand in terms relative to time. In terms of absoluteness, let us instead reference your spirit, which may wear out at some point during the upcoming instruction," Elder Stamos clarified.

Elder Stamos watched Eryana travel off into the distance, as she began her voyage back to The Residence of Angels. He then exited his hut and stood on top of a platform made of heavenly wood, raising his arms into the air. Opening his mouth, words of joy flowed through the air to the ears of each elder.

"My good friends; my brothers in Christ: the time is

now here! Let us gather and pray for the successful addition to our ranks that will complete our force. Like the image of God, we shall have one body for the Twelve Elders: separate in identity but the same in ambition."

To that proclamation ten elders came out of their abodes, in chronological order to which they had ascended through the Lake of Entrance. It started with the first of the Twelve Elders, Elder Jonas, descendant of St. Andrew the Apostle. Then there was Elder David, descendant of St. James the Apostle and also Elder Justin, descendent of St. Philip the Apostle. Out of the fourth abode came Elder Nathan, descendant of Thomas the Apostle and after that Elder Martin, descendant of St. James the Apostle, the son of Alphaeus. Number six to show was Elder John, descendant of St. Simon the Apostle, also known as Zelotes. Seventh was Elder James, descendant of St. Judas the Apostle, not Iscariot but the brother of James. Number eight and nine came out at the same time: Elder Maximus, descendant of St. John the Apostle and Elder Ignatius, descendent of St. Matthew the Apostle. Finally number ten, who was Elder Joseph, descendant of St. Matthias the Apostle, who had been the replacement for Judas Iscariot. (St. Paul and St. Timothy the Apostles had their own parts to play in the mysteries, but had no descendants, and were not of the twelve Disciples of Christ). And Judas Iscariot had his own line of descendants, which to any of the Twelve Elders remained still to be known.

Elder Stamos, descendent of St. Bartholomew the Apostle, continued to speak.

"Here with us is Elder-in-training Timothy, descendent of St. Peter the Apostle, also known as Simon. A truly special honor this is, of course not to diminish the role we all have as elders; not that an explanation is needed!

Furthermore, we must do everything in our power to prepare Elder Timothy to fill his own shoes, if you will!"

And with mention of Elder Timothy, descendant of St. Peter the Apostle, the first bishop of Rome, the gap of over two-thousand Earth-years closed between the Twelve Disciples of Christ and the Twelfth Elder to attempt at fulfilling The Prophecy of the Sacred Cross.

Eleven bright lights shone from each elder up into the dark skies, and if there were any of mortal nature to see it they would have been glued in awe to the astounding vision there shining. Like beacons of hope they reached up toward an even greater heaven, as if the heaven in which they lived paled in comparison. Their light, coming from the Light of God, made them one with God and so it was that they exemplified a true unity where their heart only knew and acted on behalf of the Will of God.

———

Eryana was on her way to visit Agread on the edge of the Borderlands, just outside of The Forest of the Wise. She had decided to travel there before the Residence of Angels, as she did not want to delay in finding Agread. As she flew low to the ground, she made crossed over the grassy hills until ahead she saw him and his host of Powers. They had formed a solid line, guarding the potential entrance of evil from any point in the forest. In the lanes traveled by the Guardian angels traffic was reduced and, reminiscent of years past, a progressive sense of evil manifested beyond to the Lake of Entrance. To the north, thousands of intelligent creatures were en route to meet Agread and his multitude: low flying birds of various kinds were flying in the sky, scouting the path forward and below them were two of every species of animal, all with their heads raised high.

Eryana landed, walking the remainder of the distance that separated her from Agread. Getting closer, she noticed that he was in a deep discussion with two very powerful creatures. The Archangels Michael and Gabriel had returned from the depths of earth with news and so they were exchanging information with the Virtuous Stronghold of the Borderlands. As she approached, they glanced over at her before flying back into the skies to return to earth. Agread stood tall upon her joining him.

"Virtue Agread, may you accept my visit during this time," Eryana said, bowing as she spoke.

"Arch-guardian Eryana, I was expecting your return at some point. I take it that Timothy has discovered the truth of his coming here? And now he must be soon titled Twelfth Elder. What details can you provide me?"

"He is ready to undertake considerable training so that he may balance his youth with the great wisdom his position requires. We were hoping to provide for him some combat and defense training, in case a dire time would warrant its use. No fighter greater than you could we think to find, save your own teacher Michael the Archangel. Would you bless us with your presence at some point during Timothy's training?"

Agread turned his head back to the forest and did not immediately respond. The words he needed to put together required an extreme intellectual energy, so that with them would carry purpose.

"Michael returned here with the companionship of Gabriel; from earth they came to speak with me. An incident has occurred with Timothy's father, Father John, and a captain of Satan. The relic, it appears, is still on the body of Timothy in a hospital and with him here in the Kingdom."

Agread paused to stare into Eryana's eyes as she nodded in agreement.

"Father John," Agread continued, "nearly had given this up to the traitors. If that had happened, as a result millions of human souls would have been lost to the will of the serpent; the last hopes of reinstating the Ancient Catholic Church would have been forfeited. Principality Jeneral, therefore, left watch of the Americas to assist Michael, as Michael could not battle the demons without greater assistance. Michael is of course still strong alone, but keep in mind that as the Light of Christ nears His return to mankind, the power of darkness increases in response to maintain the balance known as earth.

"This assistance did not come without loss, for the four natural elements that God permits to exist on earth have been penetrated by Satan's equivalent to the highest ranks of the Second Hierarchy: Judas Iscariot. Judas has power now to influence great disaster to the San Andreas Fault. Nearly all of the Guardian angels in the Western Hemisphere remain on earth as they are on constant watch; I am sure you have noticed limited traffic in the skies above.

"I too have been put on guard and the intelligent creatures are marching to this point now in anticipation of a great battle of the cosmos: greater than the War of the Heavens from ages past it may be. I am not sure that I will be able to leave my place here to assist Timothy. Please send my regrets... Eryana, you are a very talented Guardian angel. An Arch-guardian at that! You would be the next to become a Principality if loss is to ever occur, and with that shows that between you and the power of the Spiritual Armor, Timothy should be made ready and will stay well protected."

"The Spiritual Armor of Saint Paul; I should have guessed!" Eryana exclaimed, not sure she quite believed what she was hearing.

"Yes, that is in fact correct. The relic Timothy holds of St. Paul the Apostle shall form a powerful link to the Spiritual Armor. It will allow for the most powerful connection possible: the art of ceaseless prayer in order to maintain constant integration between his heart and the Holy Spirit."

Agread turned and walked over to a golden chest that was guarded by nine angelic steeds and the Powers who rode them. It opened as he kneeled down, and he picked up out of it six unique items. Turning back to Eryana, he started again to speak, handing her one item at a time.

"Here we have the Belt of Truth, to allow for everlasting wisdom; the Breastplate of Righteousness, so that he may never be mistaken by any for evil; the Shoes of the Gospel of Peace, as his path to aid in the salvation of others must be clear, without question; the Shield of Faith, for as long as he believes he shall not perish but will have eternal life; the Helmet of Salvation, to allow for the integration of his mind with his heart at all times; finally, the Sword of the Spirit, for the Grace of God shall defeat any enemy – for nothing exists without the hand of God and nothing made from God and in God can overcome the Creator who permits for its existence. Again, the seventh item is the relic of St. Paul: a shard of his hand with which he wrote in the Scriptures about ceaseless prayer; ceaseless prayer is the link that Timothy must be mindful of. Make sure that he masters the understanding of these gifts before he embarks on his journey into the Grey Mountains."

Speechless, Eryana let tears fall from the corners of her eyes. She bowed her head and maintained a position on one knee until the tears no longer were flowing.

"Justice is not void when it comes to the one true

Master!" Eryana declared.

"Go now and empower our dear friend Timothy."

Eryana followed Agread's instruction. Holding the sacred armor with her bottom set of wings, she took off into the distance, back toward the outskirts of the Kingdom of Heavenly Creatures. For the first time the east had become brighter, as a source of light now appeared in the sky.

———

Nearing the Residence of Angels, Eryana slowed down her pace. She did not want to bring too much attention to herself, as the glorious pieces she carried with her would draw enough curiosity; certainly she did not need hasty movements to add suspicion. Intelligent creatures were, after all, very sensitive to anything that they were not accustomed to. As such, she carried the Spiritual Armor along the pathway to the town center and it was immediately evident how difficult it was going to be to stay on schedule: nearly every angel stopped what they were doing and watched her walk with the radiant materials in hand. In addition, they realized that Timothy was not with her. They began to whisper to one another.

Arriving at the Cook's Hall, she anticipated that Timothy would be without friendly angelic contact for some time, let alone that he would not be able to return to the Residence of Angels before the end of his journey. Since her hands were full, she was hoping to run into Justinian again as he perhaps could suit her with some sort of carrying sack; she could trust him to not ask too many questions.

"Greetings," she called out to the first Powers that she approached.

They were sullen, nearly bereft of the usual

confidence and joy that they so perfectly had once displayed.

"Is Justinian available?" she inquired.

"No," an angel replied, "additional forces have been enlisted to Agread's Army. Perhaps you know more about this? There are quite a few rumors amidst this Kingdom and if you cannot provide us with insight, then perhaps it is true that only the First Hierarchy are privy thereto."

"I am sorry; there is nothing that I have to offer for discussion. I am following my orders and for my own part there is much that I do not know."

"That surprises us," another replied. "It seems you are quite enlightened at the moment!"

"Whatever do you mean?" Eryana inquired.

"Are you of seriousness? Sarcasm is not an angel's typical attitude, so you must be. Why don't you look over here in this mirror?"

Eryana set down the armor on top of a counter and proceeded to a mirror that was conveniently hanging on the wall. She could not see her reflection because the brightness emanating from her being was too bright. She squinted and covered her face with a wing, similar to her reaction when approaching a Dominion.

"What is going on?" Eryana asked.

"That is what we are asking you!" the two angels said, concertedly.

"Look, I need Material Potion. I haven't much time."

Eryana did not ask for a sack to carry her belongings, as she did not want to admit to the journey she had to make back to the Northern Lands. Instead, she devised a plan to convince the Powers that she was on her way to the House of Elders. Her needing to return there would be of a technical truth, as Gammond would have something for her to carry all of her items and besides, she wanted to wish him well as she would be, like Timothy, absent from the kingdom for quite some time.

"I am going to see Gammond. Can I have a package of Material Pellets please?"

Gammond, being half angel and half human, needed both types of sustenance; Material Pellets were pellets filled with a capsule of potion.

The first angel that had spoken to her handed three vials of potion and a package of pellets. Eryana then nodded and tucked the sustenance under her wings. Picking up the armor, she traveled east to the very hill that was Timothy's first resting point. There she entered into the main hall, set the armor down and walked from room to room. There was, however, no sign of Gammond.

"Gammond? Hello, are you here?"

There was no response. It was completely quiet aside from the sound of her footsteps.

"Hmm, perhaps he is out gardening... I better check upstairs first," she said, talking to herself.

"Gammond, are you up here?"

Eryana arrived to the third floor. Gammond's room was down the hall and there she often caught him resting; there was still a part of him that required regeneration. She walked down the hall and knocked on the door. Pushing it open slowly, she peeked around the corner and saw Gammond lying in bed.

"Oh there you are! Gammond: we have a lot of unexpected business going on at this moment. I wanted to let you know we, meaning Timothy and me, won't be back for some time. Oh, and also I need some sort of sack. I have a long trip ahead of me and you will never guess what Agread gave me!"

Eryana often told Gammond more detail than he needed to know, as he was so very trustworthy. Sitting down beside him, looking away toward the wall, she continued the casual conversation.

"You know, Timothy really likes you. I could tell that you were one of the most fascinating parts of his journey. And that reminds me, we saw your cousin at the Vestibule of Faith! Still ringing the bells, continuously he was. You should see the size of his arms!"

Her exclamation turned into a sudden panic within the deepest portion of her chest, as it finally occurred to her that Gammond had not been responding. Turning her head slowly, she looked down and there he lay motionless. Pressing her hand on his forehead, she found him to be as cold as death; he was breathing no longer.

Chapter 11

The Residence of the Gracious turned into a familiar scene for Timothy: a large illuminated classroom had appeared around him. He sat alone, waiting intently for instruction.

The Eleven Elders were led by Elder Stamos himself as he was closest to Timothy, having lived in a similar time period on earth; it was thought that he could best relate and respond to him. Additionally, Timothy had a very special bond with the elder, as his grandfather had been the last to see him alive on earth. This bond proved itself to be especially true because Elder Stamos was the only elder thus far who Timothy could see with any clarity.

Conferencing beyond their simple abode, the elders finally approached Timothy.

"Time to start class!" Elder Stamos declared.

Timothy immediately sensed that Elder Stamos was not articulating with his usual formal approach, as any good teacher would do while instructing a new student; he perceived it to be a sign of difficult topics to come.

"I have always wanted to say that!" Elder Stamos chuckled, as did the other elders. "Alright, let's be a little more serious! We have a lot to cover. You will be embarking on a journey through the Grey Mountains. No creature has set foot there since the fall of Satan. It is where he resided, along with the other top Archangels in a magnificent castle. All of the evil he had introduced in the heavens has there been quarantined, and if you can survive its sinister activity then you surely will pass the Trials of the Trinity. The other

Elders and myself wrestled with demons during our past earthly life, but that will surely pale in comparison to what you will soon see! Are you ready to prove yourself to be the Elder of elders? The first among equals as St. Peter himself was considered to the Disciples of Christ?"

"I am," Timothy softly spoke.

"Your voice, we are going to have to work on that. A pronounced style of speech and a beautiful voice of song you are going to need. But that will come much later."

Elder Stamos turned around as a large wall appeared before him. The other Elders, still blobs of mass to Timothy, spread out away from Elder Stamos. A large map on top of a chalkboard then emerged.

"This should help you to become more comfortable – some familiar objects I mean to say, Timothy?"

Timothy smiled and nodded his head in agreement.

"First things first: here is a map of where it is you will be going. See here, there is a secret stairway just north of the entrance to the Kingdom of Heavenly Creatures. It reaches up to the clouds that make cover over the wall, which you will be able to walk on. This will be perhaps the only instance where you might feel like an angel!"

The elders started laughing again as Timothy squinted and pouted his lips, obviously not sensing the degree of humor that they did.

"They have too much time on their hands!" Timothy thought to himself.

"Okay, let's continue. You will walk across the clouds and eventually through a forest, until you find the Fields of Horror. This will be the first of the Trials of the Trinity, known as the Trial of the Father. There you must discover how the Father could create something that permits evil. If you find the answer, then you will make your way into a large chamber for the second trial, the Trial of the Son. This is where Satan and the other high Archangels met for important matters pertaining to the plans of God. You must there discover which seat was maintained by the Angel of Jehovah. That's right, later known as the Son of God; also known as the Angel of the Lord. Are you with me, Timothy?"

"Um, I think so… I am not really following how this pertains to anything in particular. Maybe I need to understand more of the semantics?"

"Nonsense!" Elder Stamos sharply replied. "This is probably the best you will ever understand it! It cannot make sense. It is what God has to offer to you; it is too abstract even for us. Just go along with it, now. Alright, and the third trial: The Trial of the Holy Spirit. This is in the room where Lucifer dwelled and the mirror in which he saw beauty that, in his mind, was greater than God's. You must look into it and figure out the greatest of God's commandments. If through it you are able to, then the Holy Spirit by that time would have surely worked in you, as through Him you must discover the answer. If you can do those three things, of which I mean passing the tests of the Father, the Son and the Holy Spirit," Elder Stamos said, then pausing and along with the other elders crossing himself, "then you will be well on your way to your next challenge: three miracles on earth. If you fail, of course things will become real interesting. Anyhow, your first lesson today will be on seeing with your heart."

"Seeing with my heart," Timothy repeated. "Is that some sort of analogy?"

"No, actually it is quite literal. Right now you see in your mind through your eyes. That is why you can barely make out what we look like, and so we need all of these materials for you to understand what it is that we are talking about. The goal is to be able to place your mind in your heart, through the Logos, so that you can see the truth."

Timothy still looked confused, and sighed in frustration.

"Let's see now, I've an idea. Elder Jonas, could you help? You lived closest in times to the initial teachings about the Logos. Timothy, Elder Jonas lived during the latter part of the second century."

Elder Jonas, now only a big ball of techno-like colors, moved up in front of the chalkboard and cleared his throat.

"So, it is like this: part of our imagination relates to the preconceived notions that the Holy Spirit penetrated our hearts through the Will of God. This is the Truth that we know exists. It is the Word of God. It is divine; it is the Logos."

A piece of paper and a pencil appeared in front of Timothy. Taking it as a hint, he began to take notes.

"Now, have you ever thought about how you can picture something in your mind? How you can see something, without actually seeing it, forming an image of whatever it is that is familiar to you?"

"You mean if I were to look in your direction, I could think of something else and see a different image in my head, even though my eyes are looking at you?" Timothy asked, unsure of how to say what it was that he wanted to.

"Exactly! Wow, this boy is smart. No doubt he is the Twelfth. Well, there you have it. We are now in the heavens, created by God, and we are part of His Truth. Using your mind you need to access the Truth that has been implanted into your heart. Then you can see the Truth and take it one step further: relay it before your eyes. It is a rather powerful technique. You should then be able to see us! Well, at least the most transparent of the group," Elder Jonas said, finishing his instruction.

About half of the elders who thought that Elder Jonas could be referring to them did not respond, and the other half began to laugh.

"I think I understand now, strangely enough!"

Timothy was excited at the prospects of learning something new, something so abstract that he could not possibly have discovered it solely through his material existence. It seemed to him that this experience was filling a void where knowledge once had seemed to be without substance. The concepts presented to him now were not just with depth, but also seemed intertwined with an essence that could not be sensed through any ordinary experience.

"Very well!" Elder Stamos declared, returning himself to the front and center of the outdoor classroom. "Let's try for something practical, shall we? A demonstration to see how well you understand what has been taught. Stand up now."

Timothy, following instructions very well, surely did not want to delay in attaining gifts that were only at a cost of agreement. He could not yet see any drawback to moving forward and, as well, he could not see any evident sacrifice along with it. He only had to choose to accept it. It seemed to be completely without burden.

"Great, what is next?" Timothy eagerly inquired.

"Alright, now close your eyes and give it a shot! Try to see me for who I am," Elder Stamos said, challenging Timothy.

"Okay, let's see now. Look into my heart with my mind… right. I sense it beating… alright, here we go. I feel the grace!"

With every heartbeat Timothy closed his eyes tighter, until a great smile curled upward on his face. He then opened his eyes wide with intent to focus on Elder Stamos.

"I can't see!" Timothy yelped. "I can't see anything! My eyes are burning! What is this?"

Elder Stamos looked over at the other elders and sighed. Then, taking pity on Timothy, he bowed down to recite a prayer. It was barely audible to Timothy, but seemed to be delivered with a great amount of passion. Timothy's vision subsequently returned, but only to find that he had not made any progress with the challenge. In fact, he had taken a few steps backward: Elder Stamos now looked as indescribable as the other elders were and, upon realizing this, Timothy shrugged his shoulders and let out a cry of discouragement.

"Where did I fail? I tried to do everything I thought was right," Timothy pleaded, as if he was not responsible for being unsuccessful. "I learned so much about the inner-self from the Orthodox Church and my father, and about the Jesus Prayer and focusing on your heart. Surely this is what you were referring to, in order to align yourself with your heart and using the intercession of the Holy Spirit?"

"Ah, but that is where inexperience and a lack of true understanding prevail! You trust too much in yourself, my dear boy! Do not be discouraged as that is why you are here to begin with, to gain the necessary insight. There is no measurable time frame that you need to complete this by, although you cannot begin if you do not learn the skill. Start by letting your earthly cares flow from you like a river of tears."

Timothy relaxed his muscles and kept his ears open to whatever Stamos was going to say next.

"Now, you see, we have more instruction to give

you. You were taught, quite often I would suspect, about being humble. Pride is one of the deadliest traps that exist and you will find yourself easily astray if you give in to that basic building block of evil! You felt entitled, did you not? That you were now above all else, and through your own will you would be successful? No, that is not the correct way. The Orthodox Way is quite different, don't you know? Christ's Church is the true path. Rely on your faith; in the fear of God draw near!"

With that, Elder Stamos closed his eyes. He bowed his head and lifted his arms, slightly bent at the elbow, into the air. Great forces of light beamed down from the skies as if the heavens had invaded every inch around them; it was as if everything had been filled with the Glory of God and nothing could survive without it. The classroom then seemed to lift into the air, spinning ever so slowly clockwise and then sharply counterclockwise. Suspended seven feet into the air, it was certainly the entire cosmos that was revealed to Timothy. Underneath him and to his sides, dark space was filled with bright stars; constellations filled with heavenly angels and intense rays of bright hope surrounded them. Only goodness could then be found and there was only one true way understood now by Timothy. Elder Stamos had aligned his heart with the Grace of God so perfectly that it could not have been any more accurate except through God Himself. And surely it could not have been any better understood, for the glimpse of Truth revealed everything for what it was. The great sight then at once dissipated and things returned to what they were.

"Now remove all pride from your mind and do not think of anything else! Let your heart be open to the Spirit and let your mind be open to the unexplainable connection it has to your soul. Then see in your mind that which God truly made and with it replace the sight that your material eyes blind you with."

With a very serious tone, Elder Stamos' rhetoric became formal once again; Timothy did not dare to delay. Timothy naturally fell to his knees, closed his eyes and bowed his head so that his chin touched near his sternum. He let all earthly cares escape from his mind and allowed the rich blessing that the Holy Spirit had instilled in his heart – the seed that was planted in him the moment he was created – to flow into his mind. Opening his eyes, Timothy looked forward at Elder Stamos and then attempted to envision the true being that he was. Trusting fully in God, Timothy then allowed it to come to fruition as what he was seeing with his eyes became relatively inconsequential. It was as if he could now see without his eyes, yet he still could hold an image held in his mind: Elder Stamos' true form blossomed and integrated itself with the land around them.

"You are truly beautiful, as one of God's creations!" Timothy professed. "I can see you now! A perfectly symmetrical being, in every way symbolizing the love God has for us. Every hue and shade delicately complements each other and yet, at the same time, appropriately provides for contrast! Oh, a glorious glow of delicate purity that is nothing other than the true Light of lights!"

Timothy then looked for the blobs of mass, but instead there stood ten other men, five on each side of Elder Stamos. Dressed in white robes with a knotted rope circling around their waists, they stood tall yet relaxed. The vision seemed to be an archetype, which God granted to be known, that rendered insight into the cohesion of the Lord with man. This cohesion, the great Hypostasis, then revealed itself before Timothy: he could begin to see in a vague way how Jesus was fully man and fully God, and then looking at the elders he could see how man was made in the image of God. These thoughts Timothy knew to be true as he saw with definitive clarity his brothers in Christ.

Thinking back to that day on earth when he had pondered various things in front of the soccer field, he recalled having searched in the woods with eyes of wonder. He remembered how he had come across the being that was trampling through the trees and the branches. It was a beautiful, intelligent creature. Not until he had trusted in God by following Eryana through the fairgrounds had her true being and essence revealed itself to him.

"How truly connected what happens on earth is with God's Truth in Heaven, although we possess not the ability to see it so easily," Timothy said aloud before the elders.

The Eleven Elders bowed their heads to him, and his ability to see the elders in their true form remained. At that very moment they turned their heads to find Eryana travelling up the path to their abode.

"Excuse me for one moment, Timothy, I need to speak to Eryana," Elder Stamos said, being quite perceptive of troubling news to come.

He met Eryana just outside of the open grounds, into the forest. Timothy saw that Eryana had a very serious face and Elder Stamos, for his part, held his chin in his hand. He was clearly analyzing disheartening events.

As their discussion continued, Timothy had a seat. Staring forward to the other elders, he was still quite amazed at what he was able to see. What a gift it was to have these great teachers help him become acquainted with this new world. The thought occurred to him, however, that privilege comes with responsibility; with responsibility comes burden. Perhaps, he concluded, the burden was about to be revealed.

"Timothy, we are ready for the next stage in your

lessons," Elder Stamos stated, having returned from his conversation with Eryana. "Eryana has come back with some gifts from Agread. Although he cannot personally show you the ways of spiritual battle, these tools are for you to use; they will certainly help guide you along your path."

Elder Stamos turned to Eryana, signaling that it was her turn to speak. Very sullen she seemed, as if some of the brightness Timothy had once noticed radiating from her had been stole away.

"Dear Timothy, I have returned. And I hear that you have learned your first instruction quite well! Congratulations – how nice is it that you should understand your surroundings to a greater degree than before!"

"Yes, it is quite nice I have to admit. You try staring at balls of bright fire and crazy colors, eleven of them at that!"

"Indeed!" Eryana smiled, then returning to a subdued expression. "I have for you some potion. I think you are going to need a substantial amount to help you though the next series of events. Three containers I have: two for the remainder of your training and then a third for your journey forward. We assume that you can build up a significant level in your system so that you will be able to ration the rest going forward. This is surely one of the few times that we can say that indulging is acceptable. Think of it like you are preparing for a fast: all of the meat and dairy products that you could want are available for consumption until it is time to wield a bit of self-control, in preparation for an important event! Does that seem to make sense?"

"It does, but..." Timothy decided not to finish his sentence, as if he was embarrassed with what he had to say.

"It is alright, Timothy. You are with those who you can trust and rely on," Eryana confirmed.

"Well, it is just that I am nervous they might find my drinking it humorous, the Eleven Elders I mean. But, okay. Will it cause me to pass out again?"

Elder Stamos presented a great smile, and he spoke for Eryana.

"Timothy! That very same thing happened to me," Elder Stamos admitted. "I took a big sip, was not prepared and lost my sense of gravity. Do not feel ashamed!"

"That is right Timothy," Eryana continued, "it happened to some degree with all the elders here in front of you. Just the first time, is all. And for you, I think you are well suited now to handle the energy that it will grant you. You are proving yourself ready with every moment that passes by. Here, some confidence for you; for our good friend Timothy!"

Eryana handed Timothy the Material Potion. Looking over at his desk, a medium sized tankard was sitting there just waiting to be utilized.

"How convenient!" Timothy exclaimed.

He poured some potion into the cup, watched the cool steam rise and cautiously took a sip. Realizing he was tolerating it without issue, he took a few more sips, now much larger.

"That is great! I feel great!" Timothy said, taking the second and third containers from Eryana and placing them on his desk with the first. "Now, what is it that you have for me? These gifts you speak of, what are they?"

Although already advanced, Timothy's style of speech was now becoming very similar to that of the intelligent heavenly creatures; it was as if there was a local accent that had officially imposed itself onto him.

"I have for you something that will complement the sacred cross that you wear. St. Paul's relic along with the

233

Spiritual Armor that he made strong reference to in the Holy Scripture: these all symbolize the power that you can now wield."

Eryana lifted up a sack containing the armor out of her lower wings, and presented it to Timothy. Speechless, he smiled as his eyes welled up with tears. One surprise following another was beginning to overwhelm him and the burden, which he knew was about to be revealed, finally overtook him.

"Why me?" Timothy questioned, remaining humble. "Why not St. Paul the Apostle? Why not my grandfather? What have I done that is so great?"

"Remember what the Lord tells us: that the least of you shall gain the Kingdom of Heaven. And so it is that your natural ability brings you to this point. Yes, it is true that you are a descendant of St. Peter, Disciple of Christ. But who else should it be? St. Paul has his place now at the Vestibule of Faith, praying for the world and besides he is not a descendant of Jesus' Disciples. And you have your place – as an elder. It is what is to come that is of most importance and only God can see what this shall be. But that is just it. It is His plan, and it is you who bears this affliction."

Eryana, if not anyone else, was consistently proving to be an uplifting friend to Timothy. All doubt had again been removed from his thoughts.

"Let us look through what you have here. It is what you will be wearing soon enough. Are you now ready?"

"I am ready, Eryana."

"We have six pieces for you. Are you familiar with them?"

"I remember my father reading to me something about them once. My grandfather had read Scripture to him about this as well."

"These six items have their own story, but their names may reveal much to you. Here I give to you the following:" she said, handing each to Timothy one by one as she listed them off, "the Belt of Truth, the Breastplate of Righteousness, the Shoes of the Gospel of Peace, the Shield of Faith, the Helmet of Salvation and last but certainly not least the Sword of the Spirit."

After removing the items from the sack and handing them to Timothy, a small package dropped from the armor and onto the ground. Looking down, he curiously stared at it.

"Oh, what is that? It wasn't mentioned with the six items?" Timothy inquired.

"It is not significant. Just Material Pellets is all…" Eryana replied, keeping her response short.

"I did not know you referred to them as Material Pellets?" Timothy inquired, recalling how Eryana had once consumed something similar. "I thought that the material was only for the humans? I know you had some sort of pellets that you stay strong with…"

Eryana looked over to Elder Stamos, unsure if she should go into any details. He looked back at her and confidently replied.

"I think that he is mature enough to handle the situation, Eryana. It is fitting if he understands all consequences associated with his upcoming choices."

Returning her gaze toward Timothy and taking a deep breath, Eryana responded with the truth.

"Timothy, why don't you set the armor down on your desk? We will get into their details soon enough. With what I have to tell you brings along further evidence that the phase to proceed is certainly near."

Setting the Spiritual Armor down, Timothy appeared ready to listen. He took a seat and folded his hands together.

Then, opening his eyes wide, he allowed his body to relax.

"The Material Pellets were for Gammond. Gammond was half human too, remember. He required half of what you do, and half of what we do."

"That makes sense," Timothy said, not sure what the issue was. "Of course he was human... wait, you are talking in the past tense. What do you mean by was half human?" Timothy brought his hand to his chest, enclosing the relic within his fist.

"Gammond's spirit has left his body, Timothy, although I do not know how – usually that is only possible when moving from earth to heaven, not the other way around. It is true, though, that he was taken to heaven with his soul intact.

"Nevertheless, what I can confirm is that it appears that his duties here have been completed. He was assigned to care for the elders and you required little care from him during your stay here; there is nothing left for him to function for. The sin he came from – more specifically, the manner in which he was conceived – has come to claim his existence. It seems that more is tied to your calling with the elders than we could ever have surmised."

"What? I don't understand; it isn't fair! He's a wonderful creature, with a great soul! How can this happen? Because of me is what you are concluding?" Timothy said, standing up in angst.

"I do not quite understand either, Timothy. Perhaps it was just part of the great plan. We cannot know. Do not blame yourself as this loss is not easy for me either. We must trust that there is a reason behind everything."

Timothy began to weep and sat back down. He then briefly put his face in his hands.

"How about the other Nephilim?"

Chapter 11

"I do not know," Eryana plainly stated. "Much may change in Eden, possibly within the Kingdom of Heavenly Creatures itself. But you must remember something very important, Timothy. The angels and all intelligent heavenly creatures were created for one purpose: to serve man whom God loves so much. As we are the purpose of creation, creation is also our purpose. The Church, Salvation and the Sacraments: those were instituted for mankind."

Timothy gained control of his emotions and stood by his seat. Picking up the armor and looking at it intently, he had a significant realization.

"'They were to be servants of angels, saints and elders until the time of judgment,' Gammond once told me," Timothy whispered.

"I am sorry, Timothy? I did not quite hear you," Eryana replied.

"It would seem that this burden of knowledge is causing me to be mixed in how I feel. With what is perfectly good comes revelation as to what is not good. Perhaps this is just what I need to understand. My father once told me how if you can keep your mind in the trenches of the earth, you can then only look upwards from there. I think I have just realized what the second lesson for today is, as with the disheartening news regarding Gammond there is a sign of hope to come."

"Wonderful, Timothy!" Elder Stamos indicated, as if he had expected the events to turn out as they had. "Controlling your emotions and concentrating all of your energy to what is above is not an easy undertaking. But once you are able to see with your heart what is true, the next step is to find out how to contort what you now know. Congratulations, you are now ready to be instructed on the challenges that you may face during the Trials of the

Trinity!"

Eryana and Timothy looked at one another, baffled at how insightful Elder Stamos was. It made even Eryana curious as to how he would have had any sense to know ahead of time the fate of Gammond; Elder Stamos had indeed intricately integrated what would seem to have been outside of his knowing with his lesson plan for Timothy.

"The elders certainly are more than what meets the eyes, even if those eyes are looking through their hearts," Eryana concluded. "This is what you have to look forward to, Timothy!"

Timothy smiled and again took his seat. The lessons continued as Eryana explained more to him about the armor that Agread had given her. Elder Stamos then gave further training on prayer and using it to deal with temptation; he suspected that Timothy would need to have a deep understanding of the complexities surrounding it. Feeling all the wiser, Timothy did his part by remaining a good listener, making sure to not interrupt.

Although Timothy had mastered much, there was still a burning question that remained unanswered to even the elders: how would his ability to control his emotions, combined with prayer and resisting temptation, stand to the dark powers of Satan? Yes, he was now well equipped to deal with his future on earth, but he still had to make it through three difficult challenges. Fortunately, Timothy better understood the relationship between his existence in the heavens and on earth. That, along with the instruction he was to receive from the Eleven Elders, was perhaps as significant as the journey to come.

Chapter 12

Father John arrived at St. Paul's Center for Spiritual Counseling. After talking to Father Andrei on the phone, he had discovered that Father Andrei had also been contacted by Bishop David, but was unable to join them at Saint Michael's Church. Eager to hear more about the events, and also having some news of his own to share, Father Andrei encouraged a meeting in person. Since Father Andrei had no means of transportation, Father John had immediately returned to the hospital to let the staff know that he would be gone for most of the day; there was a strange connection between his meeting with the bishops and his family, and so Father John thought it would be appropriate to temporarily leave their side.

"If there is any change in their conditions, please call my cell phone immediately! I will be no more than a few hours away," Father John had told the nursing staff before traveling to Laketown early the next morning.

The temperature outside was quite cool and the days had noticeably shortened. Although this was typical for the final months in the year, the excessive gloominess seemed to hasten the sunset. This added to the sense of urgency that troubled Father John, and it was apparent from their recent phone conversation that Father Andrei felt the same way.

Father John felt sentimental as he parked just before the courtyard. It was not long since he had walked there with Timothy to see Father Andrei. Despair pierced through his heart as he wondered where he had went wrong in protecting his son. He thought about how helpless Timothy must be in a coma, unable to make decisions for himself while unaware of the situation at hand.

"If only I could be in his mind to help him wake up. I had so much more to teach him about his faith and he had so much more to do in this world. He is so innocent; he knows nothing yet about it!" Father John continued, talking to himself.

He walked through the building and started up the staircase. It seemed to be narrower than he had recalled, and the lighting above was dim. Stepping nearer to the top, the air became increasingly stale and harder to breathe. It was as if the mystical and holy presence that the building once had had disappeared. But he hardly noticed, being so preoccupied with his thoughts and concerns, and he found himself suddenly standing in Father Andrei's waiting room. And it was like a vision of the past: Father Andrei came out of the middle of the three doors to greet Father John.

"Here we are again, Father John. I am so sorry that I was not able to visit you and see Timothy and Candice. Please, come into my office; let's talk in there."

Father Andrei walked Father John into his office and looked past the door as he closed it, as if mysterious ears had followed Father John.

"After you left the council meeting in New York," Father Andrei continued, "Bishops Nikolai and David began asking me questions about my parish and inquired if I would be willing to join them in New York instead. It appears they are opening a headquarters for their mission in restoring Orthodoxy. I do not trust that it is the same mission as yours."

"As ours, you mean? No – it is far from it. I have told you very little, but what happened was of a deep coercion... they wanted me to give them the relic that

Timothy wears. There is something dark happening that they seem to be part of. And I am beginning to put it all together. Somehow I don't think it was any accident that Timothy was hurt," Father John concluded, solemn with his mannerisms.

"What do you mean? Wasn't he hurt because of a storm? Do you think his friend or his friend's father had anything to do with it?"

"No, I am referring to something even less obvious. Haven't you noticed the darkening attitudes of the bishops? How run down Metropolitan Ezekiel has seemed as of late? Something very peculiar happened back there at St. Michael's. The three of them went on to infer that other bishops and

Metropolitan Ezekiel were stepping down from their office, and some others perhaps would join them whether voluntary or not. Whatever they were trying to get me to do must have been along the same lines! What if they are being controlled by Satan, used as pawns, for something greater in his evil plans? I think this situation could be more straightforward than we initially thought, Father Andrei. All along we have been trying to look into a maze of dogmatic intricacies, when it instead could be something the Church had confirmed little about."

Father Andrei sat silently and took a few sips of coffee. Not knowing immediately what to say, he looked out of his third floor window into the skies. The look he gave suggested that what Father John was telling him was certainly not farfetched, considering the dire times that they were witnessing.

"What if instead it is purely eschatological? That the end of the world is upon us? Perhaps Satan is revving up his engine of darkness at last and we have now little chance to work on my father's prophecy?" Father John continued, swallowing as if horrified.

"I don't believe that. God's plan surely looks to protect as many as possible from the reaches of the Devil. The order of events must be proceeding according to how they should be, which would be the only reason for Satan's desperate actions," Father Andrei said, closing his eyes tightly. "Just relax, as we have time."

"If there is no rush, then what would his point have been to concentrate a great deal of energy, in order to meddle with a single individual such as my father? Surely the Devil's work in that case was for a specific reason. And now Satan is putting his energy toward Timothy, which we can safely assume is true because of how similar his situation is to his grandfather's. That would lead me to ask, why would Satan waste his time with a boy if he was not getting something more immediate from it?

"Then there are all of these events that are happening, such as the world disasters that are becoming more prevalent, and the intolerance of religious activities that is rather suggestive of the brainwashing of men! Sure, there has been persecution throughout history, but never leading to so few Christians; it had more often than not led to a stronger showing of faith. Even the United States, founded on the principles of religious freedoms, is now profoundly anti-Christian; Timothy can't even reveal a cross or pray by himself in public or else it is considered to impose on the freedoms of others!"

"God does work in all of us," Father Andrei whispered.

"I'm sorry, what was that?"

"Ah, nothing. I can see where you are coming from. So if time is running out after all, then what is the point of this conversation? What can we do in the grand scheme of things?" Father Andrei asked, sounding suddenly unconfident as he had at the monastery.

"That's it!" Father John said, standing up with excitement.

"What's it, 'this conversation?'"

"No, what you said before that: 'God does work in all of us.' If Timothy does play a significant role in this, I don't see why we wouldn't either! God never made it evident, neither through Scripture nor the teachings of Christ that Satan would have any power as to stop the Second Coming of Christ. So what Satan does have the power to do is to tempt us and steer us away, so that perhaps the Ancient Church does not reunite – and as a result far fewer know Jesus when he returns. It is probably so that there are things we cannot change that are in motion, but at the same time there are things that we can prevent or assist with! That is how God works in us."

"You make it sound so simple," Father Andrei replied, without hesitation.

"It does sounds like simple philosophy – but were we not created to be simple creatures, following our shepherd through the pasture of life? That is how he works in you and me, my friend. I have a feeling that we need to find out the truth for ourselves, starting with the other bishops. By this I mean do we know with absolute certainty that they have willingly retired? It is quite possible that Bishops David, Nikolai and Peter gave me misinformation..."

"Bishop Andrew! How could we not have paid more close attention to our own Bishop? We need to find him immediately," Father Andrei pointed out, perking up in his chair. "I am sure that we could find out all we need to know from him. He is not as timid as he lets on; if there is anything amiss, he will surely tell us. Why don't we give him a call and see if we can meet with him?"

"That would be a good start indeed, but what is our plan if we find him of no help? Should we look into contacting Metropolitan Ezekiel?"

"Let's worry about that when we get to that point," Father Andrei replied, rushing the conversation along. "As you said, Father John, we must learn more. Perhaps he has some insight into Metropolitan Ezekiel or even Patriarch Tikhon II. I doubt he is at his office, though. Most likely he would be home – and that is south of St. Catherine's. Do you have time for more travel? We will actually be closer to the hospital than we are now."

"I will have to make time. I have been praying for guidance on this matter and I am not about to assume I can analyze His plan. It is written: 'Trust in the Lord with all your heart, and do not rely on your own insight. In all your ways acknowledge him, and he will make straight your paths.' Let's give Bishop Andrew a call!"

Father John stood up and stopped in front of a window. The skies had darkened even more since he had been outside to which he made the sign of the cross.

"Sure, let's call from my phone. I have free long distance," Father Andrei offered, after taking a minute to think.

He picked up his cell phone off of a nearby table, pressing only one key to dial Bishop Andrew's home phone.

"I will put it on speaker mode," Father Andrei explained.

The phone rang, but there was no answer. Father John looked at Father Andrei, as if he was worried. The answering machine they knew he had did not pick up.

"Maybe he is on the phone already," Father John

suggested.

"Let's try again," Father Andrei said, seeming rather persistent.

Father Andrei dialed the number once more. It rang again eight times without an answer. Discouraged, Father John sighed and turned back to the window. Father Andrei then stood up behind him, placing a hand on his shoulder.

"We will get a hold of him, Father John. Just give it some time; we have plenty of time. Let's just relax for a moment, shall we?"

"Maybe you are right. This is happening all so fast. I just want answers... I hope Bishop Andrew is okay," Father John said, turning back to Father Andrei, "as Bishop David and his cohorts had alluded to a change in the other bishops' behaviors. It would be nice to know for sure."

Father John then took his seat, folding his hands together. Then, Father Andrei began to fidget and pace as his demeanor altered once again.

The phone rang. Both priests looked at Father Andrei's phone, staring at it for a few rings until Father Andrei grabbed ahold of it.

"Hello?" Father Andrei asked.

Realizing that Father John could not hear who was on the other end, he searched for the speaker phone key.

"Hold on a moment," Father Andrei continued speaking. "Alright, go ahead. Who am I speaking with?"

"Hi, this is Andrew."

"Bishop Andrew?" Father John asked, rather excited.

"You do realize that I am no longer your bishop, do you not? I retired. Actually, call me by my birth name: Jack. That will be easier for all of us."

Fathers Andrei and John paused. It was quite

awkward, especially for Father John, who had feared most the corruption of the other bishops. Additionally, it was disturbing to call their beloved bishop by any other name.

"What has happened?" Father Andrei asked, not wasting any time. "What could have caused you to step down?"

"There is no other choice. It is what God wants. I was just in the way."

"Bishop Andrew... sorry, Jack... hi, this is Father John. Look, I was just meeting with Bishops David, Nikolai and Peter. I think something suspicious is happening. Please, can we talk with you in person? There is no need to retire; perhaps there is a way out of this?"

"There is no other way. There is only this. I am sorry."

"Jack, can we please meet with you? We can help you. And you can help us. Will you be there in a few hours?" Father John continued, trying to convince his former bishop.

"There is really nothing left to say. But if you wish, I will be here. Just be prepared."

Jack finished the sentence rapidly and slammed the phone down, terminating the call. Father John and Father Andrei stared at one another once again. Standing up, Father John walked back to the window. He began to doubt that there was any hope left, and that perhaps the situation seemed more and more dangerous with every moment that passed by.

"Timothy needs you; go back to him," said a voice in Father John's head. "Give them what they want."

Turning back to Father Andrei, he let out a big sigh.

"We better go see Bishop Andrew, and now. Let's wear our outer cassocks and our pectoral crosses. And let's have a prayer before we travel, too. We should be prepared to accept strength, so that we can accept whatever it is that God will guide us to."

Father John walked out of the office and went for the lobby exit. Realizing Father Andrei was not right behind him, he stopped.

"We really must do this Father Andrei; please, let's not delay."

"Yes, we must... we must. Alright, let me get ready. Let's go to your parish to pray. I need a change in environment."

"That's what I expected. I will meet you outside."

Father Andrei partially closed the door to his office and began to get dressed in the appropriate attire. Looking at his vestment cross, he took it off from around his neck. Then, looking up in the air for a moment, he opened a drawer and put it away. He locked his office and went outside to meet Father John.

It began to lightly rain as Father Andrei stepped out of the building. Father John was sitting under a gazebo in the courtyard, looking off at the lake as the peaceful water became interrupted by the raindrops. Increasing his pace, Father Andrei decided to walk to Father John instead of projecting his voice across the way. Only steps before reaching him, the ground began to lightly shake. Father Andrei stopped moving as Father John stood up, looking around. The shaking then came to a halt.

"Did you feel that?" Father John nervously questioned.

They both looked around the grounds and up at the sky, but found nothing unusual to explain the sudden shaking.

"Yes, I did. That was strange. Perhaps there is some construction nearby? I doubt it would have been anything natural; there hasn't been an earthquake here of any noticeable magnitude for about forty years or so."

"But Father Andrei that is what I have been saying about unusual events... oh, never mind about it. Let's get going shall we? It is a long enough drive after we finish prayer and it is nearly midmorning."

Father Andrei shrugged his shoulders and they walked to Father John's car. Father John called the hospital before they took off to make sure that there was no update regarding Timothy and Candice, and let the charge nurse know that he may not be back until tomorrow. "Urgent business has come for me to attend to," he said.

Father John began to drive, his lips silent as were Father Andrei's. Then, almost to his Parish, the quietness was broken.

"How familiar are you with St. Peter's Monastery?" Father John asked.

"Oh, not extremely familiar... other than it being our usual place for council meetings. I know that it is a very attractive place for a monastery, being so isolated from any town centers or any other civilization for that matter. Why do you ask?"

"Well, part of what the bishops told me yesterday was that they wanted me to join them at their new base in New York. I was just thinking of all of the monks there. How such a sacred place could be occupied by those so evil? I didn't know if you knew of anything particularly special about the monastery, such as why would they choose it?"

"That is an excellent question. Perhaps Jack will know more about it."

"Jack? From here on out I will refuse to refer to him as that, except to him directly as he requested. He is still our Bishop Andrew, in my mind anyway."

Chapter 12

Father John seemed rather upset; his tone seemed to indicate that he found Father Andrei to be insensitive.

"Jack is still a Christian name; is it not short for John? It wouldn't bring that much disrespect to him."

"I don't know. It could be Jakin. That is Scottish, which I believe he is. But that is beside the point! I am not comfortable referring to him as anything other than Bishop Andrew."

"I'm sorry, and you are right. There is so much going on that I can't keep track of. I think we will learn more when we talk to him; that is if he is willing," Father Andrei said, looking outside at the leafless trees. "What a world it is out there, Father John. If only it was so simple."

"You know, I was wondering, perhaps we should consider our own base of operations? Maybe there are others, whether Orthodox or from other church organizations, willing to join us in the great mission that we have committed ourselves to. What if – hear me out here – what if we had some sort of school, giving children a chance to have a life free to worship and at the same time giving them an education with spirituality? If we find we are not too late, that is! What a blessing that would be. It is enough that the secular world has now robbed the lives of those wanting to live as Christians in public. But now we have what might seem to be an assault within the Church. St. Peter's Monastery is such a beautiful site and would be perfect for that sort of environment. Who knows, perhaps Timothy could be in the first class! And he could invite his friend Jacob, of course. Oh, I don't know. These thoughts are rapidly running through my mind; I don't know what I am thinking anymore."

Father John realized what he was saying was probably at the most very hopeful. He thought about how he wanted to only be by Timothy's side right now: how awful it would be for Timothy to wake up with him not there. Even worse it might be, if Timothy passed on without him within an arm's reach.

"Well, if it is as you say," Father Andrei commented, "and the bishops have already converted the monastery in New York toward their own ambitions, how do you suggest we take it over? Asking them nicely? Diplomacy at its finest…"

Father John looked straight ahead and then sighed as if acknowledging that his own ideas were irrational. He then pulled into the driveway of his parish: The Holy Trinity Church. Walking to the parish doors, hundreds of birds flew over them in the skies, heading north and east and sounding off as if in distress. Fathers Andrei and John looked up and watched them pass by, before entering through the doors. They then immediately began prayer and once they finished, Father John drove them south across the border into northern California.

Time began to pass very rapidly as Father John was deep in thought, contemplating the recent happenings in every way that he could find. It was the same road that Paul had driven Timothy and his family along to the fairgrounds just days before. Father John wondered what Timothy was thinking and how troubled he must have been by his dreams during that trip. Timothy did love nature and being outdoors, and hopefully he had enjoyed a bit of it if at all.

The further south they drove, the murkier the skies became. To Father John, it symbolized the evil that was spreading its purpose throughout the world, during an increasingly profane time when religion was considered by most simply a way to be spiritual. To connect oneself with the world and the universe after a long week, on a Sunday morning: that was the general goal he knew many to now have. In that way, religion was merely a facet of one's life instead of one's life being that of God. The principle of salvation and being moralistic based on love for one another had diminished into a tale of the past. And, no longer was it that the human race widely considered that it was possible to not have all of the answers to the purpose for existence, as scientific study was now known to be the only path to human knowledge. Anything was possible, as long as it was a focus based on egocentric principles. Yes, good and evil existed to all. The battle between morality and immorality ensued and always would on earth. The substance of it, however, would and could not be taken any other way to most than in a vain manner; good could not prevail in the lives of those who did not recognize the purpose for which it existed. And those who did consider this were labeled out of touch and old fashioned. Progressive change needed a completely different environment to thrive in, which was the far opposite of asceticism. Evil had therefore prevailed and was affecting the lives of so many, in particular Father John and his family.

"Father Andrei, wake up. Listen to this!" Father John said, turning up the radio after hearing what sounded like an emergency broadcast message. "Father Andrei, wake up!"

Father Andrei, who had fallen asleep to the low pitched humming of the car along the interstate, rubbed his eyes and listened for the sound that Father John was referring to.

"...the disaster here is unthinkable; ever-so unimaginable. I am up here in a helicopter, looking down at the utter destruction... an entire city wiped out. This is unbelievable! Oh my god, what has happened! The day has come that many prophesized about: Los Angeles has been leveled and is largely under water. Sources tell me that it was over a 10.5 on the Richter scale; can you believe that? That would beat the one off of Australia and this one's epicenter was directly under human civilization. I tell you, looking down – it is like judgment day down there. As if everything was coming to an end. Some say the shock was felt all the way up into Oregon. What sort of war is being waged on mankind; oh, what sort of war. For KLAC, this is James C., reporting and signing off. When will we wake up from this nightmare?"

In his usual fashion when unable to listen any more, Father John pressed the off-button. He then looked at Father Andrei for a brief second, whose eyes were beginning to water. It was as if Father Andrei had finally realized the seriousness of the situation. Speechless, he moved his eyes toward his window, staring outside.

"Lower your expectations, my dear Brother in Christ John... as if anything changing at this point would be possible," Father Andrei whispered, this time so softly that Father John could not hear him.

———

Jeneral, Michael and Gabriel were in pursuit of the same group of demons that had attempted to manipulate Father John at St. Michael's. Three dozen of them, led by their captain, made for their escape back to the depths of the earth. The people and the land for which Jeneral was responsible to defend had been successfully assaulted. Through the destruction of a metropolis, the angelic forces could hear the traces of evil triumph: sneers, snickers and the hisses of evil. Below, Guardian angels sifted through wreckage, performing the miracles that were ordered down from the ranks of the Second Hierarchy, who in turn had received orders from the First. This day was known to come, however, as choice and free will had allowed for it to happen. And so those who could be saved were. The remainder, and majority, of men and women who could not be saved began their journey to the Southern Lands; they were taken one by one by their respective Guardian angels. Ghost-like human silhouettes, visible only to the invisible, were lifted up toward the skies and away from the evil wrought by sin.

"They are just ahead!" Jeneral insisted, increasing the speed of his envoy.

Wisps of transparent, dark masses could be seen weaving around crumbled remnants of what used to be tall structures in the skies. Maneuvering around fire and smoke, Jeneral pointed his sword forward as a beam of light shot ahead. It had an unmistakable origin of goodness, and lifting over the group of demons it managed to sever the group in half. The captain of Satan looked backward with a disgusted face as he charged forward with still eighteen of his soldiers, making their escape into a portal to hell, somewhere near the destruction they had caused. The other eighteen, captured by the light that paralyzed their movements, were sent by the three Angels of God – by force of hand – into the Dark Chamber of Holding.

Deep within a world of its own dimension, as far away as its exact opposite high in the sky, Captain Balagad and his henchmen traveled through the barren lands of hell. Thickets and lifeless nature symbolized a place that made earth seem to be the balance between two separate forces. Once a great angel, but yet not of the same likeness of his liege Lucifer, Balagad was the chief opponent to the good works on earth and he had led many efforts to destroy the validity of faith for those who had met misfortune. It was he who had helped lead a battle between the heavens and hell, in the midst of a world war between mankind on earth over one hundred years prior.

Balagad then recalled how at that time, one hundred years prior, the great Virtue Agread had been the fiercest opponent to his attempt to hold the Lord's Army at bay in The Forest of the Wise. If Balagad had succeeded, Satan would then have brought forward the Antichrist on earth. By Satan's calculations, that would have forced Christ's return to occur before the Hand of God completed the Eldership of the Twelve, and well before the revival of the Ancient Catholic Church. Time had been in that way, as it seemed, on the side of Lucifer and Balagad's, since God's plan for the Eldership was relevant to the choice of man. But fruitless their attempts had been to push the heavenly forces into the Borderlands. It was then that Satan had realized that the Second Coming would happen in its own time, and only during that period of time could the Antichrist be revealed. And so Satan had done the one thing he could do: he focused all of his energy on damaging the Eldership, so that when Christ did return there would be far more who would succumb to the ways of the material earth and as a result suffer for eternity. Knowing their inevitable path toward defeat, it was only out of pure spite and hatred that the evil enemies had continued to take with them as many souls as possible, conceivably causing for the flooding of the world, once again, with an ocean of Holy Tears.

Balagad and his gofers finally arrived at the abode of Satan's highest ranking officer. Covered by a dark cloak and merely seeming like a hunched over frail being to his partners in evil, General Judas Iscariot's white eyes could be seen in the midst of a mask of secrecy.

"It seems that you have succeeded, and now fear will ensue and mankind will ask themselves questions. These questions will leave them to be confused and vulnerable to the next stage of our efforts," Judas told Balagad, as his host of demons stayed back in a hallway, resting on the floor.

"We lost half of our host, but great achievements we still made, that is true," Balagad responded, bowing to the man whose soul was spared from the wait in the Southern Lands.

"The stage has been set," Judas declared. "The unification of the Ancient Church seems to have been thwarted, and we have identified the location of the relic. Before Lucifer can construct the life of the Antichrist, however, we must complete more work.

"You see, Timothy Petrov lies motionless in St. Catherine's Hospital and his father, Father John, is at the same time on his way to speak with a former Orthodox bishop. The good hold St. Catherine has on that hospital building, along with the direct intercession of the Holy Spirit on the behalf of Father John, will make our work difficult. But we must hold Father John off from bringing any more protection to his son. To capture if not kill Father John would be necessary and then we will stand a better chance of stealing the relic so that we may relinquish it to the Devil. This hope of mankind, being nothing more than a silly idea that the Ancient Catholic Church will once again be unified, will then fall like dominos carefully placed in front of one another. Greater strength will then be ours in the upcoming battles!"

"I will make sure that our presence is at the meeting with the fathers and their bishop. We will not fail this time," Balagad promised.

"No. This is something Satan would like to oversee personally. Too much is at risk. Muster your army of Lieutenants, and be prepared to act on St. Catherine's Hospital. We will send additional forces if it is required."

Balagad smiled at Judas, revealing sharp fangs. His eyes turned darker, his face paler. Invigorated and empowered with evil, he took twelve of his men with him outside of the fortress.

Judas also left his encampment. He voyaged to give report to the Prince of Darkness, Lucifer. Unlike the demons and angels, Judas was still bound to laws of nature. Like a saint in the heavens, he had to walk to wherever he needed to go. In order to leave the depths of hell or return back, he required the assistance of a demon. Trickery and treachery were the special gifts given to him and, as long as Satan held power over darkness, a demonic life after his earthly death was his to keep.

Traveling far through foggy marshes, there was no sign of life; there was no nature and there was no hope. Only the occasional lifeless soul wandering aimlessly about that land could sometimes be seen. Those lifeless souls were the only exception to all who remained in the Southern Lands. After their earthly deaths, they had been claimed by Satan, having made choices while on earth that lead to a willing demonic possession. Like Judas, they had been terrible instruments of horrific acts, some committing genocide, extermination and massacre. Many had been infamous figures throughout the history of the world. Of course the Lord forgives, but they had not repented when given the final chance to be released from the chains of blackness, and so they reposed with a demon in their hearts. Lucifer considered them to be his subjects and thus they were a reserve force to deploy with the Antichrist. Until such a time, they traveled about in a limited space and served as drones to be his eyes and ears within his domain.

Judas was very uneasy when he saw one of these spirits. Perhaps it was the thought that he could have been nothing more than a roving pawn. Or maybe he was, and he did not even know it. Committing a sin such as he had, he was certainly in no position to argue as he at least was not yet awaiting the pain of death, which he knew very well to be where one must remain eternally in the presence of God after blatantly rejecting Him during one's entire earthly life. That would be the true state of hell: to unceasingly experience the Truth, knowing that you will never have any part of it for an eternity to come.

Judas arrived before the lair of Satan. Walking up steep steps, ever closer to the morbid throne, he passed thousands of armored demons. They had been Powers, similar to the angels under Agread's command. Now they were elite forces within the army of Lucifer and they served to protect their prince from any harm. Taking a deep breath, Judas entered through the dark iron doors.

Chapter 13

Timothy returned to the classroom, fully clothed in the Spiritual Armor. Eryana had spent time with him in making sure that it was secure, but not too tight. It was so fitting that the sizes were just right, as if it was all along known that he would be its bearer. In fact it was known, and the prophecy was one step closer to being fulfilled. A true warrior of Christ he seemed to be and after his next final instruction, he was as ready as he was going to be to begin the Trials of the Trinity: a series of invisible riddles and mazes that he would have to navigate himself through in order to prove his readiness. All of this he would do in order to make good his claim to be the first among the Twelve Elders.

Taking a seat and waiting for the Eleven Elders to conclude their final lesson, Elder Stamos turned to Timothy and held his arms out in the air with his palms facing up.

"Rise, Timothy! This last part you will remain standing and you should not sit again until you have completed the missions. A true elder needs no respite until he has exhausted his heart completely, finding only the ability to focus on God."

Timothy stood up with Eryana at his side. His breastplate shone brightly and his helmet stood tall. Straight was his stature, bolstered up by shoes which eloquently supported his connection to the heavenly land. His belt carried his sword firmly and the impression of might it provided perfectly balanced with his shield, which in turn symbolized passive protection against all potential forces of evil.

"You now have what you need to support your decision making along the paths through the Grey Mountains. You have learned the power of prayer and gained the ability to ward off temptation. You can calm the rise of emotion and turn it into energy toward the Lord. And along with that, your heart gives you the clarity to discern what your human eyes process before you. Our last instruction will not be an experience like any of the others, but rather a pronouncement. A discussion, if you will, of the virtues. Pay attention carefully to the following; if only all had been given the opportunity to have gained knowledge of virtue, imparted through the wisdom acquired by others then perhaps there would be more like us. Wisdom, itself a virtue, being used to gain other equally important virtues is symbolic to say the least.

"Not to be confused with the angelic Virtues, we now refer to the virtues of which the Holy Spirit planted within your existential understanding. One of these virtues revolved around the greatest commandment of all and you will learn it by the time you are finished with your journey, whether or not you are successful. Two that we will focus on which apply to you now are patience and hope. Patience, because all good things come in time, and this is why there is no time in the presence of God since at that point all good things already exist. And then we have hope. Hope, because once you find yourself patient and having received the good things that you have waited upon, you trust that what you have been given will lead to a certainty of unifying with God's will. Do you understand these two very important virtues?"

"I do, Elder Stamos."

"Very well, then. May the relic on this sacred cross

act as a spiritual compass; in conjunction with your Spiritual Armor, may it allow for the guidance of the only real weapon that you should need: faith."

Timothy, having no words he felt could be worthy for reply, gave a most basic smile. He only hoped that the virtues and tools that he now understood would help him walk in Christ's footsteps.

Elder Jonas had also provided for some context regarding those tools, as he had earlier explained to Timothy details of the Grey Mountains. (Being the oldest elder and the first to scout the Grey Mountains after Eryana had escorted him to Eden it was also particularly fitting that he should be the one to explain. But that was a different story for a different time). For example, he had described to Timothy the steps that had been taken by the Angel of the Lord through the Grey Mountains and into the Chamber of Reason, where He along with the top angels of the First Hierarchy had had many conferences long before the fall of Lucifer. It had also been explained how those same footsteps the Lord Jesus Christ had taken on earth to show mankind the Way, as the Son was referred to as the Angel of the Lord in the Old Testament.

It would have been impossible to explain and have Timothy understand anything close to the Mystery of the Trinity itself. The Eleven Elders knew very little more than any other theologian on earth, aside from the complex parallels drawn to the Angel of the Lord and Christ, between the Old and New Testaments. But what Elder Jonas could tell Timothy with absolute certainty is that there was some connection between the footsteps taken by the Angel of Lord in the Grey Mountains and the footsteps taken by Christ on earth. And in order for Timothy to survive the Trial of the Father, he would have to stick to those footsteps if he had any chance of determining how God could permit evil to exist. Timothy had responded to that particular instruction with both curiosity and confusion.

"I wish you could make it simple for me to understand, because I so desperately want to know and learn," he had told Elder Jonas.

Elder Jonas had responded with only this: "The further anyone goes toward understanding any conclusion pertaining God, the denser and more confusing the material becomes. It is partly because God is unimaginable, and partly because Satan himself cannot afford for even the very first person to be unified with God in Heaven," Elder Jonas had continued to educate Timothy. "It was quite enough a blow for evil when Christ, fully God, became fully man."

Other details of which Elder Jonas had explained to Timothy were more material, as Timothy's brain still would rely on a degree of earthly references in order to navigate through the upcoming trials.

"It will often be confusing to you whether it is day or night. One moment it may seem light, and the next dark. Still, you must adhere to the correct path. Much of what you see will, in that same way, not be entirely obvious whether or not it is of good or of evil. That is what the virtues are for: to continue on with the upward ascent toward your destination. Perhaps we will delve into these at a later point; taking control of your faculties through them will be necessary and crucial for your decision making between each stage."

Timothy then had asked him to describe more of what he could expect it to look like and Elder Jonas had explained to him that to the naked eye it would look like any normal forest would, with a strange but ordinary path leading to a door, which would lead into a castle and then to a typical room with a standard table and chairs. And an everyday type of mirror would finally face him.

"But remember, Timothy, it is not the naked eye that you have to see this with. Just pretend you are again focusing on us. Use your heart in your mind to see and you will be golden; the objects at that point will not be so normal but will rather take on greater meaning and importance."

The instruction was now complete with Timothy's acceptance of Elder Stamos' words. He followed Eryana to the edge of the Residence of the Gracious, where they were to leave the elder's encampment alone; at that point the Eleven Elders had not revealed themselves to but only a few select intelligent heavenly creatures. They had done their part through Christ in delivering some of the greatest gifts that Timothy had so far received, aside from both the great gift of life given to him by God Himself and the ability to receive through the Logos in his heart. Thus it was Timothy who would represent them as the Twelfth Elder.

Eryana and Timothy made it to the edge of the Residence of the Gracious. Turning his head back, he saw out of the corners of his eyes the great elders bow their heads with bent necks. Taking Timothy's hand, she then made an effort to hurry him along; all of the saints and angels from the Vestibule of Faith, except for the Disciples of Christ and Ss. Paul and Timothy the Apostles, who were to continue their ceaseless worship and prayer, were waiting for them just outside of the gated entrance to the Kingdom of Heavenly Creatures. A warm assembly there would bid farewell to him and Eryana did not want to delay, as it was not clear to her exactly how the other recent happenings were intertwined with Timothy's mission. Understanding Eryana's subtle gestures, Timothy began to increase the speed in which he was walking. They were once again side by side as they traveled through the forest.

They were at first silent in their journey through the Northern Lands. Looking around from time to time, Timothy noticed that the trees were no longer bending sideways. In a strange sense, he could not determine exactly if it was that they were no longer bending or if it was just that he could now understand the abstract creations in the heavens. Nevertheless, there was nothing now unusual to him about the trees and additionally there was nothing creating a physical pull of his body in two separate directions. It seemed now only natural to be where he was.

There were many parallels that the landscapes in the heavens drew to ones that he knew on earth; it made perfect sense that something so beautiful would exist in both places. After all, each was God's creation and it was only a matter of discerning between good and evil for one to determine the beauty in every created thing. It was just one more way in which Timothy could use the technique to see through his heart.

A soft breeze through warm air swept along the path that they traveled along, and the rustling of ferns and leaves on tree branches dominated the senses. It was mystically magical in every way and it calmed every anxiety that Timothy could have carried with him. Looking back to his experiences on earth, he wished he had had the ability to appreciate what it was that was right in front of him. God's gift to mankind, carefully implemented into the lives of His most beloved creation, was part of the equation that many looked too hard to find. That equation was now apparent to Timothy: in all of creation was revealed His love for man; it was only for man to figure out the correct way to use it. Perhaps, Timothy realized, the meaning of life had been right before his eyes all along.

Timothy then halted as if something was suddenly burdening him. He had caught true glimpses of beauty, but, like a light switch being turned off, his mind was now revealing to him an entirely different picture.

"Timothy, what is it? What causes you to stop?"

"I don't know for sure. I was envisioning great things. Great gifts that God has given to us are now much easier for me to recognize. But like two opposite forces pulling apart my body, now I feel that same separation within my mind and heart. I feel heavy and light all at the same time. And I feel that I am being selfish not to go back to my mother and father to tell them that I am alright, and to be there for her as she is so sick. Perhaps I can make her better! I am having second thoughts about all of this…"

Timothy then recognized, without Eryana's insight, the root cause of the doubt. It was as the elders had told him, and it suggested something very important: he must stay on his path and not let outside forces influence the relationship of his heart and mind.

"…may it allow for the guidance of the only real weapon that you should need: faith," Elder Stamos had told him.

It was also Eryana who had earlier taught him something else very profound, which was the very basic principle for which human nature permits: once you catch a glimpse of true beauty you then recognize its exact opposite. Such is the case with any journey where one tries to lift up his or her heart.

"The dream in concept represents one moving between light and darkness. For you in particular, it signified a typical path of getting closer to God: receiving a glimpse of grace only to lose it shortly after," she had told him at the cauldron filled with everlasting water.

Chapter 13

"I am fine," Timothy expressed. "I am doing well in dealing with these temptations. Let's continue. I just had a brief doubt for which I had to transform into useful energy."

Eryana seemed very pleased with how far Timothy's spirit had developed. If there were ever any doubts by her or anyone else of his ability to succeed, instances such as this would have put those concerns far away from being realistically considered.

No more words needed to be said and they departed from the forest and past the Blessed Waters. As they climbed up and over the hill, the bells from the Vestibule of Faith rang loudly. There fourteen apostles were still praying, and it was timed ever so perfectly with Timothy's descent toward the Northern Land's doorway. With their exit, he had left behind some of the last great visions of beauty he would see for some time to come.

The large hall that housed three different stairways to the south, east and north instilled into Timothy a feeling of mediocrity and yet a grand sense of longing for Truth. But there was still one more pleasant experience waiting for him, not quite like it would have been in the beautiful lands to the north, but all the same still comforting.

Eryana waited for the two heavily armored angels to open the ornate wooden doors to the courtyard. Passing through, Timothy saw before him the thousands of saints and angels who were to say good bye and grant hope for a safe journey. Cheers were transitioned by well-trained vocal chords into songs of joy as the crowd stood to the side of the one hundred archways between the wooden doors and the kingdom's gate. Horns and harps sounded off from angels flying above as the clouds rolled back and revealed a clear sky. Eleven rays of light then illuminated the path before him: the Eleven Elders were present in spirit even while they remained in the Residence of the Gracious.

Walking toward the gate he stepped onto slabs of stone, each broken up by lush green grass. The warm welcome and farewell that he was simultaneously experiencing was somewhat overwhelming and it seemed to him to be occurring in slow motion. Finally, approaching the exit, two Powers of enormous strength opened the gates of the Kingdom of Heavenly Creatures and allowed Timothy and Eryana to pass through. Clouds then returned to again provide cover over the courtyard, keeping the kingdom once again hidden from view. Walking past the stone statues and the horn that Eryana had once sounded off they took only a few more steps before hearing a voice behind them speak forcefully.

"Eryana, Arch-guardian to the elders and Timothy, first among the elders," the voice called out.

Eryana turned around and it was none other than Corinth, Chief Dominion of the Offices of the Heavenly Hierarchy.

"Your Eminence," she called out, bowing to him as Timothy followed her lead.

Timothy, no longer using plain eyes to see creatures for what they were, found himself still squinting at a source of light so bright that even his mind in his heart barely could tolerate it.

"What a special blessing this truly is!" Eryana shouted. "This is who I traveled to see when I left you with Gammond…" Eryana paused, again remembering her beloved friend.

"I heard what has happened, Eryana. Do not despair. There comes a time when you must move on. The Light has not disappeared and still remains day after day. Let us see first what is in store for Timothy, for we must have faith that all has been carefully and deliberately designed," Corinth explained.

Corinth had an ability to reassure the most destitute in a very poetic way and, when hearing his words, one could never disagree.

"And for you, Timothy, I have some special words to utter. You must be extremely careful and follow precisely what you were taught by the elders who have preceded you. I hope to sum up that which they instructed with some advice I was once given. And here it is:

"'Far above the skies, where the stars cannot even show light beyond the darkness of the universe, the darkness eventually becomes light. Everything you thought was dark is good and everything you thought was light is nothing. It is dark now, that time, but it shall soon reveal goodness. And when you thought that no light would any longer shine, you will notice that the darkness turns into gold and the light shines brighter than the constellations around it. Then it shall be revealed.'"

"My dream," Timothy said, beginning to cry tears of happiness. "You understand!"

"Keep your dream close to you, Timothy. Keep it close when you find you are to take a great leap of faith. Do not let what you thought was troubling haunt you."

"Eryana had indeed described a portion of my dream, and now I have an even greater grasp around its meaning. Thank you, Your Eminence!"

"It is my privilege to offer you advice. And it is also my privilege to see you off from this gate. Continue a ways north along the wall with Eryana until the wall turns to stone, for there will be a passage along a hidden stairway. Farewell!"

Timothy left with Eryana on a very happy note.

They traveled along the wall until above them was a sudden break in the clouds, and through the break was light shining down at an angle toward the wall. Eryana approached the wall and began to climb as if there were invisible stairs.

"How are you doing that?" Timothy inquired. "It is like you are stepping up stairs but all I see is a stone wall."

"Do not look at it as a wall. Look deeper into it, remember? You are used to optical illusions by now are you not?" Eryana asked in a playful tone.

Timothy realized again that he would need to pay attention to more than just creatures. He brought his mind to his heart again and then saw the stairs within the stone wall. Timothy climbed up with Eryana until they reached a firm pathway hidden inside of the low-lying clouds, which eventually led them to the beginnings of the Grey Mountains. It joined a winding road that was devoid of any life; rock and dirt was all to be found. The magnitude of the space they were to cross was also greater than he had expected, as was every other place in the foreign heavenly world that he had so recently encountered.

Along the way the path began to straighten out. They were now well into the mountains where there was only a view of the now rocky slopes. It was now a large valley, although still at a higher elevation than when they originally began their ascent up the stone stairs.

Darkness crept upon them as they roamed further into the forest. The trees, also similarly populated, were very much different than the others Timothy had seen so far in Eden. They were much like he remembered them to be on earth: still beautiful, but in a strange sense no longer mystical. Their material form lacked an essence and thus it was now very apparent that he had earlier been given a taste of something so profound and pure. So pure, in fact, that anything from earth had clearly seemed plain and mundane.

"This reminds me of home, Eryana, and it makes me feel rather uneasy. I suppose this is what I should have expected, but now I am left longing for something with a deeper meaning. Possibly it could be that the lands of the kingdom were filled more with God than they were materials. I know now what you meant by the fact that I would still need certain objects to be able to make sense of anything in this world, because I was not yet ready to understand the true difference in the two natures: of man and of God. I now understand that the closer one is to God, the more fulfilled your heart becomes and the fewer materials you need. Now I need materials only in the way they relate to my relationship with Him."

"Very good, Timothy, I told you that you would understand soon enough. But now you must solve even more abstract mysteries; we have gone about as far as I can take you. Even I am not prepared to go any further. I can be of no use and only the virtues and blessings you have come to understand and receive will help you to continue. Be strong – discover your depth of faith."

With that, Eryana knelt on one knee and bowed her head to Timothy.

"We exist so that one day you may be great with God in His Kingdom," she continued. "Thank you for blessing me with our recent experiences. Be well," Eryana said, saddened but with a forced smile.

Eryana embraced Timothy with a hug. Spanning her wings into the air, she graciously flew away from the forest and out of the mountains. Now alone for the very first time, Timothy at once grasped how the outcome of his final journey would largely depend on his own choices. He took a deep breath and proceeded down the open path, with trees now bunched tightly together to both his left and right.

Day had made its final transition into night, as from the horizon a moon-like half circle swiftly raised high into the sky. It was quite unlike Timothy's experience in the Eastern and Northern Lands within the Kingdom of Heavenly Creatures; for the first time the skies were not regulated to be either only light or only dark. Like the forest, he understood its similarity to earth and, along with the aspect of change, it gave him a great feeling of unpredictability.

"So let's recall more of what I was told," Timothy said, keeping himself company. "For the first trial, I believe that I am supposed to figure out why God permits evil. But how does that relate to the path ahead? Maybe I should just keep walking. Something will happen; I am sure of it!"

Timothy walked for quite some distance, but there was no indication of any beginnings of the Trials of the Trinity. As the elders had told him to expect it was a normal forest, which went on and on, and on. There was no castle and it was turning into a tiring ordeal. All that he could think about was rest. He recalled, however, that he was not to sit until he finished the trials. Timothy began to think about why that was. Was it that he was not supposed to, or that he wouldn't find himself able to? He could certainly stop if he made the choice to; it was just a matter of halting and sitting down on the ground. Considering that there was no sign of any further change in the scenery, and there was no other indication of progress besides, he decided to do just that. After all, he thought, it would be better than wasting his potion in exchange for rejuvenation.

"What makes you think that that is the right choice?" a voice called out.

Extremely startled, Timothy stood up straight as he

had only made it halfway to the ground. He looked behind and then to each side, but could not find the being that had spoken to him.

"Who said that?" Timothy demanded. "Who is there?"

Out from behind the trees presented itself a lamb. It was a typical curly haired lamb, white as light. It approached him and looked up at his face.

"I was there but now I am here; but only if you believe me to be."

"I believe that anything is possible, but I have yet to decide who you are," Timothy replied, proving to be untrusting of his new acquaintance.

"Why did you decide to stop?" the lamb inquired.

"Well, it seemed to me that nothing was changing and so I became tired and there you have it."

"I see; impatient would be a fitting word? That does not seem like a quality that one of your stature would possess. You strike me as the type that would be noble, and sensible."

"No, not impatient; that is not an appropriate word. I just needed to think, I suppose. Besides, to what occasion do I owe you an explanation? I hardly know a thing about you. Well, other than you are a lamb who talks and you are roaming about the Fields of Horror. And you don't seem to be very horrific."

"Ah, but we are still in a forest. The Fields of Horror are just ahead. And maybe I just appear to look meek? Maybe I am like your dreams. Light and dark there both existed, and so maybe I am meek but fierce."

"Like my dreams? How do you know about my dreams?" Timothy said, suspiciously.

"Well, do you not have dreams?"

Timothy stopped himself from responding directly to the lamb's question. He could sense that he was about to become agitated, and knew that he was no longer thinking clearly.

"Alright," Timothy said, after staring at the lamb for a few moments. "So, I do not know if it was the right choice to sit down. It made more sense for me to take a moment and think about where I was going and determine how in the world I would know when the Trial of the Father began."

"And what if you had chosen not to sit down? Do you think there would have been the chance that the trial you speak of would have already started by now? I suppose you will never now know. Because if you continue on now and it doesn't begin you might ponder over how a different choice could have led to a different outcome. But it will only be pondering, for you will never truly know for sure what could have been. Here is another example for you: if you choose to not embark on this journey, you can go back to your bodily life and return your father and your mother. If you keep moving on, however, you will never know for sure if your presence would have made an impact on your mother's health. Even worse still, you may never know what it would be like to see her one last time."

Stunned, Timothy looked away, as he was unable to face something that had made such an unfair statement. But the statement had struck a chord within him. The lamb had made complete sense, despite how much he wanted to ignore something that could steer him off of his path. He returned his gaze back to the lamb and, about to ask exactly what he knew of his mother, he saw that it was no longer there. He looked around like before and nowhere was the lamb to be seen.

"Well that certainly seemed to be good and evil all

wrapped in one package," Timothy thought to himself, rather shaken from such an odd scene.

Realizing what he had just said, a light set off inside of him.

"A clue," he said out loud. "I must be on the right path forward, as this revelation is certainly applicable! In this case, both good and evil seemed to exist all at the same time. It was as if the pleasant looking lamb and its evil words were attempting to balance each other out in an earth-like place like this forest; it was similar to the equation of earth that I learned about. Yes, with my heart I could see that lamb represented both; they each existed simultaneously. How it affected me was based on how I chose to respond, so it was very relative in that sense. But wait, that isn't exactly what I need to figure out. The question was: how could He create something good if it can contain at the same time something evil?"

Overwhelmed, it felt to Timothy that he was at square one again, as his analysis had brought him back to the original question at hand. Nevertheless, he realized that stopping would not solve the mystery – it would only be one step closer to failing. And no matter how much he wanted to return to his family, he had come too far to give up now. Having convinced himself, he continued walking and suddenly met the edge of the forest where three paths were seemingly laid before him, each leading into a vast open field.

"I wonder what would have happened if I hadn't attempted to sit down," he thought to himself, applying the lamb's logic to the outcome. "Certainly I made the right choice as I could have ended up still on the same path to nowhere. Clearly this is a sign I am to continue on with the Trial of the Father. Let it begin!"

Timothy took a few steps along the center of the three, but soon halted as out of the corner of his eye he caught a sign. He backed up a few steps and seeing that it pointed in three directions, he read it carefully.

"'Way of the Four – northeast', 'Way of the Worm – east' and 'Way of the Lamb – southeast.' This is strange; which do I choose? I seem to have found a bit of a riddle before the trial has even begun."

Timothy pondered the options that were placed before him. The northeast sign fascinated him, although which four it was referring to was indeed a very good question. He knew that the Bible often stressed importance on numbers, but he could not remember anything about the number four. Also, this example had no indication if the number was of good or of evil. The Way of the Worm was even more obvious. It seemed dark in and of itself; although it was intriguing in that he could not off hand recall any mention of worms in anything that he had studied before. And the Way of the Lamb seemed to speak for itself. It simply caused him to have chills; his recent encounter with the speaking animal was perhaps the creepiest part of his whole journey up until now.

"I think I will choose the Way of the Four, for I wish to know more about which four it refers to. I cannot settle on any path if I do not understand or at least know the context of all."

Timothy backed up a few more steps and proceeded along the northeast road. As he moved forward the sky became immediately brighter: the source of light turned into a full circle. The illuminated road before him, however, was not exactly comforting as he was now in the Fields of Horror under what seemed to be a full moon. Recalling prior discussions with Eryana about the validity of an earthly concept such as vampires and its relationship to the hidden dimensions, the thought of werewolves came to the forefront of his mind. He could only hope that his fears would not come to life any more than they already had.

The road ahead revealed a much more passive scene. Four men there stood, each dressed in similar attire to what Timothy wore at the House of Elders: a white robe and sandals. As he approached them, they each revealed an open mouth that was complemented by a generous smile. Both of their arms were extended forward into the air and with their left hand each held an open book. With their right hand, palms facing out, they formed the Sign of the Trinity: their index and middle fingers were pressing on their thumbs. As if about to preach, the first to Timothy's right spoke.

"Welcome, traveler! To what acquaintance are we so honored to meet?"

The second man from the right then said, in a much deeper tone.

"It has been some time since we saw another human creature, what is your name?"

"Do you come in peace?" the third spoke.

Hi, my name is Matthew," the fourth, but first to Timothy's left, at last said.

"And I am Mark."

"And Luke."

"And John! Welcome! Do you now recognize us?"

Timothy stared with his mouth gaping open as meeting those four, let alone another intelligent creature in this land, was completely unexpected. It was also clearly explained to him that he would be alone in his attempt to complete the trials. Therefore, he was hesitant to engage in a conversation of any type. Nevertheless, he cautiously proceeded to speak.

"The four evangelists; I should have known! What are you doing here? Do you know who I am?" Timothy inquired.

"Why yes, you are the boy who should prove himself," St. John continued, clearly the lead of the four. "You have come to a mysterious land that was once very active. Let me tell you of a passage. It contains knowledge of both the Old and New Testaments, but it is off the record!

"You see, Lucifer defected from God in anticipation of the creation of man. He was such a jealous angel, and it was the first time any creature had turned away from Him. When he left his seat, he trekked down the entire path between the castle and the edge of the Grey Mountains and then back again to the castle. So the entire lands, once the Fields of Beauty, turned into the Fields of Horror. It became hell, and the rest of Eden became earth. Wait a moment; are you familiar with the Toll-Houses?"

"Well, yes, now that you mention it. I learned a little about it from my grandfather. Oh, that is where I heard about worms! But the idea of it is rather foggy."

"Foggy? It sure was!" St. John continued, smirking. "Before Jesus had come to earth there was not Salvation. So, the demons and Satan, not yet having been conquered by the great King Jesus, required that all who died on earth pass through the Fields of Horror to pay for their sins. One had to pay tolls at the Toll-Houses in order to pass through to the holding area of Tartarus. These stations were quite fiery –"

Timothy interrupted. "You mean the Southern Lands?" Timothy had a seat on a nearby rock, fascinated by the story.

"No, not exactly; you are getting ahead of me! But you sure are smart. The Southern Lands are now called Tartarus, but it wasn't the original Tartarus. Now let me back up to the times before man was created. As I said earlier, after Lucifer left the First Hierarchy and this land became his, it became known as the Fields of Horror, or otherwise known as Tartarus at that time; it was the original hell-like experience. Man, however, had not been yet created, but Satan knew that he would be and that he would love God. After Satan successfully tempted the very first man in the dimension of Eden, earth transcended into its own time-based world and was no longer part of the heavens. There, in addition to Tartarus, Satan and his demons were free to roam about, often unseen. Eden itself then became just an empty land outside of the Kingdom of Heavenly Creatures.

"Tied with their fall, men had to pass through the Toll-Houses in Tartarus to pay for their sins before heading to the Southern Lands, as you have demonstrated familiarity with. In this way, Satan was connected to man through their earthly transgressions.

"Then there came our Lord and Savior Jesus Christ! He died on the Cross. And then, recall where he went before sitting at the Right Hand of God: He paid a visit to hell, or should I say the Fields of Horror, and the first battle of the war between heaven and hell began. Next, he used his death as payment for our sins: He conquered the Fields of Horror and in His Resurrection it was complete; he had trampled death by death. So no longer did man have to pay tolls for their sins and they instead were sent directly to the Southern Lands, at that point referred to some as Tartarus. As the Fields of Horror were functioning no more, there was no suffering after death to be incurred by any man or woman until facing the Judgment Seat of Christ. Satan and his demons were then permanently banished from the Fields of Horror and only were permitted to the depths of earth. They still, however, could roam about unseen.

"Of course, Satan did try to take back the lands here with his first attempt at the Antichrist. That was perhaps a century prior to now, in Earth-time. Ever hear of World War II? It was the second battle between the heavens, hell and earth. That did not work out too well for the evil creatures.

"Let me sum this all up for you: before Christ, when a person died, they had to pay for their sins with pain and punishment in the Fields of Horror. The more one sinned, the worse the ordeal was. Once through, they ended up in the Southern Lands in wait until God's final Judgment. But God is such a loving, merciful God. And so he sent his Son, the Angel of the Lord, to earth, born of the Virgin Mary. You must know about that! And Jesus, after becoming fully man while also fully God, died on the Cross, conquered hell and through the Resurrection saved your sins. He conquered Tartarus – the original Tartarus – before rising to the right hand of God. The Toll-Houses were then banished, leaving an odd balance between good and evil; it became similar to the overarching concept on earth. And instead of passing through these lands, man instead went directly to the Southern Lands in wait of the Judgment Seat of Christ."

"So what of the First Hierarchy you mentioned? Are you saying that the castle was originally the First Hierarchy?" Timothy asked, looking for additional clarification.

"That is correct, very good!" St. John continued. "It was the First Hierarchy and was the way to God. Up the stairs and into the mountains, and through the path and to the castle and then somehow, no one of course knows for sure, God dwelled near the castle. Perhaps within it or perhaps above it, but that cannot be answered. The First Hierarchy now dwells before God in order to solidify his domain from

278

possible defection. The Vestibule of Faith is the only way now to Him now. There is a wonderful new staircase built behind the altar! But it is really impossible at this point to pass through there."

Timothy exchanged glances with the four men. They were still smiling and maintained their position with their right arms extended. For what purpose St. John was telling Timothy all that information was now on his mind.

"I assume you are wondering why we are telling you all of this, Timothy," St. Matthew began to say. "Well, it is rather simple. You now know what this land is and its history. But now with your coming to the heavens, the end has been set in motion. You can return to earth to perform great works before that end, that is, if you can survive!"

The Four Evangelists began to laugh as if to suggest damnation could be imminent.

"I thought that either way I would return alive to earth and that it was just in the manner of my return that would affect the future?"

"Oh, is that what you heard? Well, you shall see! Were you not curious what the Southern Lands looked like? Perhaps you can take a journey there after paying some tolls of your own!" St. Luke added.

"Not so fast, Timothy," St. Mark clarified, "the Eldership is nearly complete, but not quite yet. And now these fields are going to test your abilities. You saw the good in us, but a balance there must be."

Timothy backed up and brought his shield in front of him, anticipating the worst. His heart did not lie, for danger was near. Bringing his mind to his heart, he looked forward: no longer did he see men. They each were spinning like a top, finally merging into one body but with four heads. Each head then one by one transformed into something very unique.

St. Matthew's face looked to be that of an angel. His head disconnected from the other three, and with his spirit he flew up into the air with great wings and then dove at Timothy. Timothy's heart, warm with thoughts of Jesus, aided him in correctly using the Helmet of Salvation. The angel was warded off, disappearing into the skies.

St. Mark transformed into a lion. He separated from the other two, and with a massive body he pounced on Timothy. But the Belt of Truth revealed that true fear was reserved only for God, and so the lion carried on into the distance.

St. Luke turned into an Ox, and separating from St. John he charged forward into the Shield of Faith. The Ox dissipated into nothingness, however, as Timothy had trusted in the protection of the Lord.

And finally St. John took his book, being the only to remain. Looking up, his head transformed into that of an eagle. Great wings spanned from his back as he lifted into the air, and with sharp talons he attempted to grasp ahold of Timothy around the Breastplate of Righteousness. But there was nothing tangible for the creature to hold on to, since Timothy thus far had proved to be using the virtues appropriately. The eagle then soared off to the horizon with a trail of dust left behind.

The dust settled in front of his face and, coughing, he waved his arm with sword in hand so as to clear his vision. A voice from beyond then spoke out, dark like his dreams.

"Not all are from God who proclaims to be. Just as it is here, so it is on earth. Your mother and father are at risk. Go back to them."

Timothy looked ahead to the northeast and the dust

soon cleared. Before him he saw a great angel, with a single tear hanging from the corner of his eye. He recognized it immediately to be the very angel he had encountered above the treetops in The Forest of the Wise. Turning away from him, the angel proceeded up along the path. Timothy charged forward, running after it as if demanding to know its intent.

Several steps later, an image soon appeared off in the distance to his side. Timothy immediately stopped to look. It was a hospital room with two beds, and there lay his mother in one and his own body in the other. His father was weeping, being escorted away by three vested bishops and a priest; neither of their faces was clear. The angel ahead of Timothy veered off the path and into the room, becoming one with the vision and lifted his mother off of her bed. Simultaneously, a leader of Satan approached Timothy's body and reached out for the sacred cross.

The scene then disappeared from his sight and all that remained was the angel carrying his mother down the Way of the Four. Timothy began chasing after them for quite a distance, until the path veered south and a sign lay before him:

"'The Way of the Worm,'" he read.

Timothy took a deep breath and pursued them on foot.

Chapter 14

Fathers John and Andrei arrived at the home of their former Bishop Andrew. It was now early afternoon and Father John did not want to waste another moment. He had now two important items on his agenda. Not only was he looking to shed some light on how exactly the remaining bishops were intending to direct the future of the Orthodox Church, he was also now hoping to make sense of their attempt to take the sacred cross that was given to Timothy.

"Father Andrei, do you have anything particular that you want to ask him? I have a whole series of questions. I have a feeling we are going to learn quite a lot."

Father Andrei shut the passenger side door and walked up to Father John, looking him in the eyes.

"No, nothing in particular I suppose. Based on our conversations I think you have on your mind what is important. Judging by how Jack sounded on the phone – I am sorry, Bishop Andrew – judging how Bishop Andrew sounded on the phone, I do not know how much information we will really obtain. He seemed awfully confused."

They both proceeded up the walkway and onto the porch. At the entrance there was a screen door preventing them from knocking, and so Father John reached for the handle to open it, only to find that it was locked.

"Let me, Father John."

Father Andrei reached for the doorbell and pushed on it with a single finger. They both waited anxiously for the door to open, but did not hear any immediate response from inside the house.

Chapter 14

"Father Andrei, I forgot to mention something: I noticed you are not wearing your cross; while we were praying I realized that you were not carrying it with you. I don't think I have ever found you to forget something so critical."

"I have a lot on my mind lately and I must have left it on my desk back at the office," Father Andrei immediately replied. "How are you able to remember crucial things during troubling times? You seem to be dealing with more stress than me."

"I think that I am more focused under pressure. I feel that I have a mission now and it is imperative that I do not lose my concentration. It may be that I am being somewhat compulsive lately."

The door slowly unlocked. As it steadily opened, through the screen door they saw Jack standing still. Both of them were taken aback, as his wavy grey hair was spread in many directions. He had not trimmed his beard for several days, and the clothes he wore were only a bathrobe over pajama bottoms and a t-shirt. Father John looked him up and down with his eyes finally resting on Jack's ragged slippers. Jack remained still and proved hesitant to open the screen door.

"I suppose I have been pacing," Jack finally said, gruffly. "I've nearly worn out my shoes."

Jack was a large man, with his stomach protruding from under his shirt. He was once jolly but now purely seemed intimidating. Something was fairly unsettling about his demeanor.

"Why don't you come in now? It looks like it is about to storm. Excuse the mess; it seems that everything started shaking and a few things became off-balance."

Jack unlocked the screen door and held it open while

Fathers John and Andrei stepped inside. They looked around his home, both appearing shocked as to how disorderly things were. Walking through the kitchen and into the living room, their eyes drew them to a single chair. It had two pieces of tattered rope, one tied and hanging from each arm rest.

"Boy, it is awful dark out. It looks like it might thunder," Jack explained, still standing with his arm propping the screen door open.

"Ouch, what was that?" Father Andrei yelped, reaching his hands toward his feet.

Father Andrei began to shake his foot, feeling something wrapped around his ankle. By the time he looked down there was nothing to be found but the bottom of his cassock. A cat then hissed and ran for the door, escaping outside.

"Hey Acts, come back! Come back! Oh, he'll never find his way out there. He is an indoor cat. Dang," Jack sighed, locking both the screen and main doors. "Oh well, let's get on with our conversation."

"What happened, Father Andrei? You look like you are in pain. Did the cat get to you?" Father John stated, sympathetically.

"I don't know; something hurts…"

Andrei took his outer cassock off and sat on the couch. Lifting up his inner cassock and then his right pant leg, he began to inspect his lower leg. Andrei pulled down his sock and revealed two puncture wounds and several scratch marks. His lower calf was beginning to bleed.

"Oh, come on now. How could this happen!"

"That cat is sneaky," Jack replied. "I don't think he cares for you."

Noticing that he was sternly being stared at, Father

Chapter 14

Andrei did not respond directly to his former bishop.

"Is there some disinfectant I could use, and a covering for my wound on top of that?"

"Jack, can you direct me to where we could find something to aid Father Andrei?" Father John asked again for Father Andrei.

"Sure, around the corner to the left over there. A cabinet above the bathroom sink."

Jack pointed in the direction he described as Father John jogged to the bathroom. Taking a seat, Jack positioned the chair so he could look out of the large bow window that captured the view of his entire backyard.

"Alright, Father Andrei, I found some gauze and other first aid items."

Father John handed over the materials to Father Andrei and then sat next to him on the couch after removing his outer cassock.

"Bishop Andrew... may I still call you that?" Father John asked, indicating that he did not care to wait any longer to begin the discussions.

"No! Not bishop. I am no longer that person. Jack, that is all, or you can both find your way back outside!"

Taken aback, Father John changed his tone to be more passive.

"I apologize – that was out of line," Father John continued. "Jack, look, we need to investigate into what is going on. It is not every day that several bishops retire from their posts and on top of it a metropolitan with them. It is most concerning. What will become of all the parishioners and their priests? What will happen now to the Orthodox Church in America? I had an exasperating experience yesterday with Bishops David, Nikolai and Peter – tell me they have not lost their minds?"

Jack continued to stare out of the living room window. He began to grind his teeth and twitch his eyes.

"We, I mean to say, the church representatives now, must make way for the Orthodox Church of Russia. Tikhon II has it under control and his policies are ever strengthening. Let's not be in his way now. All services have been ordered cancelled by Metropolitan Nikolai from here on out. Meetings will be had in New York at Saint Peter's Monastery. That is all I know. And I suggest you remove yourself from the limelight, if you know what is best!"

The room became completely silent. Father Andrei attached the final piece of tape to his leg and looked over at Jack.

"Metropolitan Nikolai? So it is true," Father John solemnly concluded, "Metropolitan Ezekiel is no longer holding his post! Perhaps this is entirely my fault as I did not know how to best go about this. I assumed our recent council was the best avenue. Now look what has happened... and my son is now lying still in a hospital bed. Don't you begin to deny that this is all related! Look, you must fight with us. We can battle this. We can bring all of the dioceses to order ourselves and use prayer to our advantage. We can become more familiar with spiritual warfare. Let's find Metropolitan Ezekiel and the other bishops."

"It is too late. You can't find them now. I am the only one that agreed to step down willingly, and look what happened to me."

Jack stood up and lifted up his shirt. Several bruises and lacerations covered the entire width of his chest.

"They are gone, I am sure of it. Get away while you can," Jack continued, presenting to Father John what he thought was the only reasonable option left to consider.

"What have they done to you? Father Andrei, do you

see this? Father Andrei?"

Father John turned around only to find that Father Andrei was no longer sitting on the couch. He then approached Jack, attempting to console him.

"My dear bishop, what has happened?" Father John wept. "Let's call the authorities. Perhaps this is the door that has been opened to stop them from the evil they are wreaking on the Church, and perhaps eventually on the world itself."

"My dear Father John, there is nothing left you can do. No one will believe you," Jack said, in a more sane tone. "It is over. Do what you can to get to your son and your wife. Protecting them is your only obligation now. Leave now before it is too late."

"Bishop, what is going to happen? What is this world turning into? What of New York? I am so confused and I feel so helpless. You are right, who is going to believe me? All I can do is pray now."

Father John bowed his head and looked down at the ground, and then lifted his head with a new idea.

"Why don't you come with us, Jack?" Father John continued after a moment. "It doesn't seem safe here. And you need medical attention. We can go to the hospital and get you looked at."

Jack looked outside once more before turning back to Father John.

"It is too late… I told you that it would be too late."

"I am sorry? I am too confused; what you are saying does not make sense. What is too late? For the Church? The world? Do you know more about what is to come?"

"For you, it is too late. I am sorry, Father John."

Father John heard footsteps approaching from behind him rapidly and, as he turned around, a blunt metal object was raised above him. It swiftly came down upon the side of his head, before he could make out who the bearer of the weapon was; a loud thump was made onto the floor. Now unconscious, the weapon was dropped next to his face. Jack then took a seat in the chair and quietly looked outside.

"Oh, Father John, you were much too trusting weren't you," Father Andrei said, in a partially sympathetic tone. "Let's get you into your car. We've got to get to the airport. You can join your other curious brothers in New York before too long. We will take good care of Timothy, don't you worry your heart."

Bishop Andrew then stood up as Father Andrei handed him the keys to Father John's car.

"Good work; you can stop calling me Jack now," Bishop Andrew told Father Andrei. "I will pull the car into the garage and we can load him into the trunk. Make sure to bind him carefully. We will certainly be rewarded with a place under Tikhon II's rule. The cross will be his soon!"

Bishop Andrew hurried out to the car and began to drive it into the garage. Father Andrei, shaken up, searched underneath the couch with his hand. He pulled out duct tape and rope, and began to secure Father John's mouth, hands and feet.

As he finished applying the tape, a cell phone rang. Father Andrei jumped up and looked around to where the ringing was coming from. Looking over at the couch, he could hear it with his eyes underneath Father John's outer cassock. He pulled it from underneath and looked at the screen.

"'Paul Stephanopoulos,'" Father Andrei read. "That is certainly interesting timing. To what curiosity would he now be calling you? Are you having your friends keeping a close eye on you, now?"

Chapter 14

Father Andrei eerily chuckled and placed the phone in his pocket. Bishop Andrew entered in from the side door and they carried Father John out to the garage.

———

Jacob, standing next to Timothy, listened as his father's cell phone rang. He called a second time, and with still no answer decided to leave a voice message.

"Hi Father John, this is Jacob. We decided to come visit Timothy here. I am with my mom and dad. I guess it has been nearly a day or so since you have been here but we were a little worried you wouldn't get here in time. Timothy's been moving his hands somehow but is still in a coma and if he woke up we didn't want you to miss it. Anyway, sorry to bother you and we hope to see you soon."

Jacob hung up the phone and handed it back to his father.

"No answer, dad. Don't you think it's weird that he's been gone for so long now?"

"No, Jacob, he has a lot of important things to take care of. He has a parish to still think about, and a few other things that I don't dare to try to understand. He will be back in his own time. I am sure of it. For now we can be good friends by being here with his family while he cannot."

"Dad, I have an idea."

"What's that, Jacob?"

"Well, do you think it is okay to pray? I mean, for those who are sick. I know we don't go to church anymore, and you wanted to protect me from being made fun of and stuff like that. But I feel like I should pray for Timothy. I don't know why. I just want to go and start a prayer group. It's all of a sudden – it just came over me."

Jacob's mother, Andrea, left the bedside of Candice and came up behind him. She gave him a big hug from behind and kissed him on his cheek.

"Always such a good boy, Jacob. You know, ever since your father was threatened to lose his job we had to do what was best for you and our family. The government does not allow its employees to practice faith. Part of me wishes we had trusted in God and faced the persecution. But you know that even Timothy faces bullying and teasing for what he believes... I worry about you, that's all."

"Well, I think I know of a few people at school that also keep what they believe to themselves. I promise I won't get caught. Timothy would do the same for us!"

"Jacob, if any teachers or the principal finds out you could be suspended. Even expelled! I am sorry but I won't allow it. You can pray for Timothy at home; I will allow for that. But no prayer groups. And no asking anyone about it at school!"

Jacob put his head down and then nodded. He went back to Timothy and held his hand. Bringing his mouth to Timothy's ear, he began to whisper.

"I know that you would have stood up for what you believe in. I am going to get as many people to pray for you as possible."

Timothy's hand twitched and Jacob looked down at it, as if feeling a great connection with his best friend. He quickly looked back up at Timothy's face with an excited grin. Finally, he turned around and walked back over to his parents.

"We can come back tomorrow afternoon, Jacob," his father instructed him. "We have work and you've got school in the morning. Hopefully Father John will be back soon."

They left the room to return home. The drive seemed

unusually long for Jacob, but he used the time to think about the next day at school. How he would ever find enough people to pray for Timothy, he thought, was beyond possible. Even if he was able to find a few schoolmates who were both willing and daring enough to try it, there was still the predicament of where they would pray. If he got caught he knew for certain he would be expelled, and he ran the risk of putting other students at risk as well: it was against the law for any school to allow prayer or any other type of religious ritual. Nearly all fifty states had passed legislation that was originally drafted by the federal government. Many states, against this proposal, agreed to some type of law regarding the expression of religion as long as they were able to craft it themselves, for fear that the federal mandates would be far too oppressive and limiting to those who had faith.

Once arriving at his house, Jacob began to play video games for a good portion of the evening. He then decided to go to bed early, but was up most of the night thinking about whom he would approach at school with his idea.

Eventually falling asleep, he experienced very vivid dreams. One particular dream that he had took place in New York, at a monastery. He was in his early thirties, sitting in an office with another man about that same age. They were sitting down across from one another and having a cup of herbal tea.

"With prayer anything is possible," the man told him. "If you can have one particular virtue at all during times such as these, it would be courage. Sometimes God opens a door for us and we are in a place of hope even when we don't see how it would be possible. Find that door, and don't look back."

Jacob woke up suddenly and it was morning. It was as if he had just fallen asleep.

"I hate it when I can't remember all of my dreams. Something about a monastery," he said to himself.

The sun was beginning to rise and, just as a rare glimpse of sunlight shone through his east-facing bedroom window, clouds then stripped it away and darkness returned to the morning. Jacob then jumped out of bed and began to get prepared for school.

Several minutes later Jacob walked downstairs as he was putting his glasses on. His nose could sense something delicious being cooked; once his eyes adjusted to his lenses, he peeked around the corner and saw his mother in the kitchen.

"Good morning, mom! Wow, what is all of this?" he said, giving her a hug with one arm.

"Well, let's see. You have been having a rough time lately so I wanted to make you your favorite breakfast! For you we have pancakes, strawberry topping and whipped cream. Oh, and a side of sausage. I have orange juice sitting there on the table. You should have just enough time to eat before the bus arrives."

Andrea turned to her son and gave him a great big smile. She bent her knees to his height.

"Look, Jacob. I can't imagine how you must be feeling about Timothy. It is also tough for me, to see his mother as she is. What a nightmare. We must be grateful for the health that we have. And by the way, I have a feeling of what you are up to. I won't tell your father. But please, be careful will you? Don't risk making the situation worse. Just use discretion."

Jacob looked up at his mother, in awe of how astute she was and how well she knew him. Mother knows best, as the saying went. She told him that often, but this time there was no need. He felt loved, supported and encouraged to be himself. Now, he was empowered to find a way at school to express how much he cared for Timothy. Just as he was processing those thoughts, he heard his father walk across the living room and into the kitchen. Jacob turned from his mother as if the conversation never happened and joined his father at the table.

"Andrea, what do you think about that awful news?"

"You mean the horrid earthquake? I don't really know, Paul. This world is such a sad place."

"Yeah, thank god we don't have family down there. I can't imagine something like that happening. I mean they are sending troops there to maintain order, even the guard from here in Oregon and other neighboring states. It is like the apocalypse judging from the scenes on the television. I am beginning to think that we need to stock up on supplies and food."

"Perhaps it is a sign to stop ignoring our faith," Andrea replied, staring at her husband.

Jacob looked up at his father, in anticipation of his response.

"That's it! I have had it with these insinuations. Look, I am going to work early," Paul said, standing up and turning toward the living room. "You know what," he said, stopping but still facing away from Andrea and Jacob, "the Orthodox Church meant a lot to me. But so do both of you. It is hard enough that we stopped going and I have to live with turning my back on something that was part of my childhood – something that reminds me of my parents and my early days growing up in Greece. But to have to live with taking it away from both of you, well that is an unbearable thought. What would you have me do?" Paul turned back to Andrea, now lowering his voice. "There is no work out there. This is my only chance at a job. Don't rub it in."

Paul walked off and grabbed his coat from the rack. The next sound to be heard was the front door slamming shut. Andrea finished cooking Jacob's food and put it on his plate.

"Eat up, Jacob. You're going to be late for the bus."

Jacob looked up at his mother who was noticeably upset. He did his best to hold in his tears, controlling any feelings that would show him to be bothered. Listening to his mother, he finished his breakfast and grabbed his jacket out of the closet. Before finding his backpack, he stopped in front of the sliding glass doors to the backyard. His tent was still standing, and beyond that lay the woods that he remembered walking through with Timothy not too long ago. If only he could finish the tree fort some day with the friend who had saved his life, he thought to himself.

"If only I could have returned the favor and saved yours," Jacob said, now out loud. "I will make sure to repay you with prayer – you cared a lot about praying. Lots of us will be thinking of you by the time I am done."

Fifteen minutes later the bus arrived. Jacob climbed in and began looking for a seat. The first person he saw was a boy who seemed disturbingly pale and sickly. It was Jason Miller, the boy from Timothy's bus stop.

"That's odd," Jacob whispered. "He doesn't usually take this route..."

Jacob found a seat a few rows back. Sitting next to him was a girl who he had a crush on, but never had the courage to ask out on a date. It was Kaylee Anderson, the most talented soccer player in the school. She could out maneuver any boy on the field. Jacob found this to be the perfect coincidence: an opportunity in disguise.

Chapter 14

"Hi, Kaylee."

Kaylee smiled at him and then returned to reading her book. A minute or so passed and then, realizing that it would not be long before they arrived to school, he continued to attempt a conversation.

"Kaylee, can I ask you a question?"

"Sure, I guess I can't get back into what I was reading now. What is it?"

"Well, do you remember a while back when we were allowed to talk about religion and God? You know, a few years ago?"

"Shhh! What are you trying to do, get me into trouble? I can't talk about that!" Kaylee put her book away in her backpack and lifted it onto the seat in between her and Jacob.

"Alright, sorry... look, I will whisper more," Jacob apologized, scooting over. "Remember when you were interested in learning more about God and Timothy's faith? And you approached him with questions about what it was like to go to church and pray for people?"

"If you are referring to the fourth grade spring dance, I was just a child. I'm not going out with you too, if that's what you are getting at... Timothy was just an infatuation, and brief at that!"

"No – I mean yes, the school dance – but no, nothing about going out with anyone... what I am getting at is do you remember dancing with him on the last slow song? And you saw something in his eyes? And it made you begin to think about religion and how you were curious about it and thought it was inspiring that he stuck to his faith regardless of what people thought?"

"Yes, I do," she replied, subtly batting her eyes. "He was very charming. And there was always something about him. Hey, Jacob, I am so sorry for your friend; I just heard about it yesterday. If there is anything I could do, I would. You know that."

"Well that's just it! I think you can. I mean, we can. A bunch of us! He's been keeping us all in his prayers for quite a while, every day I am sure. And now I have this feeling that if we can return the favor then maybe it will help him. Do you know of anyone else who has showed interest before in faith? I won't tell anyone. I was thinking we could get a group together and say a few words for him. 'There is a power in numbers,' he once told me."

"I don't know, Jacob. We could get into big trouble and that is just with the teachers. There was one kid a few weeks back who got beat up for wearing a Jesus bracelet. I don't need that sort of attention."

The bus came to a final stop. Kaylee looked around in a very paranoid manner and saw that her friends were waiting for her outside.

"Hey, like I said, I am sorry Jacob. I really am. Timothy is a great guy, and I feel bad for making you give him the break-up letter. But I don't think I can help you."

Kaylee half-smiled but did not look Jacob in the eyes. She got out of her seat and cut in front of him as she made her way off the bus.

"Let me know if you change your mind!" Jacob said, getting a final word in.

Discouraged, he grabbed his backpack and began to walk down the aisle. Not getting much further than a few seats, he felt a shove into his shoulder. Jason gave him a disturbingly nasty look and cut him off, rushing off of the bus.

"Where do these kids get their manners? Their parents should be ashamed!" Jacob shouted, louder yet toward the end of the sentence.

First period passed by, but all Jacob could think about was Timothy and how he wanted to repay his friend. Not one other person except Kaylee had yet acknowledged his friend's tragedy, and she only had after being approached by Jacob. He found it so sad how many were self-centered in that way, and the more he obsessed over it the greater he became committed to finding as many people to pray for Timothy. Even if it was in spite of the world and all who seemed to only care for themselves, he would carry on. He then knew exactly who he would ask next: gym class was third period, and there was one person whom no one paid attention to.

"Hey, Nick, hey, over here!" Jacob called out from the bleachers.

Nick Pickiss was perhaps the most teased kid in the history of school, and his last name did not help matters out. A plump boy, Nick was rather awkward in several ways. Besides the way he dressed, he had a strangely pitched voice which always alluded to the fact that it was about to change; but it never actually did. Jacob knew that despite all of this, he had a beautiful heart and was extremely trustworthy. Nick also happened to be the same boy who Kaylee had mentioned got beat up for wearing the Jesus bracelet. Jacob had a strong feeling that Nick would be more than happy to help him and his friend Timothy.

Nick walked over to Jacob, who started to tie his gym shoes.

"Were you calling for me, Jacob? What can I do for you?"

"Hey, Nick. How are you today?"

"Well, a little sore! But I have been worse. I don't know, I suppose," Nick said, pausing for a moment. "How are you?"

Jacob looked around to see how much attention Nick was drawing to them, as his voice would often become very loud. Most of Nick's school mates attributed his loudness to the limited social activity he took part in.

"Hey, let's keep it down somewhat. I have something to ask you and I don't want to bring any attention."

"Oh okay, not a problem. Sorry! What's up?"

Nick continued to stand before Jacob, swaying his arms back and forth in an uncomfortable fashion.

"It's alright, relax. Have a seat next to me."

"Thanks," Nick replied, taking a seat.

"So listen. It is about Timothy. Did you hear?"

"Yes, I did; it was in the newspaper. My grandma told me all about it and I felt so bad. Why these things happen to such good people. Are you doing okay? And have you seen him?"

"I did; I left school early yesterday and went down to see him with my dad. He is in a coma right now but seems to be stable, at least more than on Sunday. Anyway, what I have to tell you may be a strange request. But are you up for something to do with God? I know you must be a little uneasy after your incident the other day."

"Of course, I don't let other people get in the way of how I express myself. I don't cower when it comes to what I believe in!"

"Great! That is great. Nick, I am thinking of becoming more religious but am just trying to find the right way to approach it, if that makes any sense. But Timothy had been acting strange the few days before he got hurt, like there was something greater about to happen. He just didn't know what it was and it went right over my head. I have a feeling there is more to what is going on. I have this urge to get together with a few people and pray for him. He always prayed for all of us, and he told me once about the power it had. Do you think we could get together sometime, maybe during recess and hold some sort of session for him?"

"Wow, in public like that?"

"Yes, I think so. I think that it will work out, but I just don't know how. I was hoping no one would pay any attention and that maybe people being blind to God would work out to our advantage. I have asked others like Kaylee Anderson, but she said no. I think she will come around. And, I trust her. But I don't think she wants to ruin her reputation and is hesitant because of that. But surely there are others – as many as we can get would be ideal. They can't suspend all of us!"

"Gee, I wouldn't be so sure about that, Jacob. They are getting pretty tight about offending others with personal beliefs."

"Nick, do you know of anyone else?"

"I don't really think so. I don't have a whole lot of friends these days."

"Well, let me get back to you Nick. Are you in?"

"Sure, I am in! Anything for Timothy; he's a real role model for us religious guys."

"Awesome! I promise it will be great."

Jacob stood up and walked away from the bleachers. Just as he stepped onto the floor, ready for the volleyball game that they had been practicing for the past several gym classes, the assistant principal walked in with Jason Miller at his side who was pointing at Jacob. Jacob's heart dropped as he watched Mr. Tulley approach the gym teacher. Ms. Dennison nodded and then in a split second Jacob found himself being approached by Mr. Tulley, as Jason stood off in the corner.

"Jacob, could you come with me please?" Mr. Tulley firmly requested.

Jacob looked around as all of the students had stopped to watch. He caught Nick out of the corner of his eye distancing himself from everyone else. Jacob followed Mr. Tulley to the office, and Ms. Dennison immediately resumed the class.

Jeremy, the same boy who had been kind to Timothy during recess a few days back, approached Nick as he had watched Jacob talk to him just minutes earlier.

"Nick, what happened?"

Nick, shocked that a kid like Jeremy was even acknowledging his existence, mustered up the courage to respond.

"I don't know," he said plainly.

"Hey, was he talking to you about praying for Timothy?"

"Um, how did you know that?"

"I spoke to Kaylee earlier and she told me in secret about what he was doing. I tried to talk Jason out of telling on Jacob, but he wouldn't listen. He overheard Jacob talking to Kaylee on the bus. I think he just ratted him out."

"Please don't tell on me!" Nick pleaded.

"Don't worry I'm not going to. I'm sorry for what's happening. I think Jacob is in trouble. Look, keep it to yourself that we talked about this, okay? I will make sure to do the same."

Jeremy walked away from Nick before anyone noticed that they had been talking. Ms. Dennison blew her whistle and each team took their sides as the class went on without Jacob.

Chapter 15

Timothy continued east on another dirt path, hoping to catch up to the angel who had carried away his mother. The image of the tear pinned to that angel's eye was now stuck in his mind, as was a sharp pain reaching inside his chest and pressing on his heart. His mother seemed more beautiful than Timothy had ever remembered and at the same time she was helpless in the hands of the unknown. There was no sign of them, however, as all he could see was a barren path and scattered trees to the south.

The monotony of the scenery continued without any indication that he was any closer to the first trial beginning. Just like the other lands within Eden, this one provided little insight for him to gauge how long it would be to travel from point to point. The skies were in fact returning to a darker state despite the same full-circle object hanging far above, but it was surely not related to the measure of time he was searching for; rather, it was related to a measure of evil. As much as it was reassuring to him that he could be nearing the climax of the first trial, there was still a thought in the back of his mind that caused for concern: there was little context provided to him that would indicate whether or not he was even moving in the right direction, let alone what precisely could cause for his disqualification. Thus he found himself once again being tested on his ability to assimilate to the virtue of patience. It was frustrating, but he pressed on at the same pace in hopes of at least finding his way out of the Fields of Horror, if not to simply catch up to the angel who was carrying his mother.

As with every decision that he decided to remain patient, an indication of progress at once was revealed. A large gate stood in the distance that had no wall or barrier to which it was attached. It stood alone in the middle of a road that turned to the east. As he approached it and veered off of the southern road, he at once ascertained that there was a sign above the gate. The writing on the sign appeared to be that of another language.

"It looks Arabic, or something of that nature," Timothy stated, finally reaching the gate.

He reached out for the gate handle, but could not seem to grasp his hand around it. It was as if his hand went right through the gate, with no relevant material existing for him to grasp. Timothy then took a few steps backward and looked to either side. Trying to go around it, he only found that there was an invisible barrier stopping him.

"Weird... I cannot grasp the visible handle and the barrier that I cannot see is tangible. Now what should I do?"

"Are you sure you want to know what is behind that gate?" a voice called from behind.

Timothy let out a great sigh at the familiar voice. He turned around and there was the wily lamb standing still. Its mouth completely closed at first, its lips then formed a shape that caused him to suspect it was smiling at him. The lamb tilted its head as if it was connecting to his mind; it was an attempt, it seemed, to determine what Timothy's next move would be.

"Are you here to just confuse me more?" Timothy questioned the lamb, hoping to this time get a straight answer.

"No. Not in the slightest degree. I am only here when you are not sure of the next step. Just consider me... let us see, how could you understand what I mean? I am an advisor to your spirit."

"Are you one that I can find to trust?" Timothy investigated.

"Did anyone ever tell you to not answer a question with a question? I had originally asked if you wanted to know what was behind that gate," the lamb smartly replied.

"I do want to know. I want to know whatever it is that will help me find my way successfully out of this trial. Much depends on this – but if I cannot trust you, then I guess I would say that I do not want to know."

"Well, that is fair enough. Let me give you a hint: you have a text that explains about the celestial realm, do you not? I bet you did not consider that one material guide that you were told to bring along with you. This land here is considered part of the celestial realm, as you are still in the heavens. So look in your book and decide; can you trust me or can't you?"

Timothy found that explanation to be very reasonable and, feeling ridiculous for not having considered the guide for which he had yet to use, he reached for it under his armor. Under his belt, it was in a pocket attached to the white robe he was still wearing.

"I thought that the armor and virtues was all I needed," Timothy then indicated, browsing through the guide. "Alright, let me see. We have a map and a listing of the angelic hierarchies. Wow, I was right about that!"

Timothy kept turning the pages, but there were many more than what there looked to be and after turning two hundred times he was still no more than an eighth of the way through.

"You are one of those boys too smart for your own good, aren't you?" the lamb called out. "Why don't you look in the appendix? Look for the topic 'Biblical Animals.'"

Timothy looked up at the lamb, astonished at his own lack of intelligence. He hadn't even thought of his book the whole time despite it being one of two things that Eryana had indicated to him to bring with him before ascending to Eden.

"Alright, so here is the appendix. There are quite a few topics that start with B," he told the lamb, alluding to the complexity he came across while searching.

"Try 'Animals of the Bible,'" the lamb further hinted.

"That could have been useful in the first place."

Timothy backtracked to the category of words that began with the letter A. He turned through hundreds of pages, but still was only at the words beginning with Ac.

"Hold on – just give me a moment," Timothy assured the lamb. "Here it is. 'Animals of the Bible – Instructions to find: Close the book and then open the book about a third of the way. Turn two finger-widths worth of pages to the right and then half of a finger- width to the left. Then ten-hundred more pages forward.' Are you serious?" Timothy shouted, rather alarmed at the ambiguity of the steps.

"Well, what do you expect using a material resource in the heavens like this? It cannot be completely spelled out for you!"

"Fine," Timothy agreed, letting out a sigh. "Here goes."

Timothy followed the instructions as perfectly as possible.

"'And now ten-hundred pages forward.' Okay, here we are: 'Animals of the Bible.' Now what do I do?"

"Read the introduction," the lamb explained.

Timothy slapped his forehead with his hand, again

catching himself to be looking too much into the complexity of the guide.

"'Welcome to a rather important, but still overlooked piece that offers a unique correlation between the Scriptures and the Celestial Realm. (For a complete listing of all referenced animals and their specific meanings, please refer to "Listing of Biblical Animals)."

"'Throughout your journey within the Kingdom of Heavenly Creatures, you may find yourself approaching or being approached by several types of animals, all of which have a specific function and duty. Although there are exactly two of each species, a male and female, housed in the upper peninsula of the Borderlands, there are also examples of individual creatures that freely roam about the kingdom's lands. In all instances, they are only discoverable within the Fields of Horror, but since those fields no longer serve any purpose since the Resurrection of Christ there would be a rare chance you should ever find them. However, from a historical perspective, we shall cover the meanings they once had.

"'For example, if you happen to run into a dove, then it would indicate that you are near an instance where your life is going to find itself regenerated. In respect to the Toll-Houses, an average sinner would likely have made their way through its entirety before they would be regenerated into a body of holding. (A body of holding is the mode you exist in until the Day of Judgment). There are a few cases where you would not see the dove at the end of the Toll-Houses. First instance: where you committed little sin on earth, and you were to only visit a toll briefly before being sent to the Southern Lands. A second case is one in which you had committed too much sin and could not afford the tolls to pay, and thus were about to be sent directly to

Satan's domain in the depths of earth. Please note that that is a rather rare occurrence where someone chooses to be possessed by a demon and fails to repent. In both of the above cases, you would have seen the dove from the very beginning as your new mode of existence would have been obvious.' What is this getting at? And what are these modes about? I see nothing about a lamb," Timothy inquired.

"Keep reading. When will you learn, if you only would wait but a moment longer!" the lamb snickered.

"'A second example of importance is the lamb. If you run into a lamb, then that would not only signal innocence, but also the merger of strength and weakness. As noted in the Bible, the wolf will at some point dine with the lamb. Therefore, the lamb will be guiding you to a much more fierce being. Additionally, the lamb may talk to you. Unlike the dove the lamb has been given this ability and it is strongly recommended that you ask it why this is so.'"

Timothy hesitated to read any further and looked up at the lamb. Clouds drew across the sky, making it even darker still. A light breeze began to flow over the fields and the sound of it whistled in his ears underneath the helmet on his head.

"Well, are you not going to ask?" the lamb approached Timothy, drawing within only a few footsteps.

"And why is it so – so that you can talk?" Timothy asked, gulping.

"That is quite simple. Speech is a gift from God and only afforded to intelligent creatures, like you. Animals do not speak; they do not inherit the Logos, or as you know it to be, the Word – the Word of God, given to us by way of the heart. It is only how we choose to use our ability for speech that defines who we are. So therefore, what am I exactly? If I cannot be an animal because I speak, then the meek sight I present must indicate that I am to be taken as a harmless creature. But there is always a balance. So with seeing me, you must know that my opposite is near."

"And if you are not an animal, then what kind of harmless creature are you?"

"I am simply a voice of reason. I represent the Word in you; the Word in you that you allow yourself to see with an open mind. And I present to you with a way out. Beyond those gates will allow you two different choices. The first choice will be to your immediate left and is in the form of descending stairs, to which you will be able to return to earth and live happily ever after with your mother and father. This would be only for a short time as you have not yet come to know how fast time passes, but no different than it would have been had you not made your way to Eden. Or, for the second choice, you can keep going, and pay your way through the Toll-Houses. That is the only way a person may pass. You will meet my opposite if you can survive until then. And if you get even further and defeat my opposite with the only solution – that is, the correct answer – you will move on to the Trial of the Son. If you fail at any point until then you will be sent back to earth and die. You must know where you travel to at that point. And certainly you will be of no use to your family and friends on earth if you are in the Southern Lands!

"Now this may or may not make perfect sense. But if you discover the answer to the riddles of the Trial of the Father, you will have understood what I mean about opposites and the whole point to the trial. Just remember that there is a balance to everything, but only one answer."

The lamb disappeared and Timothy was left again standing alone. He was overcome by feelings that suggested to him that it might be best to return home. If taking the stairway he could see his mother and father again, and perhaps that meant that she would be okay after all. Surely the lamb, representing the Word in Timothy, would be guiding him with honesty. Also, the book indicated to trust the lamb. He had no reason otherwise not to. Timothy most certainly did not want to die and began to forget the overarching goals that he was to complete.

Maybe, he continued to think, this was all an illusion. If he would just let go of it he could return to his parents and let them know it was going to be alright. After all, during his studies of Orthodoxy he learned to not rely on one's self and fully trust in God while putting others first. Therefore, he could let God worry about tomorrow.

Timothy turned back to the gate.

"I have the answer. I can't die or I will be of no use. Let's go home," he said out loud.

Opening the book, he searched the appendix for what the sign on the gate might mean. All he had to do was get to the other side and he would be finished with the strange land.

"'Gates: For the gate to the Kingdom of Heavenly Creatures, please see Kingdom of Heavenly Creatures, entrance,'" he read out loud. "'For the gate to the Fields of Horror, please see Fields of Horror, entrance.'"

"Not again! Fine," Timothy sputtered.

He turned to the words that began with the letter F and after turning the pages several times he came across "Fields of Horror, entrance." It gave a similar type of instruction as the reference to the Biblical Animals did, and following them he eventually came to the section of the guide that he was looking for: page 30,764, in a book no thicker than a typical dictionary.

"'The entrance to the Fields of Horror can be found

along the eastern path,'" Timothy continued to read, "'known as The Way of the Worm. Alternatively you may also choose to reach this point by taking the northeast route to The Way of the Four, if you are looking for a scenic journey. Either way, once you reach the gates you will see a very specific sign that may make you think it is written in an Arabic type language. It is actually Hebrew, to be specific. Translated, it simply says, "You now have little time to enter." This means that you have only moments before you will be engulfed in flames, as the Fields of Horror no longer permits for its discovery by intelligent creatures without that said creature experiencing it.

"'Within just moments, a wave of fire would in that case be fast approaching from behind you. The author of this text certainly hopes that you have read this section before you have read the sign.' Oh no!" Timothy gasped, fearing what might soon be coming. "Okay, think… think. Wait a moment, I haven't actually read it. I didn't read it, because I could not understand it! Great thinking Tim, let's see if there are more instructions!"

"'Otherwise, in order to find your way through, you must read the sign on the gate. Good luck! This concludes the section for Fields of Horror, entrance.'"

Fear began to increase within Timothy's mind. He did not know how long the moments were, and could think of no way that he would be prepared.

"What am I to do?" he asked himself.

Timothy put the guide back in his pocket and looking down at the ground he kept his eyes from the gate. This was certainly a very strange world, and perhaps more than strange it seemed rather unfair. It was almost as if there was no way for him to logically navigate through it. Thus far he had only been able to react with choice to what seemed to present itself, which clearly did so in its own time.

"I don't understand this!" he screamed.

At that very moment, his heart began to warm and the sky lightened up. A voice called out to him from above.

"Embrace the flame and do not stray. You have humbly conceded that you cannot understand and so virtuous you are. But you also found yourself drifting from the Truth. Do not continue to be led astray, for this will only leave you feeling to be in front of the gates of hell, longing for something you once briefly knew. Embrace the flame and return to the Light."

His heart continued to feel warm, even as the sky then darkened and the voice no longer called to him. He had felt the gift of the Word and now knew for certain what he was to do, as if the indescribable was now understood not by his mind but by his heart. Timothy looked up at the sign in the fear of God, and drew near.

"'You now have little time to enter,'" Timothy said, reading the sign out loud.

Whatever light had existed was now no longer. The ground shook and the winds howled. The gate itself became illuminated, reflecting a brightness that carried with it the power to destroy anything it chose: behind him the warmth of fire became unbearable, but he stood his ground and trusted the voice that he had heard.

Visions of Truth began to circle throughout his mind as the fire approached; as if a fog had been trapping his ability to think, he suddenly felt light and able. He saw then a vision of his father who had been held hostage by two men, one of them whom he recognized well. He was being taken to a monastery where the Devil had taken over the minds of several bishops and the monks themselves remained trapped in their rooms.

Next, his thoughts revealed to him the angel who was carrying his mother. She was being transported through the Fields of Horror and into a portal, and the portal led to the Southern Lands. It was now clear to Timothy that when he had first seen the teary angel above The Forest of the Wise it had been on a mission to guard his mother's last days on earth. The angel had felt sorrow to see Timothy, unknowing of what was underway.

And then his friend Jacob, who he seemed to have all but forgotten about, was shown to him being courageous and standing up for what he believed in.

"Do not fear," Timothy called out to the image he was seeing of Jacob.

Finally, the catastrophe being experienced by southern California, the demons leading the destructive efforts and the good angels who had chased them back to Satan were the next to pass through the whirlwind in his mind. As racing thoughts, these all left him as soon as they appeared.

"Now I remember what it is I was to do and that is to follow Your will!" Timothy screamed out.

Engulfed by the flames, he was carried to the other side of the gates. With eyes now one with Truth he was effortlessly able to see what lay before him, as if he had just been fully transformed from a boy into a wise elder of knowledge. He began walking as if he had never been touched by a flame. Ignoring the first path to return home, which would have been so easily taken, he continued on. With the disappearance of the flames a burning desire for the Lord was left in his heart.

A dove then flew overhead, signaling to him the great transformation of wisdom that had just taken place. He became confused as to whether he had sinned too little or sinned too much, but looking up at the bird he was concerned no longer. It was beautifully defined: majestic like an eagle and yet no larger than a pigeon. Circling about, it lifted off into the air and disappeared into the once-again darkening skies.

"Maybe I was transformed because of something quite irrelevant to my sin," he thought. "Could it be related to my conversion to that of an elder?"

Looking forward, the land revealed several ring shaped pits, each the diameter of no more than ten yards and only several inches deep. Positioned just above the pits were tall wooden platforms that had stairs for access. Beyond that, in the distance, was the eastern edge of the Grey Mountains and a castle that was built into the rock, similar to the entrance to the Kingdom of Heavenly Creatures.

"Ring-leaders, man your stations!" a creature called out from beyond.

This creature was quite large and as it came closer to the pits, it revealed itself to be a giant demon. It was escorting several other gaunt creatures, which then each climbed up to a platform to preside over their respective pits. Letting out cheers and jeers at Timothy, they then each raised a razor-sharp javelin into the air with one hand while beginning to shake their other in the shape of a fist.

"Next!" the large demon called out. "Who is next? Let's see... you out there! Young man! Come face your sins. Pass through us if you dare!"

Timothy looked around to make sure there was not another person it was referring to, and then stepped up to the demon. He realized he had not yet figured out why evil is permitted to exist, and hoped that this was finally his chance.

"There you are! Alright, here we go. Meet your first toll: pit of fear! That's it!"

"Pit of fear?" Timothy replied, not seeing it as overwhelmingly fearful. He stepped forward and the demon pushed him along to the first station.

"Okay, stand in the center there! That's it," the demonic monster told Timothy.

Timothy stepped down into the dirt pit and looked up at the creature that was standing on top of the respective wooden tower.

"Thank you, ring-master!" the first ring-leader called out. "By the decree of Satan himself, I declare that you failed to hold fear correctly. You feared incorrectly 972 times, and 234 of those times you knowingly did so. What say you?"

"Well, I say that is quite unfortunate because I do not see what exactly fear by itself has to do with sin," Timothy fearlessly replied.

"Oh, you are one of them huh? A question and answer for everything? This will be interesting indeed. Make that 973; you failed 973 times to hold fear correctly!"

The demon set aside its pitchfork, stepped down from the high-rising platform and climbed down the stairs. It then approached Timothy in the pit.

"Do you know fear, man?" it exclaimed, opening its mouth and eyes wide. "I will show you fear!"

The evil creature transformed itself into an image Timothy had once seen in a dream: a man with a hooded cloak. The pit around him conveniently transformed into his bedroom, and he then found himself looking out the same window that he had once peered through in a dream. Unable to help or control the situation, the dream started again before his eyes as his body and mind was forced to reenact it. He tripped over his cat, looked out the window and saw a face pressed up against the glass. The scene then fast forwarded itself and Timothy, instead of standing, was lying in bed. He opened his eyes to the darkness and could see a figure approaching him. It was the same face from the window, slowly moving closer. Unlike the dream he had had, there was nowhere to run or hide: he was trapped in the corner of the room and the face, slowly moving closer, was more visible until it was only inches from him. The unidentifiable man then proceeded to scream aloud and, as Timothy's heart was racing, Timothy also cried out with an indiscernible voice.

The bedroom at once diminished as the pit returned its original form. Timothy looked around and then at himself, still dressed in the armor he was given. The hooded man spun like a tornado and transformed back into the demon.

"You did not fear God; instead you feared what He wasn't! That pleased us! But we are not who you must ultimately answer to. Do you now see what fear is?"

Before Timothy had a chance to respond, the demon speedily climbed back up the stairs and returned to the platform with his javelin in hand. Exhausted, he wiped his face dry with the sleeve of his robe and stood up tall, now able to understand in his heart that the fear being referred to was more specifically the virtue of fear.

"Yes, I see what you mean," he cried out.

"Very well, we shall now take payment! May the collectors of fear come out," it shouted, spreading its arms wide and looking down into the pit.

Timothy began to feel cold and started to shiver. Attempting to wrap his body with his arms, he realized he could not move; once again he had no control over his self. Miniature demons about half the size of Timothy then snuck up out from under the dirt and circled around him.

"Find enough memories where he correctly used fear

– to account for a number equal to half of how many times he incorrectly used fear – and strip them from him!" the ring-leader commanded the spirits.

The spirits jumped into his body and Timothy felt his heart stop. Afraid of death, a sense of impending doom overcame him and still unable to move his legs or arms he began to wince until his eyes closed. A deep emotional pain he experienced, as memories of fearing the awesomeness of God began to leak out from his mind and into the hands of the demons, leaving him to feel rather inadequate. By the time the demons found their last item for collection, they had robbed from him exactly half as many memories – in which he had properly showed fear of God – as he had memories of doing so incorrectly. They then immediately left his body and he collapsed to the ground. The creatures laughed at his helplessness.

"I feel so sad!" Timothy called out. "It is as if I feel I have not prayed and worshiped enough. I can't seem to recall any of the memories of mornings when I know I woke up for prayer. Where are they?" Timothy began scratching his head, confused.

"That is your first payment. Now you will face your Creator on the Day of Judgment, with all the less to show for! That is, if that day ever arrives... now get out of my sight you pathetic little weasel!"

As the warden of the grounds, the large demon came back to escort Timothy to the second pit. Feeling emotionally battered, he walked now much slower and was no longer standing tall with courage.

"Okay, jump into the next!" his chaperon commanded.

Timothy did not obey the command and so the demon pushed him forward. He looked up and saw the second ring-leader. This one had wings and, without delay, it picked up a scroll and began to read out loud.

"By decree of Satan himself, I declare that you failed to hold honesty correctly. You were dishonest... wait, this can't be right – only two times? Ring-master, what is this!"

"I dunno, why don't you come down here and show me. My eyes see only so far!"

The ring-leader jumped off of the platform and flew down to the master. Timothy remained quiet, particularly thankful that he had led a fairly honest life in the eyes of the Lord.

"Is this some sort of a mistake? Did you jot this down here on this parchment incorrectly?" the ring-leader scolded, accusing the master of having incorrectly documented the record.

"Why, it can't be! I set those there for you and I was the only one other to handle them... say, what are you trying to get at?"

"Two times? That is impossible. How could someone only give in to dishonesty two times? Preposterous! Are you sure?"

"Yes, leader, yes. That is correct. He must have not been properly tempted."

The ring-leader rolled up the scroll, bopped the master over the head and flew back onto the platform, continuing with the process of toll-collecting.

"As I was saying, two times; you only once did this knowingly," the demon continued, as if it was painful to speak to an extremely honest human such as Timothy. "What say you?"

Timothy thought back to the last time he was dishonest. Within his mind he began to replay the instance where he explained to Jacob about the crazy woman who had given him the book.

"So what was up with that crazy woman, Tim?" Jacob had asked him but a few days ago. "Dad told me all about it! What a strange world it is. I am almost afraid to go off on our own at the fair!"

"Oh, I am not really sure. She just mistook me for someone else," Timothy had replied.

Timothy recalled having felt extremely uncomfortable not telling the truth.

"I am deeply sorry," Timothy spoke to the ring-leader after revisiting the memory.

"Very well, but not good enough!" the winged creature responded.

It flew again off of the platform and went head-first inside of Timothy's chest. Within a short moment, Timothy put his hands on his stomach as if he was going to be sick. An extreme sense of nausea crept upwards and he immediately turned pale, bringing himself to the ground on both knees.

"I feel so sick. I can't bear this... please stop!" Timothy cried in agony.

The demon inside of him started to bounce around and Timothy looked as if he was going to vomit. Timothy opened his mouth wide and a single vision flew out: a memory of Timothy being honest. Feeling now that he had led a particularly dishonest life, Timothy cried out with sorrow as the demon returned to the podium.

"I am so sorry; I should have been honest," Timothy confessed. "I should have told Jacob about that woman. I betrayed him. Poor Jacob – I will apologize to him for certain!"

He then cupped his face into his hands and wept uncontrollably. The ring-master grabbed him and trotted toward the third ring.

On his way there Timothy found his mind to be bereft of dignity and unconditionally submitted his mind to despair. However, at the same time he felt his heart begin to warm up, which caused him to at last lift his chin up: he felt courageous once again.

Also, considering the deep warming presence in his heart, he found that his surroundings were surreal in comparison to it. It was as if the evil he could see did not exist because the warmth was so hopeful. Suspicious of the inequalities between his senses, he stopped and stared at the ring-master. He realized that like any egocentric person he had been only preoccupied with his survival and had forgotten to use the very first gift that he was blessed with. With this realization, Timothy drew his mind down into his heart and processed the truth in lieu of the material.

"Wait, what are you doing? Hurry along now. Stop staring! Hey you, I am talking to you!"

Timothy then saw the evil creatures for what they were: something only if acknowledged. Like only having been a figment of his imagination, their physicality had disappeared; his virtuous memories returned to him as he realized that their substance had evaporated into the air. All that was left was the voice of the master chastising him.

"I am talking to you now!" it continued to taunt Timothy. "You will be sorry; I will make sure you have nothing left about you that it is good by the time we are done with you!"

Timothy walked on so that he could no longer even hear the voice and he drew closer to the castle. At that very moment the dark clouds opened up and revealed a bright light as his cross began to glow. He felt a deep connection to a higher power but, consistent with his recent experiences, a disparity came into play: the ground revealed to him a completely different sensation than the skies. As the winds sped up the land beneath him intermittently shook. Weary, Timothy halted and turned his head back to find a cloud of dust inching forward underneath the earth. Instinctively, he began running toward higher ground, which happened to be in the direction of the castle. But the field inclined to a degree that caused his breathing to become labored. He felt the urge for more energy, and as if there were no time more perfect than that point, he stopped for a moment and pulled the potion out of his pocket and squeezed a few drops out of the malleable container. Running again, he covered nearly half the distance that was between him and the castle entrance, hoping that he would find the answer to the trial soon. But no further he could continue and he fell to the ground, briefly unconscious as a result of exasperation.

The fields violently shook as a potent vibration focused beneath him. Covered now by dust and the air barely breathable, Timothy looked down at his chest and saw the relic imposing its powerful glow into the surrounding area. In response, the powerful force then split the land beneath him. Forced to one side or another, he tossed himself over to the left and then all became silent.

Attempting to stand up, the surface abruptly vibrated once more and forced him back onto the ground. Lying now on his back, he saw what seemed to be a perfectly arranged order of events that finally led to an explosion of rocky soil, which only his eyes could detect. If front of him, where the cracked ground had ceased to split, a giant worm roared up into the air and towered over Timothy, sending chills down his spine. The silence was replaced by a dull ringing as fragments of stone and clumps of dirt slapped him across the face, briefly knocking him yet again unconscious. Upon gathering his senses, and at last fully functional, he saw the fanged worm ready to devour him whole.

"What do you want with me?" Timothy demanded of the worm. "What are you? I want to go home!" he began to cry out with tearless emotions.

"I am the opposite of what you seek, and I am the creator of the darkness that blinds your sight. The soul thief I am, and I have come to send you to your doom. You have failed in your task and now you shall die! You are weakened and bereft of good deeds and you shall wallow in misery. But there is more!"

The giant worm began salivating and turned itself into a serpent, decreasing in size but still able to encroach on what little space Timothy had left to himself. He drew his sword only to wield it for a brief moment; the serpent flung its wily tongue forward to knock it down. Timothy symbolically felt his own spirit fall with it.

"What do you think you possess to defeat me, the Sword of the Spirit or a Belt of Righteousness? Your virtues and powers are meaningless, as you are but an insignificant factor in the plan of God. You will be left here to wander just as your grandfather's soul did following his last earthly breath. Thus you certainly are no saint like Paul. There shall be no vestibule waiting for you to watch over the ones you love with prayer.

"And what is more, let us begin to contemplate the quandary of your dear mother… your dear mother," the serpent said, maniacally spurting off laugher, "she was attacked by a host of demons, which led to her misfortunes. And she shall also die like you, only beforehand will be possessed with wickedness to serve me until the end of days! Well, that is if you choose that for her."

The serpent transformed into a devilish man that was

the epitome of a vampire, which Timothy only otherwise knew through myths and urban legends. There was no doubt about it: he had met Satan himself. And Timothy, neither able to speak nor use any virtues or powers given to him by God through the Eleven Elders, remained helpless on the ground.

"I offer you a deal. Have you ever wanted to deal with the best – the best of the best? I can have a heart too as I can offer you choice. That is surely a display of remorse over your sorry existence. That is, if it benefits me! And what would benefit me more than having the three of you off of my domain on earth. Your grandfather, gone! You, gone! Your father… oh, he is such a detective; he is always, always playing the detective. Well he has detected more than he can handle. Would you give him up for your mother's sake? She has not quite finished leaving the earth as of yet. I can give you a chance to say goodbye to her. Oh how you would like that. But you must choose in order for me to take him. Yes, my power feeds off of your choice even when there is only one viable option."

Satan turned around and faced the castle. With a gangly hand he waved his red cape in a circular motion. Timothy watched him transform again, this time into a beautiful angel. In fact, he was more beautiful than anything Timothy had seen before on earth or in Eden; tempted Timothy was to please the demonic angel. Appearing as Lucifer, he was dressed in shining armor and had great wings that made any other angel seem rather insignificant. If it was not for him still revealing dangerous fangs, Timothy would have believed he was any good angel that he claimed to be. Two gold-framed portals then appeared behind Lucifer, which each had stairs inside of them that lead down to two very different paths.

"Choose the left," the Devil continued, "and you will find yourself saying goodbye to your mother. I promise you that she will be spared of the demonic possession that is otherwise guaranteed to occur. You will painlessly go to the Southern Lands with your father and she will join you both there. Choose the right," he went on, pointing at the other portal, "and your father can keep his life, but your mother will die under the possession of demons. And you will be tormented for the rest of your earthly life knowing you not only had failed here in these lands, but also had failed your mother. What would you have?"

The choices given to him were clearly constructed so that he would choose the path that would benefit Lucifer. Timothy stood up and, resisting the incapacitating force, walked over to his sword. Picking it up, he placed it back in his sheath and walked past the most powerful fallen angel that ever existed. Lucifer was shocked, but, raising his eyebrows, he continued to wait for Timothy's response. Pondering over his two very different choices, Timothy returned before the Devil and took a deep breath.

"Could the answer be according to the old adage that reveals the angel to be on the right and the demon to be on the left? Am I being presented with one choice that is clearly benevolent, while the other is undoubtedly malevolent? No, it would be not be any such combination. I have chosen," Timothy stated plainly.

"And?"

"I choose neither way: for you are nothing without God and the one path only knows Truth, of which you could not offer with your guileful tongue!"

Timothy unsheathed his sword, smashed his shield into Lucifer's side, and took a swipe deep into Satan's body. Lucifer's fiery mouth dropped open as he then fell to his knees. His body remained the same, but his face transformed back into the serpent he was.

"You do not exist," Timothy continued, "and neither does evil, in and of itself. Rather, evil is only the result of one steering away from the path that would have led toward righteousness – just as you were the first to initiate doom when you left the First Hierarchy in vanity. You are no more powerful here than you were the day you chose your destiny!"

Everything turned black, save the glowing relic still hanging around Timothy's neck. A wailing cry blurted out, which pierced Timothy's ears, reminiscent of the now identifiable being from his dream. After sending a shockwave of horror through the surrounding mountains, the cries slowly disappeared as if they were falling far away into the depths below and Satan's being degenerated into nothingness. The portals then shrunk in size, remaining only as a desolate ball of darkness until they finally met the same fate as the conjurer who had designed them; they dissolved into the midst of the air as a single shining star popped into the skies above, revealing only peace. Green grass and tall trees formed out of the murky landscape and glowed under the dawn and, at last to unfold, a long bridge made of purple colored silk grew out from the castle. Looking ahead, Timothy's eyes blazed with a new presence.

Landing before him were twelve stairs. They appeared to be very similar to those which he had climbed from the elevator in his dream; without delay, Timothy stepped upward and walked along the silken-paved bridge. Before too long, a transparent yet glowing image of a white-bearded man stood halfway along, holding a scepter also like in a dream he once had. Only it was not a reflection of his future self. It was a different man, whom he had not come to know as well as he would have liked to.

"Grandpa?" Timothy called out.

"I too am only a figment, but out of goodness I come to you. Do not bother coming forward, for there is nothing for you to wrap your arms around. You did well and successfully passed the first trial: The Trial of the Father. Waiting for you are the Trials of the Son and of the Holy Spirit.

"You have completed what I have not been able to do – what I was not ultimately destined for. I too once tried to pass through these lands, but it was not meant for me to fulfill the prophecy. Rather, in weakness my heart was tricked into choosing for you and your father to live on. And so I returned to earth after bartering my spirit for the sake of you both. Then, without the cross that had at one time offered my body additional protection from harm, I succumbed to the evil that was imposed on me. An earthly death I encountered and as such I wandered these lands constantly, having lost both my body and spirit. But with your ultimate success my spirit has now been freed! I may now rest in the Southern Lands in wait for my body to resurrect; in joining then with my spirit, I will find my soul once again to be complete. You have Satan's wily plan for me indeed!

"Yes you, my grandson, chose wisely – for there was really no additional risk to your father or mother other than what it will regardless be. You are one step ahead of me at a much earlier stage in life; if only I had had the insight to know that Satan holds no power over you other than that which you give him. Evil, my dear boy, is in fact only relative as you have accurately surmised. It is relative to us, but not absolute to God. It only exists as the path away from God. In essence, good is the only true thing to exist and we are striving for that in our daily lives as God calls us home.

"This trial was a representation of the balance between the two forces. Like earth, it is a middle-ground where we can choose to go toward or away from the Almighty. And now you see that evil is no more than a distraction from grace, led by a fallen angel who relies on the choices of humans on earth. And that is why your destiny is so important, Timothy… that is why you received the cross – it only took my death for me to realize it. Finish these two trials and find the remaining answers. Prove yourself to be the elder that I have failed to be. And share the gifts given to you with those whom you meet. The Second Coming will appear at the right time, in its own time. That time being something we can hardly measure."

Timothy ran toward his grandfather, ignoring his statement about being only a spiritual figment. Approaching within inches and opening his arms, Timothy grasped only the air. He looked up at the skies, crossed himself, and made haste to the castle gates. They opened without delay, indicating that the second trial was about to begin.

Chapter 16

Nighttime arrived over the western United States, ending a day of crisis that had affected tens of millions. Hospital beds had soon become full with victims in critical condition. These patients were airlifted as far north as southern Oregon, to St. Catherine's Medical Center. Canobee, a city with a metropolitan population of 300,000, had several hospitals but St. Catherine's Medical Center was the best equipped for participation in disaster relief efforts.

The moon and stars not visible, helicopters arrived on the hospital's landing pad under darkened clouds. In fact, every night since the powerful wind and rain storm had hit the region over four days prior, St. Catherine's stood without moon or starlight after sunset; only street and parking lot lights, in addition to light emanating from the hundreds of hospital windows, could be seen there by the naked eye. It was certainly more than ominous to those few who could read into such situations as the conditions were optimal for evil to travel under the veil of obscurity.

As the clock struck midnight the main entrance doors at the lower level opened, letting in a gust of wind. A small army of twelve invisible demons led by Captain Balagad entered through. Prepared they were to wage spiritual warfare against any good opposition that would attempt to protect Timothy from the demonic powers.

To the dark armies below earth, word had traveled fast of Satan's return from the Fields of Horror. Once more he had been banished, having been himself tricked into believing he could hold unconditional power over the corrupted lands. But Timothy had exposed his presence to be no more than an illusion. He had once again taken with him great rage and wrath, this time missing an opportunity to foil The Prophecy of the Sacred Cross, which would have ultimately crushed all hope for the Eldership of the Twelve. Timothy's fate was still tied to his own choice, but now was without direct influence of the Prince of Evil.

Waiting for Satan's return was Judas, who had been waiting to speak with him to determine the next steps in a battle for the ages. Balagad, the new captain who had replaced the demon defeated by Eryana in The Forest of the Wise, was already on his way to rob Timothy of his cross; Satan had revealed himself to be pleased with Judas' foresight in commanding Balagad to do so.

"If good overcame evil from above, then from below evil shall overcome what is good at whatever cost necessary. The balance must be maintained," were the words from the Devil's mouth to Judas.

Balagad led his twelve through the lower level hallways, unseen until reaching the main elevator. Then, unable to risk for the coming events to be seen by humans as supernatural, they turned into visible beings; it was expected that the demons would not go unchallenged by their enemies, and as such they were obligated to refrain from providing insight of their nature to any bystanders that could, as an unintended consequence, suggest that the invisible world did exist. Providing a reason for one to contemplate the Lord's existence was especially counterproductive to their mission. Therefore, what better was there a way than to pin evil activities to mankind? This was usually a very successful attempt at misdirecting those easily swayed by only what their eyes could see.

There standing was the group of thirteen intruders,

comprised of both the male and female gender. Their guise was, however, nearly identical to one another and to one of hyper-vigilance they could have been interpreted to be a foreign species, defeating the purpose of their initial transformation. Hair black and sleek, they wore full-length leather jackets and carried sheathed swords that were secured over their backs. Their shoes came to a sharp point, having the capability to be nearly as lethal as their blades if used in the correct manner. Finally, their faces were rather cliché: pale with sharp white fangs hanging over their bottom lip, along with dark green eyes. Together, their attributes seemed to complete the rough, dangerous image that left for little interpretation.

"We do not know what we will encounter on floor three, but let's split and each group can take one of these two elevators. I am sure that there is ample protection in hiding for the boy. Try and limit the attention we cause; we do not need to turn this into a great affair and attract any human authorities or great angelic forces," Balagad said to his crew.

History had taught him a lesson many times that it did not take much at all to create a chain reaction that would lead to an uncontrollable battle. As with every action, there was a reaction. He recalled the assassination of the heir to the Austrian throne that set off World War I, which had been a result of a demonic possession of the assailant. One event had led to another and before long a parallel battle on earth had broken out, between the heavens and the underworld. In the end, however, and more often than not, the good would prevail in direct combat and the losses proved detrimental to Satan. It was best to keep to the task at hand, winning the war in the long run using more passive forms of trickery.

Up the elevator they traveled until it at last approached floor three. The doors opened, and out they came into the intensive care ward where Timothy and his mother lay unaware in one of the rooms, dependent for protection. Balagad ordered half of the demons to wait outside at the nursing station, and, obeying, they proceeded to draw their swords at the screaming medical staff.

"Away from the phones; step back and there will be no hurt," one demon called out.

Another sprinted to a panel of light switches and placed them in the off position, as a few nurses hid under nearby workstations.

Guardian angels appeared from behind each person and remained calm. They were fully aware of their inferiority to the intruders. After all, they were the least powerful angels of the Third Hierarchy; Balagad had brought with him demons equal to the Powers of the Second Hierarchy. For a few moments, the good and evil angels stared at each other with the hope that neither side would make any drastic move. The heavenly angels then conceded, backing away into the shadows and looking on with saddened eyes; as they drew back their hidden wings that were visible to only the invisible, the smiles of the fanged creatures were wide with pleasure. Balagad, astutely aware of the most minor of details, turned his head toward the six who were watching the staff. He growled at them and they immediately wiped the smile off of their faces, realizing that revealing their unnaturally sharp teeth was not a wise idea.

Continuing on, Balagad brought the other six with him and they passed by each room until they saw familiar name labels. And not four doors down, there posted was what he had been looking for: T. Petrov and C. Petrov.

"How convenient it is that they are together," he grinned, showing his own fangs and salivating with pleasure.

Balagad opened the door carefully as the six demons

followed him into the dark. Their green eyes saw through the lightless air without difficulty, perhaps as well or better than they did when darkness was not present. As far as they could sense, no other creatures were there and so he approached the bed that Timothy lay in.

"Guard the doors, you two!" he called out. "And you two: guard the windows and intently look for any strange aura approaching. And to the remaining," he pointed at the last two demons, both female and better equipped to possess a woman's spirit, "get ready to take over his mother's soul. Satan has just sweetened the pot with another servant and when she dies, she'll be indebted to him!"

It was almost too good to be true; or rather to him it was too evil to be false – that would better suit how he looked at the opportunity. The prince would be very pleased and what a chance it was for Balagad to revive his reputation, battered after nearly being captured by the two Archangels and a Principality earlier that day. Without delay, he hunched down over Timothy's bed and reached out with long fingers and sharp nails. Lifting up the cross and ready to snatch it off of his neck, he immediately dropped it back to its original position.

"This is not it!" he screamed, piercing the night with a screech that reached to every point inside of the hospital. "It is gone; this is a fake!"

The six demons hissed and raised their heads up toward the ceiling, cursing the situation at hand.

"Take her spirit under your control now," Balagad commanded of his subordinates, very irate and not wanting to risk the chance of further failure. "We should kill the boy now, and kill her! How could this be possible – where is it... where is it?"

Balagad continued ranting, not able to control the

commotion he was creating. As he closed his mouth and walked over to Candice's bed, he calmed down and made himself ready to observe the possession. As the two demons were about to transfer their spirits into hers, a loud fuss was heard outside of the room. Frustrated, Balagad let out another cry and went for the door to check matters out.

"You two stay by the windows and you two continue with the possession. You two," he then pointed to the two demons guarding the door, "come with me now!"

They walked out into the hallway and before Balagad could assess, let alone control, what the disturbance was, he realized it was much too late to act: three men had traveled up the elevator having heard noise. After spotting the six evil men, they had tried to escape and run for help, but all except one had been immediately slain by sword.

"One escaped back into the elevator. We had to try to stop them. I think we better leave before things get out of control, captain," a demon called out, realizing the possible chain of events that could have been initiated.

Balagad looked over at the hostages. Behind them the Guardian angels were still hovering and staring. They seemed rather unsettled, as if they were anticipating further action to be near. Taking this as a hint, Balagad immediately ran back for Timothy's room. But a messenger of the Light had quickly taken over, and there battling was Jeneral himself against two of Balagad's forces. The two female demons were nowhere to be found.

The dark captain drew his sword at that very moment as the gleaning weapon of the Principality had effortlessly overpowered his combatants; the evil spells they had uttered were of no aid. They were henceforth sent to the abyss and joined their demonic predecessors who had fallen in battle before them, bound until the Judgment following the Great Tribulation.

Balagad dared Jeneral to try the same on him, as it was now just the two to engage in a fight without outside influence. The eight henchmen remaining could not risk letting the civilians free, as two were standing before the elevator, expecting the escapee's sought after recourse to return at any moment.

For Jeneral's part, he was alone in his efforts. His counterparts Michael and Gabriel would have been there with him from the start if they were to be of help. Any other assistance that could support him would potentially be on their way, but only in response to the killing of two men. That would not be for some time, however, and the time was now.

Although Jeneral was an angel of the Third Hierarchy, as a Principality he carried as much strength as that of an angelic Virtue. And so was his enemy's strength of equal force; they had each met their match as their swords clashed. Balagad's was a thirty-nine inch long two-handed blade. It was made of steel and reminiscent of a typical twelfth-century European warrior. He claimed to have stolen it from a French King upon leading him to his death, and it had been subsequently cursed and re-forged in the fires of hell. Then, it was finally blessed – with a curse – by Satan as he was pleased with Balagad's aptitude for exemplifying great acts of wrath. Jeneral's weapon of choice, on the other hand, was much more ancient and in no way originated from a material source. The ever-burning Light of Love had gloriously generated a weapon capable of defending one against the most challenging spiritual warfare that could present itself to an angel of his standing. In fact, Jeneral was the Chief Principality and presided over the three others on earth. Additionally, he had respectfully refused promotion to positions as high as a Dominion of the Second Hierarchy. His reason was simple: he loved man with such a genuine quality that he felt his mission was to remain on earth, guarding them against the destructive forces of evil. How much it pained him to witness the recent happenings on earth.

They lifted themselves up into the air, halfway between the ceiling and floor. Exchanging blows of steel packed with opposing force, they each let out cries of battle; Jeneral belted out sweet sounds of triumphant power while Balagad let out gloomy vibrations of despair. Timothy and Candice, on the other side of the room, lay still in what was an ironic disparity of peace and strife packed into one small space.

Continuing as if time did not exist, their wings flapped vigorously in an effort to keep still in one place. But the balance could not last indefinitely. Jeneral was the first to show greater strength as he distracted Balagad with sounds of grace humming from his vocal chords, which allowed him to strike his bright sword through the upper portion of Balagad's right wing. Then, unable to propel himself back into the air without unsteadiness, Balagad was forced to remain on the floor and stumbled backward into the wall. Jeneral flew in for a final blow, but his enemy dodged to the side and, with his sword, wreaked the good angel's back, inserting into it a poisonous concoction of dark magic. Jeneral was instantly weakened and, both of them now handicapped, they continued to spar in the darkness which was disturbed only by the delicate aura of grace.

Sirens were then heard from afar, as man had finally responded to the foiled covert operation. Both warriors knew of the potential unintended consequences of the spiritual warfare being exposed, but they were now both committed to being in a palpable form – Balagad had converted himself prior to the fight, and Jeneral could not fight a material being in an immaterial form.

At this point it was clear to them both that Timothy would not be harmed; most likely the fight would end with no declared winner. Each sensed legions of their own now approaching in invisible form, ready to participate in a battle that had gone already too far. But the end had come sooner than either of them had expected, for one of the hostages outside of the room had taken a stand against the undercover demons and courageously met her end attempting to escape. Jeneral, distracted for a brief moment by the human's death, found sorrow to briefly overtake him and so Balagad took the opportunity to pierce his sword through the Principality's heart. The good intelligent creature had made a fatal error and so his soul became still; with a deathly pallor he collapsed to the ground.

Balagad was aware of his own loss to injury and made a hasty escape with his eight remaining demons to the elevator. The moment the doors closed, they turned their form back to invisible evil spirits and escaped unnoticed. Police cars had just arrived, assuming the hostile group of men was still on the third floor with the hostages.

Jeneral followed suit; he also turned into an indiscernible form with the battle now over. Mortally wounded, he could not escape the room; angels and demons could perish at the hands of one another and a great angel like him was certainly not an exception. Bright rays of light then descended over him, as St. Catherine was once again given the opportunity to return to earth and, under the powers of Corinth, she carried Jeneral off to the Kingdom of Heavenly Creatures. She speedily traveled through the forest and plains with him barely alive on her back.

Chapter 16

In the end, there was not a morsel of evidence of anything supernatural left for man to find, and left to be interpreted was the unexplainable disappearance of thirteen intruders along with extensive damage done to the intensive care room, which housed a mother and son.

———

Returning back to his lair, Balagad had much news to report. On the one hand, great strides had been made on the local front. Jeneral, considered an irreplaceable angel, attending to the welfare of hundreds of millions of persons, had been defeated at the hands of evil. On the other, the sacred cross had disappeared. Although it was well known that Timothy had the parallel version in the heavens, there now would be great uncertainty as to what would happen if he were to make his descent back to earth under successful terms. The latter of the two reports was the biggest item for consideration; who had the relic was a discussion that Balagad feared to have with his superiors. Perhaps, he thought, it would not matter, as whoever might have the cross may have already miscalculated his or her efforts, unknowing of the danger that holding it could ensue. One fact was for certain: Jeneral was not the one possessing it. Although he had been in a material form and could acquire material things at that point, he was certainly too intelligent to have risked leaving with it; the cross would have more likely been apprehended by the demons as only Timothy had a certain level of mystical protection through the Holy Spirit, offering him protection in addition to the heavenly angels.

In his chamber, Balagad heard footsteps approach. Judas had just returned from the Prince's castle, in the same amount of time it had taken Balagad to return; he had no wings and was a much slower creature than the fallen angels. Judas then opened the door to Balagad's cell, entering without notice.

"Balagad, my good captain! I have heard you were hurt, and how is your wing? Let me have a look."

"It's of no consequence, General Judas. I will be fine," he replied, hoping Judas would not come too close.

Judas had the ability to make even the most foul of creatures uncomfortable. This was attributed to how close he was to the Prince of Darkness, thus having significant influence over the affairs of the underworld.

"No, it is alright... I won't bite," Judas promised, half-jokingly.

Looking at his wound, Balagad certainly had not come out of his fight unscathed. In fact, he had to be carried back by his own men, as having a broken wing meant that he would have traveled no faster than a creature like Judas.

"That certainly does not look to be good, no, it certainly is not. Who was able to inflict this deep wound into you? I will call at once for a spell-worker, who can bring appropriate integrity back to your dark wing."

"It was Jeneral, my liege," Balagad bluntly stated.

"Ahh... Jeneral you say? You had a battle with the likes of him? You are lucky, certainly in the least, to not be bound by chains at this time! Did you take him on single handedly?"

"Yes; there were no others with me. Eight were watching carefully the humans who were standing by. Two Jeneral slayed before I could stop him. And the other two I cannot account for. I did not have a moment to spare once I inflicted a mortal wound on the Principality."

"Well that is certainly unfortunate about the two... I am sorry, did you say, 'mortal wound?' Jeneral? The

Principality, Jeneral? Is no more?"

"That is what I report. I pierced his heart with poison."

Judas let out a cry of victory, spreading out his arms into the air.

"What great news! What absolutely timely news! Just think, if we were able to cause harrowing death just now to an entire region, what now without his oversight? This is certainly worth a battle victory in and of itself. Wait until Satan hears of this."

"That is not the only news," Balagad added, returning to a dull expression.

"I am sorry, what else is there? Oh, I cannot believe I did not even ask. Should I? You were able to also grab the cross and snatch the relic?" Judas said, beginning to look extremely concerned.

"I must report that before my battle with Jeneral, I bent down to take the chain holding our prize from around the boy's neck. But it was not what I sought for; it was a counterfeit. Some creature got to him before us. It was certainly not Jeneral, as his fortune was inevitably slim. We have let it slip through our fingers once again."

Judas turned away from his subordinate and began pacing, with his hands folded behind his hunched over back.

"Not good! Not good!"

"And... I am not sure of his mother, Candice Petrov. The two I cannot account for are the females I brought to possess her soul. I do not know if either one was successful."

Judas turned back to Balagad, and through his fangs he hissed in anger.

"This will not bode well. If she is not possessed, there is all the less bartering we can do if Timothy has success in Eden. There are too many unknowns, and too many variables. We must get to Father John at once. Perhaps he has the cross, or knows where it is. Oh, what now to do with him: to slay him or to possess him? Curse this man! And you, captain. You are most fortunate of your victory. That will save you I am sure from being punished for the other failures you have now admitted to."

Judas paused, staring deep into Balagad's eyes.

"You will come with me to Saint Peter's Monastery," Judas continued, "where there is work to be done. We will be escorted there for time's sake. Forget about healing, we leave within the hour!"

Judas left the cell and slammed shut the door. Balagad looked down at the ground, uncertain of how to react. Within moments he found just what he needed to effectively continue: rage. He stood up and gathered his two top lieutenants.

Meeting up with Judas shortly after, they voyaged through the tunnels beneath the earth until surfacing at the nearest portal to New York State. Soaring through the air, they arrived at Saint Peter's Monastery by dawn. It was now Thursday; seven days had passed on earth since Timothy dreamt of falling through the air. In the celestial and invisible worlds, however, so many more than that seemed to have transpired, at least from the perspective of a boy.

Changing to corporeal form, Balagad, assisted by his two aides, appeared beside Judas who himself, through the eyes of men, would have seemed to be flying through the air alone up until that point. Descending to the remote community deep in the heart of New York, they barged through the gates and there was no sign of humanity, as all of the monks had been ordered to confinement by the new abbot. That was Bishop Andrew's new post as part of his deal for leading to Father John's capture. Along with Abbot

Andrew, the only other human lives to be wandering freely in the midst of the grounds were the three bishops, who were now reporting to Patriarch Tikhon II, and Father Andrei.

A chamber that had traditionally served as a meeting room for the Abbot of St. Peter's Monastery and any high-profile visitors was holding Father John. Bound by chains around his wrists and feet tied with rope to a chair, he sat alone; he was still and weak. A very old wooden table was the only other piece of furniture in the room and sitting atop of it were John's belongings: his cell phone, cross and prayer book, along with a wallet and keys. They were systematically placed in front of him, but out of reach.

Little medical attention had been given to the laceration on the back of his head. From the wound, trails of blood had formed on the back of his neck, which soaked a portion of his inner cassock that he was still wearing. His lips were moving as he silently chanted the Jesus Prayer in constant repetition.

Unannounced, the door swung open. Escorted by the three bishops were Judas and Balagad who entered into the room. Balagad, who had concealed his wings, ordered his two lieutenants to remain outside. The five then approached Father John, who looked up to find Father Andrei and Jack not among them. He was hoping to share some words of disappointment with them.

"I would like to understand how Father Andrei and Jack could betray me like this," Father John stated, not shy to speak in front of two newcomers who he had not yet been introduced to.

"Jack? Oh, I see... Abbot Andrew? Worry not for them; they are resting after a long day," Bishop David replied, speaking for the group.

Newly appointed Metropolitan Nikolai stepped back

into a corner of the room with Bishop Peter, as Bishop David continued.

"Now, we have some visitors who would like to speak to you. Be welcoming, will you?"

His long face grew shorter with a menacing grin. Exhausted, Father John let out a sigh.

The old, cloaked man then stepped forward, his face shaded by a dark hood. He stood not much taller than the height of Father John who was sitting in a chair. Father John looked up and to the right as Balagad, who revealed grayish skin and deceiving dark green eyes, stood tall. He appeared to be something of a minder to the cloaked man.

"Father John, we meet at last. How strikingly familiar you are to your father, Metropolitan Victor. I knew him well and he knew well me, although much more than he had wished. Let me start out by saying how long we have all waited for this moment, to begin taking control of the Church, bereft of adequate leadership. Our plans to have this extension of the Orthodox Church under Patriarch Tikhon II are all you really need to know of, and I am sure all that you could comprehend."

Judas began pacing, again with his arms behind his back as he was experiencing pride and vanity. Turning back sharply and waddling fast up to Father John, he stared into his eyes for but a few seconds and continued with his inquiries.

"Do you know what it is we seek? The cross that your father gave to you, who in turn gave it to your son Timothy, is something we have been following for quite some time now. Where is it? Tell me and we may spare you serious suffering."

"You must have seen my boy then… you did not harm him? Please tell me that he is still breathing!"

"Oh you sorry, sorry man; where has your faith gone?" Judas whispered, chuckling once again. "He is as we found him, unchanged. That is, for the time being. Now answer my question!" Judas demanded, slamming his gangly fist on the table with his long fingernails clanging together.

"I don't know. I don't know where the cross is. Everything I had with me is on the table. Timothy was still wearing it last I saw him. Please, let me go and see my family."

Judas nodded toward Balagad, who then approached Father John and slapped his face. It stung like a hive of bees had fallen on top of his head. Beginning to weep, he resumed the words of prayer that had been his only source of comfort. Judas painfully did not reveal the name of Jesus to be tormenting him, as it was intended for Father John to believe that he was a man of religion, however twisted he was. Balagad, however, began to cringe, but otherwise controlled his reaction as best he could.

"You will give us the sacred cross. Your father refused to give up the cross, remember? And he soon fell ill after!"

Father John looked up at Judas with wide eyes and a quivering mouth. He then looked at the ground, finding courage to be silent and trust in the Lord.

"So you will just be quiet, will you… that is fine, that is fine. We will not stop here. There are certainly ways to find these things out. We will be back shortly! Perhaps we can use Father Andrei to help you remember. What a weak individual he is: perfect for bait!"

Judas turned around and Balagad followed. The two bishops, along with Metropolitan Nikolai, exchanged glances with Father John, who noticed they too had dark green eyes. Remembering Balagad's, he was stricken with curiosity.

Before they all left the room, Father John's cell phone rang. Judas hurried back toward the table and lifted the cell phone in front of his hooded face to see if it would reveal who had called.

"Oregon: Canobee County Sheriff," it read.

"They may find our location, fools! Who left this device on?"

Judas shrieked, throwing it at the bishops. Bishop Peter bent down to pick it up and powered it off, and looking back at Father John, he saw him reveal hope within his eyes and smile.

———

It was just past three o'clock in the morning, over three thousand miles across the country. Detective Larson had left a message on Father John's voice mail with limited news about the break-in to their son and wife's room, and additionally he had left a request for him to call the hospital. There was new news of Candice's condition, and he was hoping that that very fact might prompt Father John to return the call. Detective Larson was not ruling out a missing person case, however, as he was suspicious that there was the possibility of a link between the break-in and Father John's recent lack in communication with the hospital.

Detective Larson waited three hours. There was no response, so he finally made a decision to follow his gut feeling. He picked up his phone to call the Stephanopouloses.

"Hi, this is Paul."

"Hi Paul, this is Detective Larson with the Canobee Metropolitan Police Department. I am at the Canobee

County Sheriff's office and I have a few questions for you, if you have a moment."

"If this is about my son, he is dealing enough with the expulsion and I promise that he will not pray in public again. I also have not been involved in any way; I can assure you of that."

"No... what? I am sorry, there must be some confusion. Let me explain. You are the last visitors to see Timothy Petrov. You have visited him recently, correct?"

"Oh, my apologies. Um, yes, we did – just the other day. Two days ago I believe. Is there something wrong? I have his father's number if you are looking for it. Is everything okay?"

"No," Detective Larson replied, "that is just it. He hasn't been answering his phone."

"That is strange. My son tried calling him too and received no answer. A day or so ago it was. I didn't even think about why he hasn't returned the call.... we don't know where he went," Paul replied, becoming curious himself.

"We have reason to believe he may be missing, although we traced the location of his cell phone and it appears to be somewhere around the northeast part of the country. Do you know of any plans he made to return there?"

"No, I can't believe that would be possible. Why would he be so far away from his family? He was just in New York last weekend and left a monastery sooner than he had planned just to see his family. It is so sad. Well, do you think he is alright? Is there anything we can do to help?"

"Well, not exactly yet. There was also a strange break in at the hospital. There were some awful things that took place. I can't give you much information at this point, but could you somehow make it down here for questioning and perhaps offer us any insight? You are close friends with him I was told, and would be the best person to help us out at this point in time."

"I am on my way to work, but… anything to help my friend Father John. We are a few hours or so away. Let me see if my wife can also come down with me, she would like to see his wife Candice anyhow."

Detective Larson did not respond, knowing that Candice had had recent changes in her health. He did not want to violate any privacy laws and her current health situation was not at this point directly related to the case.

"Alright," he finally replied, "if you could make it down by noon that would be great. We will reimburse you for the expenses."

"Sure, I will do my best. Let me call into work. That is no problem, as I have a government job. I will call you back momentarily when we leave."

"Thank you, Mr. Stephanopoulos. Talk to you then."

A few hours away to the northeast, Paul stared at the wall after hanging up the phone. Rather blindsided, he had a speculative look across his face and, gathering his thoughts, went upstairs to the bedroom where Andrea was getting ready for the day.

"Hun, I have some interesting news. A detective from the Canobee Police just called. There have been some problems down at the hospital. Not sure if it relates directly to Timothy and Candice's health, but it involves them somehow. And no one has heard from Father John. Could you come down with me?"

"Now?" she replied, caught off guard.

"Yes… I believe there might be some serious things going on. Can you call in? I am about to do the same."

Andrea paused, but eventually nodded her head.

"Let me go wake Jacob up and let him know he will be home alone today. Let's not tell him what is going on. He has enough to deal with right now. Speaking of which, can we please not be too hard on him?"

Paul agreed, and they both called into work. An hour later, he spoke to Detective Larson and let him know that they would be on their way. Leaving Jacob behind, their vehicle was heard speeding down the road, during a quiet early morning in their typically peaceful neighborhood.

Chapter 17

Jacob sat alone on the living room couch. It was nine o'clock in the morning, and his parents had left to meet with the detective. Uninterested in his video games or anything recreational, he thought about what else there would be to do. A mix of feelings instead came upon him, which left him unable to make sense of the events that had taken place the day before and confused about the next step to take.

The assistant principal had taken him down to the office where the superintendent and principal were waiting to speak with him. Word had spread fast throughout the school about Jason Miller discovering Jacob's conspiracy for prayer in a public institution. It was a public institution like any other in America, where freedom of speech or religion had become limited during the past few decades. As Jacob had walked down the hall to receive discipline, it was as if all the students were peeking out of their classrooms staring at him. His own peers were then judging him; most of them did not feel any pity for him at all. An embarrassing march toward condemnation is exactly what it had been.

His mother and father had been telephoned, and within the hour they had arrived to meet with the school's administration. There was a zero tolerance policy and according to the words of the school administration, Jacob had infringed on the rights of every student in the school with his careless speech about fictitious practices, which had no scientific evidence associated with them. The law was in place for a reason, they had continued to explain, and the nation had come too far to overcome constitutional provisions that had been considerably impractical to the modern day world. His mother had shared a few tears with Jacob's many, but his father had remained stern and apologetic.

"This in no way reflects anything I condone. Those who I work with can attest to my secular values!" he had pleaded.

Without argument, Paul had led his son out of the school that would not be educating his son, at least not until the following school year. Andrea had looked back toward the principal, about to make one last comment, but she instead held her tongue, turning her head back in the direction of the exit, and had remained silent for the entire ride home.

Now Jacob was alone at home on a weekday, processing all of the events that had transpired. He had not had a lengthy conversation with one person since having spoken to Nick Pickiss the day before – not even his parents. He stood up and walked over to the sliding glass doors, observing the woods. How he longed to talk again with Timothy. Certainly he was his only true friend that could understand what he was going through. Ironically enough, he was the same friend for whom Jacob was going through these hardships.

"I wish that we had finished our work in the woods together. Boy was I lucky to have you there when I fell out of the tree house. Tree fort," Jacob said aloud, correcting himself with a smirk.

Jacob's eyes began to tear and he went back on the couch to hold his face in his hands. Determining that he hated everything about life, he settled on the fact that there was no one left to help him. Most people he had come to know were selfish and only cared about themselves, and as far as he was concerned his parents were no exception. There was no one left to pay attention to him.

"For cryin' out-loud, I am the only one trying to do something for Timothy. He can't even breathe for himself!" he then said, once again out loud.

Furthermore, Jacob thought, why is it that the people who can truly make a difference in this world are the ones that have awful things happen to them? Why is it that someone who believes something that is founded on the principles of love is not allowed to publically profess it? These questions he would never know the answer to. Who is the public enemy? Is it the person who helps others because he or she believes something that others do not, or is it the person who doesn't help others because he or she does not believe something that others do?

Certainly the world was now backward in Jacob's mind, as the fear of God had undoubtedly turned into a fear of man. Most people who still said that they believed in God of course did not deny He existed, but thought that it was more important to live life and enjoy what He gave them than to offend others with the Truth. And if that was the case, Jacob did not understand the point to anything at all: if the daily life one lived was contradictory to the most basic foundations of where his or her faith came from then what was anyone trying to prove?

"No wonder Timothy felt alone with God all the time – I just wanted to pray…" he said aloud after contemplating.

Jacob drifted off to sleep on the couch. Something merciful had begun to momentarily heal him from his thoughts.

The house phone rang after what seemed to him to be an indeterminate amount of time. Jacob quickly opened his eyes to see the clock staring at him. It was now eleven o'clock. Rising out of the couch, he wiped the drool off of his mouth and wobbled to the phone; he was somewhat off-balance from a sleep that had all but consumed him.

"Hello?"

"Hi, can I speak to Jacob?"

"Hey, this is Jacob…"

"Oh, hi! This is Jeremy."

Jacob did not respond until the silence became too uncomfortable.

"Uh, Jeremy from school? Jeremy Casey, the soccer team captain."

"Yes, I know who you are," Jacob replied, keeping his voice monotone.

"Okay… look, aren't you wondering why I am calling? During school hours?"

"The thought had crossed my mind, but I didn't think it really made any difference."

"Well, I am not at school. Neither is Nick… neither is Kaylee."

"What is this, some kind of joke? Why don't I just hang up –?"

"No, wait! It's no joke. We are all here together all alone at my house. You see, we began to talk at recess yesterday. I found Nick and we walked up to Kaylee. I told them how I have an older half-brother. He's fifteen years older, actually. And then I said how he went away to a monastery overseas because he couldn't bear where the country was headed. I remember when I was younger and he always told me that if I needed any help getting closer to God, well then I had better just let him know. So, here is the cool part: he happened to be here visiting and last night I told him about what has been going on. Anyway, where this is going is that I asked Kaylee and Nick yesterday that if I could get him to help us, then would they be willing to pray with you... and me. They said yes. They felt so horrible for you. So, my brother is going to drive the lot of us to your house. We are there for you and Timothy; the heck with Jason and everyone else who is against you!"

"Are you serious? How did you get my number? And wait, are you crazy? You all are going to get in serious trouble! Oh man, look what this is turning in to. Are you serious?"

"Yes, we are all here at my house actually, like I have told you already. My brother called school pretending to be each of our fathers, except Nick lives with his grandmother so that was a little more challenging. He said it is important that we pray for Timothy."

"Awesome! Hey, if we get done early I have this crazy new video game – it is called Galactic... wait a minute. I have a better idea. Do you have any construction skills? I can think of the perfect place for us to get together and pray: a place that Timothy would have loved us to. How perfect! Can you all help me finish my tree fort today?"

"Sure! Let us get going. Can you tell us where you live exactly?"

"Down the main road out of Grayson Village toward Laketown and the house number is 579. Can't miss it. It is right across the road from the golf course."

"Gotcha! Okay, see you soon! We are probably ten minutes away."

"Alright, great!"

Jacob hung up the phone and looked up at the ceiling.

"Thank You!" he confessed.

Certainly not everyone was selfish, he then realized.

For some, it was just a matter of courage and standing up for what one believes in. Walking a few steps over to the cabinets, he took four mugs out and heated up a kettle of water.

"Hot chocolate it is!"

Nothing but smiles, Jacob began to multitask as he was running around the house gathering supplies and work gloves from the garage. He then found in the upstairs closet a few spare raincoats, as lately it was very difficult to tell whether it was going to precipitate or not.

Just as he provided for the final details for the construction and poured the boiling water into the mugs, the doorbell rang. Jacob ran inside from the backyard and took off his jacket, throwing it on the couch. He proceeded to open the door that had at that point been knocked on several times. It was an unfamiliar face.

"Uh, can I help you?" Jacob questioned, extremely confused.

"Yes, you sure can. Would you step outside for a moment? I have a few questions for you."

Jacob skeptically stepped backward. Just then, the young man at the door began to crack up with laughter.

"I'm sorry, I am a horrible actor!" the strange young man confessed.

"Aw, Chris! You ruined it," Jeremy called out, running around to the front door from the side of the house.

Jacob changed his look of fear to a half smile, pretending to see the humor.

"Sorry Jacob, just a joke to help lift up your spirit a bit! We thought to get off to a friendly start with breaking the ice."

Jeremy looked apologetic, realizing that Jacob was not in a mood for games. Kaylee and Nick came around from the other side of the house with big, warm smiles on their faces. Jacob noticed Kaylee looking into his eyes from afar until she approached him at the doorway.

"Well?" she asked, in quite a friendly manner.

"Well? Well… oh of course, I'm sorry!" Jacob said, pulling his senses together, forcing himself to steer away from the exchange of glances. "Come on in, Kaylee. Welcome! And you guys too, come on in! Chris? Are you staying?"

"No, I am sorry but I have a few errands that I must run. What time should I pick you all up? I assume you want to get home before your parents are done with work? I know Jeremy has until five o'clock."

"My mom's working a double today. A double shift, that is. So I have at least until then. That's all I have to worry about."

"Alright, and how about you Nick?"

Nick, slow to respond, was beginning to feel uncomfortably shy. He was most certainly not used to social situations and awkwardly began to respond.

"Well… I guess…"

"It's alright Nick, they aren't going to make fun of you! Just tell them like it is! I hope we can all start out being truthful here," Jacob encouraged him.

"Okay, here goes. I live with my grandma."

"That's okay!" Jeremy quickly replied, hoping to ease Nick's discomfort. "So what does that mean for time?"

"Well, she probably won't notice the difference. So, whenever is fine."

"Alright then, I will be back at five o'clock?" Chris asked, confirming that it worked for everyone.

"How about this," Jacob added. "How about I give you a call? Can I have your cell number? My parents are out of town actually; I guess I forgot with everything going on. And I don't know when they will be back. They ran off to Canobee somewhere. Anyway, it's a long story and I don't really know much about it. So what I can do is this. I will call you if it changes. I can tell when they get home while we are in the woods because my mom has this habit of turning every light on in the house even when it isn't dark outside. I'll leave them a note saying that I took off in case they do come home while we are at the fort, so don't worry about if I am not back inside in time. And –"

Chris cut him off, politely.

"It's alright Jacob, I trust you. I just want to make sure everything is set, because I certainly do not want to get into trouble myself, aiding to the delinquency of minors!"

"Delinquency?" Jacob asked, unsure of the meaning.

"Sorry. I just want this to be a good experience for you… anything for the purpose of helping others and God. And although Timothy is Orthodox and I am Roman Catholic, I think that we have much in common. This world needs young kids like you to help restore peace. Anyway, I have to run. Take care!"

They all waved to Chris and he took off before they could say another word. Jacob then closed the door and his three new friends had a seat in the living room: Jeremy and Kaylee on the couch and Nick on a reclining chair. Jacob then took a seat on a chair across from the couch. Awkward to start, the silence was soon broken as Nick clumsily began to play with a lever on the side of the chair. He found himself propelled backward with the sound of a clang.

"Oh, I am so sorry! Jacob, that was rude of me to play with furniture."

The other three broke out in laughter.

"It's fine, Nick. I think this is the start of something

great. I haven't laughed like this in a long time," Jacob said, finishing his reply at the same time as toning down his reaction.

Nick then sat the recliner back to its original position, looking around as if it had never happened.

"I nearly forgot guys. Do you want hot chocolate? I made some and it might get cold soon."

"Sure," Kaylee and Jeremy replied at the same time.

"Awesome!" Nick then replied, a moment later.

"Okay, come into the kitchen. It is out here on the counter!"

They all jogged out to the kitchen and picked up a mug. Drinking it fast, evidence was left above each of their lips. Jacob found a few napkins and handed them out.

"Oh, crap!" Jacob blurted out.

"What's wrong, Jacob?" Kaylee said, seeming concerned and taking a step closer to him.

"Well, I just thought that I'd better wash these dishes when we are done. I can't leave anything out that will have my mom suspicious! Good thing I thought of it now. Why don't you guys head out to the backyard? Right through the sliding glass doors, right out there in the living room. It's a great view of the brook and woods past that. Just don't let the cat out! I have done that way too much. Oh, and I have a few rain coats hanging up by the doors, if you need. Or you know where to find one if you need," Jacob said, while beginning to wash the dishes. "Hey guys, thanks again for coming here! You are the only guys to ever sit here with me and drink hot chocolate, well stand here anyway... besides Timothy. That's really cool."

Jacob's eyes became teary again. Everything seemed to be reminding him of his best friend.

"Hey, no problem. I am sorry for blowing you off in

the bus. Thanks for letting us come over!"

Kaylee wasted no time in letting Jacob know that she was not the type of person he had most likely pinned her as. She had felt an overwhelming sense of guilt that had not shaken off since Jeremy had confronted her the day before. It was as if Jacob's good nature had become contagious. Aside from Nick, who seemed to always act in the same way, Jacob noticed a significant difference in his new friend's behavior.

The three went outside together and walked around. They saw the tent still propped up with two sleeping bags inside of it. Two logs remained, one across from the other, and a charred fire pit rested quietly in the middle. It was surreal for them to see because in their minds they pictured Timothy and Jacob having sat there, talking away the night before a sleepover. They couldn't have been more accurate, and the thought of someone who they could not see only added to the mystical sense that they were beginning to feel; it was about a boy named Timothy who they knew very little about.

Nick walked over to the bridge alone and looked over into the brook. He tossed in small rocks that he had picked up along the way. Still uncomfortable, he felt to be nothing other than a third wheel, as he always had when in a group, regardless of the dynamics. Although, there was something about this group that made him feel he could eventually warm up to. Seeing a few small fish floating downstream, he soon became lost in the nature until he heard a door slam shut. Looking over at the house, he saw Jacob and the rest of the group catching up to him.

"So tell me about your brother, Jeremy. What is he doing back if he left for a monastery? I thought people stayed there for years and years?" Jacob asked, just as the four of them began walking into the woods.

"To tell you the truth, he didn't really make it too long. He just came home after a few years and he wasn't a great fit. That's all he really told me. There was something else with feeling lost and that there was something more he was looking for. But I only overheard that when he was talking to my dad. My dad wasn't happy about it. My uncle was a monk before serving as priest at the old Roman Catholic Church down the road, before they closed it down. Dad had always hoped my brother would become what he never could: what his own brother was. It didn't help matters that Chris felt so lost, though. Who knows what he believes at this point. I don't know. I don't really understand it."

"Well he should talk to Timothy, or at least his father, Father John. Timothy might be only twelve but he is almost thirteen. Actually it is his birthday next week. And he is so smart, like some genius or something. When it comes to God it is even crazier. His being really smart, that is."

"Yeah, Jacob sure is right," Kaylee jumped in, trying to share her own ability to hold an in depth conversation at her young age. "I remember when Timothy first looked into my eyes at that school dance. It was like he was from another planet and I felt like I had to know more about him and what he believed. It was definitely because of what he believes that makes him act that way."

"I'm Methodist," Nick said, also jumping into the conversation. "My grandma is too and she thinks that both the Roman Catholics and Orthodox are really too strict and besides, the hymns are pretty in our church."

The three of them looked at Nick, politely acknowledging his attempt to be an integral part of the group.

"Well, I'm not really anything. My mom doesn't

believe in God, and she says that it's all a bunch of hocus pocus. God wouldn't have let her wake up all alone with three kids to care for otherwise. I see where she is coming from," Kaylee admitted, bowing her head at the ground.

"Yeah, I don't know for sure guys. My parents were Orthodox like Timothy. Actually Greek Orthodox but same difference it seems. But it is hard to believe anything these days. I am shocked that you guys even know anything about God in the first place."

"Maybe it's meant to be?" Jeremy insisted.

"Yeah, maybe! Definitely is odd how we ended up here together. I feel so bad for you all. I hope it's no worse than a suspension... that is if they find out – Mr. Tulley, anyway."

They took a few more steps until the path led them to a clearing where a great tree that housed the fort stood tall. On the ground beneath the tree were some of the remaining supplies that Jacob and Timothy had not finished carrying up, though Timothy had carefully covered them with a tarp, along with the wheelbarrow and shingles before joining Jacob back at the house after his fall. The three newcomers looked up at it in awe as it was quite a large housing. It could easily have fit ten children of their age. What a perfect spot, they all thought, to come together in peace far from the world around them.

"Hey, you have some wildlife in here! How neat! Those are deer footprints I think," Kaylee said, running over to a muddy spot at the edge of the clearing.

"Oh, you should have seen it. I remember Timothy standing just about where you are right now. I couldn't quite see him but he later told me about a deer that was 'profound,' in his words. It had antlers and everything. I can't believe it had come so close. That's when I fell out of the tree. Oh yeah, be careful up there. We have to repair part of the floor!"

"You fell out of that tree?" Nick curiously asked. "How could you have made it out without breaking something? Or even worse died!"

"I don't really know. All I remember is Timothy turning around from the deer right as I was about to hit the ground and there was something quick that happened. Like a force or something. I don't know; it was really weird..."

"Maybe an angel or something?" Kaylee said in a high pitch.

"Whatever it was," Jacob responded, "I was very lucky and I have a feeling that Tim somehow kept me safe."

Jacob began climbing the ladder again, fearless still of heights. He made it half way up and looked back at his friends.

"Alright, so is there anyone else that wants to come up with me? It will make it easier to pull the platform up and down faster."

"I'll go up," Jeremy volunteered.

"Great! I think we can get the rest up in two trips. Kaylee and Nick, you load everything up. Then we can all come up and have a hand in this! I can explain what to do at that point."

Jeremy and Jacob climbed the tree, while Kaylee and Nick began loading up the platform with the remaining supplies. Jacob showed them all of the work that he had done with his father and Timothy. He shared with them the skills he had learned and let them help with the easier tasks. Safety was the first lecture that his father had given to him, and he was very cautious when working with others who were not familiar with construction.

For several hours they exemplified true teamwork.

Chapter 17

Time passed by fast until the only work remaining was to place the shingles on the roof. Before that, they had decided to break for a late lunch. Jacob had made them peanut butter and jelly sandwiches and prepared potato chips and milk. He had pondered how he would explain to his mother where the food and milk went, but to him it was the least of his concerns. Jacob had had the time of his life and soon enough he would have a place where he could be alone to pray, free from outside distractions. Hopefully, he had thought, his three new friends would choose to come back to join him again in the near future.

Jacob was the only one to climb onto the roof to finish the shingles, but he had Jeremy and Kaylee just below inside the fort to support him if he ran into any dilemmas. Nick, assigned to be Jacob's spotter, wandered around in the clearing, not straying too far into the woods. The strong scent of pine needles and leaves fallen to the ground gave him a sense of freedom among the nature before him; remote areas such as the acreage behind the Stephanopoulos' house were a rare commodity afforded in a country now overdeveloped. For Nick's part, he lived in a small two bedroom house in a modular home community and was very intrigued by the outdoors and those who were so close to it.

A rustling sound Nick then heard further into the trees. He began to inch closer to see what the commotion was. How neat it would be to see wildlife in someone's back yard – a new friend's back yard. Nick moved a few branches and small trees as he passed through, which were robbed of water and sunlight by the larger ones around them. But he could not seem to find whatever it was that was moving about, and before long he progressed further in than he had planned.

"Oh, what's that over there?" Nick questioned out

loud.

"Hey, Nick, where'd you go?"

Jacob's voice was heard loud and clear by Nick, and looking back into the woods after peeking toward the clearing, he lost interest in what he was searching for: he walked back to the tree fort.

"Oh, there you are. It's easy to get lost out there; I was afraid you had gone too far!" Jacob yelled out, having returned to the ground after finishing the last shingles. "Check it out, will you? Jeremy and Kaylee are up there now."

"Okay. Sorry, there was something I thought was moving out there! It must have been the wind or something."

They joined the other two in the tree fort. Jacob carried up a backpack that he had brought with him after their lunch and tossed it up through the opening. Following it, he closed the hatch door behind him.

The four of them were now resting from a long day's work in the newly renovated fort. How happy and filled with joy Timothy would have been to see that project done, particularly considering that it was to promote something so good in the eyes of God.

"Alright guys! This is awesome! I can't thank you all enough. Hopefully it will stay warm enough in here as it is getting kind of chilly outside. We can go back and get blankets if we need, but I guess it is starting to get late. Does anyone have a watch?"

"I do, Jacob!" Nick said, perking up. "Let's see, it is four-fifteen. Wow, time flies!"

"Yeah, that's for sure. Alright, so I brought a few bottles of water," Jacob continued, tossing one to each of them. "And I brought a Bible, too. I guess I am not really sure how we are supposed to go about praying. I don't think

I ever have on my own. Does anyone have any ideas?"

"I do!" Nick smiled largely, excited that he could contribute to the group since he was not very much help with the actual construction. "I think it probably doesn't really matter for beginners like us. Well, I mean I pray a little, but I am not used to it with others. I just sort of bow my head and fold my hands, like this."

Nick demonstrated, and Jacob watched Jeremy and Kaylee turn toward each other with a smirk.

"It will probably be awkward. Sorry for starting to laugh," Jeremy admitted.

"Yeah, sorry Nick," Kaylee then confessed. "I don't really know how to act."

Jacob looked at Kaylee and they briefly smiled at each other.

"Hey, relax guys. We are good friends. I used to watch Timothy pray. He thought I was sleeping but I sort of snuck a look out of the corner of my eye. He would set up an icon on a table and stand before it and then would whisper. I think he would usually speak it out loud but he probably didn't want to wake me. But he would be crossing himself a lot and reading from some prayer book. He also mentioned once to me that the crossing was the opposite of the Catholics. Not sure what that means."

"Oh, I think I know that one," Jeremy added. "Catholics, Roman Catholics, cross themselves left to right like this."

He demonstrated as they all nodded, confirming their understanding.

"Okay, then we just do the opposite. With the right hand I think. Right to left, like this."

Jacob performed the sign of the cross, and then the rest of them followed. He smiled at how easily he felt it was coming to them.

"So maybe we should all stand up then? In honor of Timothy in the least, maybe we should pray how he would? He must have had some good idea or reason that he was taught that way. I really want this to be as much for him as it is for us. You know, I always wanted to tell him how sorry I felt for what my friends did to him on the soccer field. This is my way of doing that."

The four of them stood up, all facing each other. Jacob then took the lead, crossing himself again as the others followed with a concentrated effort.

"In the name of the Father, and the Son, and the Holy Spirit," Jacob then called out, feeling inspired. "Dear God, we are here today to pray for our good friend Timothy. We feel awful that he might not know he has this many friends, but please make him safe and get him better so that he can get to know them all. He's such a good guy and has real potential to be so close to You some day. Maybe even a priest like his father. Please bring him back to us; we miss him. And also don't forget about his mother. She's real sick too. How was that, guys?"

Kaylee had a tear run down her cheek and was the first to respond.

"Wow that was real emotional!"

"Yeah Jacob, that was great! Keep going if you want!" Jeremy insisted.

Nick only smiled with a wide grin and was just happy to be with everyone, knowing he had something in common with them.

"I'll say more, sure. So dear God, somehow let Timothy know we love him and are thinking of him and that whatever it is in Your plans, let it happen if it is meant to be. This world is worse off without him."

Chapter 17

A creature, resembling a deer, came out from the woods and trotted out into the clearing. Its majestic head lifted up into the air as Jacob continued his prayer for Timothy. Soon after, off in the distance, lights began to reveal themselves from Jacob's house.

Chapter 18

Timothy had been roaming along a hallway in the castle, with not a door to be found. The structure and design was quite unique in that it was not like any other he had seen before. This was certainly as he expected. Tall stone walls made up either side of the hall, and they seemed to cover the entire perimeter of the building. The rear half was two levels higher than the front, although there were not stairs but only a sharply inclined ramp to go up or down depending on which way you were traveling. Timothy had felt it natural through subconscious means to travel first to the east, then north, west and south. Now moving east again, he had completed a full trip around the outskirts of the extremely mysterious building.

"How to enter? Ah, let's look in the book again. Should be under 'room,' or 'council hall,' I think? What did Elder Jonas say exactly...?" Timothy mumbled, sifting through the robust catalog in the latter portion of the book. "'Chamber.' That must be it. There seems to be many of those. 'Chamber of... Holding. Chamber of Mystery.' Here we go, 'Chamber of Reason!'"

Timothy immediately followed the detailed instructions until he discovered the section he desired; the instructions to find "Chamber of Reason" were much more comprehensive and trying than other places. A quick thought to give up entered his mind, but he found the ability to immediately suppress it, sending it back to the dimensions of doubt where it had come from.

"'The Chamber of Reason houses seven chairs for

which the Angel of the Lord and angels of the First Hierarchy convened to discuss very important matters. These very important matters are further evidenced by the seats that they assumed at each and every time of gathering. To put it in perspective, it is estimated that the time of gathering happened every twenty Earth-years; however, it became much too frequent and at some point in the history of the kingdom it was changed to once every forty Earth-years.

"'The author of this work assumes that you have already traveled around the castle at least one time searching for a door, as it is highly unlikely you would have taken a moment to look first at instruction by those who were inspired by the Holy Spirit with insight. Therefore in order to continue, please close the book and begin to walk again around the building. This time head west.'"

The text in the book slowly disappeared and he could no longer read on. This time, however, he did not become discouraged. Timothy simply smiled and closed the book as he was instructed. With the book in hand he humbly began to walk in the opposite direction, assuming he had originally walked in the direction the manual had pointed out.

"There is something special about all of these numbers; perhaps it is yet another clue," Timothy spoke to the air. "Seven seats... If I only knew the other angels besides the Angel of the Lord, I might begin to figure out what they represent. Then I might be on to something! But this surely does not help me into the room. Well, at least I am not being pursued by demons and giant worms. And that pesky little..."

"Do not count me out quite yet, my Orthodox friend!"

Timothy suddenly stopped in his usual fashion when

caught between feelings of discouragement and curiosity. That little lamb, he thought. That pesky little lamb! He had not even finished traveling west to turn north before running again into it. There was no use standing there as that would not in the least bit make it go away. And for him to be honest, he had to recognize that the lamb had been extremely helpful in his success thus far. Surely it was more practical to seek answers to which he could carry on a dialogue for. Although, the book also did have its way of answering him when he spoke out loud or found himself desperate for an answer. It very well could be that this lamb was a part of the solution.

Timothy turned around.

"Alright, lamb... I still do not know your name. I guess this is the beginning of a friendship that is rather compulsory."

Timothy stopped and looked confused as the word compulsory was not one in his vocabulary, and out of context he had no clue as to what it meant.

"My name, you ask again. Call me Reason. As I said before, I am only a voice. The voice I represent is for only you to figure out. And that voice is the Way of the Lamb."

A unique doorway to the inner wall of the hallway appeared, gradually growing in size until the top reached only inches from the ceiling. It had an ornate wooden frame that had etchings of seven chairs and seven angels, alternating with an image of a city in between each. To his eyes it appeared to have a three dimensional appearance and as he brought his mind to his heart he could see them pop out at him. In the images, each city was being consumed by flames and each angel was carrying a letter. It then appeared that the angels were traveling from their chairs to the cities. As Timothy finally looked at each etching, the doors at once opened and in the room there was a transparent scene of an eighth city. It looked quite different than the other seven and seemed to be much more modernized. A man, not an angel, was there, and standing up from a chair he carried a letter into the flames.

Looking back for the lamb, it had once again disappeared, as no surprise to Timothy. He then looked back into the room to find that the fire was also gone. Instead, there was a large hall that contained a long council table where eight chairs stood. There were three chairs on each of the longer sides, and one on each end. The largest of the eight was on the end of the table to his right; it was crafted of solid gold.

Timothy walked into the room and the doors slammed shut behind him. He continued on, not flinching or reacting in any measurable way. Moving around the table in a clockwise fashion, he caught a glimpse of each chair. On each was inscribed lettering of a foreign language, very similar to what was on the gate to the Fields of Horror and below the writing on each was a picture of a city. It was not until he made it to the eighth and largest chair that he saw a more modern city, similar to the dimensional one he had seen before the doors had opened. This one was not labeled, however, and the city diagram was inscribed in silver – an obvious contrast to the solid gold chair.

"Which one of these chairs was maintained by the Angel of the Jehovah?" Timothy called aloud.

He walked about the room, pacing back and forth. He was determined to try to find the solution without looking at the manual, but before long it seemed to prove hopeless to rely on his own knowledge. He had not a clue as to which seat belonged to each angel, and was caught even more off guard by the fact that there were eight chairs and not seven.

A few assumptions he did make, although none gave any substance to the solution for the Trial of the Son. It was entirely possible, he thought, that the eighth chair belonged to none of the seven. Also, it would be rather reasonable for one to assume, and thus surmise, that the Angel of the Lord, also referred to as the Angel of Jehovah, was one of the seven. But that did not sit well with Timothy. Lastly, he suspected that the seven inscribed labels above each of the seven cities most likely told their names. Timothy decided to refer again to the guide, hoping that the text would be made visible again.

Through the usual routine, he turned to the appropriate place in the celestial realm's guide. Drawings quite clearly depicted each of the seven chairs, but in no way referred to an eighth. Above each drawing was a title that translated the inscriptions into a language that he could read. Timothy read them off one by one, as it certainly did not seem to cause any harm to use his voice. The worst that could happen was that the wily lamb would return.

"'Ephesus – Smyrna – Pergamum – Thyatira – Sardis – Philadelphia – Laodicea.'"

That was the order listed in the manual, and it then stated below that it was the precise clockwise order of the positions of each chair starting with the first to the right of the Golden Throne.

"The Golden Throne, that's the eighth chair," Timothy called out, realizing he said only the obvious.

He continued to browse through the book, not tempted to do anything otherwise.

"'To determine which is the seat maintained by the Angel of the Lord, you must call out the city that the correct chair represents. You may take a chance and in advance call out the one you think is correct, but if you fail you will be permanently removed from the castle. If you are here by way of the Trials of the Trinity, the game will then also end and you will return to the land from which you came. To be on the safer side, you may sit in each chair to possibly eliminate any that are not the correct answer. But beware: each carries with it a temptation of its own, some in the form of fire and light and some in the form of what may be familiar. It is also within the realms of possibility that you will not be able to overcome such temptation with the powers of virtue.

"'If you remain seated in either of the chairs for more than five minutes of worldly time, your soul will be consumed and you will then be sent to the Southern Lands having failed. Note: if at any point the temptation becomes too severe or painful, you may call out "Lord, Jesus Christ, have mercy on me." You will then also be sent to the Southern Lands.'"

"Well that certainly does not sound like fun," Timothy said, cringing and closing the book. "And that is definitely the first time that I have heard of this being referred to as a game. I do suppose that there is a prize of some sort in the end, only it is not exactly of material essence. It is so strange how everything here is like what I know on earth but yet at the same time it isn't."

Timothy stepped back from the table to analyze the situation at hand. Which chair to sit in first? He knew that it would be too risky to call out any one of the names – and for that to even be put in the manual seemed to be a temptation all by itself. That is to say, he interpreted it as such.

Patience was one virtue he felt he could master, and so he was left with two options: pondering over which chair could be where God's only Son sat as the Angel of Lord before becoming a man, hoping by miracle the answer would come to mind, or else sitting in the various chairs until the answer hopefully revealed itself. Judging from the door slamming shut, it was quite apparent that he was not going anywhere anytime soon. And this being a trial of the Trinity, it might just be as well to buck up and prove his ability by sitting in a chair.

"Okay, here goes: which chair first? There was nothing left to read in the chapter entitled, 'Chamber of Reason,' so I am now most certainly on my own."

Timothy circled around the table three times while he slowly looked at each chair to see if any would give him a hint as to what would happen when he sat down. There was nothing but images of the destruction of cities and the name of the city above them. Although they each did look different, it seemed as if they were experiencing the same fate. To think about that made him very uncomfortable.

Finally coming to a halt, he had made his decision. He would start with the first chair to the right of the Golden Throne. Before he sat down he realized that he still had some potion left and took a few sips; he had no idea how much energy he would need, but the real question was how long it would take. That would be hard to estimate with time being irrelevant and only relative to earth.

"Not any longer than just under five minutes multiplied by seven chairs. That's not so bad, is it?" he whispered.

Timothy took a seat in the very first chair. The chair of Ephesus it was, as the book so kindly had pointed out. At first he felt nothing. But, after a few moments, he began to feel rather comfortable. Then, replacing the feeling of comfort, the room around him started spinning and he was overcome by dizziness; it was so extreme that he felt nearly twice more nauseous than he had ever before in his entire life. Like a light switch turned on, settling down in front of him was a green pasture. An hourglass was resting on the grass and sand was sifting from the top chamber to the bottom.

"Oh no, that's the start of five minutes," he said, standing up. "Wait, I am out of the chair... what does that mean?"

Timothy looked around and the pasture turned into a wooded area. He began to walk forward into the trees and beyond that was a clearing. He was hearing the sound of boys and girls chatting as a cool breeze brought a familiar smell of earthly trees. It actually looked just like the land that Jacob's parents owned. Lured further in, he took a few steps and then looked up. It was a tree fort: the finished product.

"Oh how cool!" Timothy proclaimed. "I better go up the ladder here and check it out. I wonder if Jacob is in there too!"

Timothy went to grab the ladder, but realized that he was carrying the hourglass. Half the sand had fallen out of it, as it was not only pouring into the bottom chamber but also was pouring from there all over the ground. It was now obvious to him that he was in trouble. As his desire to climb the ladder grew, his hand felt as if it was burning and his heart dropped. He felt like the wind had been knocked from his lungs.

"This is the temptation? Earthly passions? Well this can't be so hard, I will just go back. I can turn away from this with no problem."

He in fact turned away from the tree house, but began to feel rather uncomforted. His soul felt burdened with a heavy weight and pins and needles over took his entire body followed by an awful metallic taste developing in his mouth. Looking back to the fort, the pain and anguish disappeared, but he had not time to experiment with cause and effect.

"This is not good... I feel like everything is happening ever so sluggishly. I can't make a decision! It is like I am running through a dream in slow motion."

The sand now was three quarters of the way to emptying itself from the top chamber. Timothy tried to turn it upside down to buy some time, but his hand was locked in place.

"Oh, this has nothing to do with any angel, especially not one of the Lord!" he cried out loud. "Cripes... think, Timothy... a virtue. Which virtue is it?"

He ran through the virtues he had been taught by Elder Stamos and the other ten elders, but none of them seemed to fit the situation.

"Wisdom? No, that's not it. Courage? No, that's not it either."

Timothy began fighting his way toward the chair, but the pain became so unbearable he felt compelled to turn back to the fort. The hourglass was nearly complete in robbing Timothy of all time left and he felt the blood rush from his head as the final moment drew near.

"This is absolutely ridiculous. I mean to say, I have no chance! Oh, I am getting much too angry."

Timothy briefly paused, and then something occurred to him.

"Angry... that's it! I know the virtue I seem to be lacking! Temperance! Here goes: let my heart settle toward its own accord through the Logos given unto me!"

Timothy bowed his head and bent his neck, relieving any stress he felt relating to discouragement. Like a magnet above a metal pin, his body shot back to the chair as the last grain of sand fell to the bottom of the glass. A flash of light then briefly blinded him. Then, opening his eyes, he found himself sitting again in the Chamber of Reason. His heart racing, he stood up and began to walk away extremely off balance.

"Now that certainly was not comfortable. Oh, I am so tired. I have no energy!"

He took out his potion again and began to sip on it, until he realized that there was only so much left and still seven chairs to go. With that said, he felt not at all closer to figuring out which chair was the one maintained by the Lord. He looked up toward the ceiling and began to pray.

"Lord, Jesus Christ, have mercy on…"

Timothy lifted his hand quickly up to his mouth before finishing the sentence, slapping his face. That was almost it: he almost lost, not paying attention. He remembered how he was to only utter the Jesus Prayer if he needed to escape.

"I can't even pray, can I?" he spoke to the ceiling. "Can't pray… well that's funny, I cannot pray. What sort of situation could you not pray in," he asked himself with a hunch. "Prayer here is of no help. That's no place of God. Nor is it of Jesus. Never mind that. What did I learn of Ephesus? The temptation was overcome by temperance. Jesus had plenty of temperance and would not have maintained a chair that caused one to act without it."

Timothy then looked in the direction of the next chair, now convinced that the chair represented by Ephesus was not one maintained by the Angel of the Lord.

"Smyrna," the chair read, as clarified by the book.

"Alright, here goes. There is not a moment to waste."

Timothy sat down in the chair labeled Smyrna and

closed his eyes. Again a feeling of overwhelming comfort came over him as he was completely relaxed; although he did not this time feel the room spinning. Waiting a few moments, he then opened his eyes to once again see something rather pleasant. It was his home, and he found himself to be walking down the hallway from his bedroom. There was no chair from which he remembered standing up, and making his way near the kitchen that smelled of baking cookies was a door to his left. It was the very door to the room that his mom had been resting in, unknown to him until recently. He wanted so desperately to open it.

"This might be my chance to say goodbye."

Timothy only half believed what he had said, but it was half enough for him to move his hand and grasp the door knob. Giving in, Timothy opened the door and felt a burning sensation on his hand. Inside was a room bereft of anything material, save for the chair of Smyrna that he had traveled on and a clock hanging above it. He noticed immediately that the clock was numbered one to five, with the gap between five and one indicating itself to potentially be the fifth minute. But as soon as he laid his eyes on it, the minute and second hand began moving backward from one. For one full minute his eyes were glued to it, watching the motion of the minute hand hitting five. Without question, the first minute had passed by and the next four were to follow until the clock returned to its original position.

"Here we go yet again!" Timothy said, projecting his voice to the other side of the room.

He attempted to move closer to the chair, but could not.

"Not that easy... why did I suspect otherwise?"

Then the exact opposite happened. He felt compelled to move to the chair, but was unable to stop himself. When he tried, the same pains returned as in the first experience: he felt tingly all over and his heart sank with a heavy burden. The awful taste then returned to his mouth.

"Come to me, Timothy," a voice called out.

A silhouette of his mother appeared to be sitting on the chair.

"Do not resist coming back to me; why don't you sit on my lap? Come and give your mother a hug."

"I don't think I am supposed to!" he replied.

The closer he came to her, the faster the clock went until it finally struck three.

"Two minutes left? I am afraid if I move any closer, the time will pass without me even knowing it!"

He forced himself this time to stop and the pain increased substantially as expected. His heart began to beat so rapidly that he became sweaty and felt faint. His mind was filled with thoughts of never seeing his mother again and of him returning to earth, only to then envision his father being harmed by Lucifer. The last statement he said about time passing by also began to resonate within his mind. He recognized at that moment that the closer he came to temptation, the faster the time went and the less he had control over his destiny.

"What a profound thought indeed," he casually stated. "Wait, I did it again! It's Wisdom! Wisdom leads to profound thinking!" Timothy screamed. "Wisdom!"

He looked up at the clock and, as it nearly hit the number one, he felt his body rush toward the chair before opening his eyes. Like the previous experience, before him appeared the Chamber of Reason. So far, he thought, the act of reason is all that had saved him from demise.

Timothy stood up and hobbled away from the chair. His legs and arms felt like jelly, and his head seemed unclear and out of focus. Reaching for more of the potion he could feel that the container was now half empty. Due to the possibility that there could be five more seats to sit through, along with a whole additional trial waiting beyond that, he dropped the potion to the ground and plopped down with it onto the crystal stone floor.

"Ephesus was not it, if my logic holds true. And Smyrna... what to make of that? I overcame wildness with temperance... and I used wisdom for profound thinking. What does that have to do with the Angel of the Lord maintaining a chair? Oh, I don't know, this has become all too complicated. There has to be something with the numbers. Five minutes for seven chairs of angels... and here I am to hopefully be the Twelfth Elder. And we have burning cities."

Timothy pondered over the concepts he had just outlined. He had the numbers five, seven and twelve running nonstop through his mind. Additionally, there were the symbols of cities undergoing disaster inscribed on the chairs that had transported him to different dimensions. What he didn't understand was what the cities indicated.

"Wait a minute – the cities have everything to do with this. What did I learn about cities and disaster? What does me being here, coming from a world that is enduring disaster of its own, have to do with being the Twelfth Elder? Everything!"

Timothy opened the trusty book that had so far not failed him.

"'Revelations: turn back twelve handfuls of pages,'" the index instructed him.

He did so, and began to read again.

"'Revelations provides insight to the end of the world as you know it. You now have made your way into the

Chamber of Reason and have experienced grand illusions if you have found this page.

"'What is important to wrap your mind around is that there were seven angels who were instructed to send letters to seven cities regarding their ultimate destruction. Those seven cities are imprinted onto the seven chairs that you have found. Also important to Revelations are the Twelve Elders. If you have come to read this paragraph, then you are indeed meant to be the Twelfth Elder of your time – not one other person can claim this title.

"'More specific to your experience now, it is also important to realize what the Twelve Elders symbolizes. Like the eleven before you, you have surpassed both human nature and time by finding your heart so close to God. You have overcome many of your passions despite both your five senses and time; time is often measured in the Scriptures by increments of seven weeks. We know this through the teachings of the holy fathers, and when you add five and seven you find how symbolic that is of the Twelve Elders. Put these pieces together with your experience in the Chamber of Reason thus far and you will see how you have been looking at this all wrong.'"

Taking a few moments, Timothy rubbed his eyes with a free hand, thinking over what he had just read.

"It is also about the five senses, not simply five minutes... I had to experience all five senses within five minutes after sitting in each chair. I was looking at this all wrong, just as the book just told me, as I was focusing my energy on the worldly minutes instead of attuning my senses to what is above. Therefore, all I could see were worldly temptations; I missed the vision of the cities themselves and ultimately the entire point of the test! I bet if I use my heart instead of only my mind, I can go beyond the realm of time and use my senses. I will then see the city itself and not some familiar place that my imagination interprets it to be! Earlier the book mentioned that I would see light and fire as well as familiar temptations, which I believe that I have yet to see in its fullness: those cities are burning as the image on the chair depicts them – how could I have overlooked this?"

Timothy was now renewed with energy and stood up. He walked over to the third chair.

"Pergamum," it read.

He sat in the chair and then closed his eyes, while looking deep into his heart. He felt this time no sign of initial comfort, for he was not moving toward anything familiar on earth. Timothy proceeded to open his eyes and, standing up from the chair, looked upon a great city standing before him. He could feel all five senses simultaneously, and there was not a clock or hourglass to hurry him along. Looking to the sky, light was beaming down from the heavens as flames equally as bright were consuming the city. An angel was circling above and in its hand was a scroll.

Timothy started for the great city. It looked familiar, but he was unable to pinpoint which city it represented. A massive old monastery lay in the very center of buildings hundreds of years newer. Forest surrounded the outskirts, but barely could one see it in their peripheral; the skyline of the city stretched for many dozens of acres. He moved in closer and could see monks and laypersons on their knees, prostrating and lifting up their hearts with nonstop prayers. The fire was beginning to consume the structures around them, but the people themselves remained unharmed as the light offered protection from demise.

"That's it," Timothy called out, "the Seven Messengers of God and the end of the world as we know it, none of the messengers being the Lord himself. I remember learning about this. I have the answer! It is none of the chairs!"

The light before him disappeared, as if a switch had been turned off. He opened his eyes and there he was sitting in the Golden Throne. The eighth chair was for him only to sit, and he recognized immediately that he was to be a messenger for a city of his own. After contemplation of the revelations given, the lamb then appeared in the center of the room and walked over to him.

"You have figured out the near impossible. Astounding! Explain it to me, will you?" the lamb requested.

"Yes, I have it. None of the seats were maintained by the Angel of the Lord. Sure, He was part of this counsel, but only as an overseer. Only at God's right hand He will ever sit. He oversaw seven angels: the seven in Revelations who were to be messengers to warn the cities of eventual destruction. And the Twelve Elders are somehow involved, too. The elders represent the eighth chair and the eighth chair represents modern day earth. And modern day earth, like the seven cities of Revelations, must also be warned. But not warned by an angel. That is because the Angel of the Lord became Jesus: fully God and fully man. The Angel of the Lord therefore represents the seven angels while Jesus represents the elders on earth. But there aren't only twelve elders... Revelations talks about the Twenty Four, as I learned from my church bible study. That was a long time ago, it seems. Who the other twelve elders are, I do not exactly know but I could guess. But we, and by me I mean myself along with the other eleven I know of, sure have our work cut out for us!"

"And so you have succeeded. In the first trial you found that evil only relatively exists. Here in the second, you find now that the Angel of the Lord absolutely exists. There is no chair that He must maintain or that could possibly hold His essence save the Judgment Seat of Christ. It is you, Timothy, like all others, who is relative to Him. And you see now that there is a great place in His plan waiting for you. You are not only meant to be the Twelfth Elder of your time – the prophecy also holds you as the Twenty Fourth. But twelve of you there shall be to complete God's work on earth and you will be the only one visibly known as such.

"The original twelve have already completed their deeds. You know of them: the Twelve Disciples of Christ. Through their lineage your work mirrors theirs, only the times now are much different. Go now, as you stay seated in the eighth chair. Close your eyes and find yourself to embark on the third trial. It is of the Holy Spirit: The Lord, the giver of life. If you can pass that, then certainly The Prophecy of the Sacred Cross will have been secured."

The lamb bowed his head to Timothy, now certainly showing more signs of respect toward him. Timothy bowed in return and closed his eyes, fully knowing that this was the last he was to see of the lamb for some time to come. It was now up to Timothy and the tools he was given: a knowledgeable book, a sacred cross, the virtues and the Spiritual Armor. Reason was now his to have without the need of two eyes.

Sitting down, he felt like he did in the third chair of Pergamum: nothing unusual at all, as if it was meant for him to be where he was. Timothy closed his eyes and brought again his mind to his heart, only this time so much easier. The chair remained in place, and his surroundings seemed to fall beneath him. Then, opening his eyes, he saw a large room before him, only he was facing in the opposite direction than in the Chamber of Reason. The most ornate of them all, the room appearing before him was a great hall filled with amenities of every kind. What seemed to be a large mirror stood across from him on the other side of the room, but he immediately realized it gave off no reflection of the room. As he stood up and approached it, he was able to see himself standing, but nothing else around him seemed to reflect itself. Magnificently he stood, armored with grand attire and for the first time he saw how he looked like he was in a body much older than his earthly one. But he soon realized the attraction was too great and so he painfully forced his eyes away; they were straining to the point that it was giving him a headache.

He roamed around the room, scoping out the beautiful wooden floors and a well-crafted ceiling that had beautiful moldings. Approaching the only window in the room, he looked out into the distance. There lay the Fields of Horror and beyond that the northern reaches of the Grey Mountains. He was on the top of the world, or so it felt. At the highest point of the castle, the beautiful room was clearly meant for a very important individual.

A small table then appeared in the corner across from him, but at the same time it seemed to always have been there. It fit so perfectly that it was almost as if the room could not exist without it. He ambled diagonally to the table and in plain English was a name plate carved out of ivory. This time Timothy had no trouble reading the inscription, and he read it aloud.

"'Abode of Lucifer: Highest Office of the First Hierarchy.'"

Timothy shut his eyes, as his heart was immediately burdened with incredible passions. The Trial of the Holy Spirit had begun.

Chapter 19

Michael and Gabriel entered into the Offices of the Heavenly Hierarchy as Corinth had requested of them. Although of the Third Hierarchy, the Archangels held a very special place in the eyes of God. In fact, they were revered by even the highest offices held in the angelic realm. As part of God's plan, it was imperative that they conduct their work on earth and, therefore, the Third Hierarchy was where they were placed. Not directly in charge of other angels, Michael and Gabriel, two of the seven Archangels, were placed under the rule of the principalities, but above the standing of a Guardian. The physical and spiritual power they wielded was second only to the Seraphim and Cherubim and equal to the thrones of the First Hierarchy.

"Welcome," Cantor said, bowing deeply before the heavily armored Archangels. "Come, follow me. There are two surprises for you waiting with Corinth, up in the Office of the High Dominion."

Michael and Gabriel looked at each other with grace and love, as they were quite hopeful as to what that surprise could be. Cantor led them through the great horizontal and vertical hallways until they were in the presence of Corinth, who was staring through a window along with two other angels. The light emanating from the two other angels was equal to Corinth's, as well as to their own. With a concerted effort the three turned around toward Michael and Gabriel, revealing very familiar faces.

"Raphael and Uriel!" Michael called out, as the four came together and gave one another powerful hugs.

Chapter 19

Corinth remained in the background with a big smile of his own, as the angelic brothers had joined one another at last.

"How long it has truly been!" Gabriel said, as they finished exchanging their greetings.

"Yes," Uriel replied, seemingly relieved after a long journey. "Long has it truly been since we lost our brother Lucifer to vainglory. Now we have completed our mission to hold the depths of hell at relative bay and here we return to resume His work on earth. We have learned much, and understand more of Satan's plan."

"And what of our other brothers, have we heard from them?" Michael inquired.

Uriel and Raphael stared at one another, neither appearing willing to answer.

"Well…" Raphael said at last, "we have not. They separated from us during the recent catastrophic event to hit North America. We have not seen them since, as it was thought they may be keeping things in order until the replacement is selected for Jeneral."

"We thought they may be in your company," Uriel added, "but it appears that is not so. This is most concerning."

"The stage has been set," Corinth interjected, walking in between the four. "We must proceed, and there is not a moment to spare in determining where they may be. Trust and hope that they look after themselves with caution in whatever evil they have found; it is possible as Raphael pointed out that they could be serving in Jeneral's absence as we speak – if the activities of the Archangels were not so covert, I could have confirmed this one way or another. I can say for sure, however, that I have heard no word of angelic adversity, aside from the demise of Jeneral. And with the loss of him you must all be ready; if the Twelfth Elder succeeds then Satan will have to instantly increase his resistance to maintain the balance we know to be called earth. We do have a replacement for Jeneral in mind, but that replacement is certainly not ready at this point to take on the role. And besides, she is undertaking a different mission at this time, vital for support of Timothy both in the now and for the future. Therefore, the four of you, if not seven as we hope, are where earth's stability presently lies.

"Set all that aside; Raphael and Uriel's work in the depths of hell is now complete. We have to be both prepared and proactive. There is one place that we cannot lose control of, as it is vital to the work of the Twelve Elders. And in that one place, there is one person that we cannot afford to lose at this point: the soon to be elder Timothy has a father who is there held captive.

"We know of a few certainties," Corinth continued, walking now back and forth along the stone floor, "of which are soon to happen. First, General Judas Iscariot is leading an effort to use Timothy's father, Father John, as bait for retrieving the sacred cross. When he finds that Father John is of no use, he will kill him to weaken Timothy. That will be extremely detrimental if Timothy returns to earth as the Twelfth Elder.

"Second, Satan, through Judas, aims to control his very first place on earth: St. Peter's Monastery. This especially cannot happen! But it becomes more complicated. If we succeed in taking back the monastery, the power of balance that Satan holds will reveal a greater aggression, as will it if Timothy soon finds victory. The race will be on to take as many souls as possible away from the heavens.

"Let me provide you with a summary. Once Timothy completes the Trials of the Trinity and St. Peter's

Monastery is secured, the last of the various battles will then have come to pass, and the final war will have begun: the Antichrist versus the Twenty Fourth Elder."

The four Archangels looked each other in the eyes, and simultaneously spanned their wings out. Corinth's words were pure and true and there was not a reply to give. They knew it was time to shine under the Light of God. Additionally, how beautiful it was for them to reunite for the first time since the War of the Heavens began, where they had battled against their brother's defection from God.

———

Father Andrei and Bishop Andrew met the others in the council hall, where not a week ago they had been sitting under the guidance of Metropolitan Ezekiel. Judas had called a meeting in preparation for an attack by the forces of good on the monastery. Demonic scouts had sent word of this to Balagad and in return he took the report to Judas. Meanwhile, legions of fallen angels were on their way to protect the beginnings of a pseudo-church: one led by possessed men. These men, now corrupt bishops and other clergy members, were soon to be joined by a large number of monks.

"Have a seat, will you? You are both now pathetic and late!" Judas said, scolding them.

The other bishops began laughing, showing not respect for Abbot Andrew. As if it had not fazed him, he immediately joined the other bishops in drinking wine and partaking in a gluttonous meal. Father Andrei, on the other hand, abstained. Judas noticed this and signaled to Balagad and his lieutenants, who in turn approached Father Andrei.

"What, you will not join your brothers in food and

drink? Are these pleasures too good for you? Judas takes care of you," Balagad said, hovering over Father Andrei with a fanged smile.

His lieutenants did the same and so Father Andrei did not risk taking part in an argument. He turned around and began drinking and eating, while the others had already begun showing signs of drunkenness. Snickering at one another, Balagad and his henchmen returned to Judas' side.

"We have little time for this meeting," Judas called out, allowing his treacherous voice to echo through the council hall. "There is word that men have begun a search for Father John. Somehow the humanly authorities have received knowledge that Father John has disappeared. And to make matters worse, we have reason to believe that angelic forces from on high are to also arrive. We have on our hands a full blown battle where these forces will try to make their attempt swiftly, before man arrives. Surely that will be in an effort to reveal an aftermath suggestive of the existence of the invisible. It is imperative that we hold out undefeated so that when these men do arrive, there is no hint at the existence of God and that there is no evidence that will make you look suspicious.

"Now, when the fallen angels arrive, you must all remain in here as we cannot afford to lose you to death. Your work on earth means too much to Satan… except for you!" Judas said, pointing at Father Andrei. "You are charged to keep Father John company. If any good man or angel makes his way near him, you must kill him. Balagad, have your lieutenants escort Father Andrei to Father John's chamber."

The Lieutenants lifted Father Andrei up by the arms. He remained expressionless as they led him out of the hall. The doors seemed to close shut on their own, sending an echo through the room.

"Now for my part, I am going to visit a small town where we suspect a boy and his friends are meddling in the affairs of something they do not understand. Thanks to our top demonic scouts, we discovered that this boy's parents gave the authorities a lead to Father John's whereabouts. As a result, we now have possible clues as to the location of the relic. Therefore, I leave you all here under the command of Captain Balagad as he will ensure your safety is not compromised. The lieutenants will lead the resistance, hopefully joined by our companions from below in due time. Do not under any circumstances leave this room! Enjoy the food and drink we have provided for you."

Judas immediately left the council hall where two escorts were waiting to transport him to Grayson Village. The bishops continued eating and drinking, and Balagad ordered the lieutenants to wait outside for the arrival of their allied forces.

On the far side of the monastery, Father John remained beaten and tired. Having been in and out of sleep, the emotional and physical pain had occasionally woken him, disturbing any benefits that rest could have provided for him. Now the middle of the night, he awakened completely. In the dark he saw only a glow of light coming into the small window of his cell. There on the east coast, the skies were still clear and had not yet been affected by the dark stormy clouds.

A familiar sound of footsteps approached the door to his chamber, and it brought memories back of meeting Father Andrei in his cell, before the emergency council meeting that past Saturday. Father John then realized that he had completely overlooked Father Andrei's strange behavior that day. He was amazed how he had not thought twice about how Father Andrei was no longer speaking in a confident tone, as he had just days before – after a session with Timothy. It was now clear that Father Andrei had at that time showed the first signs of battling demonic influence. His worry and lack of faith should have been a clear signal to Father John that his friend was struggling, and he now took pity on Father Andrei. Finishing his thoughts, the door creaked, as Father Andrei approached him with a gun in hand.

Father Andrei pulled up a chair to the opposite side of the table from where Father John was sitting. He placed the gun on the table and folded his hands together, revealing how truly empty his eyes now were. Father Andrei only stared blankly at his longtime friend, and Father John returned the look with fear and sadness.

"So, what brings you here to visit me?" Father John whispered, struggling to speak with a parched voice.

Father Andrei did not utter a word in response. A few moments passed and Father John again spoke to Father Andrei.

"Is that gun for me? You know, maybe you should think real hard about the truth of the matter. It won't be long before the authorities make their way here, you know. They called my cell phone and probably have traced it by now. You most likely have noticed worry in the eyes of those dastardly men that you accompany?"

Still not speaking, Father Andrei revealed a glimmer in one eye. He turned his head away from Father John and looked about the room. It was clear that he was struggling, but had not the ability to rationalize what he had done wrong.

"You know, Father Andrei, I forgive you. Your mind has been warped, but you know not what you have done. You have a chance to do something great here for me and my family, my brother. You can change. I know it. Poor Timothy lies sick in bed next to his mother. Remember his voice, so innocent yet intelligent? Speaking to you about the deepest secrets he had... speaking about the dreams that he had experienced and how he looked up to you as a second father?"

"Shut up! Shut up now!" Father Andrei screamed, standing up with the gun and pointing it at Father John.

Father John winced briefly but returned his gaze to Father Andrei. He noticed that his hand was shaking and that some emotion had finally returned to his soul.

"This is not you; this is not what you want. You have made a choice to give in to temptation, but it is never too late to come back to the arms of God. He loves you, and so do I. And so does Timothy."

In anger, Father Andrei wiped the table clean of Father John's personal items with his free hand. He set the gun down and marched over beside him.

"You know not a thing! You will see which side prevails in the end and will wish you had chosen what I did," he yelled, inches from Father John's face.

Father John looked up with only a smile as Father Andrei took his seat again.

"That poor boy," Father Andrei cried. "It is not his fault. But it doesn't matter! I cannot face God and Satan is my only refuge and protection at this point; it is too late. And if anyone tries to save you then you will die, do you hear me?"

Father Andrei wiped his mouth, covered by the tears and saliva that had surfaced, as a result of the intense clash of emotions that he was experiencing. In the middle of two opposing forces, he was unable to turn back. He had followed temptation, and it was seemingly more comfortable to continue to do so. Then, finding it to be extremely hot in the room, he removed his outer cassock and tossed it to the ground. He placed his hands on the table, folding them together next to the weapon.

"What happened to your wrists, Father Andrei? They look like they have been bound by rope."

Father Andrei met his glance briefly, but then looked down at the table.

"Bishop Andrew revealed to us those sickly markings on his back, clearly tortured before he had embraced insanity. But the chair in his living room isn't where his mind was taken over, was it? That chair was where you sat; the ropes hanging off of the chair arms had secured your wrists, no?"

Father Andrei brought his hands down to his lap where Father John could no longer see them.

"I know you, my good friend. Before the end you will do the right thing. You are too strong to let your soul be possessed."

The two men then looked at each other for a period of time, and their silence was broken by the sound of a crash followed by thunder that shook the very confines of the room they sat in. Father Andrei looked up and out the window to see flashes of light piercing through the darkness. He hurried to the small window, and, standing on his toes, he peeked outside to find something he had never seen before: invisible warfare between angels and demons, revealing itself in the only form that could be comprehendible to humanity. That form was of two natures: darkness and light.

"It has begun," Father Andrei called out with a quiver in his voice.

Down in the council room, Balagad stood in front of the great doors in preparation of unfriendly visitors. He felt no fear as the slaying of Jeneral gave him confidence unlike any other creature of his type had had. The bishops had stepped into the corner of the room, unaware of the awe-inspiring events taking place outside. Still human, all but three of them had not the capability to process the battle taken place, and could only hope that their side would be victorious. The three bishops who did have the capability to understand had willingly accepted the demonic possession in exchange for mental and physical powers.

Outside of that great hall, the lieutenants had begun holding back four great Archangels from taking control of the monastery. Michael and three of his brothers had already penetrated through the gates, sending thousands of demonic reinforcements to the deepest pits of hell, bound by chains and joining those who before them had been defeated in battle. With their armor, dented by poison and hatred, they still pushed on, while each taking on hundreds at a time. Their weapons came down at the speed of light and accounted for the lightning in the air, and with each swipe they took out several dozen evil creatures, causing the thunderous sounds. With every step closer to the center of the monastery, scores of Guardian angels lined up behind them, as not only insurance to the Archangel's mission, but also in preparation to return to the monks who had been held in captivity inside of their cells.

To the eye worthy of holding the true essence of the invisible, one would have seen the regal stature of the four's creaturely bodies. Each with their own set of spiritual armor that only an angel of their nature could bear, a glowing aura surrounded them as if they were in a bubble of heavenly protection, given to them directly through the intercession of their Creator. Then, in order to avoid being bottlenecked in the courtyard of the monastery, the four Archangels split up into the air, attracting an equal percent of the enemy. With force they continued to battle while only suffering the most minor of abrasions. But unable they were to make any significant progress, as for every demon they conquered two more were replaced. Into the forest they were eventually forced backward; like a tornado ripping across the land, the trees crashed down as their roots were robbed of an earthly grip.

Hours passed and the chances grew for the human authorities to arrive before their work was complete. It was three hours now until sunrise and the four Archangels were forced to call upon additional resources of power. Michael let out a glow that temporarily sealed off any demonic attack from penetrating him and equipped a great golden horn, blowing into it a song that commanded the assistance of other earthly powers: the Principalities of the Elements.

"I am the protector of Orthodox faith; may my spear penetrate through every heretical creature," he chanted.

The ground then opened and, like a vacuum, it sucked up a portion of the demons. Rain then poured down from the heavens and forced more of them to return to Satan, as they were afraid of being cleansed by grace. Wind came up over the mountain tops and then raced into the valley to send another large amount of the demons into the cracks that had appeared in the earth. Finally there was fire and, like the Light of the Spirit, it erupted and consumed even more evil creatures. In less than a few minutes the four Archangels had before them only a quarter of the original demonic company to battle. And as the forces of nature diminished, a three-fold gift of grace joined them from the skies: their brothers Salathiel, Jegudiel and Barachiel.

"My intelligent brothers," the first four called out at once.

Chapter 19

"So with miracles of God through nature, He also brings to us what completes our powerful nature. Let us continue in advance of any further greetings or discussions!" Michael commanded.

They swooped down to destroy all in their path, except for the twelve lieutenants of Balagad who were forced to retreat into the council room. The battle continued in that great hall as chaos surrounded the bishops. Before Balagad could control the situation, three bishops had escaped out of the room; Bishops David, James and Luke remained hiding in the corner, trapped behind Balagad and the lieutenants. They covered their eyes, unable to bear the sight of the great beings; the light hurt them as they had only been accustomed to darkness as of late. The twelve lieutenants then drew their swords and approached the Archangels, but they were no match for the most powerful creatures who had ever roamed the earth. The seven Archangels lifted up their great shields and charged at their challengers. In order of greatness, first came Michael with his glorious spear. Then, his six angelic brothers: Gabriel with a sword, the hilt made of green jasper; Raphael with a hammer, doused in potion bearing the healing of the Holy Spirit; Barachiel with a bow, its arrows decorated with holy rose-thorns; Uriel, bearing a rod with a steaming brand at its tip, ready to burn fire with fire; Jegudiel with a tri-corded whip bearing sharp shards of gold; Salathiel with his hands, using words of prayer to manipulate lethal instruments of the Lord.

Balagad watched as his lieutenants, which were the last to stand between him and the bearers of grace, fell to the ground and disappeared into the abyss. He lifted up his top lip, revealing his venomous teeth and, like his lieutenants, embraced the Archangels with fear in his eyes. The building shook, unable to hold such great forces clashing together. The seven great angels surrounded their enemy, outwitting and smiting him with their weapons; from the top, bottom and to each side, Gabriel at last, with his sword, inscribed a cross into Balagad's body. Jeneral was therefore avenged and Balagad met his end on earth, now only able to wait for Christ's Judgement. The three bishops looked up and stared blankly at the seven orbs of light before them, for they had not the ability to see the good essence.

"We repent," Bishops James and Luke said together, given a final chance to speak before their demise.

Bishop David, however, did not; he stood there with a closed mouth, as he had in a more willingly fashion became an enemy of the Lord. There were clearly no words he would have, and so the Archangels looked to one another and, with a concerted nod, flew out of the doors. The three were left under a collapsing building and, still under demonic possession, Bishop David met death and found himself in Satan's lair, bound with servitude to him; Bishops James and Luke were carried off by their Guardian angels who joined with them again in the nick of time.

On the other end of the monastery, the two had not spoken for hours, as Father John had again been in and out of sleep. Father Andrei then found himself in sudden silence: sunrise was near and he heard no further sound of battle. Father Andrei then reached for his weapon, ready to use it if the outcome of the battle was bleak. Father John was then woken up again by footsteps outside the chamber's door.

Father Andrei braced himself, as he was not sure who to expect. He had not a clue which forces had come out on top. Staring at the door, both of them waited equally in anticipation and suspense. Abbot Andrew then emerged from the door and closed it behind him.

Chapter 19

"It is over, Father Andrei. Hurry, complete what Judas instructed. You must kill Father John. Hurry, before we are found!"

Father Andrei looked at Father John and pointed his gun at him. Again shaking and confused, he could not make himself pull the trigger. Father John looked up at him and then gazed toward Abbot Andrew. He saw how dark his eyes were and, as he did Father Andrei, felt sorrow for him.

"I forgive you too, Bishop Andrew."

Abbot Andrew, enraged at what he had heard, pulled out a gun of his own, and aimed it at John.

"There is nothing to forgive, as I am doing the work that is necessary. Goodbye Father John."

Abbot Andrew pulled the trigger, but behind the smoke he saw only Father Andrei in his view. With a smile, Father Andrei looked down at his own stomach and then looked back at Abbot Andrew.

"I made a bad choice, Abbot Andrew, but through the Grace of God I have redeemed myself. Through this final stage of pain and suffering, I repent of my sins; may any morsel of good that remains inside of your heart find its way to bless me. I hope you find the same fortune of Love in Christ, my dear Bishop, and shall these horrible times pass quickly for all," Father Andrei said, ending with a whisper.

Father Andrei's mind ran through the recent events that had burdened him. Bishop David had summoned him the day before the emergency council meeting, and with the aid of Satan he had penetrated Father Andrei's soul with vigorous possession. But Father Andrei was a very strong and pious Orthodox Christian, and unlike the other bishops, had resisted the possession with the Logos planted in his heart. Back and forth Father Andrei had gone between good and evil during the final week of his earthly life, until, tortured, he had sat in Bishop Andrew's living room. The work of the Holy Spirit had not finished with him, however, as his tormented path had led him to still act as an instrument of God: having taken a bullet for his dear friend Father John, he then collapsed to the ground and lay lifeless.

Father John looked down at his friend Father Andrei with tears, and then again looked back to Abbot Andrew. Before Abbot Andrew could make another move, the door behind him blasted open; nearly blinding Father John's eyes were seven gleanings of light. Abbot Andrew turned around and faced the Guardian angels, feeling his spirit break down before the bright creatures. Unable to handle the force, his spirit descended to join with Bishop David's, and the Archangels carried Father Andrei away to personally bring him to the Southern Lands. Their mission given to them by Corinth was now complete.

Father John sat in disbelief, unable to process what truly had happened before his eyes. Behind him outside, he heard vehicles approaching the walls of the monastery, which were blaring out the sound of sirens through the morning fog.

———

Several hours later and three time zones across the country, Jacob woke up feeling particularly rested. It was now Friday morning and for a moment he thought he had overslept and was late for school. Rubbing his eyes, he put on his glasses and looked over at his television set that he had left on after playing video games late into the night; he had not yet spoken to his parents as he had snuck in the house and had gone straight for his room. His friends had at that point left, meeting Jeremy's brother a few blocks away.

It was another gloomy morning. The combination of the expulsion and Timothy's dire medical situation had started to wear on Jacob, but if anything had made for a positive effect on him it would have been the time he had spent with his three new friends. He was beginning to understand the power of prayer and communion with others, and how sharing moments like those could help to discover a positive connotation in the direst of situations. He had no other choice than to accept what he had been dealt. Realizing the sorrowful situation was no longer centered on himself, he was prepared to offer his support to whomever needed it.

Jacob looked at the clock and found that it was seven o'clock. How unusual it was that his parents had not checked up on him the night before; but even assuming they were angry with him, it had been uncharacteristic of them to not give him a kiss goodbye before they left for work.

"How rude," Jacob decided.

Walking downstairs, he discovered that not a single piece of evidence was remaining that would indicate they had even come home. His mother was very orderly, but it was his father who always found a way to put something out of place. In this case, not a dish had been left on the kitchen counters; not a drop of water was remaining in the sink. Everything was exactly as Jacob had left it, and if it hadn't been for the lights being turned on in the house the evening prior, he would have just assumed they were still in Canobee. Even more interesting, he found that the lights had been turned off that morning.

Walking back into the living room, he saw that the answering machine was blinking. Not having checked for messages the night before, Jacob had no sense of when the message had been left.

"Perhaps while I was sleeping," he told himself.

Just before he could press the large play button on the antique machine, the phone rang. He jumped backward and placed his hand on his heart, indeed surprised after complete silence had taken hold of the house. He let it ring twice and then turned on the phone before putting it up to his ear.

"Hello?" Jacob said, giving his usual greeting.

"Hi Jacob, this is Kaylee!"

"Kaylee? What are you doing? Are you at school?"

"No… I stayed home again. Why not have a four-day weekend?" she giggled.

"Oh Kaylee, I just don't want you to get in trouble. How are you going to get another note?"

"Don't worry about that. It will be alright. I'm going to tell my mom about it I think. Better than getting suspended."

"Wow, she must be really understanding… so what's going on then? Did Jeremy and Nick stay home too? Have you heard from them?"

"No not at all. I mean, I'm pretty sure they went to school. I didn't try to call them because I didn't want to risk anything but I thought that your parents would be at work. Did you talk to them last night? You mentioned that they all of a sudden left yesterday morning."

"No I didn't. I didn't this morning either. I had snuck in and just stayed in my room playing video games until I fell asleep. Speaking of which, I am starving!"

"Oh, well you better get something to eat until you wither away into nothing!" Kaylee again laughed.

Jacob laughed with her for a few moments, and then they were silent as they began to feel awkward.

"So hey, Jacob, what are you doing?" Kaylee said, breaking the silence. "I was thinking you could tell me more about prayer and we could hang out in the tree fort? Maybe you could even show me those video games you always talk about?"

"Oh, well if you... I mean, I think... what am I saying? Of course! Come on over! Have you had breakfast yet?"

"Yeah I just ate, but thank you just the same," Kaylee replied, softening her voice.

Blown away, Jacob's heart began to race and he became afraid to open his mouth in fear of saying something stupid.

"So how about in an hour or so? I will have to ride my bike," Kaylee informed him.

"Aw, I can't believe you would do that to hang out! It is chilly out there I think."

"Don't worry about that! I will see you soon, okay?"

"Yup! Great. Take your time and see you soon!"

"Bye Jacob!"

"Bye," Jacob ended, with a giant smile on his face. He was now convinced that he was not alone in his struggles and then folded his hands. Jacob looked upwards and thanked God for the help He was giving him.

Jacob rushed into the kitchen and cooked some breakfast. Stuffing it in his mouth as fast as he could, he then ran up to the bathroom to get ready for the day. He was so excited that the cutest girl in the school wanted to hang out with him and that she, Kaylee Anderson, would skip school just to keep him company when he most needed a friend. He was beginning to understand how the ups and the downs were becoming intertwined with each other, and he could not guess what could be next. What Jacob could say for certain is that he was really looking forward to the rest of the day.

To the minute, an hour passed by and the doorbell

rang. Jacob ran down the stairs and just before opening the door, he positioned his glasses and patted down his wavy hair. He then took a deep breath and opened the door, beholding his visitor.

"Hi Kaylee!" Jacob waved.

He stood still, leaning on the door with the arm that opened it.

"Hi, Jacob," Kaylee smiled. "Well, aren't you gonna let me in?" she fluttered her eyes, teasing him.

"Oh, well of course! Sorry, come on in!" Jacob said, closing the door for her.

He led her to the center of the living room where they both started to speak at the same time. Laughing at each other, Jacob started the conversation.

"So, it is still early; did you want to go outside? How is it out there?"

"Oh, not too bad. It was fine, really. Bring a jacket and you will be okay."

"Yeah, okay. I don't have any heat or anything like that installed yet in the tree fort. I probably won't get that!"

Kaylee smiled at him with an auspicious grin. Jacob then went to the closet and put on his coat before returning to the coffee table where he picked up a book and a chain.

"What's that?" Kaylee asked.

"Oh, this book? It's a Bible," he smirked.

"No, silly! That chain you have in your hand. It looks like a really old cross."

"Oh, that? Um, well… it's nothing. Just something I am borrowing."

"Oh okay. It is real cool looking."

"Yeah… so, let's go? We can read this Bible I have here."

"Okay! I am ready," Kaylee confirmed.

Jacob led her out through the sliding glass door and they walked through the damp grass, soaking their shoes. Into the woods again they trod, finding it becoming darker the closer they made it to the fort. A storm appeared to be heading their way, but feeling they would be safe in a place that had provided so much joy the day before, they continued nevertheless up the ladder and into shelter.

"Are you sure it is safe in here, Jacob? It looks dark out there! I thought I heard it thunder."

"It is safe. I am sure of it... don't worry! This book will help guide us. There are some Psalms in it. I found some pages that had their corners creased. I figure why not read those? Have you heard of Psalms?"

"I think so. It sounds kind of familiar."

A loud rumble of thunder crept up on them that seemed to have sent a vibration through the fort's wooden floor. They looked up at each other and then Jacob set the cross down on a miniature table, which was positioned between them. Inching over to get closer to Jacob, Kaylee stared toward the book, as if to indicate that was what she was interested in.

A bright flash ripped across the air and by the time Jacob opened to the page he was looking for, thunder again belted out its force to tell them it was heading their way.

"That was about five or six seconds. Doesn't that mean it is about five or six miles away?" Kaylee wondered.

"Yeah I think so. We aren't too far up in the tree. I wouldn't worry about it," he repeated.

"Oh, I'm not. It is alright," she agreed.

"Okay, here goes: 'Psalm 42.' I am going to bow my head a little if that's alright?"

"Sure, it makes sense. I will fold my hands and do the same."

"Cool. 'As a deer longs for flowing streams, so my soul longs for you, O God,'" he began.

At that point, it started to rain and the wind picked up. Off in the distance and out from his house a short, cloaked being was walking in Jacob and Kaylee's direction, accompanied by two dark creatures. The brook began to slow its movement, and the drops of rain then pattered down on it. Lightning struck nearby and a crash was heard but undisturbed were Jacob and Kaylee.

"'Deep calls to deep at the thunder of your cataracts; all your waves and your billows have gone over me,'" he continued, nearly halfway done with the Psalm.

The cross began to subtly vibrate, and Kaylee opened an eye, noticing its movement. Jacob remained focused on his reading.

The three creatures were now nearly halfway between the two friends and the brook. The two beings, towering over the old cloaked individual, each unsheathed a short sword and raised it above their ghastly faces.

"'As with a deadly wound in my body, my adversaries taunt me, while they say to me continually, "Where is your God?"'"

The bearers of despair then approached within inches of the ladder, as Judas stood back several feet. Reaching out with their free arm they began their ascent into the fort. Kaylee looked over at the hatch as she heard a creaking sound.

Before another motion was made by the unwelcomed visitors, a deer-like creature, which both Timothy and Nick had once each laid their eyes upon, jumped into the air with wings on its back as the water from the air beaded off of its neck. Bending its neck, it pierced its antlers into the lieutenants; with two wings near its hind legs it clasped around the head of Judas. And just before Jacob finished the Psalm, the angelic creature carried all of the evil away, sending the sword-bearing creatures to a binding fate and forcing Judas back to the depths of hell with the fear of grace.

"'Hope in God; for I shall again praise Him, my help and my God,'" Jacob finished, as he turned to Kaylee and pressed his forehead against hers.

The storm then passed by, the cross became still and hopeful smiles took over their faces in anticipation of a bright future for their hearts.

Chapter 20

Timothy felt especially ill. Sitting in a corner and far away from the mirror, he felt the strong presence of the material things in the room. It was so abrasive to his spirit that he felt as if a million shards of glass had broken apart his heart into tiny molecules. His face was pale and his skin cold. Shivering, he had to remove the Helmet of Salvation as the vibration from the metal over his skull was causing him discomfort. All hope had certainly been stolen from his grasp and there was nowhere else to go. This room was going to be the end of his journey, no matter the outcome.

He looked at the mirror across the room as it still reflected a blank image, and the table with Lucifer's name resting on its surface caused him unbearable anxiety. In a third corner was the golden chair he had arrived in, but all it provided for him was the thought of riches and confidence; those were the things riveting through his mind, peeling off with it the surface of what pumped life throughout his entire being.

"Where is your God?" a voice pulsated throughout the room.

"No matter what happens..." another said, much softer than the first.

"They cannot help you; there is no creature to send us away!" the first returned to say.

It was a rather familiar voice to Timothy, which the second time seemed to have echoed from outside – from many dozens of stories down toward the ground.

Timothy stood up and hobbled to the window.

Chapter 20

"I could have sworn it was at first calling out to me from inside this room. Who are you?" he demanded.

Only silence responded. He sat back down in the corner, where his sword and shield lay on the ground and the book and his potion sat in front of him. Looking at these, Timothy could not tell the difference between the materials that he had brought with him and the ones he found now in the room, which to all he was hurtfully attracted.

"Why am I here, I can't really remember..." he thought, unable to finish.

His eyes closed and then opened again, as he sensed the objects staring his way.

"Peter? St. Peter, I pray to you; help me find my way," a new voice cried out, speaking directly to Timothy.

"I am not Peter!" he responded in agony. "I am Timothy!"

He looked around in paranoia and began to hug himself, keeping his spirit from wandering away.

"I love you Timothy," his mother called out. "I cannot tell where I am going. These lands seem to be in the south. I am in waiting, but where? I am scared."

Timothy covered his ears with his hand and began to weep, clenching his jaw together in agony.

"Come before me and look at yourself through me! A guide is here to help console you."

Timothy looked up, finding a butterfly that was hovering about. It was at first like a dream that he had once experienced, but suddenly its bright aura darkened. Its wings were scaly, and its body was a rancid green color. Nearly ready to collapse from the putrid image, he picked up the container of potion and drank the last few drops; there was just enough energy left for him to stand up with his book in hand. He eventually opened it up and noticed some of the pages to be creased. Turning the pages backward, he found one that had not been altered.

"'The Trials of the Trinity: The Trial of the Holy Spirit,'" he read to himself.

Then below the heading he began to read more, but halfway through he found that it was speaking to him.

"Discover the greatest Commandment of God."

Timothy looked around the room, resisting his surroundings that were clearly attempting to grab his attention through the voice. Unknown to him, he was actually receiving more help than he realized: his shoes, through the Holy Spirit, had assisted him to continue with processing the guide in his hands, while his breastplate had facilitated him to decipher the tools he had brought with him to be righteous – righteous in comparison to the material things already in the room. The helmet then brought the image of Jesus back into his heart, as it reminded him of attaining salvation through His work. His belt embraced him with the Truth as he knew to believe in his ambitions. Then, the last pieces of defense and offense allowed for him to continue his faith through the Holy Spirit: the shield and sword glimmered in the air. And finally a very special relic paved the way of light through the darkness surrounding him.

"The greatest Commandment?" he asked himself, having been positively affected by the tools given to him. "Let's look in the back of the book."

The appendix gave some clear direction as he read once more, this time without a disheartening voice calling from beyond.

"'The Ten Commandments: look at this book with a different set of eyes. Start from the beginning, and turn between two sections; turn between the second and fifth book within this book, to be exact.'"

"Exodus and Deuteronomy," he spoke back to the author. "The Old Testament... this is the Bible?" he questioned, confused at what he was finding. "This is a very different book than what I thought I was instructed to take by the old, frail woman. I thought it was only a guide to the heavenly realms!"

It did not make any sense and he did not know whether to doubt the book he had seen on earth and thus far in the heavens, or rather doubt what he was now reading in the third trial. Perhaps, he thought, they were two completely different books. Despite this, Timothy began reading the chapters and contemplating the Ten Commandments, but not one seemed greater than the other. He then finished reading the rest of the verses aloud.

"'Do not be afraid; for God has only come to test you and to put the fear of Him upon you so you do not sin.'"

Timothy lowered his book, not quite finished with the entire chapter. His fingers began to feel frail and, unable to sense the tips, the book fell out of his grip. Slowly he proceeded across the room, feeling destined to appear before the mirror. His last step then led him centered before it and, out of the nothingness that had up until then showed only his reflection, a great angel came up from behind him to replace the emptiness he saw. He felt it wrap its slithery arms around him and now in the mirror he did not see himself but only the dark fanged creature. He felt again cold and the pressure on his chest seemed to be suffocating the life out of his lungs. Ashamed and despondent, Timothy gasped for any air he could get but so thin it felt as only minimum amounts of oxygen were binding to his blood. And so not just the fear of Him came over Timothy, but also the dejection caused by being without Him sifted through the deepest chambers of his humanly form.

Flames forced heat onto his skin and desperate tears flowed from his eyes; not at all did the watery streams extinguish the fire but instead they turned to steam. Timothy let out a scream but there was no other ear to validate its authenticity.

A force was now suspending him in the air as the virtual presence of the dark lord disappeared from sight and touch. Again able to breathe, he then lost the ability to see and his eyes were replaced by vivid imagery of earthly occurrences.

"Let your sin be revealed. Can any of these Commandments truly save you from it?" an anonymous voice stated, resonating through Timothy's ear drums.

Hurtful things were displayed to Timothy. As racing thoughts, one came on top of the other, pressing on him with the weight of Truth that he could not alone bear.

The first image that came into his mind was of his father being struck over the head. Father John was then carried away by false men of God who were controlled by demonic creatures. In some strange way Timothy was able to see that at least one of the two men had made a conscious choice to allow for possession to conquer him; the other had been betrayed and bound to a chair in that same room. But the faces he could not make out, as only their dark spirits could be seen. Finally, his father rested in a chamber that once had held the sounds of ceaseless prayer.

His mother, just a little girl, then appeared standing in a field of green grass, smiling as wind filtered between her hair; a barrette was holding the strands together and, like a kite, they waved up and down into the air. But she grew old while standing in place and minor wrinkles set into the corners of her eyes as she lay down on a bed of earth. Two feminine angels approached her who had long ago fallen from the sky to embrace literal darkness. They found the spirit inside of her and then took hold of the entirety of her soul, but there was no direct choice associated with their attempt and unable was she to respond to them. Inseparable still was Candice's body from her spirit.

Jacob then entered into Timothy's mind. He was walking through hallways, being persecuted by his peers in a way familiar to Timothy. Then, as Jacob was longing to be there for Timothy in an intangible way, beautiful words came from his mouth and, in communion with others, together they lifted their hearts in his tree fort. Pursued by evil, Jacob innocently continued, unaware of what lurked in the shadows.

Paul then appeared, driving to a city. Sitting by his side was Andrea, arguing about their son. They received word once meeting a detective that not only was Father John missing but his wife Candice was about to take her last breath. Paul began to cry with her as they consoled one another.

Darkness eventually took over Timothy's thoughts. He opened his eyes and could not see at first glance. A spot of light then broke open the blinding veil and standing before him was a blank mirror, where not even his reflection presented itself. Looking down, he saw that he was standing even though a floor was not beneath him. Not a wall could be discerned and black space was his ceiling. Then in front of him, replacing the mirror was a man in a white robe. He approached Timothy and embraced him from the front, in comparison to Lucifer holding him from behind. This man he then knew to be Jesus: the very being that had sat down on his bed in a dream just over a year ago. Timothy immediately lost again the ability to see, but this time it was light that was blinding him; a hopeful perspective was bestowed into his heart.

In the mirror, Paul was shown to him providing direction to a monastery for a detective; with Andrea he stayed overnight in a city. The next day, in Father John's stead, they each held Candice's hands. She then proceeded to slip away from the material world, taken to the south but not south in terms of by Satan's side. Instead, she found herself in the Southern Lands of the Kingdom of Heavenly Creatures; the demons were conquered and their possession of her was vanquished and conquered by Salvation. After all, she had not received the demons by choice and so she was not Satan's to have. Then, once again like a young girl, she stood in a small green pasture within the Southern Lands. In anticipation of Christ's return, she was now experiencing a positive environment.

His father replaced the thoughts of his mother, as Father Andrei had spared his own life to save Father John's. Out of the gates of the monastery Father John walked, escorted with Metropolitan Ezekiel by the police who had found them tied to chairs in separate rooms. Having resisted demonic possession by choice, they were the only two council members left who had not suffered a possession, aside from the Metropolitan's deacons. The Church was theirs to continue and that future then revealed itself to Timothy: Father John, now a widower, was consecrated by Metropolitan Ezekiel as a bishop.

Finally, images of Jacob exhibited themselves once again to Timothy: he saw him finish a prayer in a book with creased pages as Eryana trampled down the evil approaching. To a human eye, only a deer would be visible, but to an enlightened one, the image would be of an invisible, yet angelic, creature.

Although the sorrow for his family and friends had been trampled by triumph, the images indicative of the punishment of sin had not been fully replaced by those certain with the hope of eternal life; the mystical presence of good overcoming evil trickled away and Timothy was left standing in the room that had once overcome his senses. The objects in the room were now affecting his concentration to a greater degree, as the mirror was at last reflecting both him and his surroundings.

Looking over at the ground he saw the book he had held lying on the ground. It was facing down and was opened to a particular section. He walked over to it, finding the shoes on his feet to be light in weight. They did in fact symbolize the Gospel of Peace: picking up the book, he no longer beheld the Old Testament, but rather the New.

"'Before turning this page, walk over to the mirror and stand before it,'" it explained to him as he read the only thing written on an otherwise blank page.

Timothy proceeded to the mirror and held the book before him. As he turned the page, Love flowed into his heart.

"'The Book of John, chapter twelve, verse thirty-four: "A new Commandment I give to you, that you love each other even as I have loved you. By this all men will know that you are my disciples if you have love for each other."'"

The greatest Commandment was given to Timothy, inscribed into his core. Like super glue, the millions of pieces of his heart had been affixed together as life in his spirit pumped throughout his body. The work of the Lord had been done in him, and the answer to the Trial of the Holy Spirit was there written for his mind to comprehend.

Through the Holy Spirit and by the triumph of God

incarnate, it was all along that he only had to survive the strife of the Trials of the Trinity to capture the final solution. The solution had been quite simple all along, as it had naturally unfolded between the material and immaterial worlds. With the connection of Timothy miraculously saving his friend Jacob who, in return, offered new friends a unique experience of prayer and love, along with the willingness of Timothy to open his heart and look past what was earthly, the answer had been his to embrace. Love for others had paved a path to grace and now, with true joy, he cried in earnest for his Lord.

Looking back up to the mirror, it revealed something ever so sweet; it revealed a panoramic view for his eyes. Through his heart he processed the entirety of the company that had earlier seen him off on his journey. There standing were the hosts of angels and in front of them stood Eryana, Agread and Corinth. Timothy knew immediately in his heart that he was seeing glorious beings: a Principality, Virtue and Dominion standing tall. To their left were the Eleven Elders. Dressed as he remembered them and glowing ever still, their faces were now different and resembled their true form: their loving humanly faces made in the image of God. And to their left still were twelve more beings. The Twelve Disciples of Christ stood by the Eleven Elders' sides and Timothy realized that he was the one missing; twenty three of them were smiling. They all swayed their arms and then steadily pointed to their left – next to St. Peter was a reserved spot. And finally, there were two familiar beings who, as Guardian angels, stood smiling. It was in fact the old lady from the book kiosk and the strange man who had allowed him into the fairgrounds. They grinned and bowed to Timothy.

The entire company began singing as the harmony

was beautifully conducted and the words flowed through the gates and into the Kingdom of Heavenly Creatures. From there the lyrics of song traveled to the Offices of the Heavenly Hierarchy, where in a room Timothy could see an angel recording the song into heavenly records. Timothy at last joined along with them in song, ever so slowly:

"A new Commandment I give to you, that you love each other even as I have loved you."

The double window at that precise moment opened, calling for him to approach it. Timothy left the presence of the mirror without delay, climbing up onto the sill. He stepped out onto a flat roof and it became dark, despite having seen light through the window. It was an entirely familiar scene, as in a dream that he had not long ago in which he had been standing on what seemed to be the very same spot; looking backward he no longer saw Lucifer's lair, but rather the building's rooftop that he had once walked across. Regardless, he was now living and breathing the moment, no matter where his feet stood. And it seemed fairly hopeful.

"A better view, I must have," he called out into the air.

He turned his body now completely around, so that his back was to the thin air. Unlike his usual feeling of déjà-vu, he plunged into the recognizable night free of nausea.

In slow motion he fell as he beheld the top of the building. Then, looking straight ahead, he saw illuminated sequential numbering that had started with one hundred.

Images of his many recent dreams sparked in his mind. In one, Timothy remembered having vanished into the ceiling right in front of his congregation, just after Father Andrei, who, standing up at the altar, made reference to the six winged and many eyed angels. Next, Timothy recalled walking down a path and being led by a butterfly, eventually running into an image of his older self who inferred to him that he would find a new world.

"Pain and joy will both be found," it had told him.

Timothy then repeated it out loud, as he continued to fall: "Pain and joy will both be found."

Lastly, it now made complete sense to Timothy how one could love God with all of his or her heart, as he recalled having seen the image in Jacob's bathroom of an elder praying on his knees. The face of that elder had been only moments ago revealed to him in panoramic view: it was that of Elder Stamos.

Within Timothy's heart he pictured himself again in the Abode of Lucifer. He began moving rapidly backward; the events that had transpired within the realm of Eden were repeating, only in reverse.

He sat in the eighth chair and then, transported back to the Chamber of Reason, continued still moving backward. Next, Timothy passed through the castle, and then backward through the Fields of Horror. He saw everything with renewed clarity: four men, a lamb and then Eryana, who then moved with him out of the Grey Mountains.

At last, now having received a clear vision of the entirety of Eden, he envisioned himself standing with Eryana on the Lake of Entrance's beach. She bent down on one knee, and began to speak, only her words he had not before heard.

"In a dream an image in the water whispered, 'look out behind you.' Now that you have seen what was all along there, you can now look at what is ahead," she whispered.

His thoughts moved to the present and he then fixed his eyes on the side of the building. He was still passing by glowing numbers until the final ones appeared, as warm light shone from below.

"Five... four... three... two... one..."

Timothy lay still, with a pillow underneath his head. It was now his time to rest.

———

Saturday morning arrived. It was now the seventh day since the onset of Timothy's coma. Taken off life support just hours earlier, Timothy for the first time opened his eyes. He found himself staring at a ceiling in a very strange room, while lying in a bed with white sheets covering him. Everything about his surroundings seemed superficial and mundane.

"He's awake!" Timothy heard a voice say.

Processing it for a moment, he realized it was that of his father.

"Timothy!" Jacob yelled aloud.

Timothy lifted his head up as he was unable to find the strength to use his body to sit up. Then, observing his young hands, he realized that his body was twelve again. He sat his hands down and looked forward, as his dad and Jacob were standing in front of him and off to the side were Jacob's parents. Timothy gave a big grin, but looking around found his company to be incomplete.

"I take it that mom isn't here," Timothy stated with affirmation.

"Oh Timothy," Father John called out, embracing his son with a strong hug.

"Timothy," he then repeated after a pause, beginning to cry. "Don't you think about anything; just rest, please. I will explain everything to you. Please be a strong boy and understand I meant well. I am so sorry for what has happened."

Timothy returned the hug and with it gave his father a pat on the back.

"Dad, it is alright. I am strong, and so are you."

Timothy's eyes were glowing and a sense of peace was transferred to all in that room who exchanged his glance. His father let go of him and backed up, feeling the same tranquility that Jacob and his parents had just received.

"We aren't supposed to hold on to you for too long, doctor's orders. Some of your bones still need healing. You have been in a coma for a week now, son. But you missed so much. Once you recover there will be more to say. Everyone is now safe and we can take strides to move on."

Timothy looked his father in the eye and smiled, revealing compassion with silence, patience and joy. He then turned his head to Paul and Andrea and gave them a similar look.

"I am a bit hungry," Timothy admitted with a weak voice. "What day is it?"

"Saturday!" Jacob replied.

"Ahh, bacon and eggs!" Timothy joked.

They all started laughing as his surgeon, Dr. Morris, walked into the room. With soft eyes and a caring face, he approached the side of Timothy's bed.

"Timothy, what a miracle this is! I am sorry, is now an appropriate time? I am sure you are all very emotional at this point."

"It is fine. We have all day, doctor. Go ahead," Father John said.

"Okay, great. So how are you feeling Timothy? You have had some rough patches recently since you have been here. Suddenly yesterday, you took a turn for the better and we knew it would only be moments before you awoke. A miracle indeed!"

Dr. Morris lifted the head of Timothy's bed up a few degrees and began to examine him, looking at his pupils and listening to his heartbeat with a stethoscope.

"Wow, I would have to say that your eyes seem to have quite some life in them! You look incredibly healthy. I have seen nothing like this before," he confirmed to everyone in the room.

"I feel great, doctor. Thanks for caring for me this past week. We are blessed to have you."

"We are going to do some further testing Timothy, now that you are awake. Testing your memory and your ability to reason and interpret. That will happen over the next few days. But if everything keeps looking up, we could have you out of here in a week or two. Just make sure to rest and stay relaxed, as hard as it may be!" Dr. Morris exclaimed.

Then, turning to Father John and the other guests, he continued, "You all enjoy each other's company. I will come back later."

They all thanked Dr. Morris and he left the room, closing the door behind him. Father John and Jacob pulled up a chair. Paul and Andrea then did the same and, for a moment, the four looked over at Timothy, grateful to have him back. Timothy reclined his head and looked up at the ceiling. He appeared deep in thought, but with a kind of tranquility they had rarely seen from another human being.

"Oh... I have something for you, Timothy!" Jacob said, excitedly. "You will never guess, but I have a few friends for you to meet once you get back home. And you will never guess who! But we can leave it for a surprise! Anyway, back to what I have..."

Jacob pulled a Bible and a cross out of his backpack, and went up to Timothy as close as he possibly could.

"We were all praying for you," he continued, briefly looking at his parents who seemed more understanding than before. "I was holding onto your cross for you; I am sorry for taking it. It is just I heard those awful men who were running after you at the fair. When they rushed past me, one of them said 'the cross, we must get the cross.' Then, 'don't forget the book,' the other one said. Well, I didn't want to risk you losing either if they were that serious about stealing them from you. So when the paramedics found you under the rubble with a Bible next to you, they handed it to me and I already had your backpack and so I held onto them both. And as for your cross, I took it off of you the last time I saw you and replaced it with a chain and plastic cross from a candy machine. What a coincidence; I won it as a prize at the carnival, remember? Please forgive me. Your dad told me I made the right decision and that I followed my heart."

Jacob looked at the ground, feeling ashamed.

"Jacob, it is alright! I am sure it all happened for a reason. Can I see the Bible?"

Jacob handed it over to Timothy and he examined it closely.

"The Believer's Guide..." Timothy whispered, knowing now for certain that the book he had received at the kiosk was the Bible – more specifically, a version that which only he could see objectively as a literal guide to the heavens.

"What's that, Tim? Did you say something about your Bible?" Jacob inquired.

"Oh I am sorry, it is just something I once read," Timothy said.

"That reminds me Tim, we saw the receipt from your backpack. Whatever happened to that strange book about the celestial realm?" Father John asked, curiously staring at Timothy.

"Hmm, well – I cannot say for sure, I guess… some things are meant to remain a mystery. But this book here is surely all I need. It will guide me!"

Timothy held his cross and book in his hands, and without another thought he closed his eyes and began to pray, thanking the Lord for all the gifts he had as of late received.

Epilogue

Timothy, Jacob and their three new friends arrived by taxi at St. Peter's Monastery in New York. The first accredited Orthodox school to exist in the past two decades it was now a mystical refuge for those who wanted their children to study the Word of God free of persecution. The five students, now in the eighth grade, were pioneers in the journey to rebuild the lost Orthodox ranks from recent years. They were now aspiring to be priests, deacons and a deaconess in a new community that served as more than a monastery; it was their home away from home.

Abbot John personally greeted his son at the gates to the monastery, miles away from the nearest main road. Hugging Timothy, he genuinely smiled at his friends and led them through the long stone road that served as a path to each building within the gates. As they approached the rear of the encampment, the wall was broken open. Beyond that, construction was ongoing all the way into the beginnings of the forest. A new community was underway as the monks and volunteers were taking advantage of the last right they had: the ability to own and maintain private property – as long as it was kept private. Plans there were for a city with a skyline as high as the forest, so far unchallenged by the government.

The young teenagers – all now over the age of twelve – rushed into the Residence of Young Orthodox Students and climbed the stairs to the fourth floor. As Timothy had requested, his father arranged for their rooms to be near one another.

Epilogue

"Hall of Wisdom," the plaque read, each floor having a distinct name.

Timothy and Jacob shared one room and Jeremy and Nick another. Kaylee, for her part, was still waiting to hear who she would be rooming with for the remainder of the school year. After setting their items down in their respective quarters, they met up in Timothy's room and had a seat on the two couches.

"So, did you all check out your new devices?" Timothy questioned.

"Devices? What do you mean?" Jacob inquired, as he became intrigued.

"Oh, you did not hear? Well, we have an engineer in the community. They found an Orthodox man who is skilled with computers and programs. They developed what is called an Ascetic Advisor. It is a little tablet next to each of your desks, sitting on a pedestal and it gives you different Scriptures to read daily, shows you your class schedules and really conveys any information you are looking for."

"Cool!" Nick responded.

"Yes, anyway, I just looked at mine. We have a meeting in a few moments. They are going to give us our new names and let us meet our instructors. I think there are eleven classes we have! Five are on one day and six the next; the amount alternates in that manner."

"Oh, that is the initial assembly we thought we were going to miss today?" Kaylee asked.

"That is the one!" Timothy confirmed.

"I hope they are more pleasant than the teachers at our old school..." said Jeremy. "That's what made me focus more on sports I think. I couldn't stand the teachers."

"These ones will be much different; I am sure of it!" Timothy replied, comforting them.

"Did you feel that?" Jacob uneasily asked them.

"Yeah it felt like the ground shook a little," Kaylee replied.

"I didn't notice anything..." Nick said. "Maybe it's the construction?"

Timothy remained silent on the topic and stood up to look out the window.

"Well, let us head down soon? Maybe we can get a good seat," Timothy suggested, keeping them all on schedule.

"Sounds good," Jacob agreed.

The five friends walked through the hall and down the stairs, heading outside and toward the other side of the monastery. The assembly hall was close to the classrooms, and neither of them were anticipating the hike to class during the winter season, just months away. Regardless, there was something about each other's company that made them look forward to their experience together and for every negative thought one had, the other found a positive one to match it.

"What's that building?" Nick asked, overwhelmed by all of the different structures and signs that made the community seem like it had already become a small city.

"That's a food store, where you can get hydration and small snacks – in case you need energy throughout your busy day!" Timothy explained. "There are all sorts of buildings and rooms here, each with a purpose to help us have what we need through our years. Over there," he continued, pointing, "that is our uniform shop. They have them pressed and cleaned and altered or repaired. And over there is the book shop, with all sorts of helpful texts."

"Hey... how do you know all of this, anyway?" Nick asked.

"It is in a strange book I once got from..." Timothy

started to say, suddenly stopping himself.

Jacob looked at Timothy, lifting one eyebrow up.

"You can find a map of the monastery in the device I showed you, if you want," Timothy explained, steering his friends away from his initial comment.

They continued walking to the assembly. They saw dozens of other kids of various ages entering, ready to start any grade from sixth on. Timothy and his friends then arrived inside, finding seats together on the bleachers. The wood was cherry and hand-carved. The auditorium in general was a beautiful sight; it was a new facility that had in every way the touch of their Orthodox brothers and sisters: artisans, carpenters and painters. There was at least one community member for each skill imaginable.

A few minutes passed by and Abbot John entered with the staff. As they took their positions, standing to his right were eleven instructors and to his left the various administrators. As Timothy looked at the teachers, each one seemed to have something special about him or her. Additionally, there was a positive vibe that each one offered.

"Good afternoon, students!" Abbot John said with a forceful voice. "You mark the first two-hundred students to study here at St. Peter's! Welcome!"

The students all cheered, and the instructors and staff joined in by clapping.

"Let us start off with a prayer," Abbot John continued. "Dear Lord, help us to embark this year on a positive note, keeping You close to our hearts and allowing You to guide us through the Holy Spirit. Thanks be to the Father, and the Son, and the Holy Spirit, Amen."

"Amen," they all repeated.

"So here is the agenda for the next few hours. Each instructor is going to introduce him or herself and which subject he or she is teaching. There will be the same eleven subjects for all students regardless of grade, but there will be varying difficulty levels associated with each and additional projects may be added as you grow here with us. Here are the eleven courses."

Abbot John opened up a scroll, and allowing the bottom of it to drop to the ground he began to read the contents.

"Ancient Language, Arithmetic and Numerical Association, Prayer, Church History, Secular Issues, The Modern-Day Role of the Church, Virtues, Humanitarianism, Tradition versus Modernization, Science and its Relationship to the Soul and, last but not least, Spiritual Warfare.

"Each of you can find your upcoming schedules with your Ascetic Advisor. I now turn to your first instructor, Father Bartholomew."

"It is my honor to teach you all. We have quite a year ahead of us. I will be teaching Spiritual Warfare."

Timothy smiled as the rest of the students looked on and listened carefully; they all seemed excited and intrigued at the same time. This school year was going to be like no other they had ever experienced, and they could only imagine the teachings they would receive.

From beyond the buildings and halls a bright sunny afternoon led to the shimmering of light through the western reaches of the over one hundred acre forest. Quiet was the land and sky as the daylight traveled west; to the east came night, and with it dark clouds and the slight rumbling of thunder.

Bio | Peter Silas

Peter Silas was born in September, 1980 in the North Shore, MA area. Moving to New Hampshire in grade school, he there resided until joining the armed forces in 1998. Peter made his way through college studying computer science before switching paths and graduating with a nursing degree, having only written poetry throughout his child and adulthood. Employed as a registered nurse and inspired by faith, he tirelessly worked morning and night around his day job to complete his very first novel, *The Prophecy of the Sacred Cross*. An Orthodox Christian, Peter is fascinated by theological topics and through self-studies aims to bring conservative Christian topics to his newly formed blog. Peter still lives in New Hampshire with his wife, Katie, and their two cats.

Visit Peter's web site to find bonus content, his blog and to follow him via social networks: http://www.petersilas.com